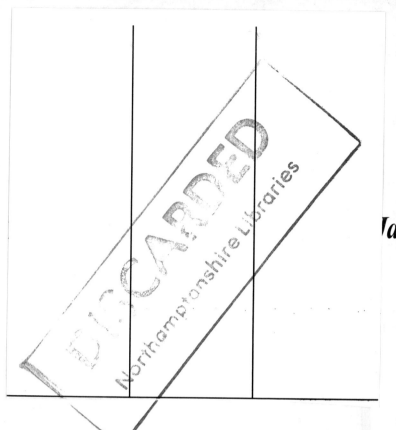

Jarrow

D0260594

80003212961

Published by MacLeod Trotter Books

New edition: 2011

ISBN 978-1-908359-01-8

www.janetmacleodtrotter.com

For my special, special daughter Amy - with all my love

***

*Many thanks to the welcoming members of The Jarrow & Hebburn
Local History Society for all their kindness, help and encouragement.*

***

Janet MacLeod Trotter was brought up in the North East of England with her four brothers, by Scottish parents. She is a best-selling author of 15 novels, including the hugely popular Jarrow Trilogy, and a childhood memoir, BEATLES & CHIEFS, which was featured on BBC Radio Four. Her novel, THE HUNGRY HILLS, gained her a place on the shortlist of The Sunday Times' Young Writers' Award, and the TEA PLANTER'S LASS was longlisted for the RNA Romantic Novel Award. A graduate of Edinburgh University, she has been editor of the Clan MacLeod Magazine, a columnist on the Newcastle Journal and has had numerous short stories published in women's magazines. She lives in the North of England with her husband, daughter and son. Find out more about Janet and her other popular novels at: www.janetmacleodtrotter.com

Chapter 1

1861 - Lamesley, County Durham

Rose clung on to her grandmother's gnarled hand, terrified of being swept away by a sea of dresses and buffeting legs. A cannon exploded deafeningly, and the tiny girl screamed and burst into tears.

Her grandmother swung her up into comforting arms and grinned at her toothlessly from under a huge faded bonnet.

'Hush, hush!' she soothed. 'You mustn't cry on Miss Isabella's weddin' day! I'll treat you to a twist of barley sugar if you stop your wailin'. Look, see how grand they all look? Isn't it a sight to warm the heart? And look at them horses - gleamin' like marble. No one keeps a stable like Lord Ravensworth.'

She pointed with a rough, calloused finger at the procession of horse-drawn carriages trotting smartly through the crowds of villagers and estate workers, snaking their way out of the wooded hillside.

Rose now gripped her grandmother's neck tightly; convinced the horses would sweep them away. Why was everyone cheering and waving so happily when her ears were hurting from so much noise? The women were turned out in their best bonnets and print dresses, and men wore their Sunday breeches. Bigger children than she were running around shouting and knocking each other over in their eagerness to see the grand gentry from Ravensworth Castle, that mysterious cluster of towers gleaming over the newly budding trees.

Rose felt she had been waiting there for ever and wanted it all to be over. They saw smartly dressed soldiers in scarlet tunics clatter into the church, their swords flashing in the spring sunshine.

'She's marryin' an officer,' Granny shouted over the raucous noise of a military band, pointing at a tall man with thick side whiskers. But Rose buried her face in the old woman's shoulder and refused to look at these stern men, who Granny said had fought against the Russian Bear in the Crimea.

Granny was full of stories for anyone with half an ear to listen. She knew everything about these godlike people, for she had worked at the magical castle on the hill since she was a girl. Rose loved to sit on her knee and listen to her talk of this place of many bedrooms and countless fires to lay, of beautiful dresses and important people who spent their days banqueting or riding the hills of County Durham.

'I was there when the Duke came to stay,' Granny would say in a voice full of reverence. 'He saved us all from the French bogeyman.' Rose was particularly scared of the bogeyman, who Granny said would catch naughty children if they did not do as they were told. 'They feasted for days when the Duke of Wellington came to stay,' Granny would cackle. 'Rode all over the county feastin' - and back at the dead o' night by flamin' torchlight!'

All around them, cheers went up as the carriages stopped outside the squat-towered church of Lamesley and a footman rushed to open the door of the first carriage. An elderly man in a tall black hat stepped down and Granny cried out, 'God bless you, Lord Ravensworth!'

Rose waited for the man to call back to her grandmother, but everyone was making such a noise, he did not seem to hear and did not reply. Then the small girl caught her breath and stared at the beautiful lady who climbed out next. She was a shimmer of white satin and silk, her billowing skirts catching in the April breeze, flounces of lace and ribbons fluttering like butterfly wings. Just then, a shaft of sunlight broke from behind the racing clouds and set the headdress of orange blossom aglow.

Rose gaped open-mouthed at the heavenly vision, her fears forgotten. She yearned to see the face of this angel, but it was hidden behind a gossamer veil.

Granny grew garrulous. 'Bonny, bonny bride!' she kept repeating, wiping away tears of emotion. 'Your mammy could have been workin' for the likes of the mistress, if she'd listened to my advice. A good job she could have had in the kitchens, just like me. I would have put a word in for her. But no, your mammy knew better. She lost her head over that Irishman McConnell. Now she's feedin' pigs and diggin' leeks in that terrible place - like the jaws of Hell. You could've been runnin' all summer with the village children,' Granny ranted, 'breathin' in God's fresh air, instead of all that smoke and filth in the town. I wish I could keep you here wi' me in the almshouse for ever, but it's not allowed. Cryin' shame!' But no one around her was listening.

Rose was straining to see where the angel had gone, and wanted to follow. She didn't like all her grandmother's talk of the filthy town and the jaws of Hell. She knew she had been sent to stay in the village because there was fever in the town, and fever was bad because it could kill children between sundown and sunrise. Rose wriggled out of her grandmother's hold easily, for the old woman was tiring of carrying her, and pushed her way through the forest of legs to the church wall. Someone lifted her up so she could see the entrance, but the beautiful lady had disappeared and the doors were firmly shut.

Just when she was growing bored with waiting, the church bells erupted in a deafening peal and the church doors flew open. The angel appeared on the arm of the stern soldier and this time her face was visible. For a brief moment, the face of the angel looked up, noticed Rose sitting on the wall, and smiled. Rose felt bathed in warmth like the heat from the kitchen fire. It was a feeling she would never forget. She knew she could never now be taken away by the fever, because she was friends with an angel and this figure in dazzling white would always protect her. For the first time in her young life, Rose McConnell felt brave.

As the band struck up and the villagers threw handfuls of rice on the newly wedded couple for good luck, she waved and clapped from her perch on the wall. Older children ran behind the bridal carriage, scrabbling in the mud to pick up the coins that the groom threw to them from the open window. Rose gazed after the procession until it was lost once more in the trees, and would have sat there all day if Granny had not ordered her down.

The villagers set about celebrating with races in the fields for the children, and much drinking of beer at old Ravensworth Arms, the village coaching inn. Rose sucked her sugar stick and drank milk that was still warm from the cow, content with her new surroundings. She had almost forgotten what home looked like: a blackened wall under a pall of grey smoke, hens perched on a steaming midden, windows too filthy to see through. Here, as daylight waned, she could see stars pricking a velvet sky. Never had she seen such brightness in a night sky.

'What's that?' she asked Granny sleepily as she was carried home on the old woman's stooped back.

'Why, lass, have you never seen the moon before?' Granny cried in amazement.

'We don't have one in Jarrow,' Rose yawned.

'It's there,' Granny snorted, 'you just can't see it for all that smoke.'

'Like an angel's face,' Rose murmured, her eyelids heavy. As she fell asleep on her grandmother's back, the moon became confused in her groggy mind with the smiling face of the angel bride. It would always be there to protect her even if she could not see it, Rose thought. Granny had promised it was so.

For young as she was, Rose was already aware that she would need protection when she returned to the land of smoke and fever that was her home.

Chapter 2

1872 - Jarrow, Tyneside

'Well, one of you will have to go!' Mrs McConnell snapped, her nerves frayed at her daughters' bickering. 'Your da promised those cabbages to Mrs McMullen and she's a dozen hungry lads to feed. Maggie, get yourself over there sharp if you don't want to feel the back of my hand.'

'Why can't Lizzie or Rose go?' Maggie protested, beginning to cough. Rose noticed how her sister always began coughing like a consumptive when she did not want to do something. It made their mother fret and forget about being cross with her.

'I went over to the cottages yesterday,' Lizzie answered. 'It's my turn to feed the hens.' She went back to her sewing. Rose knew how her other sister hated to get her hands dirty at all and was always complaining about the amount of muck around their parents' smallholding. But they were luckier than most in their part of Jarrow. Their father helped out at a local blacksmith's as well as tending the plot of land he rented from the tenant farmer. They had regular food on the table and did not have to take in lodgers when there was a slump in the shipyards. Yet when the dock gates of mighty Palmer's closed for lack of orders, the whole town suffered.

This spring there was growing agitation along the riverside for a nine-hour day among the steelmen and mechanics. Rose had heard her father say so. There would be hardship the length of the River Tyne if it came to a strike. Talk of strike action made Da angry, for he held no truck with union agitators. As a youth he had been one of many brought over from Ireland by Lord Londonderry as a strike-breaker in the pits, and had done well enough finally to rent a piece of land and buy his first cow. When the talk on street corners was of squaring up to the bosses, it was best to humour McConnell or keep out of his way. Both Rose and her mother understood this, but Rose's younger sisters seemed oblivious to the tension gathering about them like storm clouds. Lizzie and Maggie played and fought like young kittens and left the worrying to their fourteen-year-old sister.

Her mother threw Rose a despairing look.

'I'll go,' the tall girl offered, already reaching for her shawl. It was faded, fringed and old-fashioned, but had belonged to her dear grandmother and when Rose wrapped it about her and pulled it over her dark hair, she felt the dead woman's strength and was comforted. 'Never fear the dark,' Granny had always told her. 'God sees everything, even in the pitch-black of night.' And soon what daylight there was on such a gloomy day would be gone, Rose thought anxiously. The quicker she got the delivery over, the better. She had no desire to be stumbling around Jarrow's dirty unlit lanes or be caught anywhere near the Slake. Rose shivered to think of the putrid, stinking inlet, known locally as the 'Slacks'. It had to be crossed to reach the old pit cottages where the McMullens lived.

'Thanks, hinny,' her mother said, as Rose began to load up a basket. 'And take a few eggs to sell round the doors while you're out.'

Rose's heart sank, but she did not waste time protesting. The steelworkers and

4

dockers were their main customers and the McConnells would have to put by all the pennies they could get now, if they weren't to suffer later. Rose felt impatient with her sisters for not realising this, but as she went, felt a stab of envy for their carefree laughter and ability to live for the moment.

Rose went into the henhouse at the back of the cottage and collected half a dozen eggs, which she put in a basket over her arm. The heavy vegetables she balanced in an old fishing creel on her head. She was used to going about the town like this, selling their produce from door to door. She would chivvy her sisters into helping her scrub the vegetables and arrange them nicely, so that people were more tempted to buy. Customers seemed to like her quiet, polite way of speaking and her shy smile. Rose would sometimes allow her regulars credit, keeping a tally in her head of who owed what.

The poorer they were, the better the customer, Rose had discovered, for they were prisoners in overcrowded tenements, burdened down with children and often denied credit at the shops. Rose brought a cheerful greeting and a winning smile into their drab day, knowing they would find the pennies for her by the end of the week.

The McMullens were another matter. Rose felt mounting nervousness as she skirted the centre of Jarrow and made her way downhill towards the Don, an oily slick of a stream that emptied into Jarrow Slake. She doubted she would receive any payment from the McMullens, despite several of the sons now old enough to be working as labourers in the docks. Old McMullen, or 'the Fathar', as they all called him with fear in their voices, was a burly brute of a man who worked in the ironworks carrying the heavy 'pigs' of iron from their moulds to waiting wagons. Strong men were needed for such a back-breaking job and McMullen had come over from Ireland to do just that. He hailed from the same part of Ireland as Rose's father and so McConnell insisted on helping them out where he could.

'We've both known the Famine,' McConnell had told his daughters, 'and I'll not see our people starve when we've got food growing beneath our feet. We're from the same village.'

Rose's mother had muttered, 'Aye, and that McMullen seems to be doing his best to father his own village! With all them lads, isn't it about time they paid for some of our food?'

But McConnell had given her a sour look. 'They'll pay when they can. At least he's got plenty to carry on his name.'

Rose felt troubled when she thought of her father's barbed remarks about his lack of sons. Her mother got all the blame. Rose often lay awake at night listening to their hissed arguments.

'I'm past giving you bairns,' her mother had said wearily.

'No you're not,' her father had protested. 'It's your duty. Hasn't Father Boyle told you often enough?'

'I've done my duty!' Her mother had grown agitated. 'It's not my fault if scarlet fever carried off my two bonny lads.'

'Maybe if you'd kept this place cleaner...' Rose's father had grumbled.

A sob had caught in her mother's throat. 'Don't you dare blame me! Blame yourself for bringing me to live in this terrible place. We should have stayed in Gateshead like I wanted - or gone back to Lamesley.'

'And have you be at the beck and call of that old witch your mother?'

Rose had buried her head under the blanket in distress at hearing her dear grandmother called a witch. She'd tried to block out their tired bickering, but she'd heard her mother protest that daughters was all he was going to get. 'Bearing another bairn now would kill me. Then who would run this place for you or bring up your lasses to be hard-working and respectable? Ask your precious priest that.'

'I ought to take me belt to you for your cheek!' Da had growled.

'Aye, just like McMullen?' Ma had scoffed. 'I don't care how many sons he has, there's nowt manly about beating his missus. If you want me strong enough to lift tatties from the ground you'll leave us alone and let me get some sleep.'

Rose hurried on as fast as her load would allow, her heart thumping at the memory of her parents' argument. What was it that her da had wanted her ma to do? And why was her mother's voice filled with such disgust at the idea? What went on in the marriage bed beyond the thin partition, Rose was not really sure, and was too frightened to ask. Occasionally there would be creaking and restless movement, but, more often, whispered protests or exhausted snoring from both parents.

As she neared the foul-smelling Don, Rose's mind went back to that blustery spring day in Lamesley when she had seen Lord Ravensworth's daughter married to an army officer. She had been so clean and beautiful in her white dress, her face suffused with happiness, tinged pink with excitement. Rose had thought of her for years as a guardian angel, conjuring her up in her mind when she was frightened or unhappy. When I marry, Rose promised herself, I want to look like her. She might never be able to marry a handsome officer in a scarlet coat, but she would work hard to afford a pretty dress and choose a man who would bring her happiness and security.

Putting down her burden, she rested a moment in the blackened shadow of the ancient ruined monastery, St Paul's. Once this had been the home of St Bede in a golden age of Christianity, her Sunday School teacher had told her. Even at the time when Queen Victoria had come to the throne, in Granny's lifetime, it had still been a place of fields, small boat builders and sail-cloth makers. Now it was hard to imagine it had ever been anything else but this hellish landscape.

The sulphurous smell from the chemical works was overpowering, and the sky was an oppressive grey haze from the belching chimneys of chemical factories, paper-mill, coke ovens and steel mills. The leaden horizon was peppered with steaming salt pans, jutting coal staithes and a forest of rigging and cranes on the river's edge. Even from this distance, the clatter from the docks and the thump of giant hammers in the rolling mills carried loudly over the blackened rows of houses.

Rose felt the metallic taste on her tongue that soured her mouth whenever she drew near to the ironworks. Below her the Don oozed its way into the muddy Slake where the ebbing tide had left its flotsam of seasoned timbers stranded like a shattered vessel after a shipwreck. In the gloom she saw children playing on the precarious network of planks, jumping from one to another and daring each other to follow. She would never allow her future children to play in such a dangerous place, she determined. When she married the kindly man of her imagination, she would live well away from this sinister part of the river, with its uneasy ghosts.

She knew from her grandmother that this part of the riverside was haunted. Apart from those who had slipped and drowned in the fetid waters of the Slake, it had been the site of the last public gibbeting. Granny had told her about the miner Jobling who had been hanged for his part in the murder of a magistrate during a terrible strike. They had brought his body from Durham Gaol, smeared it in black pitch and trussed it up in an iron gibbet for all to see.

'Stuck it right there in the muddy waters where the tide comes in,' Granny had told her, 'to be a lesson to the pitmen and their families that they can't take the law into their own hands. They say Jobling's widow could see him swingin' there, from her very doorstep. Aye, and people came from all over to see the terrible sight. Soldiers guarded it night and day,' Granny had continued in an eerie voice, 'but there was something devilish about that pitman. One day it disappeared - the whole lot - body, gibbet an' all! Nobody could have cut it down - it was solid iron - and anyone who tried was threatened with seven years' transportation! Some say it were his pitmen friends who risked their lives to do it - buried him out at sea. But I think it was witchcraft. On windy nights you can still hear Jobling's ghost moanin', and see him swingin' there when there's a full moon. That's what I've heard. So you stay away from that place!' Granny had warned. 'He'll get you like the bogeyman if you stray down too close to the river.'

Rose felt familiar fear weaken her knees. Many nights she had lain awake thinking she could hear the groaning of Jobling's unhappy ghost carried to her on the wind. 'Will he be in Hell or Purgatory?' she had asked her mother, deeply troubled that the pitman had not had a Christian burial.

'That's not for us to judge,' her mother had answered shortly.

'But he was a murderer, Ma, wasn't he? And he never got properly buried. That's why his ghost still haunts the Slacks when there's a full moon, isn't it? Granny says witches must've carried off his body.'

'Stop talking daft,' her mother had said impatiently. 'And don't go repeating such tales to the priest, or he'll think we're a family of heathens.'

Rose glanced up at the sky now, but there was no way of knowing if a full moon was on the rise or not. She took a deep breath in the acrid air and told herself not to be so fanciful. It was just one of Granny's stories that she liked to tell over a winter fire, and Ma had told her not to believe half of what Granny had said. Besides, the moon was her friend. Why should she be frightened on such a night?

All the same, Rose decided to go the long way round and doubled back up the hill, skirting the banks of the Don until she could cross it higher up near the turnpike road that led all the way from South Shields to Newcastle.

By the time she reached the long rows of pit cottages, she could hardly see to pick her way over the stagnant pools that collected in the rutted, uneven lanes. Rose pulled her shawl over her nose to try to deaden the stench of rotting household slops and sewage that leaked out of the earth closets and oozed into the yards and through the walls of the ancient cottages. They had been abandoned long ago by mining families when the Alfred Pit had closed, and no landlords had bothered to spend any money on these hovels that now housed Jarrow's poorest. Whole streets were taken over by Irish labourers, their wives hooded in thick shawls that they pinned under their chins.

Several of these hardy women were now lined up patiently at the standpipe at the top of the street, waiting to fill kettles and pails of water. Their quick chatter and sharp calls to their scampering, barefoot children rang through the murky twilight.

'Is that you, Rose McConnell?' one of them shouted.

'Aye, missus,' Rose called back. 'I'm going to Mrs McMullen's. But I've a few eggs spare. Fresh as they come. They'll be a treat for your man's tea.'

'Give me three, Rose - the babies can have the tops, so they can. Call by when you're done at McMullen's.'

'I'll pop them in on me way down, Mrs Kennedy,' Rose said quickly, thinking she'd have nothing left to sell if Mrs McMullen saw them first.

It was a long way to the end of the row, and the further downhill the houses, the more they were sunk below the level of the road. The McMullens' could only be reached round the back of the house, for at the front only the roof tiles showed above ground level. A candle was already lit in the window and as she slithered down the bank to the back gate, Rose was greeted by a cacophony of voices.

A horde of boys were chasing a tin can or pot up and down the back lane, whacking it with sticks and bits of old fencepost. They screamed and bellowed at each other, cursing and encouraging in language that made Rose blush.

In her hurry to get past them unnoticed, she slipped in the mud and her basket of cabbages toppled to the ground, bouncing across the filthy lane and into the open gutters. Rose gave a shriek of alarm.

One boy tripped over a runaway cabbage and went sprawling, face down in the mud. He cursed foully as the others laughed and pulled him to his feet. The tall youth threw them off and rounded angrily on Rose. She sat on the ground, still winded with shock.

'What you do that for, you daft bitch?' he shouted.

Rose flushed with humiliation and offence at his words. 'I didn't mean t-to,' she stuttered.

He came to stand over her, glaring. 'Bloody lasses!'

The other boys began to crowd around her too. Rose tried to scrabble to her feet, feeling threatened by their closeness. Her dress and hands were covered in filth and her shawl had slipped from her head. She pulled it around her defensively.

'It's not my fault you don't keep a decent path to the house,' she replied, almost in tears.

The tall boy lunged at her and grabbed her arm. 'Are you blaming me for you landing on your arse? Eh? It's you that tripped me up, you stupid little cow!'

His angry face was so close to hers now that she could see him clearly for the first time. His dark hair was shorn close to his head and there was the

8

beginnings of a moustache on his snarling upper lip. His thick eyebrows were drawn together like storm clouds, but his glowering eyes were startling. They were a vivid green, like the sea at South Shields on a summer's day, belying the aggression that marred the rest of his face.

Something about those eyes lessened her fear of him for a moment. Indignation ignited inside her. She threw off his hold.

'You tripped yourself up by not watching your step! And what about me cabbages?' she cried. 'They're all ruined! There'll be hell to pay from me da if they don't get to Mrs McMullen's.'

He gawped at her, dumbfounded by her answering him back. The crowd around them began to snigger and jostle, sensing trouble.

'Don't you know who I am?' he shouted.

'I don't care if you're the Pope,' Rose replied with spirit. 'I just care about me cabbages.'

'I'm John McMullen! And nobody - least of all a skinny lass like you - makes a fool out of me.'

He moved as if to grab her again.

Suddenly, a voice cracked behind them like a whip. 'What's the meaning of all this noise? John, is that you there? Mary, Mother! What in the name are you doing with that girl?'

In an instant a small terrier of a woman was amongst them, pushing boys aside like a prizefighter. 'I'll box your ears if you've laid a finger on her, so I will!' She reached up and grabbed John's collar, hauling him backwards with the strength of someone twice her size.

At once Rose recognised the wiry figure and flushed face of Mrs McMullen. She was bareheaded, with her skirts hitched up and tucked into a thick belt to avoid the mud, revealing a coarse woollen petticoat and a pair of outsized man's boots. She talked breathlessly, as if she could not get rid of her words fast enough, cursing the youth in her clutches and flaying out at any others who dared to get in her way.

'You great big bully! What's this you've done? Knocked over the lass's basket? Is that you Rose Ann McConnell? By the saints, John, you'll pick up every one of those cabbages if you have to crawl through your own filth to find them.' She gave him a big push. 'And the rest of you can help your brother instead of standing around laughing like loonies.' She aimed a kick at a younger boy beside her. He howled in protest. 'And if there's so much as one damaged or missing, I'll set the Fathar on to the lot of you. You'll not sit down for a week.'

Immediately the boys began to search around in the half-dark for the scattered vegetables, with barely a word of protest. Even the tall John did not challenge his mother, but bent to the unsavoury task. Rose just stood there mutely, amazed that this wild tribe could be so easily tamed. Within a couple of minutes the basket was full once more.

'Now, take those cabbages up to the tap and give them a good scrubbing,' Mrs McMullen ordered.

'Who, me?' John asked indignantly.

'Aye you, you great big lump! And don't twist your face at me,' she added, swiping him with a dirt-ingrained hand.

Rose winced as she heard the sharp smack on his jaw. She saw him tense but

9

he did not answer back.

'Rose Ann, come inside a minute while the boys wash those cabbages,' Mrs McMullen ordered. 'We'll share a cup of tea before you set off home. And I've a bag of cinders that the boys collected - you can take that back for your mother.'

Reluctantly, Rose followed her through the back gate and under the low doorway. She hated the McMullens' overcrowded home, with its pungent smells of the midden and sweaty men. Usually she dumped her produce at the door and hurried on her way, not really distinguishing between the many faces that stared at her, just aware that they were all boys. She steeled herself to enter.

There was hardly a bare inch of brick floor to be seen, for their one living room was taken up with a rough kitchen table surrounded by upturned boxes for chairs. In the corner was a large iron-framed bed with someone sleeping in it, while clogging up the hearth was a scattering of ill-assorted boots. Damp washing was strewn everywhere, hanging limp and steaming from lines of string. A ladder led up through a gaping black hole in the ceiling to the loft, where Rose supposed most of them slept.

She looked at the bustling Mrs McMullen and noticed in the firelight how deep lines scored her face. Outside in the gloom, she had seemed young, with her quick movements and springy black hair, and a girlish flush on her cheeks. But now, as she reached for the big black kettle and poured into a handleless cup, her shoulders were stooped and her face was that of an old woman.

'We don't have a teapot since young Michael broke it,' she explained, 'so I make up the tea in the kettle. There! You get a bit of warmth inside you, Rose Ann. Sit yourself down, and tell me the news. How're your mother and father? And those pretty sisters of yours? I'd like to think some of my boys might go courting the McConnell girls one day, eh?' She winked and laughed at Rose's startled expression. 'No, I don't blame you for looking so worried after that carry-on outside. But they're grand boys at heart - hardworking like their father and good to their mother. Bit wild at times, but they'll grow out of it, I'll see to that.'

Rose sipped at the flavourless tea, wishing the boys would hurry up with her basket so she could be gone. She felt a stab of pity for Mrs McMullen, struggling in this tiny cottage to provide for so many hungry mouths, and she wondered how her own mother could begrudge them a few extra vegetables for the pot. But the thought of either herself or her sisters courting any of these rough McMullens filled her with horror. She had heard from her mother how old McMullen took the belt to his wife for the slightest fault and how the boys were getting a name for fighting. 'Like father like son,' Ma would say in disapproval when her own husband was out of earshot.

Rose had seen enough of the McMullen temper - especially in that tall John - to know that none of them could fit the picture of the man she would marry. After a few more minutes of Mrs McMullen's questioning, Rose was thankful to hear boisterous shouting grow louder till it reached the door and several boys clattered in. John dumped the basket at Rose's feet and gave her a stormy look.

'Done,' he muttered. 'As clean as a baby's arse.'

Rose avoided his look and got up quickly, grabbing the cabbages and putting them on the table.

'Ta for the tea, Mrs McMullen,' she said, swiftly emptying the creel. 'I'll be off now.'

'Hold your horses, Rose Ann,' Mrs McMullen cried. 'Remember the bag of cinders? John, fetch them from the yard. You can carry them back for Rose Ann.'

'Oh, no, I can manage,' Rose said in panic.

'Nonsense; it's nearly dark and I'll not have you breaking your pretty ankles falling in some pothole. Your mother would never forgive me. Away you go, John, and see the girl home with the cinders. It's the least you can do for all the trouble you've caused.'

Rose thought he was going to burst with fury. But without a word, he stomped out of the house and left her to follow. He picked up a sack by the back wall, swung it over his shoulder, just missing her head, and set off down the lane without a backward glance. Rose balanced her empty creel and egg basket on her shoulder and hurried after his retreating figure. Pulling her shawl over her head in the biting wind, she was disgusted to find it damp and stinking from being dropped in the liquid refuse that leaked out of the privies. Damn John McMullen! This was all his fault, yet he was treating her like a lump of dung from his foul midden. Well, he could rot in Hell, St Theresa forgive her for the thought.

By the time she caught up with John at the bottom of the hill she was out of breath and furious.

'Stop!' she panted. 'I can see mesel' home. I'm not ganin' to run after you like I'm your slave, John McMullen. So give us the bag of cinders.'

He turned and looked at her for the first time since leaving the rows. She could not read his expression in the dark, but he suddenly seemed very tall, looming over her. Behind him the night sky was lit with lurid flashes belching from the furnaces of Palmer's mills. It could only be late afternoon, but it seemed like the dead of night, there were so few people about.

Then Rose realised where they were. Jarrow Slake. She could tell from the noxious mix of smells: chemicals, effluent, a faint whiff of the tide and ships' timbers. Pitch. The dark, resinous smell filled her nostrils and the spectre of Jobling's rotting, pitch-smeared corpse leapt to mind.

John must have seen the sudden fear cross her face, for he came closer still and demanded, 'What's wrong? Are you frightened of me or some'at?'

Rose gulped down her panic. 'I'm not!' she retorted. 'If you'll just see us across the Slacks, I can manage the bag after that.'

'Scared of the Slacks, then, are you?' he asked, amusement creeping into his voice. 'Worried that the ghost of Jobling is ganin' to get you?'

'No!' Rose cried, but could not prevent herself from looking over her shoulder at the treacherous inlet.

'Yes you are!' John said with glee and let out a piercing howl that made Rose jump. He came at her, making wailing noises, pretending to be a ghost.

'Stop it!' she screamed, which made him laugh out loud.

She dodged past him and began to run towards the Slake. John grabbed at her shawl and pulled it from her shoulders. 'I'm coming to get you!' he

11

threatened in an echoing voice.

'Leave me alone!' Rose shrieked. 'I hate you!'

But this just made him laugh harder as he chased after her. Rose hardly knew where she stepped, she just wanted to get away from him and across the Slake as quickly as possible. She plunged forward and found herself knee-deep in freezing water. The tide was in, so there was no way of squelching through the mud to the far side. In desperation, she clambered on to some of the floating timbers that were lashed together like a raft. Running to the end of it, she jumped on to the next group of planks and nearly toppled into the water. They bobbed and turned and she crouched down to hold on.

'Wait!' John shouted behind her. 'What do you think you're doing, you daft lass?'

'Don't you come near me,' Rose wailed.

But John was already on the raft behind her. 'Stay still!' he commanded. 'Unless you want to bloody drown.'

'I don't care,' Rose sobbed. 'It's better than being left here with you!'

In an instant he was reaching across and gripping her arm hard, pulling her back towards him. She thought in terror that he was probably going to kill her. He yanked at her arm, nearly pulling it out of its socket, and the next minute they were both toppling off the timbers into the icy Slake.

Rose tried to scream but the breath was frozen in her chest. How long does it take to drown? she wondered, paralysed with fear that the water would engulf her at any moment. But John was still hanging on to her and trying to drag her through the water. She was as heavy as a sack of coal, her thick woollen skirts drenched in water, but somehow he managed to heave her to the bank and push her to safety.

For a moment Rose struggled for breath, then she rolled on to her side and retched.

'You mad bitch!' John panted. 'You nearly had us both drowned!'

Rose gasped and spluttered. 'Me?' she croaked. 'You pushed us both in!'

'No, I never!' he argued. 'You were the one who led us out there. What you want to run away for?'

'You, pretending to be Jobling's ghost...!' Rose began, and then burst into tears.

John said nothing. He stared at her nonplussed, breathing hard. 'It was just a bit of carry-on. Not my fault if a lass can't take a joke.'

Rose cried louder, part in relief at still being alive. 'It wasn't funny,' she sobbed. 'I thought you were going to—'

'What?' John demanded.

'Hurt me,' Rose accused.

He reached out and she flinched away. 'I wouldn't have hurt you,' he said in a sullen voice, but his look was almost bashful. They sat in the dark, regaining their breath, each wondering what to make of the other. Rose could tell he was not used to girls. But for all his uncouth manners, she thought he was trying to say sorry by his awkward words.

'I'll take that as an apology then,' Rose sniffed, and hauled herself up before he could argue. She was cold, aching, smelly and very tired.

'I'll walk you up the top road,' John said quietly, reaching for the bag of cinders and the shawl he had thrown down before leaping after her.

'Don't bother,' Rose scowled.

'Please,' John said with a softness of tone that surprised her. She regarded him suspiciously for a moment and then nodded, taking the muddied shawl he held out to her.

It was only when they were halfway up the slope, walking apart and in silence that Rose suddenly remembered. 'I've lost me baskets in the Slacks,' she gasped. 'Ma will kill us!'

John put a steadying hand on her shoulder for a second, then let it drop. 'I'll fetch you over another creel. Tell her it was my fault for acting daft about the ghost,' he said, then added with a grunt, 'she'll believe that. Doesn't think much of us McMullens, does she, your mam?'

'I wouldn't know,' Rose mumbled, avoiding his look. John just snorted and carried on walking.

They did not say much as they walked back to the McConnells' smallholding that evening, just enough for Rose to discover that he worked as a puddler's helper in the foundry and that he missed the fresh air of Ireland, even though he had not been there since he was a small boy.

'It smells of the grass and the earth,' he enthused. 'And the rain - it tastes good enough to drink. Not like the dirty black stuff you get here.'

'If Ireland's so grand,' Rose couldn't resist teasing, 'why do you stop in Jarrow?'

'To help me family, of course,' John replied defensively. 'There's no work back home.'

'I've never been further than Lamesley,' Rose mused, 'and that was like a world away. I can't imagine going anywhere as far as Ireland.'

'Well, I'm going back one day,' John determined. 'I'm Irish and proud of it,' he told her with a stubborn jut of his chin. 'And I'll knock the brains out of any lad who speaks against Ireland or the Pope!'

Rose did not doubt it. 'Aye, well, you Irish lads are too keen by half on fighting,' she dared to voice her opinion. She thought this might rile him, but rather he seemed to sink into his own thoughts again.

Then, as they reached the gate of the McConnells' squat cottage, he suddenly asked, 'Don't you think of yourself as Irish?'

Rose hesitated, looking back at the sprawl of Jarrow town below them, dimly lit by gas lamplight. From here, she could see right along to Shields, where the River Tyne merged into the sea. At night, the poverty was unseen and the blackened buildings disappeared into a galaxy of soft lights from shops and pubs. The clamour of the day subsided into the comforting night noises of a train's whistle or a distant ship's bell.

She turned to John. 'No, I don't feel Irish,' she answered. 'I'm a Jarrow lass and this is me home.'

At that moment the strong wind tore a hole in the blanket of cloud overhead. Fleetingly, the moon peered through, illuminating the rough ground around them. Rose caught the look in John's fierce green eyes and knew that she had disappointed him. For a moment she was sorry; then she remembered how much he had frightened her. The unease she had felt with him earlier returned. Why should she want to please this tall, brawny bully of a lad? She

13

did not care what John McMullen thought of her.

'I'll face Ma and Da on me own,' she told him abruptly. 'Ta for the cinders.'

He leant towards her as if he would say something, but she drew away and he thought the better of it. Dumping down the sack, he muttered, 'Suit yourself.'

Without another glance he turned and strode off down the hill, his ill-fitting boots kicking up loose stones as he went. Rose felt relief at his going and yet he perplexed her. He seemed so angry with everything - everyone. Yet for a brief while, as they'd trudged up the bank together, he had shed his taciturn nature and spoken of his homeland with a simple passion that had impressed her. He had seemed almost gentle. But the impression had vanished as swiftly as the night clouds had smothered the elusive moon.

Rose sighed, picking up the sack of cinders. She was far too weary to care what it was that ate into John McMullen's soul. All she wanted was dry clothes, a hot drink and to fall into a warm bed beside her sisters. Let those troublesome McMullens look after themselves, Rose decided.

Chapter 3

Rose was roundly scolded for losing the creel and spent the next fortnight selling vegetables from an old wooden box that was much more cumbersome to carry. She waited for John McMullen to turn up with a new basket for her, but he never came. Instead, like a malign spirit, he would intrude on her thoughts and disturb her humdrum life. She would lie awake at night, troubled yet excited by the memory of his stormy-eyed look and his passionate words about Ireland.

When she hawked her wares around the pit cottages, Rose sometimes glimpsed a tall figure with a restless stride and for a moment her heart would miss a beat. Then the man would turn and, with a mixture of disappointment and relief, she would see the face of a stranger. She wondered why she thought of him at all. She disliked John - was even frightened of him - but at the same time felt drawn to him with the same dangerous fascination as the treacherous tide in Jarrow Slake.

But he was never at the McMullens' when she called with offerings from her father, and Rose became increasingly annoyed at the thought of him and his broken promise about replacing her basket. After a month, she made excuses not to go.

'It's getting too dangerous down them streets,' she protested to her father. 'There's always fighting - and it's as likely to be the lasses. The men just stand around and watch like it's a dog fight.'

Her mother backed her up. 'It's true. I've seen them draw blood like wildcats. It's the drink, of course.'

'And now with the strike,' Rose pressed, 'I'm not getting paid regular - I'm just giving it away.'

'Aye,' Mrs McConnell agreed. 'We're not the Parish. Can't afford to give charity.'

Rose's father muttered at them ill-temperedly, but relented. 'I'll take a bag of tatties to McMullens', you can try and sell round the town where there's still work. And we can all pray to the saints that this carry-on is sorted out before we're all queuing up at the workhouse gates.'

Rose felt a chill at her father's words. Her grandmother had told her about the 'visitations' of fever - cholera brought from Europe by sailors - that had swept the area when her mother was a baby. They had left so many destitute that hard-pressed parishes had set up Poor Law unions to cope with the numbers. As a small child, Rose had been sent to Granny's for safekeeping to escape an epidemic of scarlet fever, but other families had not been so lucky. These visitations often seemed to strike when there was a trade slump on the river or a lock-out at the works. Rose had seen skilled men reduced to the humiliation of stone-breaking and clawing at the ground with their bare hands in order to feed their families. But those without breadwinners were even worse off. She had seen families pawn every last possession and stitch of extra clothing and then disappear into the workhouse, never to be seen again.

How right her father was to tell them to pray they never had to enter such a place! It was the nearest thing to Hell that Rose could imagine - families split up and doomed to lives of humiliating incarceration and servitude. Father

Boyle had told her that plagues and misfortune were a result of the sinfulness of the people and that she must confess her sins or suffer the flames of Hell. When she saw the belching smoke from the workhouse chimneys, Rose knew how close by Hell lurked.

That summer she spent a lot of time praying in church for herself and her family and those of the strikers who were jeopardising their immortal souls. The Protestants and Dissenters were past saving anyway, but there were good Catholic families who were also caught up in the strike for a shorter working day. The Fawcetts for instance.

Mr Fawcett was a steelman from the Midlands and his family were regular attenders among the large congregation at St Bede's. Mr Fawcett had been active in the lock-out seven years ago when the employers had tried to reduce wages and extend hours. He was a burly, straight-talking man, who had taught himself to read and spent what little spare time he had in the library at the Mechanics' Institute.

Rose was friendly with their daughter, Florrie, ever since they had paddled together on the sands at South Shields on an Easter outing. She admired Florrie for being able to read and write and add up figures, which was why her friend had a job in a haberdashery shop on Ormonde Street. Florrie was always smartly dressed and knew about fashion, and Rose was grateful for any small trimmings of ribbon or spare buttons that Florrie could give her. Living on the isolated smallholding and having to work from an early age, Rose had had little opportunity for making friends and largely relied on her younger sisters for company. She suspected that the friendship was more important to her than it was to Florrie, but accepted that she had less to offer. Rose's mother approved of the Fawcetts, who lived near Croft Avenue, the sought-after part of Jarrow, and encouraged the friendship, despite her father's grumbling about them being union agitators.

'They're a good family,' Mrs McConnell reproved her husband gently, 'never miss Mass on Sundays.'

'Look down their long noses at the likes of us,' McConnell muttered.

But Rose admired their long noses, especially that of Florrie's brother, William, who was an apprentice at the rolling mill. She did not like to admit that her devout attendance over the summer might have something to do with William. But she loved to kneel in the quiet of the large church, smelling of candles and incense, and watch the light glinting on the statues of Jesus and the Virgin Mary. While outside there was grey drabness and dirt, inside was richness and colour and cleanliness.

William was fair-haired and red-cheeked, with a lusty singing voice that Rose could have listened to for hours. They had hardly exchanged more than a dozen words in the past year, but until the strike, he had worked punishing hours at the steel mill. Florrie told her that sometimes he would work from six in the morning until midnight, instead of the ten-hour shift he was supposed to.

But when the rash of strikes for a nine-hour day broke out in May, William was often to be seen around St Bede's church, doing small repair jobs. Rose did not know why she should suddenly have become interested in boys, but they occupied her thoughts more and more. At the same time, she could feel her body changing, her hips and breasts swelling. Last year, she had alarmed her

16

sisters by bleeding in the bed, and their screams had brought their mother rushing in panic. But her mother had declared she was not dying and should expect the same every month.

'It's the lot of womenfolk,' was all the explanation Rose was given. 'And I can see we'll have to widen that bodice,' her mother had added, giving her an appraising look. At times Rose felt dizzy and sick at the pace she was changing, and soon she was wearing old dresses of her mother's that she tried to make less drab with Florrie's cast-off ribbon.

As the summer wore on with no sign of the dispute with the Tyneside bosses being resolved, Rose offered to help out in the soup kitchen set up by the youthful, more liberal-minded Father O'Brien, to help the hard-up striking families.

One day William caught her staring at him. Rose had detoured through the church to fetch water in the hopes of seeing him. To her delight he was there, busily occupied as usual, content in his own company. His fair head and strong upper body were bathed in muted sunlight as he bent to the task of mending a chair. He looked like an angel. William sensed her presence and looked up, his large blue eyes focusing on her in the shadows. Rose's heart thumped like a drum and she had to stop herself crying out at the shock of his beauty.

He blushed, then gave her a quick bashful smile before carrying on with his work. It was scant encouragement and the moment was over in seconds, but Rose felt a thrill of excitement surge through her that lifted her step and made her smile at everyone she met for the rest of the day.

But the next day when she hurried to the church after selling her basket of vegetables, there was no sign of William. She struggled to hide her disappointment. It was not until Mass on Sunday that she caught a glimpse of him again, by which time she felt sick with anticipation. Rose gazed at his handsome face. He seemed so lively and animated when singing, she found it hard to believe he was normally so shy and tongue-tied. Florrie said her brother was very devout and had once wanted to train for the priesthood.

As the summer wore on, Rose measured the time in William days. On ones that she saw him, she felt full of energy and a lightness of heart. But on days when she caught no glimpse of his boyish good looks, she was irritable and sullen and snapped at her sisters. After a few weeks, he would nod to her as they passed and give her one of his quick smiles that made her skittish as a kitten.

The numbers using the soup kitchen were growing daily. The millers and bakers in the town were refusing to give the strikers credit and children were falling sick with summer fevers in larger numbers than usual.

Rose felt detached from the tension at home, her parents worrying over business. Neither did the increasing hardship around the town dampen her spirits. Whenever she felt fear for the future, one passing look or smile from William was enough to fill her with giddy optimism that soon all would be well. She ignored her father's criticism that she was spending too much time at St Bede's and not enough looking for custom.

'You've turned holy all of a sudden, Rose Ann,' her father grumbled, throwing her a suspicious glance. 'Are you thinking of becoming a nun?'

Rose's sisters giggled at the idea, but her mother defended her.

'You and Father Boyle should be happy with that,' she snorted. 'Our Rose is a good lass.' Yet she eyed her eldest daughter's reddening cheeks and pondered on the reason.

Rose did not care if her mother guessed her motive for spending so much time at St Bede's. It was as if she were smitten with a summer fever over which she had no control. Her body was transforming into a woman's before her very eyes and with it came womanly feelings - thoughts of William that plagued her and left her restless.

She would wake in a sweat on hot June nights next to her sleeping sisters and throw off the covers, her nightgown damp against her body. If she dreamt of him, she would hug herself in the warm afterglow of her dream and try to recapture it. On other occasions she would wake, gasping in alarm for air, wondering why she should feel such panic. Then she would remember that it was John McMullen's surly, brooding face and piercing green eyes that had forced their way into her dreams. Her hammering heart would calm down as the relief of being awake engulfed her.

She had no idea why she should be dreaming of John, or even thinking of him at all. Rose had not set eyes on him for months. It was distasteful to think of him in the same way as William. He was everything that the good-natured, quiet, diligent William was not. Rose pushed uncomfortable thoughts of John from her mind and concentrated on trying to get William to notice her more. She wondered whether she should confide in Florrie and ask for her help. But Florrie was working long hours in the shop to supplement the Fawcetts' meagre strike pay and she was never alone when they met at church.

Then one day at St Bede's, her hair tousled from the steam of cooking and her apron full of vegetable peelings, Rose was confounded by William saying, 'You're doing a grand job.' By the time she realised he must be speaking to her and not to the statue of the Virgin Mary behind, he had passed on and the moment to reply was lost. Rose was nearly in a frenzy of frustration at the missed opportunity. She had daydreamed for weeks of what she would say if he ever stopped to speak to her, and now it had happened she had stood and stared at him like a simpleton. That's probably what the Fawcetts thought of her anyway. Rose had never felt her lack of education or social graces so keenly as at that moment. She wished she had had an ounce of the schooling Florrie had been given.

She determined that the next time she saw William, she would be the one to speak first. The following week, the weather played a mischievous part in her plans. The hot spell of early June, that had seen the strikers wandering the fields beyond Jarrow and enjoying the unaccustomed fresh air, broke. On the morning of the eighteenth, it grew still and airless, the heat in the church hall oppressive. They laboured on over the midday meal, but as the helpers cleared up in the early afternoon, it grew so dark they had to light the lamps. Rose felt edgy, but she had seen William go to fetch water and so refused Father O'Brien's attempts to get her to hurry home.

William appeared carrying two pails of water he had fetched from the pump. 'Storm's nearly here,' he said quietly to no one in particular. Rose darted forward and helped take one of the buckets.

'Be good to clear the air.' She smiled at him, her hot face burning even more fiercely at his arrival.

'Think you should get off home,' he said in concern. 'Looks as black as night over Newcastle way.'

'Don't really want to gan out there when it's so dark,' Rose answered. 'Think I'll stop till it's over.'

He looked at her directly for the first time. 'I'll walk you up the hill if you like,' he offered.

Rose's heart thumped in shock. She felt suddenly tongue-tied again, but forced herself to reply before he took her silence as rejection.

'Aye, please,' she answered.

They smiled at each other bashfully and then Rose was pulling on her shawl in a hurry.

As they reached the top of the street, lightning streaked across the sky to the west, followed swiftly by a low rumble of thunder. Rose knew that they would get caught in the rain long before she reached home, and glanced back at the large church.

'Grand, isn't it?' William followed her look. 'My father helped to build it when we first came to Jarrow. It's more special being built by ordinary men, isn't it?'

'Aye, it's beautiful,' Rose agreed, amazed at this sudden burst of conversation. 'Do you think we should turn back?'

William looked at the brooding sky overhead. It was an unnatural green. The town had suddenly emptied and the streets were eerily quiet.

'Let's hurry,' he decided. Rose nodded, unsure if he was just keen to get the job of taking her home over, or whether it meant something more.

As they made their way through the dense streets away from the river, lightning flashed again and the thunder grew louder. Minutes later, slow fat drops of rain began to splash around them. Within seconds, rain was falling from the sky as if a sluice had been opened, pounding the cobbles around them and soaking their clothes. Rose slipped, but William instantly put out a hand to catch her and she grasped it in delight.

Hand in hand they ran and slithered along the road, laughing out loud at their folly as the thunder boomed overhead like cannon-fire. As the streets thinned out into rows of cottages and the roads turned to tracks, they soon became bogged down in a squelching sea of mud. Then the rain turned abruptly to hailstones, huge balls of ice that cut at their bare faces and hands, and made it impossible to see where they were going. All at once, William stopped and pointed to a small wooden hut on the edge of rough ground that marked the pull uphill to the McConnells' smallholding.

'Let's gan in there!' he shouted over the din of the storm.

'It's a pigeon loft!' Rose cried in distaste.

'I've nowt against pigeons, if they don't mind us,' William replied, and pulled her after him.

Rose laughed, not caring how bedraggled or mud-spattered she looked, just giddy with the adventure. Lifting the latch quickly, he pushed her inside first. There was a trill of protest and a flapping of wings in the semi-dark, but they sank on to the dry ground thankfully.

As they regained their breath, Rose rubbed at her sodden hair with her shawl and patted her stinging face. 'I'm sorry. This is all my fault.'

'No, we should have stopped in the church like you said.' William was generous. 'It's just...'

Rose detected something in his voice. 'Just what?' she asked, curious. Even in the gloom she could tell he was blushing furiously.

'I wanted the excuse to walk you home,' William admitted softly.

Rose's pulse quickened. 'You did?' she gasped. On impulse she put out her hand and found his. 'I wanted you to, an' all. I didn't mind how much of a soaking I got.'

They both laughed in bashful delight and she felt him squeeze her hand. His shyness seemed to evaporate in the dark shed and they chatted happily as the birds cooed around them and the hail drummed noisily on the roof. They swapped stories about their families and people they knew around Jarrow. She made him laugh with tales of the characters she met while selling her vegetables and he talked of his hopes for a better life once the strike was over.

'I've no time to myself,' he said ruefully, 'just all day working at the mill. But once we've won the battle over working hours I'll have more time for other things.'

'Like what?' Rose probed.

'Like ganin' to watch the rowing, or helping at St Bede's - the things I've been able to do these past few weeks since the strike began - but to do them without the worry of how we're going to get through the week without pawning Mam's china and Dad's best suit.' She listened to the eagerness in his voice as he talked of a brighter future. 'When my apprenticeship's over, I'll have a good skilled job at the steelworks. It's what working men deserve. We're the ones who put in all the hard graft every day; it's only fair we get a decent share of the bosses' profits.'

Rose had hoped for a more romantic answer, but was prepared to be patient. They might be too young to start courting, yet Rose knew she had found the lad she wanted. He was hard-working and ambitious, gentle in manner but quietly determined. He talked with the knowledge and fluency of someone who was educated, and to top it all, he was a devout Catholic and good-looking into the bargain.

Rose was the first to notice that the storm had subsided and that bright chinks of light were cutting into their shelter. But she said nothing, not wanting to stop William's chatter now he had started. Only later, when he began to sneeze and they both felt chilled in their sodden clothing, did they stir.

'Haway, it's time I got you home,' he said, helping Rose to her feet.

They emerged from the hut into bright sunshine, yet the air was still cold from the freak icy storm. As they hurried uphill and the McConnells' home came into view, William retreated into his usual reserve. They arrived to find Rose's parents in bad temper and standing outside surveying the damage. The summer vegetables had taken a terrible battering and two windows had been smashed by hail. Her mother took one look at Rose's dirty, soaking dress and shrieked.

'Rose Ann! You look like you've been dragged through the midden! Where've you been? I thought you were safe in the church. What's the meaning of all this?' she demanded, staring suspiciously at the pale-faced youth at her side. 'You're the Fawcetts' lad, aren't you?'

'William,' he nodded. 'Sorry to worry you, Mrs McConnell,' he answered politely. 'I offered to see Rose home but the storm came on that bad, we took shelter till it was over.'

Mr McConnell shouted over. 'She knows the way home without you having to show her.'

'I was frightened of the storm,' Rose muttered. Her father snorted in disbelief.

'Get yourself inside and change out of that dress before you catch your death,' her mother fussed. 'It was good of you to take care of her, William. Will you come in and dry off?'

By now, Maggie and Lizzie had appeared to stare at him with interest. Rose knew he would refuse.

'I can see Mr McConnell needs a hand fixing up that fence,' he replied. 'I'm handy with a hammer.' He strode over to Rose's father and picked up a plank of wood before anyone could argue. The older man grunted in acceptance of the offer and in silence they set about repairing the storm-damaged plot. Rose was full of admiration at the way William had effortlessly gained her father's approval, but was disappointed at the end of the afternoon when William again refused to enter the house.

'Better be off,' he said quickly, and she only had time for a brief wave from the doorway before he turned and hurried away down the hill. He looked tired and chilled, and there was no hint of the warm intimacy that they had shared a few hours ago. Rose wondered anxiously if he had found their home too coarse, or her sisters too rude in their giggling inquisitiveness. She determined that she would find a way to speak to him again soon.

But she developed a cold after the drenching and her mother kept her confined to the house for several days. Eagerly, Rose hurried to St Bede's once her feverish head had cleared. To her dismay there was no sign of William, not even at Mass on Sunday. In alarm she sought out Florrie.

'Would you like to go for a walk this afternoon?' Rose asked tentatively. 'We could go up the fields at the back of ours.'

Florrie looked pale and tired. 'I don't think so...'

'We could paddle in the stream,' Rose urged. She was determined to get Florrie on her own and find out more about her elusive brother.

But Florrie seemed distant. She shook her head. 'Not today. It's too hot and the walk's too far.'

Rose looked at her in concern. 'Are you sickening for some'at?'

Florrie shrugged.

'Is that what's wrong with your brother?' Rose blurted out. 'Is he ill?' She flushed at Florrie's look. 'I just wondered, him not being here. It's just he's always here. And he was kind to me the other day - walking me home in the storm.'

'William's been poorly ever since,' Florrie told her bluntly. 'He came back in a terrible state - couldn't stop shivering.'

'How poorly?' Rose asked in alarm.

'Very,' Florrie said shortly. 'Head's as hot as a furnace - and he's got a bad cough. Mam's frightened it might be pneumonia, but we can't afford to call out the doctor.'

Rose saw the tears welling in Florrie's eyes. 'I feel terrible,' Rose gasped. 'What can I do to help?'

'Nothing,' Florrie replied, turning away.

'Please!' Rose insisted. 'I'll bring round some veg - make a warming soup. Mam's good at making remedies for all sorts. Me granny taught her.'

'Father won't accept charity,' Florrie told her bleakly.

'Not charity - just helping out friends,' Rose said. 'It's the least I can do. William only caught a chill because of me. I'll come round this afternoon.' She hurried after her mother and sisters before Florrie could protest.

Later, with her parents' agreement, Rose took a basket of produce down to the Fawcetts in James Terrace. She was curious to see the house, for she had never been invited inside, despite her friendship with Florrie. Mr Fawcett was genial enough, but Mrs Fawcett was always distant in manner and spoke with an accent quite foreign to Tyneside. But instinct told Rose that she would have to impress this sharp-featured woman and she had spent half an hour scrubbing the soil from under her nails and from the grooves of her calloused hands. Overawed for a moment by the grandeur of the whitened front step and gleaming brass door knob, Rose rubbed her boots on the back of her legs before knocking.

Florrie came to the door and hesitated before letting her in. 'You'll not be able to stay long,' she said, with a hasty glance up and down the street. Rose had the uncomfortable feeling that the girl did not want her to be seen entering their house.

'I can't stop more than a few minutes any road,' she answered to save face.

Through an open door she could see a neat parlour with a carpet and a piano in the corner. Mr Fawcett was dozing in an armchair by the unlit fire. Florrie whispered for her to follow. She took her into the kitchen. It was orderly but sparse, with a meagre fire burning in the grate and no smell of cooking from the well-polished stove. Two pairs of working boots stood gleaming but idle on the hearth like soldiers waiting for action.

'Just put the basket on the table,' Florrie said as if talking to a servant.

Rose pursed her lips as she plonked down her offering. 'Where's your mam?'

'Not feeling very well - she's resting,' Florrie said, her fair face blushing easily, reminding Rose of William. They looked at each other awkwardly. Rose took her time unloading the basket, thinking that Mrs Fawcett had looked perfectly well to her at Mass that morning. Was the woman avoiding her because she blamed her for William's illness?

Rose took off her shawl and hung it over a chair.

'What are you doing?' Florrie asked tensely.

'Going to help you prepare these onions and carrots for a canny pot of broth. Ma's put in a nice ham knuckle. We'll need to stoke up the fire a bit, mind.'

'No!' Florrie said in alarm. 'I can manage. We've already eaten, so we'll keep this for tomorrow. Thank you.'

Rose was baffled and a little hurt by her friend's frosty attitude. She had been looking forward to them making the soup together and chatting about William.

'Is there any chance . . . ? Could I... er - see your brother?' She tried to hide her embarrassment.

Florrie looked scandalised. 'Oh, no, you can't go upstairs. I mean he's much too poorly to have visitors. At least at the moment. Maybe when he's on his feet again. . .'

'Aye, of course,' Rose said, feeling foolish for having asked. Suddenly she wanted to get out of this unwelcoming house as quickly as possible. 'Well, I'll be off then.' She put on her shawl. 'I hope William's better soon. You'll let me know if there's anything else we can do? Ma and Da are only too pleased to help out,' Rose added pointedly.

'Thank you, but I'm sure we'll manage,' Florrie replied.

Rose noticed for the first time how her friend lifted her chin haughtily and remembered her father's comment about the Fawcetts looking down their long noses at the likes of them. She felt sudden annoyance. She came from a respectable family and was here to help them out, not the other way round. Having airs and graces and living in a posh house in James Terrace boiled down to nothing when there was a strike on and not enough food on the table. It was then that friendship and neighbourliness counted for everything.

But maybe Florrie did not even see her as a friend, just someone she knew from St Bede's? Rose realised she was always the one who approached Florrie first, never the other way round. What did their friendship amount to? A few minutes of chatter at church and someone to play with on rare social outings. Occasional titbits of ribbon bestowed on her with the showiness of a queen to a humble servant. And she had been so grateful! Now Rose felt only humiliation.

Quickly she grabbed the empty basket and marched out of the kitchen. Turning at the front door, Rose said in a loud voice, 'You'll tell William I was asking after him, won't you?'

Florrie nodded, looking flustered, and glanced into the parlour to see if her father had been disturbed. Rose lingered on the doorstep, perversely enjoying the girl's discomfort. 'And please tell Mrs Fawcett I'm sorry to have missed her - and hope she's better soon an' all.'

Florrie nodded vigorously, while trying to edge her out of the door. As soon as she was clear of the step, the door was closed behind her. Rose stepped on to the hot pavement and turned to glance at the upstairs windows, wondering if William lay behind one of them. There was a blind pulled down at the smaller window above the door. Just as she was turning away, she saw the lace curtain at the larger window lift a fraction. For a brief second, she saw the becapped head of Mrs Fawcett staring down at her, then the curtain was quickly dropped back into place.

Rose flushed furiously. She was not ill or resting; that woman had been hiding upstairs all the time! Hurrying up the street she felt waves of anger surge through her at the Fawcetts' rudeness. It was quite plain that they did not want to be seen associating with a common labouring family like the McConnells, let alone receive help from them. They had done everything to discourage her, apart from throw the vegetables back in her face.

Rose fumed all the way home at their treatment of her and the slight to her hard-working and upright family. It was painfully obvious that the Fawcetts would not see her as a suitable match for their only son. She had been mad to entertain such a dream. As she neared home, Rose began to doubt William's feelings for her. All he had done was offer to walk her home in a storm. He had been polite and friendly, but then he was like that with everyone - it was in his nature.

She was sure he would not have been so begrudging of her gifts and help, had he known of them. But that did not mean he would cause upset with his parents by courting her in earnest when they were a little older. It might never have crossed his mind to court her, and even if it had, he probably did not look on her as a suitable match either. By the time Rose had toiled up the hill and reached home, she felt the hopelessness of her situation.

Ever since she was a small girl watching the wedding of Lord Ravensworth's daughter, she had harboured dreams of a fairytale marriage that would lift her from the drudgery of manual work on her parents' smallholding. Did her mother ever regret leaving Ravensworth to marry her father and live in the town? Rose thought how different life would have been had she stayed - how different for all of them had her mother persuaded her father to return to Ravensworth when they were younger. She still had a vivid memory of children playing in sunny fields around Lamesley, and her granny ruing the day her headstrong daughter chose to follow McConnell into 'the jaws of Hell'. When she looked at her mother she saw a woman already worn out before she was forty. Rose wanted more from life than that. But with heavy heart she realised that William Fawcett was beyond her reach. She would have to lower her expectations and look elsewhere.

Banging through the gate, she caught sight of her sisters running around and playing with a skipping rope.

'Haway, Rose! Come and join in,' shouted Maggie.

'You take this end and I'll jump in the middle!' cried Lizzie.

Rose grinned at them, dumping her basket quickly by the fence. She would forget about lads for a while and be content with her sisters' company. When friends turned out to be fickle, she could always rely on family, Rose thought gratefully.

Chapter 4

1877

Rose jostled with Maggie for a place in front of the cracked mirror. For this special occasion she wore her hair tied up and caught in a chignon as she had noticed fashionable women doing. The girls had spent the last week adapting two hand-me-down dresses of their mother's - coarse linen, but better than the plain woollen skirts and sacking aprons that they wore all day in the field.

'Let me see!' Maggie cried impatiently. 'Does this bonnet suit me?'

Rose surveyed her. Today her sister looked pretty, her face flushed with excitement at the thought of the McMullen wedding. Too often in recent times, Maggie had looked pinched and grey-faced under a large man's cap and a moth-eaten shawl that had belonged to their grandmother.

'You look bonny as can be!' Rose encouraged, retying the ribbon for her so that the bow framed her cheek.

'Can't wait to see Lizzie,' Maggie said in excitement. 'Do you think she'll bring us some'at from Shields? Like that glass necklace she bought for your birthday?'

Rose touched the coloured beads at her neck and smiled. 'Maybes she will. It'll just be grand to see her again.'

It seemed an age since their sister had gone into service. Rose knew that Lizzie did not like living away from home, but she seldom grumbled about the foreman from the chemical works for whom she worked. No doubt it was to stop her family worrying, Rose thought, for there had been too much worry and distress these past two years. What terrible times!

For a while, their world had seemed more secure, after the lengthy strike five years ago. Despite the shipbuilders and bosses trying to bring in blackleg labour from abroad, they had finally capitulated and introduced the nine-hour working day. Rose had watched the riverside grow ever more crowded, with larger ships being launched, churches being built and tenement houses mushrooming. Their own market garden had prospered and they had had money to spend on going to the fair during Newcastle's Race Week, on new hats and even a sewing machine.

Their mother had been suspicious of such an innovation, but the girls had revelled in making their own clothes from whatever cheap material they could find. If they heard of a bargain in a neighbouring area, they would ride the coal wagons to secure a nice piece of cloth. Lizzie was especially adept at sewing and made beautiful quilts that Rose and Maggie would hawk around the town to the better-off households.

They had avoided the Fawcetts in James Terrace, though, for Rose had no intention of being humiliated by them twice. It seemed a distant memory when she had been so smitten with love for William. A calf love, Rose now thought of it, a silly childish hankering after the impossible.

She had not seen him for weeks after that futile visit to his house. Either he was avoiding her or he took a long time recovering from his illness. If she had been able to write properly she would have sent him a note to tell him how sorry she was that she had caused him to catch a fever. But she determined not to give the Fawcetts the satisfaction of laughing at her lack of education.

So it had been September before she saw William again at St Bede's and by that time apologies had seemed too late. She knew that his family must have been suffering great hardship after five months of no work, but pride made them keep their trials to themselves. William had looked painfully thin, his large eyes dark-ringed and his face pale as milk. He had nodded at Rose in a self-conscious way, but had not spoken and she had not gone out of her way to try to speak to him. It was as if their moment of friendship in the pigeon loft had never been and she was embarrassed now to think of it. William was now a brethren at St Bede's, his spare time given over to the Church, and she assumed he had no interest in lasses.

Likewise, Rose had put thoughts of lads from her mind. She discouraged any interest from youths such as the McMullens, who could be playfully bawdy with her and her sisters given half the chance. All except the moody John, who shied away from girls and was teased by his brothers for his tongue-tied gruffness.

Now Michael McMullen was marrying Jenny Kennedy and there would be as big a celebration as their scant resources would allow. How her mother would have enjoyed a party! Rose felt tears spring to her eyes as she thought how swiftly and cruelly their mother had been taken from them the year before. Hunger and destitution had come again to the rows of Tyneside houses as a slump in trade had blighted the area. Hardly a ship was launched from Palmer's and most of the workshops had been closed. A sinister silence had settled on the town. Then, as if that were not punishment enough, typhoid fever had spread through Jarrow like a fire, paralysing every family in fear.

Their hard-working mother, the rock of their family, had returned from visiting a sick friend and gone to bed. Within three days she was dead. Still numb with shock, they had made a pyre of her bedding and nightgown and set fire to them, while their father had crouched by the fence and wept like a child. They might have all starved if Rose had not rallied her sisters to take over the digging in the garden, while their father sank into deep mourning. She missed her mother deeply, and the fear that her life and those of her sisters might go the same way haunted those dark months. It had spurred her on to make a difficult decision.

'Lizzie, hinny,' she had taken her sister aside one day, 'you're the most domesticated of us lasses. You'll have to gan into place. We need the money badly. Me and Maggie are stronger at the labouring and Maggie's good with Da.' She tried to cheer her sister. 'You'll be better off than stoppin' here.'

Lizzie had nodded like a wise old woman and they had gone together to see Father O'Brien, who had taken over from old Father Boyle, to ask if he could put in a word for her. By the end of the year he had secured her a live-in position as general maid to the Flynns in South Shields, doing all their cooking and cleaning and back-breaking chores. Rose had never seen the cramped attic boxroom where Lizzie slept, but she knew her sister worked long hours and got little time to herself, for she rarely came home. Rose missed her lively sister and felt guilty for having sent her away, but knew they had no choice. Once a month they would see Lizzie for half a day. But today she had been given special permission to attend Michael McMullen's wedding.

Rose stared critically at her reflection. At nineteen, she was large-featured with prominent cheekbones, a broad forehead and a full mouth. Her brown eyes were her best feature, framed by dark lashes and eyebrows. She patted her dark head of hair, catching a glimpse of calloused, dirt-ingrained fingers.

'Eeh, look at these!' she cried in dismay. 'They're workman's hands.'

'No one'll be looking at your hands,' Maggie assured her. 'They'll not see past your bonny face.'

Rose gave her sister a grateful hug. Maggie was full of kindness and optimism, always looking on the bright side. Rose wouldn't have been able to keep going this past gruelling year if it hadn't been for her sister's humour and encouragement.

'Here,' Maggie smiled, 'try on the hat.'

Rose took the round blue hat that they had snapped up for Lizzie in a second-hand clothes shop, and placed it on her head.

'I think it's too small for my big head,' Rose giggled. 'Anyway, it's for our Lizzie.'

'She won't mind,' Maggie insisted. 'You never buy anything for yourself.' Maggie readjusted the hat for her, securing it to the back of her head with a large pin. 'That's how you're supposed to wear them - tipped back - not on top like a bird's nest!'

They both laughed. 'Haway, let's go and see if Da's ready,' Rose said, with a last swift glance in the mirror. 'I can hear him swearing over his collar.'

The sisters bustled into the kitchen where their father sat cursing over the unaccustomed restrictions of his best shirt and antiquated breeches. But Rose was glad that he had agreed to come to the wedding at all, for he had hardly left home since their mother's funeral over a year ago, shunning any company but theirs.

They fussed around him, helping him with his buttons and tie, until he was presentable. Finally, they set off together into the warm September sunshine, eager to meet Lizzie at the church.

'Mrs McMullen says Michael's going to be living with the Kennedys until they can afford to rent a place of their own,' Maggie chatted. 'Makes you wonder why they didn't wait a bit longer.'

'I don't wonder,' Rose answered. 'It'll not be half as crowded as the McMullens' place.'

'Aye,' Maggie laughed, 'that's one more lodger Michael's mam'll be able to squeeze in after today.'

'Can't have the beds getting cold,' Rose joked.

Maggie sang, 'And the little one said, "Roll over, roll over!" And they all rolled over and one fell out. ..'

'That's enough!' their father growled. 'You'll show a bit more respect for our own people. They're fine stock, the McMullens, and they do what they can to survive - just like the rest of us. It was thanks to your dear mother's good housekeeping that we never had to take in lodgers, not because we're any better than the likes of the McMullens.'

'And Rose too.' Maggie spoke up. 'We've got by because of her since Mam —'

Rose gave her a sharp jab in the ribs and a warning look. She did not want to spoil the day by stoking up one of their father's black moods by mentioning their mother's death. Her parents had argued about many things, but now her mother was gone, her father seemed lost and forlorn without her.

A hazy sky hung over St Bede's that Saturday afternoon and, once in the town, a black dust soon settled on the men's white collars and the women's bonnets.

'There she is!' Maggie cried, and they rushed towards Lizzie, hugging her in delight.

'Grand hat,' Lizzie said to Rose.

Rose blushed. 'It's for you - you can have it after today.'

'Don't be daft,' Maggie said quickly, 'it suits you. She can keep it, can't she, our Lizzie?'

Lizzie gave the hat a brief longing glance then nodded her agreement. 'Mrs Flynn gave me this old bonnet of hers - it'll do for now.'

Rose felt a rush of affection for her younger sister. Impulsively she reached out and squeezed her arm. 'No, after today this hat's yours. I can wear Mrs Flynn's one for church.'

They talked nonstop as they entered the church and filed into the pews behind their father. The church was stuffy, filling up with friends and relations. Half of Jarrow seemed to be crammed in to witness the wedding. As the McMullens clattered in, Rose caught a glance from John. He had grown a moustache since she had last seen him and strutted in defiantly. There seemed little trace of the gangling, awkward youth of five years ago. He was a man in his twenties, broadened and hardened by heavy physical work. No doubt he would soon be taking a wife, she thought with a quickening of her pulse that she could not understand. He was handsome enough, but he would be nothing but trouble to whoever took him on. She had heard about his fighting around the pubs of Jarrow, and how neither the priest nor his mother could get him or half his brothers to church. This was a rare occasion to see so many McMullens trouping into St Bede's in an array of ill-fitting suits and caps.

Rose glanced down, feeling uncomfortable to be singled out by John's harsh stare.

'There's Jobling's ghost,' Lizzie sniggered, and dug her in her ribs. Her sister had teased Rose for years about the incident down by the Slake. 'Did you see the way he looked at you? Still sweet on you, Rose Ann!'

'Ssh! No he's not,' she hissed. 'We haven't spoken in years. Any road, I don't care for him.'

'I sometimes see him,' Lizzie whispered, 'queuing at the dock gates for work when I'm taking the tram. Seems hard-working to me.'

'Aye, and hard-drinking and hard-fighting, from what I hear,' Rose snorted.

'A lass needs a man who stands up for himself and his own kind,' Lizzie teased.

'I don't need a man at all.' Rose flushed.

With the arrival of the bride, they stopped their arguing over John. After the ceremony they were invited back to the Kennedys' house. With a son at Palmer's mill and another a joiner at the shipyard where trade was picking up again, the Kennedys were doing well enough to have left the old pit cottages for a house nearer the town centre. Rose knew Mrs Kennedy kept a strong grip on the purse strings and had been putting a little by for her daughter's wedding day for years.

There were ham sandwiches and savoury pies in the small kitchen, a barrel of beer and flagons of whisky in the back yard, and the oilcloth rolled back in the front room for dancing. A fiddler had been hired to play all night or until the last guest went home. Rose and her sisters found the house bursting with people, all intent on this rare break from the daily grind of work or lack of work and scraping by.

They greeted the bride and groom and then squeezed their way through to the food, tackling it with enthusiasm. Later, when her father was steered into the back yard to sit on a crate and drink with old McMullen, Lizzie pulled her sisters into the dance room. They jostled into someone behind the door.

'Sorry,' Rose said, turning to see who it was. Standing, looking out of place in a smart suit and clutching a small glass of beer, was William Fawcett. Rose gasped in surprise and felt colour flood into her cheeks. She had not seen him arrive or noticed him at church.

William's eyes widened too. 'R-Rose,' he stuttered.

'What are you ...? I mean, I didn't know you were ...' she floundered.

He smiled almost apologetically. 'I work with Danny Kennedy at the rolling mill,' he explained. 'Don't know many people here - except you.'

Rose felt her insides lurch. She had not stood this close to William since the day of the hailstorm, all those summers ago. He was taller and leaner, his face almost gaunt. A wisp of a moustache shaded his upper lip, but his smile was still boyish and his blue eyes lively. She did not know what to say, aware that her sisters were watching them with interest.

After a pause he said, 'I'm sorry about your mother passing on.'

'Thank you,' Rose murmured.

'Is your father keeping well?' he asked quietly.

'He's grown old all of a sudden,' Rose found herself confiding. 'The shock of losing Ma - and things haven't been easy this past year. Mind, they haven't been for most people.'

'Rose has been grand at looking after us all,' Maggie piped up. 'We haven't wanted for anything.'

'Aye,' agreed Lizzie, 'and today she could do with a bit of fun - like a dance maybes, and a bit of attention from a lad.'

Rose went puce at her sisters' interference, but William just smiled.

'Better ask her quick then - before I miss me turn,' he teased back. 'Rose, will you dance with me?'

'You don't have to take any notice of them,' Rose said, quite flustered.

'I wouldn't want to get on the wrong side of the McConnell lasses,' he grinned. 'Come on, Rose, show me how to dance your Irish dances.'

Lizzie and Maggie pushed their sister forward and William took her hand. Rose felt light-headed at the contact, and soon they were turning and spinning around the cramped dance floor to the merry music of the fiddler.

When the dance finished they were both out of breath and Rose felt her body glowing with heat.

'Want to stand outside for a minute?' William suggested. Rose nodded and followed, ignoring the grins on her sisters' faces.

They walked to the end of the terrace and stood against the shaded gable, letting the cold brick cool their backs. Beyond the next terrace they could see the blackened ruin of St Paul's, Bede's monastery. A strong smell of sulphur wafted to them on a warm breeze that sent dust dancing in crazy circles around their feet.

'How's Florrie?' Rose asked a little awkwardly.

'Canny,' said William. 'Still at the haberdasher's. She's courting a lad from the bank.' He slid her a look. 'And you, Rose - are you courting yet?'

Her heart thumped at so direct a question. The boy of five years ago would never have been so forward, but then William was now a man.

'No,' Rose admitted while gazing intently at her feet.

'I haven't seen you at any of the church socials,' he said.

She could tell he was watching her, but she dare not meet his gaze. Had he been looking out for her?

'Don't have time,' Rose answered, 'now I'm helping Da with the digging and that.' She caught sight of her large, rough-skinned hands and quickly slid them behind her back. But William saw the self-conscious movement and reached out to take her hands. He held them gently in his own warm, work-hardened ones and rubbed his thumbs over her blistered palms. Rose caught her breath at the delicious tingling sensation this caused.

'You shouldn't be ashamed of them,' William said, 'or the hard graft you put in to help your family. I admire you for it.'

Rose looked up and met his blue-eyed gaze. It was full of warmth and understanding.

Rose gulped. 'Do you really?'

William squeezed her hands in his. 'Aye, I do. But then I've always admired you - the way you look after your sisters, your friendliness. That day of the storm - it was the first time I'd ever really spoken with a lass apart from me sister. You were so easy to talk to, so full of life. I stopped feeling shy with you. But afterwards ...'

Rose saw the doubt on his face. 'Afterwards?' she whispered.

William shrugged. 'Well, you kept out me way. I could see that day of the storm hadn't stuck in your mind like it had in mine.'

Rose gripped his hands in return. 'But it did!' she cried. 'I came round to see you when you had pneumonia -brought stuff for a broth - but Florrie wouldn't let me near you. Couldn't get rid of me quick enough. And your mam hid upstairs so she didn't have to meet us. Did Florrie never tell you?'

'No!' William replied. 'At least I don't remember ... I was feverish for a long time. They were afraid I was going to die. But it would have cheered me to know you had come. Maybes they just forgot.'

'They wouldn't have,' Rose retorted. 'It was obvious they thought I was too common to be seen coming to your house.'

'Florrie's not like that,' William protested.

'Then why did she never invite me round to her house?' Rose asked. 'She was always welcome at mine - but she used to make excuses not to come.'

They dropped hands and looked at each other uncertainly. Rose felt wretched that she had spoken out so swiftly against his family, but it had rankled inside for years. She saw William frown and took it for disapproval.

Suddenly, he slipped his arm through hers and said, 'Let's walk for a bit - down to St Paul's.'

Confused, she allowed him to lead her away towards the ruined monastery. The light was beginning to dim, a hazy orange glow settling over the rooftops behind them as early evening closed in. William did not speak again until they were standing under the arch of the long-abandoned monastery.

'I love this place,' he said softly. 'I like to imagine St Bede walking around the cloisters, working at his books. Sometimes I can almost hear the voices of the monks singing - echoing round the stone.'

Rose kept silent. All she heard were the distant shouts of children in the streets and the clanging from the shipyards. To her the place was empty and full of frightening shadows. But she let William carry on in his quiet voice, telling a story of early Christians working the fields round about, fishing from a river as clear as glass and praying in the calm of the evening. She marvelled at his imagination. How could he see such beauty in this dirty, soot-covered landscape where nothing grew?

Looking at his animated face and listening to his mesmerising voice, Rose felt again the rush of love for William that she had experienced when they were younger. It must always have been there, buried under her disappointment and rejection by his family. When he fell silent, Rose stepped closer and looked directly into his dreamy eyes.

'You're a very special lad,' she whispered. 'I'm glad we met again.'

William gazed at her in surprise for a moment, then he smiled. 'So am I.'

The next instant they were leaning towards each other and brushing lips together. It was such a tentative kiss, like the touch of butterfly wings, that Rose was not sure they had kissed at all, but it filled her with a warm excitement. She yearned for William to kiss her again and for longer, but he seemed unsure and drew back.

'Better get back to the weddin',' he said with a bashful look, 'in case your father's worrying where you are.'

'He won't be worrying about anything if he's still drinking with Mr McMullen,' Rose answered. But to her disappointment, William turned back up the street.

When they reached the Kennedys', many of the revellers had spilled out into the street and were dancing and drinking outside in the dusk. The noise of celebration rang around the cobbled lane. Rose saw Lizzie dancing with one of the McMullen boys.

'Would you like me to see you home?' William asked.

Rose hesitated. She would like nothing more, but she could not leave without her family.

'I'll have to wait for me sisters - and make sure Da gets home in one piece,' she answered.

William nodded. 'I'll go and say goodbye to the Kennedys then.'

'Aren't you staying?' Rose said in dismay.

'I'm helping at St Bede's this evening,' he explained. 'I'll see you at Mass tomorrow, though?'

Rose nodded. She would have to be content with that, though she was in a fever of confusion over what William really thought of her. Had he regretted their brief kiss in the shadow of St Paul's? Did he fear what his parents might say if they knew he had walked out with her? But he was gone and she was engulfed in frustration.

For a while, she stood around in the half-dark, watching the dancers, and was on the point of going to find Maggie and her father when someone lurched out of the shadows and grabbed her arm. Rose smelt a waft of whisky on the man's breath and recoiled before realising it was John McMullen. He held on.

'Dance with me, Rose Ann,' John ordered, his grip tight and bruising.

'Leave go me arm, you're hurting me!' Rose protested.

'I want to dance wi' you,' he growled.

'All right, I'll dance,' she gave in, 'just don't hold me so hard.'

He relaxed his iron-fisted grip a little, as he swung her into the throng of dancers. He was a touch unsteady and she knew at once he was drunk, but he swirled her around with more assurance than she would have thought him capable of. With William gone, the excitement had drained out of the day, but dancing at least would fill in the time until her sisters wanted to go home. Rose could not help smiling to think she had been asked to dance twice in one day. It was more than she had danced in the past two years!

'Glad to see you're enjoyin' yersel',' John shouted above the noise of the revellers, in mid reel.

'Aye, I like a good weddin',' Rose called back.

When the dance finished, John took a quick swig from a jar of whisky while holding on to her with his other hand. Rose looked around for Lizzie but could not see her in the dark. The fiddler struck up again and John pulled her into the next dance.

'Since when have you been so keen on dancin'?' Rose teased.

'Depends on the company,' he said, giving her a drunken grin. She had never seen him so animated.

They danced again and at the end Rose insisted, 'I need a sit down.' She went and squatted down on a neighbouring doorstep.

'We could gan for a walk,' John suggested. 'Promise it won't be the Slake.'

Rose looked at him in surprise. Why was he showing her all this attention? Could Lizzie's teasing remarks about him being sweet on her really be true?

'I'm too tired to walk,' she replied.

He flopped down beside her. 'You weren't too tired an hour ago.' He nudged her. 'I saw you ganin' off with that stuck-up Fawcett lad.'

Rose blushed. 'He was telling me about the monastery. It was very interesting.'

John laughed in derision. 'Didn't look like he was giving you a lecture from where I was standing.'

Rose was incensed. 'Were you spying on me, John McMullen?'

'Your father wouldn't like to hear you'd been wanderin' off with a lad, now would he? I was worried for your safety.'

'It's none of your business to worry over what I do!' Rose replied at once.

'But I do, Rose,' John said, leering over her. 'What do you see in that lad any road? Don't you want to be kissed by a real man?'

Before Rose could dodge away, John had hold of her roughly and covered her mouth eagerly with his. She was enveloped in his sour breath, his wet lips hungry for hers. After a moment, Rose managed to shove him off and turn her face from his in disgust.

'Don't you dare try that again!' she hissed, not wanting to draw attention to them.

John laughed. 'Just a bit fun on me brother's weddin' night. It's not asking much.'

'I never heard you asking,' Rose retorted, trying to stand up. He grabbed at her skirt.

'Haway and sit down wi' me! Didn't mean to upset you. You must know I've taken a fancy to you?' John slurred.

'I know it's the drink talking,' Rose said, wrenching her skirt from his hold. Her heart was thumping with something that felt like fear. Why did he always make her feel so uncomfortable?

'Think yourself above us McMullens, don't you, Rose Ann?' He turned suddenly aggressive. 'Well, your father would think you lucky to have the likes of me - a real Irish patriot - and true to the Faith!'

Rose laughed scornfully. 'When's the last time you went to confession?'

He staggered up and blocked her path. 'Not like your little altar boy, eh? Pure as the Virgin Mary,' he taunted.

Rose was offended. 'Watch your tongue!' She pushed past him and hurried to the safety of other company. Behind her she could hear him cursing her for a prude and a snob. Hot with the shame of the encounter, she looked quickly for her sisters. They were sitting in the parlour singing with Danny Kennedy and some of John's brothers.

'It's time to get Da home,' she told them brusquely. They knew from the look on her face not to argue.

A few minutes later they were out on the street, steering their maudlin father between them, as he sang snatches of half-forgotten Irish songs. John was still there, taunting her as she went.

'Ta for the dance, Rose Ann, and for the kiss!' he shouted.

Lizzie and Maggie giggled.

'Don't look back or say anything,' Rose ordered.

'By, you've had a time of it!' Lizzie said in admiration. 'Lads falling over themselves for you.'

'That's all John McMullen's good for,' Rose snapped, 'falling over.'

Later, when they had tucked their father into bed and climbed into the one they shared, the sisters talked about the day and who they had met and danced with.

'Fancy our Rose Ann being courted by two lads at once!' Lizzie crowed.

'I'm not courting either of them,' Rose protested. 'John was drunk and won't remember the fool he made of himself - and you forced William to dance with me.'

'We didn't force him to walk out with you,' Maggie reminded. 'You'd like to see him again, wouldn't you?'

Rose sighed, 'Aye, I would. But his family'll not allow it.'

'That William has a mind of his own,' Maggie encouraged. 'You shouldn't give up hope.'

Chapter 5

The next day, Lizzie went back to South Shields, promising to visit before the winter set in. Rose went eagerly to church with Maggie, but William did not seek her out after the service as she had hoped. The Fawcetts left together. William merely glanced in her direction, and allowed his mother to bustle him out of the church. Rose swallowed her disappointment and trudged back up the hill, determining to put William from her thoughts for good. Even Maggie could not think of anything to say.

That afternoon, while their father snoozed by the fire, the sisters went picking blackberries and stayed out until dusk. When they returned, they found a small bunch of flowers and twigs on the doorstep, gathered from the surrounding hedgerows. Rose picked them up, quite puzzled. Rushing into the house, half expecting to find a visitor, she saw only her father sitting staring into the fire.

'Da, have you had company?' she asked. He looked up at her blankly. 'Has anyone called while we've been out?'

He shook his head. 'Have you been out?"

'Aye, for hours, Da!' Maggie exclaimed. 'We've picked a canny few blackberries. Have you been asleep all this time?'

'Must have,' he yawned and stretched.

'So you didn't see who left these flowers on the doorstep?' Rose asked in frustration. Her father shook his head again.

'Are you courtin'?' he asked, suddenly suspicious.

'No, Da,' Rose answered swiftly, but could not help a twitch of a smile. William must have come to see her after all. Only he could have made such a romantic gesture. Hope flared within her once more. She would encourage William to court her and help him stand up to his parents. Rose was convinced that they would be happy together.

All week, as they worked on the smallholding, Rose planned. On Saturday evening, she washed and dressed in the clothes she had worn for the wedding and set off for St Bede's, knowing she would catch William after evening benediction. To her relief none of his family were with him. She waited around, approaching him from the shadows in the entrance.

'Rose!' he gasped in surprise.

She came straight out with her invitation. 'We'd like to ask you up for tea tomorrow,' she gabbled. 'Maybes go for a walk in the fields first - if it's fine. The blackberries are grand just now - we could pick some. Then you could stay for tea and maybe you could sing to us - me and Maggie would like that. And Da would like to meet you again. I just thought that after you had - well, you know...' She tailed off, her cheeks on fire.

William was looking at her in astonishment and she thought he was going to rebuff her like Florrie had done so often in the past. Then suddenly he was smiling.

'I'd like that very much,' he said, touching her lightly on the shoulder. 'I'll come after Sunday dinner - when my parents are taking a nap.'

Rose grinned back at him. 'Grand! I'll see you tomorrow then.' And she turned on her heels and almost ran into the dark, before he should change his mind and decline the invitation.

So began Rose's courtship with William, fanned into life by the gesture of the flowers on the doorstep. After the first successful Sunday afternoon visit, William called regularly for tea at the McConnells' home at the top of Simonside. All through the autumn they strolled through the fields on bright, chilly afternoons, or sat round a cosy fire and made toast if the weather was too wet. They revelled in each other's company, Rose enjoying William's stories about history, while he delighted in her quick talk and observations about people in the town. After tea, they would sing together, and Maggie and her father would clap enthusiastically, calling for more.

'It would be canny to hear you at the piano,' Rose suggested one day. 'I wish we could sing around your piano.'

They all watched William for his answer. Rose's great happiness was only marred by the thought that he had avoided inviting her round to James Terrace. She wanted their courting to be official and acknowledged by his family.

He hesitated, then nodded. 'We'll do that.'

'When?' asked Rose in excitement.

'Soon,' William promised.

But the weeks wore on and Christmas came and went without any invitation to visit the Fawcetts. William made excuses that he was too busy at the church and they should wait until the New Year. Lizzie came home for a brief visit and spoke her mind.

'They've no right to treat you like they do. You tell him if he wants to carry on courting he's got to take you home and do it proper, like.'

Rose repeated this to William. 'It's as if you're ashamed of me and me family,' she complained.

'Never!' William protested. 'I care for you, Rose. I care very much.'

'Then show it,' she challenged.

At the end of January, William finally came with the invitation to call round on Sunday afternoon to James Terrace. Maggie spent hours helping Rose to get ready, combing out her hair and tying it up neatly, scrubbing her hands until they were raw and stinging.

'Put on the glass beads and Lizzie's hat,' Maggie said. 'Wear everything fancy we've got.'

Rose was in a turmoil of nerves and anticipation as she approached the house in the gloom of that January day. William let her in and steered her into the parlour with a nervous smile. His parents sat stiffly in chairs either side of the fire, while Florrie set the table for tea.

Mr Fawcett asked after Rose's father and sisters, and then the room fell silent. Rose turned to Florrie.

'I hear you're courtin', an' all,' she smiled.

Florrie clattered the crockery and her mother gave her a sharp look.

'Careful, Florrie. You're so clumsy,' she scolded.

Florrie seemed too flustered to answer the question, so William intervened to break the awkwardness.

'I'll play something on the piano,' he said eagerly. 'Rose, would you like to sing?'

Rose did not know if she could manage a squeak, so dry was her mouth from nervousness. But she nodded and stood up, keen to be near him. They sang 'Linden Lea' together and for a moment Rose lost herself in the beauty of the music, even though her own voice was nervous. At the end, William smiled at her in encouragement. But when he suggested another, his mother interrupted sharply.

'It's time we had tea. Florrie, help me fetch it in.'

They bustled about and brought in plates of beef sandwiches, a ham and egg pie and a sponge cake with jam filling.

'Come and sit up, William,' his mother ordered. It was only as Rose stood up to come to the table that she realised it was only set for four. She hesitated in confusion. Mrs Fawcett glanced at her and pointed to the horsehair sofa where she had been sitting.

'You're fine where you are,' she said brusquely. 'No need for you to wait in the kitchen while we eat. Florrie, give the girl a cup of tea.'

Rose felt herself shaking as she sat down again. She stared at William, but he was sitting with his back to her, bent over his plate. Mr Fawcett was already eating. Florrie handed her a cup of tea with a look of embarrassment. Rose felt like hurling it at the table, but she merely took it with a mumbled thanks. Inside she was sick with fury and shame. Who did these people think they were? They were humiliating her for no reason other than pure snobbery!

To think how William had been welcomed into her home like one of the family, sharing as much food and companionship as they had to give. Why was he allowing his mother to treat her with such contempt? She glared at his back, but he did not look round. She attempted to drink the tea, but it stuck in her throat and she could not swallow.

Suddenly Rose could not bear to be excluded any longer. Abruptly, she stood up. William was weak and she would not have him if this was how little he thought of her! Stepping over to the table she slammed down the cup and flowery saucer, slopping tea on to the starched white tablecloth.

'Mind the china,' Mrs Fawcett said in alarm. 'And you haven't finished, girl.'

'Oh, I've finished!' Rose glared. 'And I'll not stop here another minute where I'm not wanted,' she said in a voice that trembled.

Mr Fawcett looked quite bemused, while Florrie's mouth fell open in shock.

'There's no need for rudeness,' Mrs Fawcett tutted, the ribbons on her cap fluttering as she wagged her head in disapproval.

'The rudeness isn't mine,' Rose replied, pulling her shawl tight about her. 'We McConnells would never tret a visitor like this - keeping me from the table like I'm worse than muck. What are you afraid of- that I don't know how to eat from a plate?'

'Really!' Mrs Fawcett said, going red in the face.

'Well, I do. I used to envy Florrie living in a house like this, with fancy furniture and a piano in the parlour. But not any more. It counts for nowt compared to a house with love in it - however poor.'

'Now, now...' Mr Fawcett said ineffectually.

'How dare you speak to us like that?' Mrs Fawcett cried. 'William, how could you bring such a girl here to insult us? I told you she was a common little thing.'

All this time, William had not looked round at Rose, but had sat, shoulders hunched, as if he could protect himself from the confrontation. Now he turned and she could see his lean face was quite ashen. Rose knew in that moment that she had lost him, that he would never stand up to his censorious mother for her sake. She swallowed the bile of anger that threatened to choke her and strode to the door.

'Stop!' he said behind her. Rose checked her step but did not turn round. 'Don't go,' William said more firmly.

'She can't stay now,' his mother protested, 'not after the way she's insulted us!'

Rose turned to see William confront the older woman, his face reddening.

'We're the ones who've done the insulting,' he said quietly. 'I'm ashamed to think you could begrudge her a bite of tea. And there's nothing common about Rose. She's got more kindness and decency than all the folk who live round here and think themselves better.' He looked at Rose at last and she thought she would faint at the smile he gave her. 'I'm sorry. Please forgive us.'

Before Rose could answer, Mrs Fawcett was on her feet and shouting. 'Forgive *us*? How dare you? She doesn't belong here!'

William did not take his gaze from Rose's. 'Well, she will soon,' he said stoutly. 'Rose and I intend to marry.'

This time it was Rose who was completely taken aback. She gawped at him, quite speechless.

Mr Fawcett let out a belch that went unreprimanded. 'That's a bit sudden, isn't it? You hardly know the lass.'

'It's out of the question,' Mrs Fawcett snapped.

William stood tall, his shoulders braced against their opposition. 'I've known Rose for years - and I've seen enough of her to know she's the only lass I'll wed. She's a good Catholic and I'll have no other.'

Rose felt tears sting her eyes as she stepped swiftly to his side in support. He grabbed her hand.

'You can't,' his mother gasped. 'She's not good enough for you. You're too young - you need our permission.' She looked at her husband beseechingly. 'Tell William he can't do this!' she wailed, then sank back into her chair and began to sob.

Mr Fawcett said, 'Florrie, comfort your mother.' Turning to William he asked, 'Have you asked Mr McConnell?'

William flushed. 'I mean to - just as soon as I get the chance. It's just come a bit sudden.'

His father grunted. 'So sudden, I think it's taken young Rose here by surprise an' all.'

Rose quickly spoke up. 'I'm of the same mind as William. I'll be a good wife to him - just as he'll be a grand husband to me.'

Mr Fawcett nodded. 'We'll see what McConnell has to say.'

'So you won't stand in our way, Father?' William pressed.

'I have no objection to the lass,' he replied, which provoked an increase in wailing from the other end of the tea table. 'Pull yourself together, Mrs Fawcett,' he said in irritation. 'If this is what William wants, you'll just have to learn to get on with the lass.'

Rose and William exchanged triumphant looks. He squeezed her hand tightly in his. She felt her whole body shaking with relief. Rose wanted to kiss him there and then, but thought the shock might send his mother into a fit.

'Let's go and ask your father now,' William grinned, light-headed at their boldness.

Rose could not escape fast enough. Moments before she had been convinced she would leave alone with a heavy heart and never return. Now she had William beside her and the promise of a future together. She thought she would burst with joy.

They tumbled out into the dark evening, unable to contain their laughter. The street was lit by a bright moon that made the frozen cobbles sparkle like crystals, and clouds whipping past made it appear to move. Clutching her hand, William looked up at the full moon and cried out, 'I'm so happy! Race with me, Rose!' He began to run, pulling her along behind.

'You've gone mad!' Rose gasped, laughing in delight. 'What are we racing?'

'The moon, Rose, the moon!'

As they skidded along the road, clinging on to each other tightly, Rose thought she had never been so happy. She had William's love, and the moon - that angel-faced guardian of her childhood - was beaming down on them, blessing their union.

'You're a madman, William Fawcett!' she cried as they ran like the wind after the elusive moon. What she meant, but was too bashful to say, was; I love you with every inch of my being.

Chapter 6

Rose and William were to be married that spring of 1878. Once Mrs Fawcett saw she was outnumbered, she accepted the situation with bad grace and tried to influence proceedings as much as possible.

'Of course my William can't go and live in a workman's hut in the back of beyond,' she protested at the idea of them starting married life at the McConnells'. 'She'll have to come and live here where I can keep an eye on her - teach her the ways of a good wife.'

It rankled with Rose that her future mother-in-law continued to speak about her as if she was not in the room and never referred to her by name. But she curbed her tongue for William's sake. It would be a temporary arrangement until they had saved enough to rent a place of their own.

'Better this way than not at all,' William reasoned, trying to cheer her. 'We don't want to give them the time to change their minds about us getting wed. And it will be handier for work living here.'

Rose found an unexpected ally in Florrie. She offered to move out of her bedroom and sleep in the narrow boxroom at the top of the stairs where William had been.

'It's not much bigger,' said Florrie, 'but it doesn't seem right, you starting off married life in a cupboard. It'll be hard enough living under the same roof as Mam.'

Rose was surprised by her frankness. 'That's canny of you, Florrie; ta very much. I can make it nice and homely for the two of us.'

The other girl nodded. 'Somewhere to escape to.'

Rose raised her eyebrows. 'I thought you were happy here?'

Florrie gave a short laugh. 'I'm counting the days till I can get married too. As soon as Albert has enough put by I intend to marry him and start a home of my own.'

Rose gave her a shy smile. 'It'll be canny having you here until then. I hope we can be friends again?'

Florrie glanced over her shoulder before answering. 'I always wanted to be,' she admitted in a hushed voice, 'but it would have caused too much fuss. Mother never wanted me to visit your house - said I would catch some illness from all the muck and animals. And it was always easier not to invite anyone back here for tea in case she took a dislike to them.'

Rose felt sudden pity for William's sister. What a lonely upbringing she must have had in this stark, spotless house, imprisoned by her mother's censoriousness and obsession with order.

'I'm sorry,' Rose said. 'I was wrong about you. From now on we'll look out for each other, shall we?' The girls hugged in agreement.

The wedding was not as Rose would have planned it. Her father wished to kill a pig and lay on a meal for everyone they knew up at Simonside after the service. But the Fawcetts, being teetotal, shunned the idea of too much drinking and too many Irish.

'Da, William's parents won't come if we hold the feastin' up here,' Rose tried to explain. 'I can't fall out with them over it - I have to gan and live there. Please let them arrange it their way.'

'I'll provide for me eldest daughter's wedding, so I will!' he blustered.

'Me and William want it in Lockart's - just a quiet tea, and maybes a couple of dances,' Rose said stubbornly.

'Dancing without the drinking!' he exclaimed, quite baffled. 'No one'll come.'

'We don't want many there, Da,' Rose said, tiring of the constant arguing. She had had enough of that with the Fawcetts. She silently agreed it would be a strange occasion, toasting their marriage with tea and cocoa, but if that was their way, so be it.

He shook his head. 'Well, Rose Ann, I shall give a party for your wedding day whether you come to it or not.'

Rose sighed. 'Just as long as you come to Lockart's first,' she pleaded.

'Lockart's Cocoa Rooms,' he muttered. 'Jezus, what's the world coming to!'

On a blustery spring day, Rose and William were married at St Bede's by Father O'Brien. Rose wore a white dress of material that Florrie had secured for her cheaply and Maggie had made up on the sewing machine. It was not the silk dress of her childish dreams, but Florrie had persuaded her mother to lend a small bustle of horsehair to make the dress fuller and more fashionable at the back. They trimmed it with lace and made a veil decorated with orange blossom, just as she had always wanted. The Fawcetts paid for a colourful posy of flowers.

At the church there was a large turnout of friends from the Irish community to wish her well, despite the Fawcetts' intention of keeping it a small, select affair. Rose noticed two rows of McMullens as she came down the aisle, but knew there would be no drunken behaviour from John to mar the day. Maggie had heard from Danny Kennedy that John had disappeared one day in January. A week later his mother had been given a message from the knife grinder that John had joined the army. He had up and left without a word of goodbye to anyone. No one knew why. Now nobody knew where he was. Rose thought it just confirmed what a strange and cussed man he was, and then put all thought of John from her mind.

Walking towards William, looking so handsome in his smart suit and shining fair hair, Rose felt she would burst with happiness. She wished her hard-working mother could have been there to see her a grown woman, marrying so well. And she knew by the proud squeeze of her father's arm and the glistening of his eyes that he was thinking the same thought.

The tea party at Lockart's Cocoa Rooms on Ormonde Street was pleasant, if a little subdued at first. There were two dozen guests, mostly friends of William's father from the steelworks and neighbours from James Terrace. But Rose's sisters, along with Florrie and Albert, Danny Kennedy and a couple more of William's workmates soon enlivened the afternoon. After a few stilted words from Rose's father and the cutting of the cake, the younger guests persuaded William to play the piano and they all gathered round for a singsong.

Rose liked nothing better than to stand at William's side and sing along with him, their voices mixing in easy harmony. It was something at which she could equal him, despite her lack of education, and it filled her with a sense of wellbeing and contentment. The more she heard his strong voice, the deeper her love for him grew.

But the room was only reserved for an hour and soon it was time for them to leave. Rose kissed her father and hugged her sisters goodbye, knowing they would be returning up the hill to continue the celebrations with others of their friends who awaited them there.

'It's been the best day of me life, Da,' Rose told him, feeling suddenly tearful. 'Ta for everything. You will come and visit, won't you?' she asked, worried that he never would.

'You come and see us when you can,' her father answered with a gruff smile. 'It'll be terrible quiet without you, Rose Ann.'

'I'll stop by on me next half-day off,' Lizzie promised.

'Aye, do that,' Rose smiled, then turned to Maggie, whom she would miss the most. 'Take care of Da -I know you will. I'll be up often to see if there's owt I can do.'

'We'll manage fine,' Maggie reassured. 'You look to your new life - you deserve your bit of luck.'

They hugged again, Rose trying to swallow the tears that flooded her throat. How she would miss Maggie's company!

'Come on, Rose,' William said, tugging gently on her arm. 'My parents are waiting outside.'

They got into the small brake that the Fawcetts had hired to take them back to James Terrace in style. William had already loaded up Rose's small mound of possessions - a bag of clothes and the bundle of linen, including the patchwork quilt that her sisters had made her for a wedding gift. Wrapped inside was an old copper warming pan that had belonged to her grandmother, and secured inside this was a silver tea caddy spoon and set of bone-handled cutlery from her father that had been her mother's pride and joy. There were other household items gifted by the Fawcetts' more prosperous friends, which would have to be stored until Rose had a home of her own.

Ignoring Mrs Fawcett's sniffy remarks about looking like tinkers on the move, Rose sat close to William, waving to her family until they were out of view. It was only when they arrived and disembarked outside the house in James Terrace that Rose was seized with nervousness. From now on she was going to be living in this place under the rule of her critical mother-in-law, day in, day out.

She busied herself helping William carry her belongings up to their bedroom and took as long as possible sorting them out. There was a small chest of drawers, mostly full of William's clothing, and a washstand with his shaving brush and razor. The small wardrobe in the corner still held Florrie's dresses, for she had nowhere else to put them, so Rose hung her hand-me-down skirts and frocks over the end of the iron bedstead. She spent an age smoothing out the quilt over their bed, her insides somersaulting at the thought she would soon be sharing it with William. Feeling suddenly giddy, she sat down quickly.

She had an idea of what consummating a marriage meant; she had seen pigs rutting noisily and observed the fluttering fuss and commotion of birds mating. She could hardly imagine William behaving like that, but it was something they would have to do. The priest had told her it was her duty as a wife and a good Catholic to have babies. Rose liked the thought of babies - lots of golden-haired infants with sweet smiles and voices like William's. Conceiving these babies might take a few undignified moments of flapping and grunting, Rose was not entirely sure, but it would be over swiftly, that she knew.

Then she remembered the strange whispered wrangling from her parents' bed, protests from her mother to be left alone, that she would give her father no more bairns. Rose realised now that her mother must have been putting her immortal soul in danger for refusing to do her duty. With a stab of anxiety she wondered why her mother had found it such a hardship. Perhaps such urges were seasonal? Sitting on the bed, trying to regain her composure, she wondered how much William knew about these things.

'Penny for your thoughts,' William smiled nervously, hovering by the door.

Rose flushed. She could not possibly tell him what she had been thinking. She covered her mouth to hide an embarrassed smile.

'Nothing,' she murmured.

'Florrie's made some cocoa,' he said.

'More cocoa!' Rose laughed. 'Don't tell me da.'

William grinned. 'I'll bring it up, if you like - say you're tired.'

Rose gave him a grateful look. She had been delaying having to go down and sit with the Fawcetts in their dreary parlour, while up the hill her family and friends would still be celebrating her wedding day. She felt a pang of disappointment that they were missing out on the dancing, then remembered how lucky she was to have William. All she wanted was to be with him, whatever the circumstances.

'Please,' she smiled at him. Then more coyly added, 'Could you take the warming pan and put some coals in from the kitchen fire?'

William nodded, reddening at the hinted suggestion they should get to bed.

By the time he returned with two cups of steaming chocolate, she had drawn the curtains against the dusk, changed into her nightdress and got in between the chilly sheets. Her long dark hair was loose and draped around her shoulders like a shawl. He gazed at her, quite overcome by the sight.

'Where's Granny's warming pan?' Rose asked.

William cleared his throat. 'Mother says it's unsafe. Might set fire to the sheets.'

'Doesn't want a speck of soot on her precious linen, you mean!' Rose said crossly. 'I've used it for years without any trouble.'

William handed her a cup. 'I'll buy you one of them china "pigs" to warm the bed,' he promised. 'Any road, we'll soon warm it up,' he grinned bashfully. 'Get that cocoa down you.'

Rose blushed, her annoyance instantly dispelled by his good humour. He was so good-natured, it was impossible to be cross with him for bowing to his mother's wishes. After all, it was the Fawcetts' house and she had to fit in with their ways. Things would be different once they had their own home, Rose determined.

As she sipped her chocolate William began to undress with his back to her.

'Do you want me to look away?' she asked in alarm.

He glanced round and laughed. 'Only if you can't bear the sight of me in long Johns.'

'I could look at you all day long in whatever you wear,' Rose giggled.

William speeded up his undressing and quickly climbed in beside her. For a few minutes they lay there, well covered in underclothes and nightdress. He lifted the covers and looked at her.

'By, you're wearing more than you did when you were dressed!' he exclaimed. 'You're ready for a Russian winter.'

Rose laughed. 'Well, it was always cold up Simonside - specially if you had to run to the privy.'

'You don't have to do that here,' William said in amusement. 'There's a pot under the bed.' Rose had noticed the gleaming china chamber pot with interest. Her father had always said it was healthier to go outside, so they had never had one. She was also looking forward to using the proper boxed privy in the backyard, which was emptied regularly by the midden men. There would be no more sodden earth closet or spreading of rank-smelling refuse on the fields for her.

'So what do we do now?' Rose asked.

William hesitated. 'I suppose we get to it,' he suggested. 'If I can find me way past all this nightwear.' They both laughed.

Rose looked at him fondly. 'Kiss me first, will you?' she whispered, beginning to shake with nervous excitement.

William smiled and, leaning over, began kissing her tentatively on the lips. Rose shuffled closer and they spent several minutes kissing and stroking each other's hair and faces. Then William began to fumble with her clothing and with his buttons, but took so long that Rose began to help him. Eventually he straddled her, but got caught up in a maze of twisted petticoats. It was all taking a lot longer than Rose had anticipated. Suddenly he found a way through and what Rose assumed was the consummation began. At first it was uncomfortable, even painful, but then they settled into the same rhythm she had observed in the animals at home.

Shortly afterwards it was inexplicably over. William sighed and rolled to the side. Rose lay still a while longer in case there was something else she was supposed to do. But that appeared to be it. She felt triumphant. It had not been too unpleasant and it had warmed her up twice as quickly as Granny's bed warmer could have done. Best of all, she was now truly William's wife.

In the days that followed, Rose began to look forward to the time she and William could escape to their room in the evening. It was a haven away from the strictures of Mrs Fawcett's downstairs domain and William's gruelling work at the rolling mills. Once Rose had washed up the tea dishes and banked the fires, she was free to go upstairs.

Sometimes they would lie on top of the bed with the evening breeze of early summer fluttering in under the lace curtain, while William read to her. He would smuggle in mildewed books and torn periodicals that he had picked up from second-hand bookstalls and kept in the bottom of the wardrobe. They were not the serious, improving works that Mr Fawcett read in the Mechanics' Institute, but sensational stories by Charles Dickens or mysteries by Wilkie Collins. Whatever William read, Rose loved to hear his voice and marvel at the words that poured from his mouth. Later, they would pull up the covers and make love quietly, Rose trying not to imagine her mother-in-law sitting below doing needlework or polishing her already gleaming fire brasses.

Within a month, Rose felt the difference in her body, the tender swelling of her breasts and a queasiness in her stomach. When she went early to bed, her tiredness was no longer an excuse. By June, she realised that she had not had a monthly bleed since just before she was married.

One evening, while William was reading to her, she lurched over and was sick into the chamber pot.

'What's wrong?' he asked in alarm. 'Is it something you've eaten? Shall I get me mother?'

Rose grimaced and shook her head. 'No, it'll pass in a minute.'

'Has this happened before?' William demanded, reaching over to rub her back. Rose nodded. 'Then I'm going to get Mother. She'll know what to do.'

'There's nothing to be done,' Rose answered, trying to smile in reassurance. 'William, I think I'm expectin'.'

He gaped at her. 'Expectin'? A bairn?' Rose nodded again. 'But how can you tell? You've never been . . .'

'Aye, I know. It's just some'at I feel.'

Suddenly he was hugging her to him. 'Our first bairn already! By, that was quick work, Rose Fawcett,' he crowed. 'Father O'Brien will be pleased with us.'

'Forget Father O'Brien,' Rose laughed. 'What about you?'

He kissed her tenderly. 'I'm over the moon!' he declared.

Rose kissed him back. 'Aye, so am I.' Then she frowned. 'But what about your mother? She'll not want all the mess of a baby around this house.'

William defended her. 'She's had bairns of her own, remember. She'll be pleased to have her first grandbairn and show him off to the neighbours.'

Rose slid him a look. 'Maybes by then we'll have a home of our own. I know it's more sudden than we thought, but isn't it a good time to be looking for our own place?'

William frowned. 'We'll have to see.' He must have caught the look of disappointment on her face, because he added, 'If the work's good and regular through the autumn and winter, we'll move out, rent somewhere small.'

Rose kissed him in delight, thinking how life was growing better with each day.

But as the baby formed inside her and Florrie had to help her let out her skirts to ease the discomfort on her spreading waist, Nature acted to thwart Rose's plans of escape. The blustery autumnal weather of October turned to harsh winter by November. A terrible frost gripped the area, turning the earth to stone and the iron on the docksides to ice. Trade stagnated while men were once more laid off from the shipyards. The iron could not be touched without it ripping off the skin from the men's bare hands. Never could Rose recall such a cold autumn. The Fawcetts huddled round the kitchen range, trying to keep warm. They went to bed with as much clothing on as they could wear, and no one protested when Rose filled her antiquated warming pan with coals to take the icy chill from their bed.

Rose's father and sister could not till the frozen ground or bring out the winter vegetables. They lost a pig, and several hens were carried off by starving foxes. Rose went up with food parcels until she was too advanced in pregnancy to manage the toil uphill in the cold. For the first time ever,

McConnell and Maggie came into the relief soup kitchens in the town for food.

When William and his father went on short time at the rolling mill, Rose abandoned any hope of moving out of James Terrace before her baby was born. Now she began to fret about how her baby would survive in such a cold world. When it kicked, she put protective hands over her womb and willed it to stay there as long as possible. William forbade her to go out in case she caught cold.

Their first Christmas together was an anxious one. Rose insisted that her father and Maggie should be invited for Christmas dinner, but on Christmas Eve Maggie came with a message that their father had taken to bed with a fever.

'He'd been over to see the McMullens,' Maggie explained, 'worried how they were managing. Old McMullen's been at the stone-breaking - there's so little work at the docks. I think he picked up some'at from there.'

Rose felt breathless, her pulse racing uncomfortably. 'What can I do?' she asked helplessly.

Mrs Fawcett interrupted. 'You can't do anything. You'll not go gallivanting up there in your condition, catching the fever. You've my grandchild to consider.'

'That's right. Stay here and keep warm,' Maggie insisted. 'I can look after Da, and Lizzie will be back on Boxing Day. So don't you worry.'

'I'll make us some tea,' Rose said, dragging herself to her feet.

But Maggie said quickly, 'I can't stay - I just wanted you to know.'

Rose knew her sister did not intend to cause trouble with Mrs Fawcett, but she was not going to let Maggie go empty-handed. 'You must take half the ham to keep you going and some of these sweet mince pies.'

'We've nothing to spare!' her mother-in-law protested.

Rose defied her. 'Maggie and me da would have eaten it here if they'd been well enough - I'll not see them go without at Christmas time.'

Before she could argue back, William came stamping in from the frozen back lane and as soon as he heard Maggie's predicament he intervened.

'Of course you must take some food. I'll walk back up the hill with you,' he insisted, 'make sure you've enough fuel in to keep the fire going.'

'But, William, you've a weak chest,' his mother fussed. 'You mustn't go near Mr McConnell if he's poorly!'

'I'll not stay long,' William said, 'just make sure he's all right.'

Rose gave him a grateful look as she parcelled up the food for her sister. When they went to the door they discovered it had started to snow. The dark afternoon sky was heavy with fluttering snowflakes that sank to the ground and stayed.

'Hurry,' she urged William as she waved them away, but even that brief minute on the doorstep left her feeling chilled. She sat huddled by the hearth trying to warm up, but felt increasingly unwell. Neither the decorations that she and Florrie had hung up nor the thought of the next day's festivities could lift her spirits. She worried about Maggie and William out in the snow, and watched the time creep by on the black clock on the mantelpiece. As they sat on in the darkened kitchen, Rose felt sharp pains in her belly.

'He should never have gone!' Mrs Fawcett grumbled, making Rose feel irresponsible and wretched.

'I think I'll go and lie down,' she said breathlessly, but her mother-in-law did not seem to notice her discomfort. The bedroom was arctic and she lay under the covers fully dressed, alternately shivering with cold and clammy from hot flushes. She could not get comfortable, and all the while the pains inside grew sharper and more frequent. Rose cried out in distress, but no one came. Florrie was still at the shop and Mr Fawcett was keeping warm in the reading room of the Institute. Only her mother-in-law was there to help and she did not seem to hear her cries.

Rose lay tossing in the bed, frightened at what might be happening to her and longing for William to return. She could not possibly be having the baby yet; Mrs Fawcett had told her it would be at least another month when she had complained of recent twinges.

'Please come back,' she whimpered in the dark damp room, the inside of the window frozen with ice. 'William, I need you!' she sobbed.

Then Rose thought she heard voices in the street below and she struggled to sit up. If she could get out of bed and knock on the window, someone might come and help her. She heaved herself to the side of the bed and swung her legs over, feeling dizzy at the sudden movement. A spasm of pain made her double up in agony. Then all at once she felt a rush of liquid between her legs that soaked her underskirts. Rose tried to scream, but the air seemed trapped in her throat and all she could do was gasp. Gripped by fear that it might be blood pouring out of her, she crawled towards the window.

'I'm going to die!' she sobbed, as her insides were seized in a vice-like pain. 'Oh, my baby!'

At that moment, singing rose from the street below, the clear joyful voices of carollers. 'Good KingWenceslas looked out, on the feast of Stephen ...'

Rose, panting in agony, tried to raise herself to knock on the window, but could not. She sank back, crouching on the bare floorboards like a wounded animal. The pain ripped down her body. It felt as if she was being stabbed with hot needles between her legs. Terrified, she squatted on the floor, waiting to die. She felt too winded to cry out any more.

But as she struggled to catch her breath, she became more aware of the singing from the unseen carollers. The mix of voices, young and old, was comforting, giving promise of new life. They were singing now of the Virgin Mary giving birth in the stable. It suddenly dawned on Rose that that was what must be happening to her. Her baby was coming. She felt it now, pushing hard between her legs, forcing its way out. She began to weep with both fear and relief.

Instinct made her scream. She yelled so loudly that the singing below halted. Rose screamed again. Within a minute, William's mother was rushing in.

'What's all the noise about?' she demanded, brandishing a candle in the dark. 'Where are you?'

'Help! Me baby's coming!' Rose cried, almost fainting with pain.

'Not there on the floor!' Mrs Fawcett squealed in disgust. But Rose was past caring where she had it. All she wanted was to push and scream and for the agony to be over. 'And stop making such a fuss!' She bustled to the door.

'Don't go,' Rose panted. 'Please don't leave me—'

'I'm going for brown paper and to get out of this dress,' she replied, and plunged Rose into the blackness once more. Outside was complete silence. The carollers must have moved on, their footsteps muffled in the newly fallen snow. Rose fixed her mind on the image of the street, wrapped in a glistening white blanket of clean snow, glowing under a bright moon. She imagined William hurrying through the snow towards home, unaware of what was happening. He would soon be here. Rose took deep breaths, calming herself with the comforting thought. She must stay strong for her baby and William.

By the time her mother-in-law returned, protected in a large apron and bearing brown paper and a bowl of water, Rose's baby was already thrusting its head between her legs. She howled in pain as Mrs Fawcett yanked her on to the brown paper that she laid out on the floor and pulled her skirts out of the way. The older woman squeezed water on to her face, but it was icy cold and Rose gasped in shock.

'That'll stop your noise,' Mrs Fawcett said grimly. 'Now show a bit of breeding and get on with it quietly.'

Rose gritted her teeth to hold back the screams that wanted to tear out of her throat. She panted and pushed, sank back and started again. If she had known how much torture this was going to be, Rose thought, she would never have let William anywhere near her. At that moment, Rose wished she had become a nun. Being stuck in this cold room being scolded and splashed with cold water by Mrs Fawcett was worse than any nightmare she had ever had as a child.

Then suddenly, the blockage between her legs gave way and she felt the baby slither out of her in one quick gush. Her body throbbed in relief.

'He's here!' Mrs Fawcett cried in satisfaction, covering her hands in old cloths before lifting the newborn up for inspection.

Rose peered through the flickering candlelight, panting with exhaustion. 'Let me see him!' she croaked. 'Is he alive? Is he all right?'

The older woman gave the tiny bundle a sharp smack and it gave out a small bleat.

'Oh,' she said, her voice dropping in disappointment.

'What's wrong?' Rose gasped in anxiety.

For a moment there was silence as William's mother wrapped the baby tightly in a piece of old blanket. 'We'll have to get this mess tidied up before William's allowed in here,' she sniffed.

Rose was almost in tears. 'What's wrong with him?' she demanded, shaking from head to toe.

'It's a girl,' Mrs Fawcett said disapprovingly. 'That's what's wrong with him.' She thrust the baby at Rose.

Rose grabbed at the bundle and squeezed it to her with a sob. She stared down at the tiny features peeping above the rough wool blanket. Her daughter, Rose thought in triumph. She had a little lass! She did not care in the slightest if it was not the longed-for grandson that would carry on the Fawcett name. Her baby was alive, she was alive! They had a Christmas baby. She wept with euphoria.

Shortly afterwards, Florrie appeared and was soon rushing around obeying her mother's orders to get the room cleaned up. The brown paper with the stench of childbirth still on it was rolled up and thrown on the kitchen fire, while the floor was washed down and Rose and the baby put to bed. Mrs Fawcett insisted that the bed should be lined with clean brown paper so as to save the sheets from more blood.

Rose fell into an exhausted sleep and when she awoke, William was sitting on the side of the bed, illuminated by soft candlelight, cradling their daughter in his arms. They smiled tenderly at each other and Rose unexpectedly burst into tears. William carefully placed the baby in her arms and leaned over to hold them both.

'Don't cry. She's as bonny as her mother,' he assured her. 'I don't mind that it's not a lad.'

'That's not it,' Rose sobbed. 'I'm crying 'cos I'm happy!' She laughed and cried at the same time. 'I was that scared - I thought I was dying. I wanted you to come back ...'

'At least Mother was here to help you,' William said.

Rose kept to herself how unhelpful his mother had been. It was all over now and she vowed that Mrs Fawcett would never 'help' her in childbirth again. 'And your father's comfortable. I made sure there was a fire going before I left and plenty of coal in the hod.'

Rose smiled at him through her tears. 'Oh, William, you're a grand man. I'm that glad I've got you!'

He kissed her gently on the lips. 'You'll always have me,' he promised.

Chapter 7

That winter was the cruellest in memory. 1879 was heralded by heavy snows that did not melt for weeks, turning Jarrow into an arctic wasteland. Nothing could move through the deep frozen snowdrifts. Ships were icebound and trains marooned. Coal could not be transported to the docks. Many a fireplace stood cold and empty, forcing people to find what warmth they could against a wall that backed on to a neighbour's fire.

Schools were closed and children bundled into bed together in the middle of the day, while their mothers went out in search of fuel. As cupboards emptied, starvation crept into homes like a pestilence. Men queued up for outdoor relief and waited their turn around a heap of stones to earn ninepence for piecework as stone-breakers. Some went mad with idleness and lack of food, and threw themselves into the icy oblivion of Jarrow Slake. The workhouse filled up with families that could no longer pay the rent and had nothing left to sell.

Mrs Fawcett wept when they had to pawn their china and shiny brass fender to put food on the table.

'We'll buy them back when work picks up again,' her husband promised.

Then the piano had to go. Rose watched a grim-faced William struggling with three others to secure it to a flat cart and drag it off across the treacherous black ice to the pawn shop. Mrs Fawcett sat in the stark parlour, head bowed in shame at such a public display of their difficulties, but Rose's heart went out to William, who would miss the music the most. Afterwards, a spark was extinguished from her husband's eye and lethargy crept over him. Always one for whistling or humming snatches of songs, he soon stopped singing at all.

Rose was housebound for weeks with baby Margaret, hibernating in bed or by the kitchen fire, anxious that her supply of milk might dry up for lack of food. Margaret was tiny and found it difficult to suckle, and the priest swiftly came to the house to christen her in case she was carried off by the pitiless winter like scores of other infants. Rose prayed fervently to the Virgin Mary to save her first-born, shuddering with horror at the thought of losing this trusting, snuffling creature with her delicate face and hands. Only Margaret could keep her arms warm and her heart comforted during this bleakest of times.

At first, William would walk miles each day searching for casual work, doing odd bits of joinery for the wealthy of South Shields. He would accept payment in food, a piece of meat or a couple of loaves and some jam, bringing them home triumphant as a sea captain with his treasure. But then he caught a chill, which settled on his chest and brought on bouts of painful coughing that left him exhausted. A bed was made up for him by the kitchen fire and Rose watched him with mounting alarm as all his energy and interest in life seemed to drain away with the sputum he spat into the bowl at his side.

By March, with no sign of the earth waking from the frozen spell of winter, Rose bundled up Margaret in as many layers as she could and went out in search of work. Such was the lethargy among the household that no one asked her where she was going. She thought of the Liddells, the new rector of St Paul's and his young wife, who lived in the blackened rectory between the ruined monastery and the stinking Don.

The Reverend Edward Liddell had startled the Fawcetts by calling on them one day to introduce himself as rector of the parish. Mrs Fawcett had quickly dispatched him with the sniffy reply that they were of the 'true faith' and not to bother calling again. But from what Rose had glimpsed of the young smiling rector, retreating with good grace and a faithful collie dog at his heels, she thought he might be sympathetic. If they were new, they might be in need of domestic help.

As Rose picked her way carefully over the slippery cobbles, she was aghast at what she saw beyond James Terrace. The streets were strangely quiet, with little traffic and no singing of birds or cries of children. At a church door, emaciated, thin-lipped men stood silently in line, hands thrust deep into pockets, waiting for the relief kitchen to open. Rose hurried on to the end of the street towards St Paul's. Off in the distance she could see figures crawling over the empty railway line that led down to the docks. Women, hunched in their shawls, were scrabbling at the iron-hard ground with bare hands for any discarded nuggets of coal.

Rose stopped in her tracks, appalled at this twilight world of suffering. For weeks, she had been out only on the occasional Sunday to attend Mass. She had heard of what was going on in the town from William and Florrie and occasional visits from Maggie to reassure her that her family were still alive, but she had not witnessed it for herself. She thought they had been badly off, but at least they could afford to keep a fire going. She hesitated, wondering if she dare go to the Liddells asking for work when there were so many worse off than she.

On the point of turning back, Rose glanced down at baby Margaret, muffled in her blankets, grizzling. She felt a strong protective anger. Her baby could die if she did nothing! Their daughter would not last long if William's illness continued and he could not get out to find work, however menial. He needed medicines and they all wanted food. She worried about Maggie, coping with her father, weakened by influenza. They all needed what little she could bring in to tide them over until the mills and docks stirred into life again. She would do anything to protect her own! Hugging Margaret tightly to her breast, Rose walked on resolutely towards the rectory.

No one answered her knocking at first. Finally a young maid came to the door. 'The rector's at a meeting and the missus is visitin',' she said, eyeing Rose with suspicion.

'Can I wait?' Rose asked, before the girl could close the door on her. 'I belong in this parish.' The girl opened the door and nodded for her to come in, then left her standing in the draughty hallway and disappeared.

This was how Mrs Liddell found her when she returned. As the older woman stamped the dirty slush from her boots, she was startled at the sound of Margaret whimpering.

'Goodness me! Who's that?'

Rose stepped out of the gloom. 'Sorry to bother you, Mrs Liddell. But the rector called on us the other day and I wondered if you might have a bit work for us. I can do anything - cleaning, washing - just an hour or two if you like. Me husband's ill and so's me da, and I've a bairn now and I can't think how we're going to manage. We live with me husband's people, but they're out of work an' all...' Rose stopped. The woman's face looked cross and exhausted, creased in worries of her own. What a fool to think she would get work here among the Anglicans, Rose thought; they would surely look after their own kind first. 'Me name's Rose Fawcett,' she added in a desperate attempt to appear respectable, feeling shame that she should try to hide behind her English name. But she thought she stood no chance at all if she were marked out as Catholic and Irish.

Rose watched the well-dressed woman shed her thick red velvet cape with a look of worried exasperation.

Margaret chose that moment to increase her wailing. Suddenly, Mrs Liddell put out a hand and touched the fretful baby.

'Sounds like she's hungry. How long have you been waiting? Jane shouldn't have left you standing here on your own. You'll come into the kitchen and have something to warm you,' she insisted. 'You can feed your baby too.' Suddenly she smiled and her whole face lit up, softening her features. Her eyes shone with kindness.

'Ta, Mrs Liddell,' Rose answered with a cautious smile.

For the next half an hour, Rose sat in the homely kitchen around a large table, thawing out from the cold and eating biscuits dunked in piping hot tea. The rector's wife unwrapped Margaret and inspected her, rocking her gently on her shoulder until Rose's hands had lost their numbness and she could hold her to her breast and feed. As Jane seemed to have disappeared on some errand, Mrs Liddell stirred the soup on the range and insisted Rose had a bowl before she went out into the cold again. All the time she asked her questions and spoke in a beautiful voice which Rose could have listened to for hours.

'Is Jarrow very different from what you're used to?' Rose could not help asking.

Mrs Liddell laughed shortly. 'Yes, very. I come from the north of Scotland, but my husband and I have been living down near London - in the country. His family are from near here, though. Ravensworth.'

Rose gave a gasp of delight. 'Eeh! Me grandmother used to work for Lord Ravensworth. I remember visitin' the village as a bairn - saw Miss Isabella gettin' wed.'

Mrs Liddell smiled. 'Fancy! My husband was probably there too. He's a cousin of Lord Ravensworth's.'

Rose looked at her in astonishment and could not help blurting out, 'A cousin! Then what's he doing living in Jarrow, Mrs Liddell?'

The rector's wife laughed. 'What indeed! Most of his family think we're quite mad.' Then she sighed. 'He felt a strong calling to come and minister here, Rose, where there is so much need. The troubles of the people are so enormous, the task sometimes seems to overwhelm him. But he had no choice. He didn't choose Jarrow. God chose him for Jarrow. It would have been a betrayal of God's plan for him to stay on in a comfortable parish in the south of England, and an easy life.'

Rose thought how William would like and approve of these people. 'It's very brave of him, Mrs Liddell. And you. Leaving behind all that you know, for somewhere you don't.'

'I used to think so,' she said reflectively. 'But it's nothing to the courage we witness here every day, believe me. Life's not about taking the easy path - but then you know that already, don't you?' She gazed at Margaret sleeping in her mother's arms and tears welled in her eyes. 'It's all about using your energy and gifts as best you can for your fellow man - not just your loved ones,' she added softly. 'That's why we're living in this damp old rectory and not on a country estate.'

Rose looked away, embarrassed at the woman's frankness. Why had she confided in her like that? Rose wondered. Perhaps it was a mark of how lonely she was in this strange, blighted town so far away from her own family and the places she loved. When Rose looked up again, Mrs Liddell was vigorously stirring the soup.

'Well, Rose,' she said, in a more businesslike way, 'we have someone who does our laundry and Jane is supposed to do the cooking and cleaning with the help of Widow Bradley. But perhaps you could come in and help them lay the fires and do some polishing from time to time?'

'Anything!' Rose agreed quickly. 'I lay a grand fire and I can do the heavy work - fetching water, filling baths, gettin' in the coal. I'm used to that.'

'And what about baby Margaret?'

'I - I can leave her at home,' Rose said, a little unsure.

'If it's difficult you can bring her with you,' Mrs Liddell said kindly.

Rose was overjoyed. She left with the agreement that she could come the next day for two hours. The raw air outside did not seem so biting as she hurried away. She did not care if the Fawcetts disapproved of what she had done - there was no one going to stop her coming to work for the Liddells, even if it was scrubbing floors for Anglicans.

Christina Liddell watched the young woman leave, her undernourished baby wrapped tight in her shawl. Edward would probably groan at her weakness in taking on another girl they could ill afford on his meagre pay, but she did not have the heart to deny her. There was something about Rose Fawcett that had touched her. The girl was friendly and showed a lively mind. She was tired of the suspicious looks and closed doors that she had encountered so often since their arrival. The people seemed bowed down by the burden of trying to keep alive, of the brutal seesaw between endless shifts or no work at all. Their employers appeared not to care what happened to them once they left the work gates or how they lived their lives. Where were the public parks and well-endowed libraries? There was no isolation hospital to stem the tides of fever or even a dispensary in the town. No one had even thought to build them a theatre or music hall where they could enjoy a respite from the relentless daily grind.

Edward privately fulminated against the laissez-faire attitudes of employers like Palmer's.

'They don't even have anywhere to get a warm drink in the morning,' he had told her angrily. 'Is it any wonder they shelter in the pubs before work? The publicans profit from it nicely - opening in the early hours to catch the men before Palmer's gates are unlocked.'

'Why don't you set up a cocoa stall for them?' she had suggested. Edward had instantly seized on the idea, but then the winter slump had thwarted his plans.

They had never seen such poverty or such drunken oblivion as on these streets. She had witnessed grown women fighting like animals, half-naked children begging for food, skeletal men digging for stones with hands that had learnt a skilled trade.

Today had almost been the last straw. She had come from a house in the parish where an Irish woman had died. She had been found with her feet in the cold ashes of a long burnt-out fire where she must have crawled to try to seek a trace of warmth. No one deserved to die like that! Coming home to their wretched house by the putrid barren ground above the Slake, on the point of bursting into tears, she had felt like giving up. The task was a hopeless one, the misery too great for them to make an ounce of difference. How she hated this benighted place! Then Rose had stepped out of the shadows. Here was an eager, lively young woman, in far worse straits than herself, willing to try anything to help her family.

Rose had made her ashamed of her own woes and self-pity. She had shown her what real courage and endurance was. Watching Rose dealing with her baby, she had glimpsed the goodness that existed among the evils of this industrial town. How could she think of turning her back on them? She would help Rose Fawcett by giving her work and she would redouble her efforts to get their wealthy acquaintances in the town to contribute more generously to the relief funds. By God, she and Edward would make a difference in the lives of Jarrow folk if it killed them!

Rose weathered the storm of protest at home for daring to go out and get a cleaning job.

'And with them Protestants!' Mrs Fawcett said in a fluster. 'She'll be bringing in washing next.' The men felt their pride was at stake too.

'It's bad enough our Florrie being the only wage earner,' William fretted. 'It's my job to provide for you and the bairn.'

'How?' Rose demanded. 'If the mill started up again tomorrow, you're in no fit state to gan back. You can hardly get up off that bed!'

William grew agitated, his breathing noisy as a pair of old bellows. 'I'd manage—'

'You're not going to stop me,' Rose declared, 'me mind's made up and I've promised Mrs Liddell I'll go. I'm lucky to get the work and I'm not so proud as to think I'm above doing a bit of hard graft. I do it round here for nowt,' she added with a defiant look at William's parents.

Seeing how upset she was making William by her stand, she softened. 'I'm doing it for you and the bairn. I want to buy you medicines for your chest - pay for a doctor to visit. The sooner you're well again, the better you can take care of me and Margaret. I'll give up the cleaning when you're back on your feet,' she bargained.

All through March and April, Rose went to the rectory. She looked forward to getting out of the claustrophobic house in James Terrace and grew to enjoy her work. Jane became friendlier, and Rose was grateful for the extra food that was offered her in the kitchen whenever Mrs Liddell was there. Occasionally, Rose saw the rector dashing between meetings or visits, grabbing a quick bite to eat, Verger the collie always at his side. He was up early and out before she arrived, supervising the cocoa stall he'd managed to get started by the docks, then helping run a soup kitchen at midday. But he was always cheerful and his thin boyish face reminded her of William. Rose mused that if the men had been born in the same class they would surely have been friends.

Her strength returned and she worked hard, endearing herself to the wheezing Mrs Bradley by offering to do the heavy chores. The women made a fuss over Margaret, but Rose liked to keep her with her, carrying her around in a kitchen drawer while she polished the brass stair rails or laid fires.

'You have a lovely singing voice, Rose,' Mrs Liddell surprised her by saying one day while she was scrubbing the tiles in the hallway.

'I like a good singsong,' Rose smiled. 'But me husband's got a much better voice than me. He sings like a lark, Mrs Liddell. You should hear him at church—' She bit her tongue for her foolishness.

But Mrs Liddell did not appear to notice. 'How is Mr Fawcett?' she asked.

'Much better, thanks,' Rose said hastily. 'The rolling mill's opened again. Me father-in-law's doing short time and I'm hoping William will be soon an' all.'

'I'm so glad,' Mrs Liddell smiled. 'Let's pray the worst of it's over.' She stepped past Rose, then turned as if remembering something. 'Oh, I met someone who knows you.'

'Me?' Rose faltered.

'A Mrs McMullen. She's been coming with some of her boys to the soup kitchen at St Paul's. Said she'd heard from your sister that you were working at the rectory. I was to tell you it's time you brought Margaret round to show her.'

Rose felt the blood draining from her face. 'I used to deliver vegetables round her way, that's all.' She tried to make light of the connection.

'She's had a very hard time of it,' Mrs Liddell continued. 'But it seems one of her sons is in the army and sends back his pay. That seems to have kept them out of the workhouse.'

'John?' Rose asked. 'They've heard from him?'

'Yes, John, that was the name. I don't know if they hear from him directly. All Mrs McMullen knows is that he's out in India.'

'India!' Rose exclaimed. 'Well, the saints—' She clapped her hand over her mouth and coloured in confusion.

Mrs Liddell said gently, 'It's all right, Rose. We know you're Roman Catholic. You don't have to pretend. It doesn't matter to us in the least. Don't ever be ashamed of who or what you are. We're all God's children, after all.'

Rose went crimson. 'Ta, Mrs Liddell.' She bent her head and began scrubbing vigorously. As her employer moved on, she wondered why she had found it so disturbing suddenly to hear news of the McMullens. She had hardly given them a thought in months. John's stormy face and whisky-breath kiss came back to her as if it had been yesterday. What had possessed him to run off and join the army and end up in far-off India? Perhaps there was more to him than she had ever given him credit for. She had thought he was just full of fighting talk and no action beyond a drunken brawl in the back lanes of Jarrow.

Rose chided herself that she should hear of the McMullens second-hand through this woman who hardly knew them. It was shameful that Mrs Liddell had taken more interest in the McMullens' plight than she had. It made Rose realise how much she had cut herself off from her old friends in an attempt to fit in with the Fawcetts and their more well-to-do neighbours. She had been so preoccupied with the baby and her own troubles that she had not even been to see her own father and sister in months. Rubbing the tiles furiously, she resolved that in future she would pay them all more attention.

By May, William was recovered enough to begin work again and, as if signalling an end to the misery of the past months, spring finally broke through the hardened earth. Flowers burst from the hedgerows around Simonside and blossom on the trees. Rose went up to help Maggie on the smallholding, so that she had produce to sell that summer. Her father's grip on the spade was more feeble and she knew she was going to have to help them out more. He was no longer capable of heavy work at the forge.

On a visit to Mrs McMullen to show off Margaret, she suggested that one of the boys might like to earn a bit of extra food by helping her father with the digging.

'That's a grand idea,' Mrs McMullen agreed, rocking Margaret in her lap. 'I'll send Joseph - get him out from under me feet. I wish I'd had a little angel like this one here. But not one girl among the lot of them!' she cackled.

'I hear John's in India,' Rose said bashfully.

'Aye, taking off without a word to his mother!' she cried. 'I'll box him round the ears when he next comes home. Michael thinks he might be fightin' the Afghans. Read something in the newspaper about his regiment marchin' with General Roberts. Now he's an Irishman, by all accounts. I says to Michael, wherever your big brother is, he'll be fightin' someone, so he will!'

As life grew easier again that summer, Rose resisted pressure from her in-laws to give up working at the rectory. She tried to make William understand that she liked working there and enjoyed the company, though it was getting harder to manage with Margaret. The baby was now thriving and was no longer content to lie still in her small drawer. Once she had rolled off the bed when Rose had been laying the fire in an upstairs bedroom and yelled the house down. Now she was crawling and had to be constantly watched.

Then something happened that brought Rose's small taste of freedom to an end. One day when she was polishing the banisters she felt a terrible pain shoot through her. She clutched her stomach and cried out in agony. Jane, who was passing through the hall, came running.

'Whatever's the matter?' she demanded.

Rose gasped for air as the pain shot down between her legs. 'I need to lie down,' she said in agony. The girl helped her on to the hall floor, where she lay feeling sick and dizzy.

All at once, Jane screamed, 'You're bleedin'! Down there!' She ran for Mrs Bradley, who helped carry Rose into the kitchen. By the time they had her lying in front of the hearth, Rose felt ill enough to die.

'Where's Margaret?' she fretted.

'Divn't worry about that bairn,' Mrs Bradley told her. 'It's the one you're carryin' you should be thinking of.'

'What d'you mean?' Rose asked, light-headed.

'Looks like you're miscarryin',' the old woman said glumly. 'I should know; it happened enough to me.'

Rose's heart thumped hard in shock. 'But I didn't even know I was expectin'!'

she wailed.

'Well, you are,' Mrs Bradley confirmed. 'The only thing you can do is take to your bed and pray you keep it.'

All August, Rose lay in the stuffy upstairs bedroom with the window open and the blinds drawn, listening to life going on normally in the street below. Time dragged and she thought she would go mad with boredom. The bleeding had stopped, but the doctor had ordered complete bed rest and William forbade her to move. Mrs Liddell had called with a basket of fruit, but Rose had heard her turned away at the door.

'She's too delicate to have callers,' Mrs Fawcett had rebuffed her before closing the door.

Rose lay in frustration, listening to the sounds of her mother-in-law coming and going with Margaret in the new pram bought since the men were working full time once more. For months she had resented the older woman's disinterest in the baby for not being a boy, but now she feared her position as mother was being usurped. These days Mrs Fawcett monopolised Margaret. Occasionally she would bring the baby in for a feed, but Rose's milk was dwindling and soon Margaret was sucking from a bottle more often than from her mother.

'If you brought her up for a feed more often, me milk would come in grand again,' Rose dared to protest.

But this swiftly provoked a lecture. 'It's working like a skivvy for them Anglicans that stopped your milk. Yes, and it might cost you your unborn baby too. You'll only have yourself to blame - we all told you to stop. But would you listen? No, you always know best. Pride and disobedience are sins, girl,' she tutted. 'From now on, I'm going to make sure you're a dutiful wife to my son and a good mother to his children. You'll not be carting Margaret over to that rectory any more and letting strangers take care of her while you neglect her.'

'I've never neglected her!'

'And what about that time she got a bump on her head falling off the bed?' Mrs Fawcett accused.

Rose flushed. 'That could have happened anywhere—'

'Well, it didn't,' William's mother said sharply. 'Now hand her over. I'm going to take her out to that new park to get some air. You should be more grateful that you've got me to help out while you lie in bed like a queen all day long.'

Rose wanted to scream with annoyance, but bit back an angry retort and let go of her daughter. That afternoon she tossed restlessly on the bed, wishing she was the one pushing Margaret around the new recreation ground gifted to the town by Sir Walter and Lady James. She had heard the Liddells talking about the wealthy local patrons, for it was the Jameses who had asked Reverend Mr Liddell to take up the position at St Paul's in the first place. Rose was sure the kind Liddells must have had something to do with the sudden bequest to the townspeople of open ground where they could walk and play sport away from the strictures of the crowded back lanes.

As she listened to children playing in the street below and the call of the ice-seller further away, Rose determined that as soon as she was on her feet again, she would go looking for a home of their own. She could not bear the thought of another winter cooped up with her censorious mother-in-law. It would be an endless wrangle over what was right for Margaret, or William, or the new baby if it survived. She was tired of kowtowing to this woman who was wheedling her way into Margaret's affections and treating William as if he were still hers alone.

Placing her hands on her stomach, where she felt her baby flutter, she hissed, 'Please don't die! Prove her wrong and live!'

On a raw morning in late November, Rose went into labour. William went rushing for the doctor, for he had worried about her and the baby ever since the threatened miscarriage. Despite his anxiety, his mother ordered him off to work.

'We can't pay the doctor if you get the sack!' she scolded.

To Rose's relief the baby came easily and with a healthy wail, soon after one o'clock.

'What are you going to call this pretty little maid?' Dr Forbes asked in his cheerful way.

'Elizabeth,' Rose smiled at her new daughter, 'after me other sister. She's going to be all right, isn't she?'

'She's perfectly healthy. You must keep her warm, and try and feed her as soon as you can - especially while your mother-in-law is keeping Margaret occupied downstairs. Or would you like me to send them up?'

'No,' Rose said quickly, 'not yet. I just want to lie here with the bairn. She's taken that long to come -I just want to look at her.'

'It'll be a nice surprise for William when he gets back from work,' Dr Forbes smiled. 'He didn't want to go this morning.'

Rose sighed. 'I know he would have liked a lad ...'

The doctor turned from rinsing his hands in the washbowl and dried them on a linen towel. 'Knowing William, he'll just be pleased the pair of you are alive and well.' He gave her an understanding look. 'And it doesn't matter what anyone else thinks.'

Rose gave him a grateful smile.

William was delighted with his second daughter and would have nothing said against her. This time they had a proper christening at St Bede's, with all the family invited, and afterwards laid on a fine tea at James Terrace. This year the family were able to celebrate Christmas with presents for each other and have Rose's family round for a meal, but Rose felt tense and tearful at the small criticisms she endured from her mother-in-law. One minute she was told she wrapped the baby too tightly, the next that she did not keep her warm enough. Her gravy was too lumpy or too thin. She neglected Margaret in favour of the baby or she spoilt her eldest with too much attention.

How Rose hankered for a place of their own! But she had not been strong enough to go searching alone that autumn. Worryingly, William showed no great desire to move house. Florrie was engaged now, and planning to marry in the spring, and Rose felt a rising sense of panic that her one ally would soon be gone.

'Margaret can have Florrie's room soon,' William had said, when Rose had brought up the subject. 'Give us more time to save up.'

'Why do we need to save?' Rose demanded. 'We can afford the rent on somewhere small now.'

'It's always best to have a little put by,' William advised. 'You never know what's round the corner.'

'If work slackens off again, we can just move back in here,' Rose argued.

William took her hands. 'I want to provide for you and the bairns properly,' he insisted. 'I'll know when the time is right for us to move.'

Rose tried to pull away, annoyed by his intransigence, but he would not let the disagreement escalate. He pulled her towards him with a grin. 'One day we'll have a big house all of our own, full of bairns,' he promised. 'Now give us a kiss!'

She could not be angry with him for more than a minute, for he still made her heart beat faster just by her looking at his handsome fair face. Rose kissed him back and soon she was thinking of nothing else beyond the taste of his mouth and the comforting closeness of him lying next to her in bed. They had not resumed love-making since Elizabeth's birth, but he was tender and affectionate, and she felt stirrings of desire for him, despite the rawness of childbirth and the tiredness of feeding. She loved him deeply and wanted nothing more than to be with him and the girls. Rose resigned herself to being patient.

In the spring of 1880, Florrie married Albert in St Bede's and they had a grand reception in Lockart's Cocoa Rooms. The Fawcetts hired the whole of the upstairs for the occasion and there was a band laid on for dancing, and a monumental tea of delicate sandwiches, cakes and scones. Rose could not help comparing it with her own modest wedding, but she was pleased to see Florrie so happy, and grateful to her sister-in-law for inviting Maggie and Lizzie. Besides, William had treated her to a new dress for the occasion. Rose felt like a real lady in her green striped gown and fashionable new hat that sloped forward over her high forehead, decorated with flowers and lace.

She had spent hours grooming Margaret's fair hair and keeping her white dress spotless, while the baby was trussed up in a profusion of lacy skirts and bonnet. William looked as handsome as ever in his best suit, with a new watch and chain in his waistcoat. Rose was so proud of her growing family!

They danced to the band and Rose caught up on news from her sisters and Danny Kennedy, who was being particularly attentive to Maggie. Lizzie was not so happy.

'Mr Flynn's in bad health,' she confided. 'Terrible trouble with his breathing. All them chemicals at work, his missus says. She wants him to gan back to Ireland where the air's better and they've family to look after them. I'll be looking for another place shortly, wouldn't be surprised.'

'Well, you've skivvied for them long enough,' Rose declared.

'They've been canny enough in their own way.' Lizzie was generous. 'Kept me on when times were hard.'

'Well, now's your chance to find some'at better,' Rose said, determining to help her if she could.

When the time came for Florrie to depart, Rose was suddenly tearful to see her go. She was moving across the river to Wallsend, where Albert had recently taken up a new position as assistant manager in a bank, and she had given up her job in the haberdashery. Rose had grown to care for her shy, diffident sister-in-law and been grateful for Florrie's quiet support these past

59

two years.

'I'll miss you!' Rose said, as they hugged. 'You will come back and visit when you can, won't you?'

'Yes, of course,' Florrie promised, then added in a lower voice, 'I'll look forward to seeing you in your own house some day soon, eh?'

Rose grinned. 'Aye, soon.'

The days that followed were dull and humdrum after the excitement of preparing for Florrie's wedding. Mrs Fawcett was more querulous and demanding than ever, but for once Rose understood why. She was missing Florrie and nothing else could fill the emptiness in her life. Rose thought how bereft she would feel without Margaret or Elizabeth and yet they were still tiny infants. Imagine what it would be like to see them grow up and leave home! Feeling unaccustomed pity for the woman, she decided to delay her plans for moving out of James Terrace that summer. She did not think her mother-in-law could cope with losing William so soon after Florrie's departure. Instead, she determined to enjoy the greater freedom that summer would bring.

Rose took her daughters for walks around Jarrow Park and for visits to Simonside. She helped her father prepare for a flower show, and lay in the meadow, chewing grass and gossiping with Maggie, who was now courting Danny Kennedy.

One day in late May, William came rushing in and scooped up Margaret.

'Haway! If we hurry we'll see the Cornelia going out to sea!'

Rose grabbed the baby and ran out after him, infected by his enthusiasm and Margaret's squeals of delight. They had watched the pleasure yacht, built for the Durham landowner, the Marquis of Londonderry, being launched in February from Palmer's yard. Now its fittings were complete and ready for the steamer's first sea trials.

'Why don't we go up Simonside?' Rose suggested. 'We'll get a view of it all the way down river.'

William agreed and they hurried out of the town, climbing past the now derelict pigeon loft in which they had once taken shelter.

'Remember that?' William winked as they paused for breath and scoured the riverbanks for sight of the steam yacht.

Rose laughed. 'Doesn't look that romantic now, does it?'

'It'll always look romantic to me,' William grinned, hoisting Margaret on to his shoulders. He told his daughter, 'That's where I lost me heart to your mam.'

Rose giggled and gave him a shove. 'Nearly lost your life, more like! Catching pneumonia.'

'It was worth it,' William said, kissing her on the cheek.

Suddenly, Margaret started to jig excitedly. 'Ship! Ship!' she said quite clearly. They both gazed at her pointing finger.

'There! She's right,' William exclaimed. 'Do you see the three masts?'

Rose caught sight of the schooner, unfurling its white sails as it reached the mouth of the river and turned north into the choppy sea. It was too far to hear the throb of its engines, but it was racing at a jaunty speed.

'By, she's sharp-eyed,' Rose said in amazement.

'Like her mam,' William smiled.

'Clever like her dad,' Rose insisted. 'Words coming out of her little mouth already.'

'I want the best for our lasses,' William declared. 'I want them to gan to school and learn things - get a good start in life.'

Rose thrilled at his words. How proud she would be to have educated daughters who could read and write and get a good position in an office or marry well like Florrie. They would be shielded from the insecurity of slumps in trade and the fear of the workhouse that hung over the poor like a black cloud. Her daughters would not have to make a living digging or hawking vegetables in the freezing cold like she had, or wearing themselves out skivvying for others like Lizzie. All this, William would give them. How the saints had smiled on her the day she and William had taken shelter in that drab little hut.

She was struck by a sudden desire. 'William! Let's go and call on the Liddells. They've been good to me - sending treats for the bairns. You'd like them. They're full of education. Won't you come and meet them?'

William pursed his mouth and said nothing. Rose knew he felt awkward at the mention of the people she had worked for. It reminded him of a time when he was too weak to look after his own. And he was a devout Catholic, a brethren of St Bede's, who should not be seen entering the rectory.

'They're good people,' Rose persisted. 'They'd do anything for Jarrow and working people. And the rector's canny. His favourite saint is St Bede - just like you.'

William looked at her holding Elizabeth, her face flushed and eager, her dark hair escaping from its coil in the wind and snaking around her large eyes and sensual mouth. She was still as pretty as the young girl who had caught his attention at church eight years ago. He loved her for being the simple country girl that she was at heart. But more than that, he loved her liveliness of spirit, her sudden unexpected whims and her joy for living.

He smiled. 'Haway then. Take me to see your saintly Liddells, or I'll get no peace.'

Rose kissed him in delight. They strode off down the hill, William singing and Margaret joining in with her own babyish humming.

By the time they reached the rectory, Rose's arms were aching with carrying the baby. William pulled at the brass bell handle. They stood and waited. The face of a small boy peered out from the bay window, then darted out of sight.

'Ring again,' Rose urged. On the second ring, Jane answered the door and the boy darted out in front of her.

'Who are you?' he asked, his dark eyes inquisitive.

'Don't be cheeky,' Jane scolded. 'Hello, Rose. Is that the baby? Eeh, look at the size of Margaret! Come and give Auntie Jane a cuddle.'

She reached up. William carefully lifted Margaret from his shoulders and handed her to the maid.

'Uncle Edward's not in,' the boy announced, jumping on and off the top step. 'He's gone on the boat.'

'Aye,' Jane confirmed. 'They've both gone on the Cornelia - be away all afternoon. The mistress will be that put out to have missed you.'

'I can't go 'cos children aren't invited,' the boy continued. 'But I'm going to be a sailor when I grow up.'

'You were going to be Viceroy of India five minutes ago,' Jane said, rolling her eyes in exasperation.

William bent down to his height. 'Good for you, lad. And what do they call you?'

'Alexander Pringle,' he answered. 'What do they call you?'

'Don't be cheeky,' Jane warned.

William just laughed and ruffled his dark coppery hair. 'William,' he replied, 'William Fawcett.'

'Have you got any boys for me to play with, William?' Alexander asked in hope.

'Not yet,' William laughed and winked at Rose.

'Can we come in for a drink of water?' Rose asked, feeling suddenly faint. She handed Elizabeth into William's arms.

'Are you all right?' he asked in concern.

'Just need a sit down,' she panted, her pulse racing uncomfortably.

'Come in the kitchen,' Jane said quickly. 'Alexander get out of the way! You'll trip someone up.'

The boy hopped after them. 'I'm a pirate with a wooden leg!'

They went through the gloomy dark hall smelling of polish, and through to the familiar kitchen. Rose was hit by hot air from the range and sank on to the bench by the table.

'Don't go giving us all a fright like last year,' Jane cried, pouring her some water from an earthenware jug, Margaret still clamped to her hip.

'What happened last year?' Alexander piped up, but no one answered him.

Rose drank the water while William stared at her. She looked over at him. 'Am I going to feel like this every summer?' she asked weakly.

'Like what?' he asked.

She grimaced at the familiar wave of nausea. 'Expectin',' she whispered.

William sat down quickly. 'Already?' he gasped. She nodded.

'Look at me, William!' cried Alexander, wobbling along the other bench with his hands outstretched. 'I'm walking the plank.'

'Get down!' Jane gasped. 'Eeh, Rose, another bairn on the way. Wait till I tell the mistress!'

'That's grand!' William declared, recovering quickly from the shock.

Jane fetched biscuits and handed them round. 'Here, this'll stop the sickness.' Margaret grabbed one and soon had sticky crumbs all over her face and the furniture as she explored around her. Alexander sat on the table kicking his legs.

'We're sailing to the Spanish Main looking for treasure,' he imagined. 'This is all we have to eat - biscuits in a barrel.'

Rose smiled, feeling better. 'Where have you come from?' she asked him.

'England, of course,' he answered, and began to climb on the table again.

'Hoy, down you get, you little monkey,' Jane ordered. He jumped down and hid under the table. 'He's sending me mad. Under me feet all day, never stops with all his questions.'

'Who is he?' Rose asked, dropping her voice.

'Some sort of cousin of the rector's.' Jane shrugged. 'His mam was related - but she died last year. As far as I can make out he's been shoved from pillar to post ever since. He's here for the summer - or until the family can agree what to do with him.'

Under the table they could hear him singing some made-up sea shanty.

'Poor bairn,' Rose sighed.

'Has he no father?' William asked quietly.

Jane leaned forward and whispered, 'They say his mam ran off with a coachman called Pringle and the family wouldn't have anything to do with them. Well, her being a Liddell and one of the gentry, they wouldn't, would they? Now the father's sent him back to her family - says he can't afford to keep him.'

'Look, William!' the boy called. 'I've found a cave - come and see.'

William handed the baby back to Rose and crouched down to join him under the table. As they played together, Jane continued in a whisper, 'I think Mrs Liddell would like to keep him - them having no bairns of their own. But the rector says he'd be better off at Ravensworth or with one of the richer cousins. Says it's too unhealthy here and they're too busy with the parish. By, the master works himself night and day! The mistress worries about him overdoing it.'

Rose's heart went out to the little boy play-acting under the kitchen table. She could see how much he needed a father and was enjoying William's attention. And losing his mother too!

'Tell Mrs Liddell we came to see her,' she told Jane, 'and brought the bairns.' She stood up and William crawled from his cramped position, insisting on carrying both the girls.

'You'll take it easy, lass,' he insisted. 'Ta-ra, Alexander. I hope you find your treasure.'

'I'm Captain Pringle!' he cried, leaping out and hitting William on the leg with a serving spoon. 'You can't go, I've captured you!'

'Give me that,' Jane intervened, and swiped the weapon from his hands. 'Now say you're sorry.'

Suddenly the boy's eyes filled with tears and his chin began to tremble. He gulped, 'Sorry,' then burst into tears.

William put an arm round him. 'That's all right, Captain.' But the boy struggled free and dashed out of the room, his sobs echoing down the stony back corridor. A door slammed. William and Rose exchanged helpless glances.

'Don't worry about him,' Jane said brusquely. 'He'll be back to pester me soon enough.'

'He seems a canny bairn,' William said ruefully.

'Aye, well, the rector's been schooling him since he came here and the mistress teaches him his manners,' Jane sniffed. 'But underneath he's still a wild Pringle, if you ask me. There's no escaping your breedin'.'

At the beginning of June, Finder's Circus came to Jarrow. For several days before the performances, Rose took the girls in the pram to watch the large tent being erected and to view the wild beasts in their cages. Rose was quite alarmed and felt nauseous at the animal stench. But Margaret came home making roaring noises, not the least in awe of the strange sights and smells.

'Let's take her when it opens,' William said, entranced by her mimicry. 'She really wants to go.'

'You mean you do,' Rose teased. 'I'll stay at home with Elizabeth.'

'Haway, Rose,' William encouraged. 'It's not often some'at this exciting happens round here. You deserve a treat. Mother will mind the baby.'

Rose did not need much persuasion.

The day before they were due to go, William appeared preoccupied. 'I was wondering ...' he began.

'What?' Rose asked.

'That lad - Alexander. Stuck in that house with no other bairns - no mam or dad.' He hesitated.

'You want to take him to the circus,' Rose guessed.

William looked at her cautiously. 'What d'you think?'

'I think you're a canny man,' she smiled, and touched his face in affection. 'I've been thinkin' about the bairn as well. I can call round in the morning and ask, if you like.'

When Rose called at the rectory the next day, Mrs Liddell welcomed her in like an old friend. She seemed taken aback by their offer, but Alexander showed so much enthusiasm that she quickly agreed.

'I'm going to be a lion tamer!' he declared, cracking an imaginary whip.

'Makes a change from being a lion,' Jane muttered as she poured them out some tea in the kitchen.

Alexander was in a fever of excitement by the time they came to collect him in the evening. They took him by the hand, but he could not keep still and kept dashing ahead. Rose prayed they did not lose him in the crowds. But when they got to the tent, the boy kept close to William and held on to him, suddenly overawed by the press of people and the noise. Rose thought it all magical in the soft flare of lamplight, and gasped in delight at the acrobats. Margaret soon fell asleep while Alexander giggled at the clown. But the animals disappointed him.

'When will the man get eaten?' he kept asking, to William's amusement.

Afterwards they bought him a bag of nuts from a street stall and he talked all the way home.

'I'm going to be a hunter when I grow up,' he enthused. 'I'm going to chase bears and lions and tigers.'

When they handed him over at the rectory, he was tired but reluctant to see them go.

'Maybe Rose and William would like to bring their children on the church outing to Ravensworth?' Edward Liddell suggested, appearing in the hallway. 'Repay you for your kindness,' he smiled.

Rose was as excited by the idea as Alexander. But William was wary. 'It wouldn't be right - us not being from your church.'

'You're in our parish,' the rector said amiably.

'Please, please!' chanted Alexander. Rose looked at her husband in expectation. She would love to revisit the place where her grandmother had lived, that dreamworld she had treasured from early childhood memory.

'It would be canny for the bairns,' she added.

'Agreed then?' Edward questioned.

'Aye, agreed,' William smiled bashfully.

Chapter 9

In the end, William did not go on the outing to Ravensworth. He made excuses about having jobs to do at St Bede's, but he stood up to his mother's objections to Rose and the babies going.

'It's a chance for them to get out in the fresh air - see a bit of the country,' he reasoned. 'It'll do them good.'

On the Saturday, Rose clambered into the horse-drawn brake, a girl on each knee, and settled back to enjoy the journey. She was so entranced by what she saw that she was not bothered about the bumping and lurching of the carriage along the turnpike roads. They turned their backs on the smoky, gas-smelling air of Jarrow and its blackened streets and headed into open countryside. Rose marvelled at the lush green of fields and trees, and the abundance of buttercups and daisies in the meadows. Wild blue and yellow irises sprouted out of ditches, while the hedgerows were overrun with wild briars, their small star-like roses wafting up heady scent as they passed. The distant moors were a haze of purple and white clover, and crowning them all were the forests of the Ravensworth estate. Rose was glad of Jane's company, for the young maid was in high spirits and helped entertain Margaret on the journey.

When they reached the village of Lamesley, Rose cried, 'There's the church! I remember watching the wedding sat on that wall. It doesn't look half as high now,' she laughed.

She saw again in her mind's eye the procession of carriages and the wedding party in their grand dresses and uniforms, and felt once more the excitement of that far-off golden day. She never thought to see the place again, yet here she was with her small daughters, about to drive up the magical road that snaked into the trees from where the wedding party had emerged. It was every bit as beautiful as she remembered. Rose hugged Elizabeth to her in anticipation as at last, they turned up the steep hill that led deep into the woods.

They entered a dark tunnel of overhanging branches and the children went suddenly quiet, overawed by their surroundings. All except Alexander who shouted, 'This is my castle! I'm a knight and I'm going to chop off all your heads!' Christina Liddell hushed him and tried to sit him on her knee, but he struggled from her hold and flung his arms around Uncle Edward.

'Look, Alexander,' he coaxed, 'see who can spot the first tower.'

They drew up sharply under a vast archway and called for the gatekeeper. He emerged from the lodge and pulled back the heavy gates to let them through. As they trundled up the drive, straining for a sight of the castle, Rose was struck by the resinous smell of newly cut logs.

Suddenly it loomed ahead out of the dense trees - a vast array of gleaming towers and golden walls caught in the sunshine. Myriad windows winked in welcome. The passengers gasped and the children shrieked in delight at the enchanted castle. Before it lay soft green lawns and flowerbeds bursting with colour. The visitors passed under a huge archway with a clock tower and into a warm open courtyard lined with stables and outhouses, where they all piled out. The children had to be restrained from disappearing in all directions at once, eager to explore. Edward took

Alexander by the hand.

'Follow us,' he smiled broadly. 'We know where the food is! We'll take it out on to the lawns.'

Jane swept up Margaret, and Rose hurried behind with Elizabeth.

'Let me.' Mrs Liddell appeared at her side and reached out for the baby. 'You shouldn't be carrying her in your condition.'

Rose said, 'I'm used to it.'

'I know, but today we're going to spoil you,' Mrs Liddell answered, taking the baby in her arms. The two women exchanged smiles.

As they walked around the high walls, Rose mused, 'Me granny used to work here in the kitchens - she was full of stories about the place. But I never thought I'd see it meself.'

'Well, what's the use of the rector having grand relations if he can't put them to good use?' Mrs Liddell whispered conspiratorially.

'It's like stepping into Heaven,' Rose enthused, as they followed the others down a pathway towards a lake. Fish jumped in the clear water and butterflies fluttered out of the long grass in front of them.

'It's a good break for all of us,' the rector's wife sighed in contentment, watching her husband up ahead, directing some of the children to help lay out the picnic.

Rose was filled with a strange sense of belonging. Here her ancestors had lived and worked for generations, courted, married and died. Had fate taken a different turn she might have been living here too, just like her grandmother. What pleasure it would give her to see her own daughters growing up away from the dangers of the town, breathing this clear air.

But had she grown up in Lamesley she would never have met her beloved William, Rose reminded herself. Jarrow, with all its teeming, noisy, precarious life, was what gave William a living. Jarrow was her lot. Perhaps one of her daughters would return to Ravensworth one day and live out her dream, Rose mused, stroking Elizabeth's soft cheek. If not her, then one of her family.

Rose said impulsively, 'I wish me sister Lizzie could work somewhere like this.'

'Is she not happy in South Shields?' Mrs Liddell asked.

How typical, Rose thought, that she should instantly remember where her sister was in service, though she had never even met her.

'She doesn't complain,' Rose confided, 'but the Flynns are moving back to Ireland and soon she'll be out of a job. Do you think . . . could you ... ? I know I shouldn't really ask.'

'I don't have as much influence here as you might think,' Mrs Liddell replied gently, 'but I'll see if I can put in a word for your Lizzie. It might help that her grandmother once worked here.'

'Ta very much, Mrs Liddell.' Rose beamed in gratitude.

The day passed swiftly in the sheltered grounds of Ravensworth, with the rector organising races among the children and taking trips out on the lake in a rowing boat. Young people strolled under the canopy of beech and sycamore trees and mothers lay dozing in the shade. Before leaving, they were all served tea in the servants' hall, a couple of hymns were sung, and then they reluctantly piled back into the open brake.

Alexander ran away and they spent ten minutes hunting for him. Rose and Edward found the boy in one of the stables, sitting high up on Lord Ravensworth's grandest carriage.

'I'm a better coachman than my father,' he declared. 'I drive for Queen Victoria.'

'Of course you do,' Edward smiled, hiding his anxiety at the boy's disappearance. 'Now it's time for you to drive us home to Jarrow.'

'Jarrow's not my home,' he shouted petulantly. 'It's dirty and smelly and there's no one to play with. I want to stay here.'

'We all want to stay here,' Rose laughed, 'but none of us belong.'

'I do,' Alexander grew tearful. 'Why can't I stay here? And why didn't William come? He said he would come. He's spoilt everything! I hate you all!'

'You mustn't speak to Mrs Fawcett like that,' Edward said, growing impatient. 'Come, come, everyone's waiting for you.' He stretched up and took his young cousin firmly in his arms. Alexander struggled for a moment, then allowed himself to be carried outside. By the time they had reached the gateway through the woods, he was asleep in Edward's lap.

Rose looked back at the lengthening shadows and the turrets retreating behind their fortress of trees, and sighed. It had been a perfect day and she wished William had been there to share it too. Next year, she would make sure he came on the outing. Her cheeks glowed from the warmth of the sun, and Elizabeth and Margaret slept contentedly after the unaccustomed fresh air.

Dusk was descending on Tyneside and a stiff breeze blew off the river by the time they rattled down into Jarrow. The countryside withered as it neared the town and the familiar smell from the chemical works was more overpowering than ever. The infants woke, stiff and fractious, and began to cry.

William was there to meet them and took the girls swiftly from Rose. With cries of thanks to the Liddells they trouped back to James Terrace. Rose felt suddenly overwhelmed with dissatisfaction for the house she had to call home. Here she was hemmed in, not only by the tightly packed cobbled streets, but by the strictures of her mother-in-law. She had tasted freedom today and it had left her hungry for more.

That night in bed, William kissed her and said, 'You still smell of the countryside - hay and wild flowers.' He buried his head in her long dark hair.

'It was a glimpse of Heaven,' she murmured, her body feeling pleasantly tired, not with the exhaustion of heavy housework, but from hours in the sun and fresh air. She stroked his face. 'I want us to have our own place,' she urged. 'Somewhere I can grow a few flowers, where the bairns can play without fear of them being trampled on by the coal carts.'

William kissed her. 'We'll look for somewhere soon.'

Rose pulled away in frustration. 'That's what you always say!' she accused. 'I want us to start looking now, William. By Christmas we'll have another bairn - I want it born in our own home. I'm sick of waiting.'

He looked at her in dismay. 'What's brought all this on?'

Rose looked at him keenly. 'Today I've seen beyond Jarrow. I'd forgotten what life was like outside these few streets - but it all came back to me. Trees - proper trees thick with leaves - and grass you could get lost in. Just how I remembered the country from when I was a bairn. I want our lasses to know what that's like. I want them to have a bit of Heaven, however small.'

William stared at her. She waited for him to ridicule the idea as being quite impractical, to remonstrate with her for having gone on the outing and come back so dissatisfied with her lot. He was forever telling her they should be grateful for what they had compared to the majority of working-class families in the town.

But he did not rebuke her. 'Where do you want to live?' he asked quietly.

Rose continued eagerly, 'Somewhere up Simonside, above the town. Maybes with a little plot of land like me da's where I can grow things.'

William nodded. 'We'll see.'

Rose was not content with this. She gripped his arm. 'Promise me, William! Promise me we'll be out of here before the bairn's born?' She searched his face for the telltale signs of weakness, the way his look would slip from hers, the apologetic shrug that came when he gave in to his mother rather than her. But he held her look with his keen blue eyes.

'If it means that much to you,' he said gravely, 'aye, I promise.'

Chapter 10

By October, William had paid a month's rent in advance on a small house in Raglan Street. It was not the house on the edge of the countryside that Rose had hankered after in her daydreams, but it was neat and respectable. It was one of the newer properties away from the stench of the river and had a tiny patch of ground between the front door and the street on which she planned to grow flowers. A short walk away lay the Recreation Ground, as Jarrow Park had become known, and it was ten minutes in the other direction to William's place of work.

'We'll never see you!' Mrs Fawcett had repeated melodramatically for a fortnight before they moved. Her husband had tried to placate her.

'Course we will. We'll see them every Sunday at St Bede's, and I'm sure Rose will be glad of your help with the babies during the week.'

Rose had smothered her real feelings and said she would be happy if her mother-in-law called round to see them whenever she wanted. But as she suspected, the older woman seldom did, unless she knew that William would be there. Rose had to put up with William calling in to see his mother on his way back from work more frequently than she would wish, but she was so relieved to have their own house that she did not complain.

Even though she was large with their third child, Rose busied herself making their house in Raglan Street into a cosy home. Maggie came to help her paint the walls and put up blinds and scrub the floors before putting down clippy mats and rugs. For the first time, Rose was able to unpack their wedding presents and put them on display: a china tea service with blue birds of paradise; brass tongs and coal scuttle for the hearth; a green baize cloth and glass cruet set on the table. Above the second-hand piano hung a gilt-framed oil painting of farm workers bringing in the harvest that reminded Rose of Ravensworth. They made up the bed with fresh, crisp linen and put colourful quilts in the girls' cots and patchwork curtains at the windows.

Rose revelled in her new home and in the freedom she felt at being solely in charge. She was careful with William's wages and was able to buy small treats at the end of the week: an extra piece of meat, some calico for the girls' dresses or a piece of sheet music for William. She thanked the saints that her husband never stopped off at any of the numerous pubs that he passed on the way home from work or drank away half the housekeeping like others did.

In early December, a few days after Elizabeth's first birthday, Sarah Ann was born safely. She was a contented baby, undemanding and easy to feed. Rose wondered if this stemmed from her own contentment and feeling of wellbeing that had settled on her since their move to Raglan Street. But she soon realised how tiring a baby and two infants could be in a house she now had to run herself, and her temper began to fray. William went to Maggie in concern.

Two days later, Lizzie came to help out with the older two, before taking up her new position as chambermaid at Ravensworth. Mrs Liddell had personally recommended her for the job. She was excited at the prospect and Rose had sent round a cake to Mrs Liddell as a thank you for her intervention.

'Eeh, three daughters!' Lizzie marvelled as she fed porridge to Elizabeth on her knee, while Margaret banged a spoon in her high chair and squirmed to be out.

'Aye, just like us three,' Rose sighed where she lay on the truckle bed suckling Sarah. 'I hope they all get on as well as we did as bairns.'

'We didn't always,' Lizzie declared. 'You were always bossing me and Maggie about - sending us off on errands.'

'I was the one doing the running around,' Rose protested. 'I'd walk for miles with a basket on me head while you two ran off and played.'

'We were helping Ma around the house,' Lizzie contradicted.

'That's not what Ma used to say,' Rose snorted.

Margaret, tiring of her confinement, threw her spoon across the kitchen and yelled. Rose winced as the sound jarred her taut nerves.

'Listen to her! You've no patience,' Lizzie said, wagging a finger at the wailing child. 'Just like your mam,' she teased. Plonking Elizabeth on the floor, she reached over and hauled her eldest niece from her chair. The girl ran immediately to her mother and began pulling at the baby.

'I want up, Mammy!' she cried.

'Careful!' Rose scolded as the baby blinked in alarm. But Margaret pulled herself up on the bed and clambered over her mother, making it impossible to feed. 'Get down,' Rose ordered weakly. Elizabeth crawled over to see what was happening.

Lizzie swept down and lifted her up, then grabbed Margaret by the hand and hauled her protesting from her mother's side. 'Haway, we'll gan out for a walk, let Mammy get some rest.'

Margaret howled in resistance.

'Go on,' Rose snapped, pushing the petulant girl away.

'We'll see if the chestnut seller is up the street,' Lizzie coaxed.

'Ta,' Rose said above the din, collapsing back.

Lizzie eyed her. 'You'll have to find someone to help you when I'm gone. Can William's mam not lend a hand for a bit?'

'No,' Rose cried in alarm. 'I'll manage. I'll be on me feet again by Christmas.'

'Well, I can only stop another week,' Lizzie reminded. 'Maybe Maggie can call in and help with the washing and ironing.'

Rose closed her eyes. 'I'll be grand, the baby's no trouble.'

'Aye, but these two are a handful,' Lizzie said, struggling to get her nieces into their coats. 'Don't work yourself into an early grave like Ma did.'

'Ma died of typhoid,' Rose pointed out.

'And overwork - and too many babies too soon, more than likely,' Lizzie said forthrightly.

After she had gone and the noise of the girls grew faint, Rose lay back thankfully with her baby nuzzling at her breast. Maybe Lizzie had a point. She felt achingly tired despite Sarah being a tranquil baby, and the thought of William's attentions in bed beginning again made her sigh with exhaustion. She felt no appetite for lovemaking any more, but was sure this would pass as she loved her husband deeply. Besides, she knew it was her duty and would not be able to deny him for ever. But for now, she was happy to lie in the warmth of the kitchen on the truckle bed, rather than in the chilly bedroom upstairs. She did not need to retreat to their bedroom for privacy as she had done in James

Terrace. As Rose drifted into sleep, she determined to delay the move back to the marital bed as long as possible.

On Christmas Eve, Margaret's second birthday, the family were invited round to the Liddells' home for a magic lantern show with members of the Sunday School. Rose took the small girls, and Margaret was entranced by the coloured pictures of the Holy Family resting in the stable, and shepherds and wise men travelling to see them. Edward Liddell gave a running commentary, and afterwards Mrs Liddell treated the children to mince pies and cocoa.

'Where's Alexander?' Rose asked, thinking of the boisterous small cousin whom she had not seen since the late summer.

'He's not with us any more,' the rector's wife answered with a look of regret. 'He was sent south to start school. He's living with another of his mother's cousins now.'

'I bet it's quiet around here without him,' Rose said.

'Yes,' Mrs Liddell sighed, 'especially after Verger was knocked over—' She broke off, her eyes welling with tears. Rose had heard of the rector's beloved collie being trampled under the hoofs of a dray horse that autumn. She still pictured Alexander rolling on the ground with the friendly dog and giggling as it licked his face. 'Never mind,' Mrs Liddell said more briskly, 'no doubt we'll see Alexander when we next go south to visit.'

'Aye, well, say we were asking after him if you do,' Rose said, surprised that he had not come to say goodbye to them. There again, he was young and had probably not given them a second thought since the summer outing to Ravensworth. Thinking of that day prompted her to add, 'Our Lizzie's that happy going to place at the castle. Ta very much for all your help.'

'I'm glad.' Mrs Liddell smiled once more and, with a touch on baby Sarah's cheek, turned to see to the other children. Soon afterwards, Rose thanked them for the special treat and trouped out into the dark afternoon, thinking how tired and pinch-faced the Liddells had looked despite their cheerful welcome. She hurried home to prepare tea for William.

Rose had wanted to host their first Christmas in their own home, but had to concede she did not have the energy. So they went to the Fawcetts, taking the girls there after church for a lunch of turkey and potatoes, bread sauce and winter greens, followed by a large Christmas pudding and white sauce. The day was enlivened by seeing Florrie and Albert and hearing their news from across the river. William's mother fussed over her favourite, Margaret, making a great show of presenting her with an expensive doll's house. Rose felt aggrieved at being upstaged. William had worked hard at making their eldest a pull-along wooden lion in a cage with a red-coated lion tamer, which Margaret had delighted in that morning. Now it was forgotten in the excitement of her very own doll's house. But soon Elizabeth was trying to climb inside it and eat the miniature table and chairs, and the house had to be removed. Margaret burst into tears of frustration and would not be placated.

'We'll keep the doll's house here in the parlour,' Mrs Fawcett ruled. 'I can see it'll only get broken at your house. Margaret can play with it when she comes.'

But this only made the child howl the louder, until Rose smacked her in frustration. They ended up taking the children home early instead of staying for

71

tea. Margaret's tantrum had blown over by the time they reached Raglan Street and she made no resistance at being put to bed. With the girls asleep upstairs and the baby lying swaddled in a soft woollen shawl on the truckle bed, Rose sank into her chair by the fire.

William disappeared into the yard to fill up the coal scuttle. He woke her from a doze with a soft call from the back door. 'Come and look, Rose. There's a grand moon out the night.'

She roused herself and went to the door, yawning and pulling her shawl about her. It had turned bitterly cold since their walk back home. William was standing by the gate to the back lane, his golden hair illuminated in the moonlight like some angel. The moon was so bright it cast shadows along the street, its icy white light more brilliant than the winter sun. A sharp frost covered everything, turning the drab lane into a carpet of white and the rooftops sparkling silver. Straight pillars of smoke rose from chimneys, filling the air with their acrid scent.

Rose went to him and slipped her arm through his, feeling the returning pressure. Neither of them spoke, as if spellbound by the beauty of the moonlit landscape. They listened to the sounds of the night: footsteps ringing on the frosty cobbles in the next street; the screech of cats on the prowl; the muted sounds of neighbours having a singsong across the lane.

William kissed her head tenderly. 'Are you happy, Rose?' he whispered.

She leant into him, thinking of their cosy home and three daughters who looked like cherubs when they slept. She thrilled at the feel of his warm hold about her. Tonight even Jarrow looked magical in the moonlight. She looked into his anxious eyes and knew how much she was loved.

'Aye, I am,' she assured, 'I've never been happier.'

And saying it out loud, she realised how true it was. She might feel overwhelmed at times with tiredness and the demands of three small infants, but that would pass. She had everything she ever wanted right there: a secure home, healthy babies and a husband in work whom she loved and who loved her in return.

William smiled bashfully. 'Me an' all,' he said. 'You make me that happy. I'd do anything for you, Rose - for you and the bairns. You know that, don't you?'

'Aye, I do,' Rose smiled back, and lifted her lips to kiss him.

'Come back upstairs tonight,' William urged. 'I miss you next to me. Granny's old bed warmer isn't the same thing,' he joked.

Rose hesitated, feeling embarrassed. She glanced down the lane, but there was no one in sight to overhear their intimate conversation. 'I want to,' she said, 'but...'

'What?' William asked. 'You do love me, don't you?'

'Of course I do,' she answered quickly, 'it's just – I don't want any more bairns. At least not just yet.' She saw his face flush in the moonlight. 'We've had three babies in less than three years and it's enough to cope with. I know what the priest says about it being our duty, but I'm tired out.'

William did not speak for a moment and Rose feared she had offended him. Then he squeezed her to him. 'I'll leave you alone,' he whispered. 'I just want to lie with you and baby Sarah, that's all.'

She hugged him back in relief. At that moment a small whimper started up in the kitchen. 'Haway, then,' Rose said, shivering, 'let's take her up to bed.'

Chapter 11

Heavy snowfalls and deep frosts that kept the streets treacherous and many labourers idle saw in 1881. Then February brought a thaw and Rose emerged from a state of hibernation to take the girls out to the shops and park. By the spring, trade was buoyant along the river and the town was thriving once more. In early June, the talk was all of the centenary celebrations to mark the birth of railway engineer George Stephenson. As trade union members, William and his father were involved in the procession, and a huge number travelled from Jarrow to join in the festivities upriver in Newcastle. The family decided to go. Extra trains were laid on, and Maggie met Rose early at the station to help with the children.

Rose had managed to persuade her mother-in-law to take baby Sarah for the day.

'You'll not catch me in Newcastle for anyone's centenary,' Mrs Fawcett had shuddered. 'All those crowds! I think it's dangerous taking the children.'

'Maggie's ganin' with me,' Rose said, keeping her temper with difficulty. 'We'll manage fine if you'd keep Sarah till tea time.'

It took an appeal from William for Mrs Fawcett to consent to the idea. 'Well, if William wants you all to be there, I suppose ...'

Rose was as excited as the children as they clambered aboard the crowded carriage and steamed into Newcastle. William had left with his father at the crack of dawn.

'Don't suppose we'll ever manage to meet up in this crowd,' Rose said, as they gawped at the sea of people making their way into the city. All the bridges and roads snaking across the Tyne and up the steep bank were packed with revellers.

'I've never seen so many folk in all me life!' Maggie exclaimed, holding Elizabeth up for a better look.

Margaret, dressed in a new sailor suit and straw hat, pressed her nose to the window and peered through the smoke of the engine. 'Where's me da? I want to see me da!'

Rose hugged her tight. 'You stay close to me, do you hear? We'll find your da. He's going to be carrying a banner and following the band.'

'I want to follow the band!' Margaret jumped up and down with excitement.

'We will, hinny,' Rose promised with a kiss on her cheek.

They were carried forward in the sea of people wending their way through the streets of Newcastle, following the grand procession of trade union banners, civic dignitaries dressed in rich robes and representatives of railway companies from around the world. Finely groomed horses pulling models of engines, stamped and snorted behind military bands. The noise was deafening and Rose clung on tightly to her daughters and sister. But neither girl seemed frightened, each peering around wide-eyed at the spectacle, pointing and squealing at the horses. It was far too crowded to catch a glimpse of William, though Margaret insisted she could see her father every few minutes as another banner swept past.

To Rose's relief, they managed to find William and his father on the Town

Moor where the procession ended, listening to a rousing speech by the Mayor of Jarrow. Afterwards they shared the picnic that Rose had brought, then milled around looking at the exhibition of locomotives. William took Margaret on a pony-and-trap ride around the open park, which so thrilled her that she refused to climb down at the end. Only Maggie's bribe of a sticky piece of liquorice enticed her from the carriage.

As the afternoon waned, they began to make their way back down to the station for the journey home. As the family stopped to watch a Punch and Judy show, Rose took the opportunity to disappear behind a bush and relieve herself. When she re-emerged she could see no sign of Margaret. She had been holding hands with her grandfather.

'Where's our Margaret?' she asked him at once.

He looked taken aback. 'I thought she'd gone with you—'

'No she didn't!' Rose replied. William turned at the sound of her anxious voice. He had Elizabeth on his shoulders; Maggie was still gazing at the entertainment, quite absorbed.

'She's gone,' Rose gasped, fear choking her. 'Where's she gone, William?' She spun around, grabbing bystanders by the arm. 'Have you seen me little lass? Fair hair - wearing a straw hat - white and navy ribbons,' she gabbled. People turned to look but shook their heads.

William thrust Elizabeth into his father's arms and shouted, 'Stay right here and don't let her out of your sight! Maggie, you look around here - we'll gan back to where we started.'

Rose looked around at the moor, still packed with revellers, some of them now well inebriated from a day's drinking in the town. 'We'll never find her in all this!' she sobbed.

William took her by the hand. 'Yes we will. Pray to St Anthony to find our little lass.'

Rose's panic was stemmed by his strong conviction. She ran with him through the crowds, searching and shouting for Margaret. They pushed their way back against the flow of trippers making back for the town, straining for a glimpse of straw hat or fair cheeks among the tired children being carried or led home. All the while they stopped people to demand if they had noticed a little girl in a sailor dress, but nobody had.

Rose felt herself ageing by years in those terrible minutes of gut-wrenching panic. How could they have lost her so quickly? She must have been snatched! She would never have just wandered away from her family. She might have been knocked over by one of the steam engines! Maybe at this very moment she was being trampled underfoot by a startled horse, just like the Liddells' dog . . .

Suddenly an idea hit her. She seized William's arm and gasped, 'The pony - the pony and trap!'

Without another word they ran in search of the carriage that had been giving rides across the moor all day long. A young boy had been left in charge when William had taken his daughter for a ride. At first there was no sign of it and they feared the boy had gone. Then William spotted it next to the platform where the speakers had been which was now being dismantled.

They rushed over and shouted to the boy holding the pony's reins. He was eating a pie and had his mouth full. The carriage looked empty. Rose felt dashed.

'Have you seen our bairn?' William panted. The boy chewed and swallowed.

'Is that her?' he asked, nodding at the trap. 'Didn't know who she belonged to, but she said you'd come and fetch her.'

They peered in. A small figure was curled up on the bench already fast asleep.

Rose let out a sob of relief. 'Margaret!'

William reached in and gathered the child to him. She stirred sleepily, muttered something about the pony and then settled against his chest.

'You naughty lass!' Rose cried, quite shaken. She wanted to scold her into never doing such a thing again and crush her to her breast at the same time.

William shushed her. 'She's alive, that's all that matters.'

Rose burst into tears. What worse fate could happen to her than to lose one of her precious children! She clung on to William and Margaret all the way back to the others.

After such a scare they hurried for a train home, not waiting for the evening's fireworks. Picking up Sarah from James Terrace, they all colluded in not telling William's mother about losing Margaret. Their nerves were shattered enough without Mrs Fawcett berating them further.

From then on, Rose was nervous about them venturing as far as Newcastle again. She was happier staying within the boundary of the town and being content with local entertainment, for Jarrow continued to mushroom as new waves of workers and their families arrived on the Tyne to fill the expanding shipyards. Dominating all was Palmer's.

The wealthy shipbuilder and local MP owned the means of production from the raw material to the finished ships. Sir Charles owned the ironstone mines in North Yorkshire, the port where the iron ore was loaded and the boats which carried it to the Tyne. He possessed the iron works, the blast furnaces, the puddling mills and rolling mills. He employed the fitters, riveters, platers and boilermakers who built his mighty vessels, and the joiners and carpenters who fitted them out. At his beck and call were the army of casual labourers who queued at his gates in the early morning for the chance to fetch and carry, shovel and haul, load and unload until dusk. Jarrow was a company town, its fate inextricably linked with Palmer's success or failure.

Idealists like William might rail against Palmer's autocratic hold over his workers, but there was no escaping that their own prosperity and survival was bound up with that of their distant employer who lived far away in North Yorkshire.

'He wasn't always so grand,' William pointed out that autumn as they made ready to go to view the launch of the Virginia. 'Did you know he's the son of a master mariner from Gateshead? Now he's one of the gentry with a fortune to his name - a fortune made for him by hard-grafting working men. The only time he shows his face round here now is at a launch or election time.'

Rose ignored his aggrieved remarks. She was glad of this rare day off work together when they could take the girls on an outing. The late summer had been wet and the Durham Agricultural Show on the Recreation Ground had been washed out. They had taken the girls to see the animals and listen to the

Royal Artillery band and another from a training ship, but had been beaten home by the incessant rain. To Rose's alarm, William and the girls had caught chills, which had lingered on their chests and caused them to cough for weeks. But now they seemed recovered and she was determined to enjoy the day.

'I think it's canny giving you a holiday to gan and see the ship. Let's make the most of it,' she said cheerfully.

William's mood soon improved when they joined the throng of spectators heading towards the river. The expectation of the crowd was infectious. Never before had such a big ship been built at Jarrow, and newspaper boys shouted out the news. Rose and William clutched Margaret firmly between them, while Elizabeth rode high on her father's shoulders and Sarah clung to her mother's hip.

The girls revelled in the lively bands and clapped their hands. Jubilant workers threw their caps in the air as the vast steamer was cut from its moorings and edged into the grey water of the Tyne.

'You've been a part of that, William!' Rose gasped in awe as the steel-plated ship groaned and sighed its way into the pewter-coloured river. She felt brimming over with pride that his long hours of labour should have helped produce such a large and imposing vessel.

'My da's ship!' Margaret began to chant. 'My da's ship!'

Rose caught William's look of bashful pride and they both laughed.

'Let's pray there'll be plenty more like that one,' he said with a wry smile.

That evening, William surprised her with a treat. Maggie came to look after the children and put them to bed.

'Where are we ganin'?' Rose asked in excitement.

'Put your best dress on, Mrs Fawcett, we're going out,' William grinned.

Rose dressed hurriedly in the green frock she had worn for Florrie's wedding that hung in the large wardrobe and smelt of mothballs. Margaret demanded to know where she was going and that she should go too.

'When you're older,' William placated her, 'I'll take you, an' all.' He swung her up and kissed her, then handed her to Maggie. 'Tonight your mam's getting the treat she deserves.'

Rose laughed as she kissed the girls good night and headed out on William's arm, determined to ignore Margaret's protests at being left behind. As they walked up the street under the soft gaslight, she tried to guess where they were going.

'Some'at's on at St Bede's?'

William shook his head.

'We're meeting Florrie and Albert?' she guessed again.

'No,' William answered with a secretive smile.

'Lockart's Cocoa Rooms?' she asked in the hope it was something musical. But again he shook his head. Rose's heart sank. 'It's not one of your lectures, is it? It's nowt political?'

William laughed. 'Not exactly. But it will be stirring - something good for the soul.'

Rose tried to hide her disappointment. 'It's a temperance meeting, isn't it?'

William just squeezed her arm in reply. They carried on through the town in silence, Rose trying to recapture the excitement she had felt earlier. At least it was an evening out with her husband. They were dressed up and free from domestic chores for an hour or two. What more did she want?

As they turned into Ormonde Street, Rose was struck by how busy it seemed. A large throng of people were gathered on the far side. But then the town was bound to be full on the evening of a launch day and the pubs would have been doing brisk business. Yet this was no rowdy crowd full of drink. A moment later, it dawned on her they were gathered outside the new Royal Albert Hall. Her heart thudded.

'William!' she gasped, hardly daring to hope. 'Are we ganin' in *there*?'

He smiled at her and steered her across the road. 'The bands from the launch are playing tonight - and there's singing too.'

Rose let out a cry of delight. Jarrow had never had a theatre or music hall before and she had watched with interest as it was being built. Yet it had not occurred to her that she would ever go to a performance there. She had never been anywhere like it before. Any socialising they did was usually at the church. William would go out with his father to talks at the Mechanics' Institute, but the theatre was considered frivolous and frowned upon in the Fawcett household. Maybe that was why William had asked Maggie to mind the children for them. She suspected his parents knew nothing about this trip to the Royal Albert.

They stood in line for tickets, Rose fretting they might be turned away.

'It's huge, Rose,' William assured her, 'seats for eleven hundred.'

Soon they were in and clutching a programme; William had splashed out and bought shilling tickets for the dress circle. They were ushered in by the proprietor himself.

Rose gawped in amazement at the vast auditorium below with its tip-up seats and the distant balcony above where the cheapest seats were. There was a hum of excited voices as people settled down and watched the bandsmen setting up their instruments on the raised stage. William helped her off with her cape and Rose glanced around. She recognised one or two shopkeepers, well dressed and middle class. Others were obviously prosperous working class like themselves, the elite of Palmer's workforce.

'I feel like the aristocracy,' she joked. 'Tell me what's in the programme.'

But before he could do so, the proprietor came on and began to banter with the audience. People shouted loudly from the balcony above to get on with the entertainment. Soon it started and Rose felt swept along by the music. A military band played rousing martial pieces and a colliery band played jaunty local tunes. A men's choir sang popular songs that brought Rose close to tears, then a comedian came on and had them laughing, provoking ribald exchanges with those in the pit stalls. A singer joined him and they gave a rousing comic duet. The evening finished off with the colliery band playing once more.

Emptying out into the street, Rose and William felt their ears still ringing with the music, and people around them repeated the jokes they had heard inside and laughed again. The couple went home arm in arm, humming the tunes of the evening.

'It was the best night ever,' Rose declared.

'We'll go again soon then,' William said, his spirits quite lifted by the experience too. It was so seldom that they had any time off to enjoy together away from the demands of work or daily chores. Tonight they had seen a whole new dazzling world that existed right on their doorstep, a place of music and make-believe hidden behind Jarrow's grimy streets. What harm was there in escaping to its bright, welcoming interior once in a while?

That night, still giddy from the experience, William and Rose made love for the first time in months. Their heads were full of music, their bodies energised rather than achingly tired. They made love with vigour and enthusiasm, their usual shyness at such an act quite dissolved. Afterwards, they lay cradled in each other's arms, wrapped in deep contentment. Rose wondered, before falling asleep, if they had created new life that night. What a passionate and loving baby that would be! A baby made from sweet longing and deep affection, a baby with music in its soul and laughter on its lips.

The following summer, as the roses outside their house burst into bloom, their fourth child was born.

Chapter 12

Lizzie happened to be home visiting from Ravensworth the day the baby bellowed its way into the world. Lizzie had come down with Maggie and her father to visit Rose and the girls. They found Rose pacing the kitchen, unable to get comfortable, while the girls played about on the backdoor step. Margaret leapt up in excitement at their appearance and took charge of the cinder toffee that her Auntie Lizzie held out.

'The bairn's on its way,' Rose told them matter-of-factly, between grimaces of pain.

'Get yourself upstairs now,' Lizzie ordered. 'Maggie, boil up the kettle - and fetch newspaper.'

Old McConnell looked alarmed and raised himself up stiffly from the chair by the hearth. 'I'll take a walk down to the Queen Victoria . . .'

'No you won't, Da,' Lizzie told him. 'You'll stop and give a hand with the bairns while me and Maggie see to our Rose. You can do your celebratin' later.'

He grumbled to St Patrick but sat down again, allowing Sarah to pull herself up on his knobbly legs. 'Can you manage a boy this time, Rose Ann?' he called after her. 'I've had a lifetime of being bossed around by women, so I have.'

'Spoilt rotten, you mean!' Rose managed to shout back, before another spasm seized her.

Her sisters set to work stripping the linen from the bed and lining it with newspaper, while Rose got out of her clothes and put on her nightgown. She felt huge with this baby, like an overgrown marrow that was ready to burst. With the others she had felt nauseous and tired, but with this one she was always ravenous. For months she had had the appetite of someone who worked in the fields and she had satisfied her cravings with anything sweet: mounds of bread and jam, scones and cakes. There was plenty of work at the mill, William was bringing home a steady wage and they had fed well all year. The girls were thriving, William was happy and Rose felt luxuriantly fertile when he touched her full body and complimented her on her plumpness. Now this greedy baby, whom she felt sure must be a boy, was ready to leave the abundance of her belly.

The first part of labour came swiftly and her waters broke, but then the time dragged on and nothing happened. Rose grew weary and fretful, weighted to the bed like a sack of stones. She had expected this one to come quickly, with the same ease as her pregnancy, but something held it back.

'Maybe we should send for the midwife,' Lizzie murmured to Maggie. 'She's all done in.'

Maggie agreed - 'I'll fetch Mrs Kennedy' - and went hurrying off for help. A while later she returned with Mrs McMullen, with a shrug at her sisters. 'Danny's mam wasn't there.'

'I said I'd come as soon as I heard,' Mrs McMullen said, bustling to the bedside. 'Now what's the problem, Rose Ann? Can't be anything I haven't seen already. Mary Mother! You look like you've got room for three or four in there! I was never that big, even with the triplets.'

Rose looked at John's mother in alarm. 'Don't say that,' she panted, sinking back on the bolster in exhaustion. She found the woman's presence unsettling. Despite her good intentions, Rose was hardly in touch with her any more, except to nod to or exchange a brief word outside church after Mass. She was a reminder of the past, of hawking vegetables in the bitter cold, of a time when all her clothes were second- or third-hand and when poverty had been an ever-present threat. She was aware of the woman's shabby clothes and grimy hands, the smell of the lanes about her. She stirred up uncomfortable memories of John, mixed feelings that made Rose sweat even harder in the stuffy bedroom.

She tensed as Mrs McMullen prodded her belly and felt for the unborn baby. 'It's breech,' she announced. 'Baby's trying to come out feet first, just like my John. It'll be awkward like him, so it will.'

The sisters stared at her. 'So what do we do? Call for the doctor?'

'Not a bit of it,' Mrs McMullen dismissed the idea. 'I can manage fine. It just needs a bit of a sharp talking to. Now help me get Rose Ann propped up more - the baby won't come if she's lying down like the sleeping.'

Rose had no idea how long she crouched there on the bed, supported by her sisters and cajoled by Mrs McMullen into pushing her baby out. She roared with the pain and swore to the Virgin she would have no more children. No sooner had Maggie wiped her face than her eyes were once more blinded with salty sweat. It poured down her body like a stream. She screwed her eyes shut and surrendered to the red-hot hammers that thumped in her head, the pistons of pain that throbbed through her body. She vaguely remembered hearing Margaret and Elizabeth wailing at the door to be let in and Maggie leaving her side to go and placate them.

After each attempt to push she sank back weaker than before.

'I'm going to die!' she sobbed in despair. She could see the look of fear on Lizzie's face.

'Hush now,' Mrs McMullen said briskly. 'There'll be no one dying here today. I can see it coming - just another push so I can get a hold of somethin'.' But even she began to pray urgently under her breath to a litany of saints, and Rose whimpered in fright.

'Haway, Rose!' Lizzie rallied. 'Try again!' She propped her up with strong arms and gripped her hand in encouragement.

Rose gathered every ounce of strength left to her and pushed for her life.

'Here come the feet!' Mrs McMullen cried. She yanked at them so hard that Rose screamed at the searing pain. 'One more time, Rose Ann,' she shouted. 'You push and I pull!'

Together they made so much noise they startled a horse in the street below. It reared up whinnying, then bolted, shedding from its wagon a sack of flour that burst on the cobbles. Children ran to play with it and chuck handfuls at each other. The flour rose on the breeze like a sandstorm settling on windowsills and wafting into open doors.

By the time Rose's baby was out, she could taste flour on her parched lips. She sank back, utterly spent. She did not even have the breath to ask if the baby lived. But a moment later her worry was dispelled by a lusty cry.

'St Theresa be praised!' Mrs McMullen beamed in relief.

Lizzie peered eagerly for a look. 'It's another lass,' she laughed in amazement.

'By heck, it's a strappin' one, our Rose!'

Rose felt a wave of disappointment. She could not summon the enthusiasm to open her eyes and look at her fourth daughter. How she had longed for it to be a son for William. They had been so certain that it would be that they had not even chosen a girl's name.

'Haway, Rose,' Lizzie chided, 'look at your new bairn. She's got dark hair like you. She'll be the bonniest of them all.' The baby howled louder as if trying to gain its mother's attention, but Rose felt pinned to the bed by exhaustion and disappointment.

'Leave her be,' Mrs McMullen said gently, 'she needs to sleep. We'll go and show off the bairn to her big sisters.'

They left her alone. Rose could hear the buzz of excited chatter downstairs and the clamour of the children to see the new baby. The fetid room smelt of childbirth and flour and horse dung from the street below. She was hot and thirsty, but past caring of her discomfort. Within minutes she was wrapped in a blissful sleep.

Rose took several weeks to recover from the birth and Maggie came down frequently to help with the children. They paid for a girl called Bella to come in and do the washing and ironing and black lead the range. But Rose's initial rejection of the baby was short-lived. She found herself enjoying the enforced rest upstairs, feeding and cuddling her newborn. William chose to name her Catherine, but somehow the name was too formal for the noisy, bright-eyed infant, and from the first she was known as Kate.

'She's got your bonny dark hair,' William said, rocking the babe proudly in his arms.

'She's got your lusty lungs, but!' Rose laughed. 'We'll have another singer in the family.' Her mind went back to their evening of passion after the Albert Hall concert when she was certain Kate had been conceived. Looking at the pair of them she felt a surge of affection. When William held Kate up to his face to be kissed, she saw the same oval shape in miniature, the same fairness of skin as his. This daughter had taken the best features of them both and melded them into one. Rose prayed she would have William's sweet nature and her own common sense.

By the end of August, Rose was back on her feet again and gaining her strength. Bella continued to come in and help on Mondays with the washing, for Rose found her hands full with the four small girls. She strove hard to keep them clean and neatly turned out, well fed and polite, though often Margaret's bossy manner and Sarah's exuberance would manifest themselves when their Fawcett grandmother came to call. Margaret was strong-willed and intent on organising her sisters into games they did not grasp. But she was already a help to her mother in fetching her sewing box or mixing ingredients or standing on a stool and handing out pegs when Bella hung out the washing.

Elizabeth was milder natured, fair and bashful like her father, slow in picking up speech. She usually did what Margaret commanded without much protest, happy with the odd small bribe of a lump of sugar or being allowed to hold Margaret's doll. Elizabeth treated her baby sisters like dolls, combing Sarah's wavy hair and trying to lift Kate from her crib to hold on her knee.

Their third daughter Sarah had lost her babyish contentment and was forever trying to explore and escape to the dangers of the street. She would climb upstairs and not be able to come down again, or be found under the heavy oak sideboard eating a lump of coal. William had to make a special fireguard to keep her from climbing into the fire or playing with the bellows. Once when Bella dashed out to collect in the washing as rain began to pour, Sarah had staggered halfway down the back lane before they realised she was missing. She was a constant worry to Rose. But Kate at least lay where she was put, gurgling happily at the faces which came to peer at her.

The christening was delayed because St Bede's was being enlarged and new bells installed. In early October the refurbished church was opened again with a special service to bless the bells, and Kate was christened a week later. It was a happy family occasion, but Lizzie came with news from Ravensworth that the Reverend Edward Liddell's health had completely broken down.

'He was staying with his lordship for a couple of weeks, before harvest,' Lizzie told her. 'It seemed to upset him - being that close to Jarrow but not allowed to gan back to his work. So he went south again.'

It confirmed rumours locally that his health was in ruins. Rose had been disappointed that the summer trip to Ravensworth had been cancelled, for the Liddells had been absent. Yet there had been a big ceremony in the parish on St Peter's Day, when the Bishop of Durham had come to preach and open a new church in the more run-down area near the river. Mr Liddell had been made an honorary canon of Durham, and Rose had slipped along to watch them coming out of the new St Peter's. Jane, the Liddells' maid, had told her how proud Mrs Liddell was of the rector that day.

The week after Kate's christening, Rose bundled the girls into coats and bonnets, put the younger two in the pram and set off for the rectory to see for herself. Jane let her in.

'The mistress isn't seeing visitors,' she warned, 'but I'll tell her you're here with the bairns.'

They were ushered into the drawing room, which was cold and bleak, half the furniture covered in dustsheets. Rose was shocked to see how drawn and pale Mrs Liddell looked, but she rallied at the sight of Rose and the children. She made a fuss of the new baby and told Jane to bring in some tea and biscuits for them all.

'We're leaving,' she said abruptly, turning to stare out of the soot-speckled window. 'The rector needs a long period of convalescence.'

'I'm sorry,' Rose said, trying to stop Sarah from exploring under a dustsheet. The older two fidgeted on the seat beside her. 'Will you be gone for long?'

When Mrs Liddell turned round her eyes were full of tears. She nodded. 'We won't be coming back,' she whispered. 'It's been too much for my husband - he's made himself ill caring for so many.'

Once she started speaking of her anguish she could not stop. 'He's given his best years to Jarrow - down at the docks before dawn, doling out hot drinks, preaching in the streets, visiting everyone who called for his help no matter what time of day or night! There's hardly a home in the town he hasn't been into to hold the hand of a sick child or a dying man. Never once did he spare himself. He drove himself until he dropped and I couldn't stop him! God forgive me, but sometimes I get really angry and ask, why him? Why did God give him this great challenge and then rob him of his health so he cannot complete it?'

She let out a terrible sob and Rose wanted to go to her, put her arms about her. How lonely she must be to be telling such things to the likes of her. But Rose was inhibited by this woman's social position; it was not for her to make such an impertinent gesture. So she sat and gripped Sarah in her lap, thinking of the rector striding about Jarrow with Verger at his heels, greeting everyone he met by name and with a cheerful smile. It was tragic that such a good man had been beaten down by the very conditions he sought to improve.

'We're put here to endure,' Rose answered simply, 'not to ask why.'

Once she might have believed that ill health was a sign of a person's sinfulness, but she could not think that of the rector, even if he was an Anglican. William had made her less tolerant of such ideas. 'It's bad conditions that cause disease that are sinful, Rose,' he would say, 'not the diseased.'

The rector's wife bowed her head as if ashamed of speaking such thoughts, and reached for a handkerchief.

'He'll be greatly missed round here, Mrs Liddell,' Rose mumbled. 'You an' all.'

Christina Liddell put her hand to her mouth to stifle another sob. 'Thank you, Rose. We'll miss you all too.' She sighed heavily. 'When we first came, I thought it the end of the earth - wanted to run away at once. But Edward felt akin to the people here. He hated the way they were forced to live, but never the people. Wherever we go next, half of him will always be here.'

Rose was moved by the woman's sadness, but said, 'At least you and Canon Liddell have somewhere else you can go.'

'You're right,' she said ruefully. 'Yet he doesn't see it as escape, he sees it as a job left undone, his people abandoned.' She looked at Rose regretfully. 'This may be hard to understand, but to my husband it will be a kind of exile.' She paused, then added in a whisper, 'And to me it is the end of a dream.'

Rose stared at her in surprise. She had never heard of anyone who looked upon Jarrow as a dream fulfilled, except maybe her starving Irish forebears escaping the Famine.

'What do you mean, Mrs Liddell?' she asked gently.

The older woman swallowed hard. 'I - we had hoped to adopt Alexander - had almost promised him,' she explained. 'But now with my husband's illness and no permanent home to offer, it's all too uncertain. We've abandoned the idea. And I had so wanted to. . .' She broke off, quite overcome.

Rose felt tears sting her own eyes. 'Does Alexander know?'

Mrs Liddell nodded. 'He took it badly - shouted and threw things about. We feel so awful at letting him down.'

'You mustn't,' Rose said quickly. 'You did what you could for him - and he's got plenty other relations to take care of him.'

Mrs Liddell hung her head. 'Condemned to being passed around like a parcel. Besides, he's fast running out of relatives willing to put up with his unruly ways.'

Rose instinctively put out a hand and touched her briefly in comfort. 'Maybes Canon Liddell will recover sooner than you think and you can give Alexander the home he wants.'

The older woman looked up and smiled in gratitude. 'You are a kind girl, Rose.'

Bashfully, Rose withdrew her hand and muttered she should be going.

Mrs Liddell stood too. 'Alexander was very taken with you and William,' she admitted. 'He once asked if he could go and live with you both rather than be sent away south.'

'With us?' Rose exclaimed.

'It made me a little jealous, I must confess,' she smiled.

'W-we couldn't have taken him in,' Rose stammered.

Mrs Liddell was quick to reassure. 'Of course not. We wouldn't have expected you to take on such a burden. It was just Alexander's fanciful idea.'

Rose bristled. 'We wouldn't have minded because of the cost,' she said proudly. 'It's just him being one of the gentry - it wouldn't be right.'

'No, I suppose not,' Mrs Liddell sighed. 'Poor Alexander. He doesn't really belong anywhere.'

Soon afterwards, Rose gathered up the children and left the forlorn house that had once been so welcoming to all who came. She was saddened to think she might never see the Liddells again or know how Alexander's life turned out. They had been a link with a broader world outside the confines of Jarrow town and St Bede's church. This kind couple had given her friendship and work when needed, and a glimpse of paradise in that summer trip to Ravensworth for which she would always be grateful.

How strange, Rose thought, that the Liddells should have chosen to leave the security of Ravensworth for Jarrow, just like her mother. But Jarrow had taken these gentle people and drained the life out of them like a thirsty beast. Only the hardiest of people survived its appetite.

As she pushed the girls home, all perched on the pram, Rose pondered what Mrs Liddell had said about exile. She knew what the rector meant. If she were to leave Jarrow tomorrow and never come back, it would be like a slow death. It was not so much the familiar buildings or this particular stretch of river or even the hazy horizon of Simonside she would miss. It would be her family and friends. They were her reason for being, she thought with a fierce, protective urge. To be separated from your own people must be the worst punishment in the world.

She thought of young Alexander being shunted from pillar to post with no one really to care for him. He might be better off than they, but wealth did not seem to have brought the boy happiness. Her heart ached for him and for a brief moment she daydreamed about William and herself taking the rejected boy into their home. Impossible, of course. His own kind would have to take care of him.

On the way home, Rose stopped in at the church and lit a candle for the Liddells. She prayed for their broken health and sore hearts to be mended. She prayed for Alexander, that he might find someone to love him. Then she hurried back to Raglan Street, thankful that she had her young family around her.

Chapter 13

With 1883 came a further year of prosperity for William and Rose, and their young family throve. Rose was kept busy from dawn to dusk looking after the lively girls, and it was a source of great pride to see them turned out clean and tidy in new clothes from the Co-operative store. That summer the weather was fine for days on end and they spent as much of it as possible outdoors.

She would walk the children up to Simonside to play around her father's smallholding and picnic in the meadow. On Sunday afternoons, William would take the older girls paddling in the stream and catch small fish in a jam jar. If there was racing on the river, he would carry them on his shoulders to go and watch the rowers pit their strength against boatmen from as far away as the Thames.

On a glorious sunny August day, Jarrow was packed with crowds marching behind bands and banners for the laying of the foundation stone to the new Liddell Dispensary.

Rose had never seen so many townsfolk turned out to demonstrate their solidarity for the new clinic and their admiration for the former rector who had done so much for them. Every trade and friendly society in the town was represented and the Fawcetts marched with the crowds to see mighty Charles Palmer lay the stone.

'Can you see any sign of Canon Liddell?' Rose asked William, straining on tiptoe to catch a glimpse of the dignitaries.

He shook his head. 'They're saying something about him now,' William told her.

Word spread back that the rector was travelling abroad for his health, and once again it saddened Rose to think of the warm-hearted couple in their solitary enforced exile. She wondered briefly where Alexander was now. In all likelihood they would never see the boy again either.

Putting sad thoughts from her mind, she and her family followed the procession to the Recreation Ground for the speeches, and the children ran around in the sunshine.

Her sisters lifted the babbling Kate from her pram and attempted to get her to walk, staggering along either side of her.

'Let her alone,' Rose chided, seeing the pain in the baby's face as they dragged her forward. Kate began to whimper and protest.

'She can't walk proper, Mammy!' Margaret cried in annoyance.

'She's still a baby, hinny,' Rose defended.

'Her foot's funny,' Elizabeth added, as they plonked Kate on the grass.

Rose stared at the red-faced baby, holding up her arms to be carried. She saw with alarm how the child's foot was turned in awkwardly. She had noticed her sitting like that before, but had convinced herself it would straighten in time, once she was on her feet and walking.

William bent down swiftly and lifted Kate into his arms. 'There's nowt wrong with her foot,' he declared, avoiding Rose's look. 'She'll walk canny in her own time.'

Rose knew how he doted on his youngest and would have nothing said against her. But from that moment, Rose knew there was something wrong with Kate's limb. Deep in her heart she had known from birth that the child's foot was damaged; it had never looked quite right. She suspected it was from the way the baby had been yanked from her womb, feet first, by the frantic efforts of Mrs McMullen to ensure both she and the baby survived.

Over the months she watched her daughter develop and grow into a lively infant with a sunny nature and infectious giggle, but she was slow to walk and preferred to pull herself along sideways like a crab, her crooked foot tucked in behind her. They all felt protective towards the baby of the family. Her older sisters mothered her and William made more of a fuss over her than the others. Rose bristled at the slightest comment on Kate's foot from other mothers, especially Mrs Fawcett.

'She should have her leg put in callipers, that one,' William's mother advised, 'straighten it out before it's too late.'

'She's still a baby,' Rose retorted, 'and she's not ganin' to be put in any irons.'

'She'll be a cripple,' Mrs Fawcett sniffed, 'spoil her chances of getting work or a husband.'

'She's not a cripple!' Rose cried, and snatched Kate from the woman's critical inspection. 'She'll run as fast as the rest of them in time, you'll see.' And Rose determined there and then that she would.

Nevertheless, Rose took the infant to the doctor, not wanting anything to mar Kate's chances of getting on in the world. He advised against doing anything until she was older.

'We don't want her to undergo the surgeon's knife so young. Wait and see. It might correct itself in time.'

The year ended in terrific gales and storms, which carried on into the January of '84. Chimneypots were blown off and shop windows shattered; a brig broke from her moorings and was smashed up against the quay. A man at the ferry landing was blown into the river and drowned, while a woman and her two children were killed by the gable end of their house falling on top of them. It seemed an inauspicious start to the new year and Rose shuddered at how swiftly and brutally fate could destroy a family's security.

But in the spring Margaret started school and Rose was filled with pride that they could afford to clothe their eldest in smart shoes and starched pinafore and send her off clutching a penny to the Catholic school. Elizabeth missed her playmate so much that soon she was tagging along with her to the school gates until the teacher relented and allowed her to sit in class with her older sister. Margaret revelled in this new world of slates and chalk, and came home chanting her spellings and tables.

Rose enjoyed the few hours when she had Sarah and Kate to herself, and she took them to the park as often as possible, coaxing her youngest to walk and keep up with the inquisitive Sarah. She saw what an effort it was for the small girl, but Kate never complained and it surprised Rose how determined the easy-going Kate could be. In June came Race Week, when Tynesiders flocked to Newcastle's Town Moor for the horse racing and Temperance Fair. After the scare of losing Margaret there as a small child, Rose had no wish to go back and William could not persuade her to change her mind.

'The bairns would enjoy the side shows,' he encouraged, 'and we've got enough put by. Let's spoil them a bit.'

'You do plenty of that already,' Rose replied, but with a smile that told him that she did not mind. 'I'd rather take them to the seaside - the youngest two have never been.'

William was easily persuaded. Rose was thankful that he would never be the kind of man who treated Race Week as an excuse to gamble and get drunk and spend their hard-earned savings. So instead they dressed up, took a picnic and the train to South Shields and had their picture taken in a studio. They spent an afternoon on the beach, splashing in the shallows and digging in the sand. They ate fresh winkles washed down with ginger beer and saw a clown performing along the pier. For the first time, Kate ran six paces along the sand, holding hands with Margaret and Elizabeth, before her weak foot buckled under her.

Rose clapped in delight and William swung his dark-haired daughter high in the air and kissed her for being so clever. After that, they raced the girls, clutching Kate between them and lifting her off her feet every few steps.

'See, you can fly, me bonny little nightingale!' William cried, and the small child threw back her head and squealed with laughter.

By the time they climbed on board the train back to Jarrow, they were all tired out, their cheeks ruddy from the sun and sea air, their toes gritty with the sand in their shoes.

'Can we go again next week, Mammy?' Margaret pleaded, while Elizabeth's head already lolled sleepily on Rose's shoulder.

'Soon,' was all she would promise, smiling across at William, who cradled the sleeping Sarah and Kate in his arms.

Margaret turned her attention to her father. 'Can we, Da? It's canny at the seaside.'

'We'll gan again soon, like your mam says,' he grinned.

Rose thought how glowing with health he looked that evening as they jostled home on the train. He still looked so boyish, despite his moustache and the thinning of his fair hair at the temples under his respectable bowler hat. She felt stout in comparison, having never regained her slim waist since Kate was born. But the way he looked at her made her feel girlish and desirable. How lucky she was to have such a husband, she thought, drowsily content. At that moment she wanted nothing else in the world, for Rose believed she had it all.

By the autumn, a slump in trade hit Tyneside, spreading hardship along the river and into the surrounding towns and villages. Relief funds were set up and soup kitchens opened once more to feed the hungry. Rose was thankful that through her careful housekeeping, they were able to live off the money saved during the past two years. She managed to scrape together enough to keep the girls going to school, for both she and William were determined that they should be educated. Christmas came, but there was little entertainment or celebrating in the town and the girls had to make do with second-hand toys and less meat on the table.

William tried to be optimistic with the dawning of 1885. In January, Palmer's launched the three-masted schooner, the Surprise, the first built by the company for the Admiralty.

'I may be on short time,' he reasoned, 'but there's work ticking over.'

There was a further launch in February and in June, the Dovenby Hall was completed, the largest sailing ship ever built at the Jarrow yard. Trade limped on, but there was an air of stagnation about the town and Rose grew used to seeing small shops boarding up their windows and removal carts piled with the belongings of those who could no longer afford to pay rent. They were just getting by on William's reduced wages and by limiting themselves to meals of bread and tea rather than meat and milk.

Then Rose's general unease turned to fear when a smallpox epidemic broke out in the summer and the dilapidated fever hut on the edge of town that served as an isolation hospital filled up rapidly. When the cases of smallpox slackened, the hut was hastily disinfected and prepared for a new wave of typhoid cases. Illness plagued the town and the sombre sight of horse-drawn hearses rumbling down the streets became commonplace.

Most alarming of all was an outbreak of infant diarrhoea that swept in with the hot weather and brought many deaths in its wake. Rose watched Kate like a hawk and when the child woke hot and feverish one afternoon, she went rushing for Dr Forbes.

'Are you still feeding her yourself at all?' he asked.

'No,' Rose blushed, 'she likes the bottle - I keep it warm for her on the stove.'

'You mustn't do that!' the doctor said sharply. 'Germs can multiply in warm milk. Throw away the bottle, Rose, she's old enough to drink from a cup. And steer clear of grocer's milk till the hot weather is over. Give her boiled water that's cooled off in the pantry. Keep her cool at night too.'

Rose wanted to ask the doctor about Kate's foot again, but she could see he was frantically busy and preoccupied with stemming the tide of disease around him. So she hurried home and followed his instructions, coaxing her daughter to sip the sterilised water. Kate was fretful and listless for a couple of days then, to Rose's relief, suddenly perked up as if nothing had been the matter.

Rose tried to protect her family by feeding them what she had and denying herself. Some days she would eat nothing until William returned at tea time. Whether he had work to go to or not, he stuck to the routine of going out and keeping himself occupied, doing odd jobs at the church or reading at the Mechanics' Institute. But he noticed how the weight was dropping off her and insisted on sharing what she put on his plate.

'We can't have you going sick for lack of food,' she cried at him anxiously. 'You have to bring in a wage.'

'And how will me and the bairns manage if you waste away?' he pointed out. 'Now get some food down you.'

With autumn, the raging fevers abated. Luckily for the Fawcetts there was still work at the steel mills, if not in the yards. In November, a large gathering of businessmen met at Palmer's steel works for a special ceremony of tapping a new steel furnace, which was done by Mrs Palmer. William brought home enough for them to celebrate Christmas, but Rose's spirits were dampened by the obvious distress of so many around them. The unlucky ones had spent all their savings and pawned everything they owned to try to keep roofs over their families' heads.

Two skinny boys came knocking on Rose's door begging for food on Christmas Eve. She hurriedly wrapped up a loaf of bread and a couple of apples and sent them on their way before her own inquisitive children could ask too many questions. She wanted to shield them as much as possible from the hardship and poverty of the outside world that lapped at their door.

The year turned again and they prayed for better times. But the winter of '86 was unrelenting. In March, cold winds blew in from the east, bringing ferocious snowstorms that lasted for three days. The gales were arctic and the town disappeared in a white storm that kept people trapped indoors, as if Nature fought to take repossession of the polluted and despoiled land. Rose was too fearful to go out for food or fuel and kept the girls bundled up in bed together to keep warm. Margaret organised them into playing the Snow Queen, and Rose was thankful for the girl's imagination in keeping her sisters occupied for hours on end. For two days, William struggled down as far as the end of the street before he was beaten back by the weather. He could hardly retrace his steps in the blinding icy blizzard. He stumbled over the frozen corpse of a nag that had slipped and been abandoned to the smothering snow.

By the fourth day, when they had run out of supplies, the winds dropped and he dug his way out of the back door, emerging into a Siberian landscape of deep snowdrifts and sparkling icicles. He came home with a bag of coal, some stale bread and tinned fruit, which was all he could find at the grocer's. Rose quickly got the fire going again, seeing he was frozen through from standing in line for food.

'There's nowt moving in the streets,' he said between chattering teeth. 'Some of the snow's the height of a man. It'll take days to clear.'

The children clamoured to be out in it, but Rose would not let them for fear they disappeared under the suffocating blanket of snow. She worried about her father and Maggie marooned up the hill.

'Don't worry,' William reassured, 'they always have a store of food for the bad weather. I'll go up and see them tomorrow if you like.'

But the next day he was shaking and feverish, and Rose put him to bed. He lay listless, as if all the energy had been drained out of him in his battle against the snow. Rose tried to get him to eat, but he had no appetite and when she spoon-fed him like a child, he coughed the thin broth back up again.

Rose kept the children out of the bedroom to give him rest, listening to his persistent cough from down below. After two days she found him struggling into his clothes, looking thin and wasted. A caller had been round shouting that the mill was open again.

'What do you think you're doing?' she demanded.

'I'm ganin' to work,' he panted.

'You haven't the strength to walk across the room, let alone gan to work,' Rose remonstrated. 'Get back into bed!'

'I need to work,' he gasped, setting off a bout of coughing. 'And I haven't been round to Mam's for a week - they might need some'at.'

'Your father can take care of your mother for once,' Rose retorted. 'Your first duty is to us, William. You get yourself fit for work - you're no use to me as an invalid.'

When she saw his unhappy look, she was sorry for speaking to him so sharply, but seeing him in such a weak state made her frightened. If he was off work much longer, she would have to think about going out and finding work herself. Then who would look after the girls? she fretted.

'I'll go round and make sure your parents are managing,' she relented, 'if you promise to stay in bed and keep warm.'

Later in the day, she popped the younger two daughters into bed with William and, wrapping up the older girls in as many warm clothes as she could find, set off for James Terrace. It took them over half an hour to wade through the blackened snow drifts and icy slush piled up at the side of the road. Delivery horses slithered around on the treacherous cobbles and Rose had to keep hauling the girls out of the snow when they took refuge from passing carts and horse-drawn trams.

When they finally reached the Fawcetts' house, Rose was exhausted and the children soaked and numb from the melted ice in their boots. There was no reply. Rose hammered harder, annoyed that she had trekked all the way over only to find them out. Why hadn't they thought to come over and see if their precious William and his family were all right? she thought angrily. Mrs Fawcett had never forgiven her for persuading William to stand up to his mother and move out of the family home. She could expect no help from her petty, spiteful mother-in-law.

Margaret began to shout for her grandmother and stamp her feet in frustration.

'It's no good, we'll have to go home,' Rose sighed. 'They're not in.'

But Elizabeth clambered on to the top step and poked her runny nose through the small brass letterbox. 'Grandma! Grandpa Fawcett! It's me and Margaret. Let us in, please!'

'Haway, hinny.' Rose pulled at her hand.

'They're in there, Mammy,' Elizabeth insisted, stubbornly refusing to move.

Margaret barged her sister out of the way, for a better look. 'There's someone coming,' she announced.

Just then the door opened a fraction and Mrs Fawcett peered out. Rose was struck by how old and forlorn she looked. 'Who is it?' she asked querulously.

'It's us, Grandma!' the girls chorused.

Rose saw the expression of confusion on the woman's face. 'Mrs Fawcett, it's me - Rose. We've come to see if there's anything you need fetchin'.'

'No, not today, thank you,' she replied as if speaking to a tradesman. Rose was perplexed.

'Can we come in for a minute? The lasses are cold and we've walked all the way in the snow.'

As Mrs Fawcett struggled to reply, the girls dashed in under her skirts. 'Where's Grandpa? Is he at work?' Margaret asked. 'Da's not at work - he's sick in bed.'

'Look!' cried Elizabeth. 'He's in the parlour. Grandpa!' The children clattered into the cold parlour where their grandfather sat in his chair.

As Rose followed them in, Mrs Fawcett said in a frightened voice, 'He's resting. You're not to disturb him.'

Halfway into the parlour Rose stopped in her tracks. She gasped in horror at what she saw. Mr Fawcett was colourless like marble, his mouth drooping open as if frozen in surprise, his eyes half open. She knew death when she saw it.

'He's cold, Grandma,' Elizabeth said in concern, reaching him first. Margaret stopped still, sensing something was wrong.

'Come over here, lasses,' Rose called to them sharply. 'Leave your grandfather alone.' She turned to Mrs Fawcett and saw the confused childlike bewilderment in her expression. 'How long has he been like this?' she whispered.

'He's been sitting all day,' she said, trembling. 'I can't wake him up.'

Rose stepped towards her and said gently, 'He's gone, Mrs Fawcett. You know that, don't you?'

Her mother-in-law met Rose's look for the first time and let out a terrified sob. 'I didn't know what to do!'

At once Rose put arms round her and held on while she wept in distress and disbelief. The girls crowded about their grandmother. Rose pulled them into her hold.

'Grandpa's gone to be with baby Jesus and the saints,' she told them, and turned their faces away from the dead man in the high-backed chair.

Chapter 14

The funeral had to be delayed until the iron-hard ground had thawed out enough for burial. By that time William had recovered sufficiently to work again, though Rose worried at his emaciated look and the cough that he could not shake off. His mother buckled under the shock of losing her husband so swiftly. In her widow's weeds she looked an old woman and it was decided that she should move across the river to live with Florrie and Albert.

The house in James Street was packed up, some furniture sold and the rest transported by cart and ferry to Wallsend. Rose promised to bring the children to see her and for a while they visited once a month. But Florrie was finally pregnant with her first child and Rose could see what an increasing burden it was to feed and entertain their large family. When she suggested that they visit Jarrow instead, Mrs Fawcett refused to travel.

'She hardly goes out any more,' Florrie complained, 'and she never lifts a finger to help me around the house. Just sits there brooding by the fire, talking to herself.'

William was saddened by how little interest his mother took in her granddaughters. When they clambered around her she grew irritated and snapped, 'Why can't they behave themselves?'

Even the favoured Margaret could not please her. The child's attempts to entertain her grandmother with recitations of poems she had learned drew the response, 'What d'you need to learn all them words for? You're just a girl. Don't bother me with silly rhymes. They make my head ache.'

Eventually when they called they would find she had retreated to bed.

'There's nothing wrong with her,' Florrie remarked in annoyance. 'She just likes playing the invalid. Wants the attention, now Father's not here to give it to her. Well, I won't be able to run up and downstairs all day long once the baby's arrived.'

One time Rose went in to speak to her alone. It distressed her to see William so upset at his mother's withdrawal and she determined to put aside her dislike of the woman for his sake.

'Mrs Fawcett, why don't you come and stay with us for a bit when Florrie's baby comes? The lasses would be pleased to see their grandma.'

William's mother fixed her with chilly blue eyes. 'Stay with you?' she asked querulously.

'Aye, for a week or two,' Rose encouraged.

Mrs Fawcett pursed her thin lips. 'Never!' she hissed. 'I wouldn't stay under your roof if it was the last one standing on Tyneside. You'll always be a common Irish labourer's daughter to me, no matter how much you dress yourself up.'

Rose flinched under the look of pure hatred. She was so taken aback, she could not speak.

But Mrs Fawcett went on. 'I'll never forgive you for taking my William away from me and I'll never understand what he saw in you. So take your brats and be gone. I can't be bothered with them any more.'

She turned back to staring into the small bedroom fire and didn't look up again.

Rose stumbled from the room, stung by the venomous words. She had not realised how deeply the woman had resented and despised her. She felt utterly humiliated and hurt at the way her children had been dismissed. She refused to tell William what had been said, but he could see how upset she was and they swiftly left.

Soon after, Florrie and Albert were surprised and delighted by the arrival of boy twins, David and Peter. Absorbed in their busy lives, contact between the two families grew more infrequent. A year after Mr Fawcett's death, William's mother refused to come out of deep mourning. She would venture forth once a week to Mass and then retire to her room. On rare visits to Wallsend, the girls would hover at the door listening to her talking out loud to the saints, afraid to go in.

William, who had been subdued and fatigued for months after his father's death, sighed one day, 'What's the point us visiting when she won't come out her room? I don't think she even knows who we are any more. She won't speak to the lasses. We'll not come again,' he decided. 'Florrie and Albert can bring the bairns to see us in future.'

Rose could hardly suppress the feeling of triumph she felt that William had finally shaken off his mother's hold. For nearly ten years, she had put up with the older woman's critical interference in her marriage and in the way she brought up her children. Now they were free to live their own lives with their growing family. They did not need her or her petty bullying, did not have to put up with her reproachful comments ever again. It was over. Let the old woman stew in her own bitterness!

Sarah had joined her sisters at school, delayed by a year because of the slump. But now there was plenty of work along the river and there were grand plans afoot to celebrate the Queen's Golden Jubilee later that year. William seemed full of renewed energy, with no repeat of the worrying fever and persistent cough of the winter before. Rose's optimism for the future soared when she recognised tell-tale changes in her body. She was growing plump again and her breasts were swollen and itchy against the constrictions of her tightening dress.

In the early summer she told William, 'I'm expectin' again. This time I'm ganin' to give you a lad.'

He hugged her round the waist in delight. 'A lad to carry on the Fawcett name!' he declared. Rose knew that since the death of his father, this seemed to matter more to William than before. 'And what a lucky lad he'll be to have such canny sisters to take care of him,' he grinned, seizing Kate - who had rushed in from outside - and chucking her up in the air.

Kate, who was now nearly five, screamed in delight as her father caught her.

'When's the baby coming?' she demanded.

'Eeh, you shouldn't have been listening!' Rose said in embarrassment.

'Will he be here in time for tea?' Kate persisted.

William laughed. 'Not this tea time.'

'The morra? Will he be here for tea the morra?' she persisted.

'You and your questions!' Rose cried. 'You'll plague the life out of those poor teachers when you gan to school.'

'He'll be here in the autumn,' William winked, 'in time for blackberry pickin'.'

'Do babies eat blackberries?' Kate asked doubtfully.

William pinched her cheek. 'No, so you and your sisters can eat more, can't you?'

'Will you come pickin' an' all, Da-da?' Kate asked excitedly.

'Course I will, little nightingale,' he promised with a kiss on her wavy dark ringlets.

Rose watched them both with affection. Kate never stopped talking from the moment she woke up to the time she bedded down with her sisters. She was turning into the loudest and most boisterous of them all; even Margaret found it hard to get a word in edgeways. She was clumsier than the rest, ever eager to keep up with them despite her limp, but often tripping and dropping things. When Rose grew irritated and tried to curb her youngest's exuberance, William would defend her.

'Let the lass be. She's high-spirited like her mam, that's all,' he teased.

But now as she saw Kate sitting on William's knee, chatting about babies and blackberries, she felt a surge of love towards her. Kate was full of William's loving nature. She followed him like a devoted puppy, hating to let him out of her sight. Kate would wave her father away, running down the back lane in that strange half-skipping way of moving she had developed to disguise her crippled foot. She would watch for him coming home, playing out in the street for hours until she recognised his lean shape and ambling walk turning the corner. She would rush forward to greet him, arms outstretched, and jump into his hold, and they would race the last few yards hand in hand till they reached home. He would take her for walks down to the ruined monastery and tell her the story of St Bede and the early Christians. Then he would point out the Slake and recount the grisly tale of Jobling on the gibbet and how the friends of the tragic pitman had risked death by rescuing his body.

'The working man always has to fight for whatever he wants,' William told his small daughter. 'No boss is ever going to hand it to him on a plate.'

Rose would chide him, 'The lass is too young for such talk.'

'It's never too early to learn about the saints - or the rights of the working classes,' William answered stoutly.

'Well, don't go filling her head full of dreams - or tales that'll stop her sleepin' at night,' Rose warned.

But neither of them took any notice of her words. Kate was not frightened by talk of Jobling's ghost as Rose had once been. Her oval eyes opened with interest and she squealed in delighted terror. Kate continued to demand stories and William supplied them. Some nights, a childish enthusiasm would grip him and he'd seize his daughters by the hand and pull them out into the dark street.

'There's a full moon the night!' he whispered eagerly.

'How can you tell?' Margaret demanded. 'It's too dark and cloudy to see.'

'But it's there,' William insisted. 'Haway, hold Elizabeth's hand.' He grabbed Sarah and Kate tightly by their hands and they all started to run.

'Race the moon!' they cried as they ran laughing up the street, startling passers-by returning home.

Rose just shook her head, remembering the early days of their courtship when William had done the same with her. She felt she had aged with the bearing of babies and the responsibilities of keeping their household running through some difficult times. But William appeared as young at heart as when she had first met him. Paler and thinner maybe, but still with the spirit of a young boy.

Summer came and everything stopped on 21 June for Queen Victoria's Jubilee Day. The night before, Rose bound up the girls' hair in strips of rags so they would have bonny ringlets for the celebrations. In the morning she dressed them in their smartest frocks, pinafores and stockings, and nagged them to keep clean and not to play in the street. Rose's father and Maggie, who was finally engaged to Danny Kennedy, came down to visit.

'Lizzie's had to stop and work at the castle,' Maggie told a disappointed Rose. 'They've got dozens of visitors and a grand banquet the night. She'll maybes get a day off next month.'

By the time the afternoon came and they marched the girls down to the school, they were bursting with excitement. There were thousands of children converging on the town schools and the streets were already packed with crowds of onlookers.

For once, all social distinctions between the people of Jarrow were put aside as the whole nation was gripped in a frenzy of patriotism and wellbeing towards their queen and each other. Rose noticed that well-to-do managers and their wives had volunteered to wait on the children along with the schoolmasters and -mistresses. To the children's amazed delight, they served out a special meal of buns and spice loaf, milk and tea. Then every child was presented with a jubilee mug.

'Look, Mam!' cried Margaret. 'It's got pictures of the Queen on. My very own cup!'

'Aye.' Rose beamed to see her so happy. 'There's Queen Victoria when she came to the throne - and look on the other side - that's what she looks like now.'

'She looks like Grandma Fawcett,' Elizabeth observed. 'Do you think Grandma would like my mug? Stop her feeling sad all the time?'

Rose touched her daughter's head in affection. It was so typical of Elizabeth to think of giving her prized possession away without a thought for herself.

'Grandma's got plenty china,' Rose told her. 'You keep this mug to show your children and grandchildren what a great queen we had.'

'What's that say?' Kate asked, waving her mug precariously in the air.

Margaret pointed to the letters as she read out the inscription: 'Jub-i-lee, Eighteen eighty-seven, Jarrow-on-Tyne. That's where we live,' Margaret said importantly.

Rose thrilled at the sound of her eldest reading out loud. It made her so proud to think she had a daughter who was getting an education. One day Margaret would secure a good job in a shop or an office and maybe she would better herself enough to marry a man of business or one with a profession. Oh, that one of her daughters should marry a gentleman!

Soon after, there was a scramble to get outside and follow the Temperance Band through the streets. At the junction with Ormonde Street, they converged with another huge procession headed by Henderson's Brass Band and jostled together towards the Recreation Ground. Rose clung on to Margaret and Elizabeth, while Sarah rode on Danny Kennedy's shoulders and

Kate on William's. Maggie took her father's arm to steady him in the crowd.

'Look how grand it is,' Maggie cried as they made their way under the archway to the park, gaudily decorated in bunting and flags. There at the entrance, waiting to greet them, was the Mayor, wearing his chain of office and flanked by aldermen, councillors, clergy and the gentry of the town.

'For once in our life, we're the important ones,' William said gleefully, as he passed the dignitaries waving to the crowds. 'You're a lady, Rose Fawcett!'

Smiling, Rose led the older girls over to where they were to line up with the other school children. Margaret took her younger sisters by the hand and pushed them into position. Rose knew they had been practising all week. She stood back with the others and her heart swelled with pride to hear her girls among the vast choir singing the Jubilee Anthem. Then everyone burst into a loud rendition of the National Anthem.

'Three cheers for our queen!' someone shouted. The crowd erupted in spontaneous cheering. This was followed by, 'Three cheers for the Mayor!'

Soon after, the ranks of children broke up and they ran off to prepare for the races and sports. Their energy seemed boundless that day, the girls keeping going until long into the evening. Kate was as determined as the rest of them to compete, and came away with a prize of sweets for a sack race. She could jump as enthusiastically as any of the children her age. Her sisters' pride turned to a touch of jealousy when she also won a prize in a singing competition.

Rose and William tried to take them home, but they begged to be allowed to stay up for the fireworks and bonfire. William relented. 'Well, they'll not see the likes of this again in their lifetime,' he reasoned.

As darkness descended the sky was peppered with flashes of light and colour that made the crowd gasp and Kate scream, half in wonder, half in fright. At half-past ten, they watched for the lighting of the bonfire on the Bede Burn slag heap. Wagonloads of timber and barrels of tar had been amassing on the spoil heap for weeks and the police had been vigilant in keeping scavengers at bay.

'There it gans!' William called out, lifting Sarah and Kate for a better look, as flames leapt into the air. The night was lit up with lurid orange light as the fire took hold and roared away. Further up river, they could see another bonfire burning on a ballast hill at Hebburn and, across the river, the high ground was studded with distant fires.

'Jarrow's is the best,' William declared. 'It'll be burning till mornin'.'

'Will it be burning the morra?' asked Kate.

'Aye, and the day after,' he joked.

'And the day after that?' Kate smiled.

'All week!' he chuckled. She laid her head on his shoulder and yawned widely.

'And the week after...' she murmured. By the time they reached the gates of the park, she had fallen asleep and had to be carried all the way home.

Chapter 15

In the autumn, Maggie was wed to Danny Kennedy and the celebrations went on at Simonside for two days. There was much drinking and dancing and telling of stories. When the fiddler tired of playing, Rose's father and old McMullen would recount ancient legends of Irish heroes and drink to their old homeland. Rose was heavy with her unborn child and had to sit out the dancing, but she enjoyed the gathering of family and friends. She was pleased that Danny would now be living at Simonside and helping with the running of the smallholding, for her father suffered from rheumatism and was increasingly frail. Maggie had found it difficult to manage these past two years.

'Why aren't you dancing?' Rose teased William.

'I only like dancing with you,' he smiled, and sat down beside her. He looked tired, his eyes shadowed.

'It's time we took the bairns home,' Rose decided. 'It's been a long day for us all. This lot'll not go home till the beer runs out.'

Maybe it was due to the exertions of the day and the long walk home, but Rose went into labour that night. She could not rouse William from a deep exhausted sleep, so got up and went downstairs, preparing a bowl of hot water with which to wash herself and laying out brown paper on top of sheets on the truckle bed. In the flickering firelight she clung on to the back of a kitchen chair while contractions seized her, and tried not to cry out in the night.

But Margaret must have heard something, for the girl appeared in her nightdress out of the dark.

'What's wrong, Mam?' she asked anxiously.

'The baby's coming,' Rose gasped.

Her daughter looked around, puzzled. 'Who's bringing it?'

Rose smiled despite the searing pain. 'I am.'

'But Francie at school says babies get delivered,' Margaret insisted, 'like coal.'

Rose grimaced. 'The bairn's coming out of me, hinny, and it's in a canny hurry. Will you gan down the street and fetch Bella? She'll help with the delivery.' She buckled over as another contraction gripped her. 'Quick, hinny!'

Margaret rushed to the back door, pulling on her boots but not bothering to lace them up and throwing on Elizabeth's coat, which was nearest to hand. She was out the house in seconds and Rose could hear her running off down the lane in the still frosty night. By the time she returned with Bella, who had often helped out with chores since Kate's birth, Rose was crouched on the bed and panting in the throes of labour.

Bella dispatched Margaret quickly upstairs and told her to keep the other girls from coming down should they wake.

'But I want to stay and help,' Margaret protested.

'Plenty time for you to help your mam once the baby's here,' Bella replied, and bustled her through the door.

Half an hour later, as the mantelpiece clock struck five, Rose gave birth to her fifth child. It let out a petulant whimper.

'Let me see him,' she gasped, raising herself with the last ounce of strength left in her aching body. Bella said nothing as she wrapped the baby in a cotton sheet and put it into Rose's arms.

Rose gazed at the pink crinkled face and damp dark hair and felt a surge of triumph. He looked just like Kate had done. A boy who would grow up with handsome chestnut curls but with his father's blue eyes.

At that moment a sleepy-eyed William appeared in the doorway, blinking in confusion to see Bella standing in the gaslight. He looked at Rose clutching their baby and gave an astonished cry.

'I wondered where you were - you should have woken me, Rose! Can I see . . . ?'

She smiled at him wearily. 'Come and look at him.'

'A lad?' he gasped in delight. Rose nodded, not noticing the look on Bella's face. Even when the young woman shook her head and stuttered, 'No, Mr Fawcett,' Rose did not realise her mistake.

William was leaning over the baby and touching it gingerly with one finger when Bella shattered Rose's dream. 'It's not a lad, Mrs Fawcett. It's another lass.'

'A lass?' Rose whispered in confusion. 'But you said it was a lad.'

'I never. You just had it fixed in your head,' Bella protested. 'I didn't like to say owt.'

Rose pulled away the swaddling sheet and stared at the skinny body beneath. Disappointment engulfed her as she saw that Bella's words were true. William said nothing. Rose screwed up her eyes, feeling overwhelmed by failure. She had been so sure this one would be a boy to carry on the Fawcett name! She did not think she could ever go through another pregnancy and birth. She felt as old and as worn out as an old nag. Rose bent her head and began to cry, long racking sobs that came from deep within and would not stop.

'It doesn't matter,' William said quietly, but she could hear the regret in his voice. 'She's bonny - and there'll be others.'

'No there won't!' Rose said savagely and turned her face to the wall. 'I don't want any more.' Someone lifted the unwanted baby from the bed, but she did not see who and did not care. No one spoke to her.

'I'll stay and see to the bairns if you like,' Bella offered.

'Ta,' William replied, then left the kitchen, his footsteps thudding heavily as he retreated back upstairs.

Chapter 16

The baby was christened Mary Ellen, but Rose could not find it in her heart to love her. She felt tired and morose for weeks after the birth and the baby could do nothing to please her. Every cry and whimper irritated her frayed nerves; every suck of the breast seemed to sap her of what little energy she had left. She would leave the baby to lie for long hours, ignoring her fretful cries, while she tried to get on with all the other chores that did not cease.

Life was one relentless round of washing, ironing, cleaning, cooking and feeding. Bella stayed on to help until Christmas, but there no longer seemed time to take the girls up to Simonside to see her father and Maggie, and it was too cold or too wet for the park.

William was kind but distant towards her, leaving her alone at bedtime as if he had taken to heart her bitter words about wanting no more babies. She was thankful that he did not bother her, but she missed the comfort of lying in his arms and falling to sleep wrapped in his warmth. She was so bound up with her own cares that she did not notice at first how his cough had returned. But one night in early January, she woke to find the bed soaked in his sweat and William bent over the side, wheezing and gasping for breath.

She got up, boiled the kettle and gave him a steam infusion in the china wash bowl, his head smothered in a linen towel. But this just made him cough all the harder. When Rose removed the towel, she stared in horror at the steaming water. It was flecked with mucus and blood. A cold terror seized her, but she would not allow herself to question what it might mean. Hastily she got him back to bed and bathed his face and body, which now felt as hot as a furnace. The baby woke and began to cry, but Rose ignored her. William was shaking as if with cold and winced when she touched him.

'See to the bairn,' he rasped, and began another bout of coughing.

Rose fled from the room with the crying baby and sat in the kitchen, attempting to feed her while she listened to William's painful coughing above. The night sweats and fever went on for a week and anything he ate turned to liquid in his bowels. The bedroom stank and she was constantly nagging the younger children to stay out of the way while she cleaned up with Margaret's help. Kate would sit on the stairs, shouting to be let in to see her father or throw a tantrum if she was denied. Only Elizabeth seemed able to calm her down and distract her by playing with Margaret's old doll's house or bashing on the keys of William's piano. But their father grew so weak that Rose finally went against his wishes and sent for Dr Forbes.

'He's aching all over,' she told him in concern, 'and he can't keep anything down. He won't even let Margaret feed him.'

She waited downstairs with the children, worrying over what the doctor might find. When he returned, his face was sombre. He sat at the kitchen table and told her quietly, 'William is not at all well. His lungs are diseased - that's why he's coughing up blood.'

Rose went numb. 'His lungs?'

'I'm sorry, but your husband has tuberculosis.'

Rose refused to believe it. 'It's just a fever! It'll pass. He's been ill like this before.'

The doctor gave her a pitying look. 'He needs to be kept isolated from the children. You have some sickness insurance through his union, don't you? I could arrange for him to be sent to the hospital.'

Rose put protective arms about Elizabeth, who had crept near at the sound of fear in her voice. 'The isolation hut?' she gulped. Most people who went in there never came out alive, she thought in horror. 'I'd rather look after him meself than have him gan in there.'

The doctor sighed. 'He needs fresh air and rest - cleanliness and good food. It might take months of convalescence before he's back on his feet again,' he added with hushed urgency. 'How can you manage that with all the children and him not working? You might need to find work yourself, Rose,' he pointed out.

Her eyes stung with tears. 'Will I be allowed to visit him if he gans in the hospital?' she asked, her look pleading.

'I'll do my best to arrange it,' Dr Forbes promised, 'but not with the children.'

Rose swallowed hard, trying to stem the panic rising in her throat. She met the doctor's look and nodded in agreement.

Two days later, an ambulance pulled up outside the house and William was carried downstairs. He gazed at her with large feverish eyes, his face the colour of clay. He tried to speak, but his breath was ragged and all she could hear was his chest heaving like bellows. She put out a hand and touched his cheek.

'Don't worry about me and the bairns,' she said. 'You just do as the doctor says.' She wanted to kiss him but felt inhibited in front of the neighbours who had come cautiously to their doors to watch. She saw the fear in their faces at the sight of a man with consumption, as if by coming too near they might be touched by his disease. 'I'll visit soon,' she promised, trying to smile.

William said nothing, but he did not take his look from her until he was lifted into the back of the ambulance. The children pressed around, clinging to her arms and skirts.

'Where's he going, Mam?' Sarah asked. Rose could not answer for the dread that pressed on her chest like a ton weight.

'To the hospital,' Margaret answered, 'so they can make him better.'

The ambulance door clanged shut. Kate let out a howl. 'I want to gan with me da!' And she dashed forward into the road.

'Stop!' Rose sprang after her, pulling her back just before an iron-bound wheel rolled over her feet. She gripped the five-year-old with one hand and slapped her with the other in fright. 'Don't you go doing that again, do you hear?'

'I want Da-da!' Kate wailed. 'I want me da!'

At this, Sarah burst into tears and Elizabeth began to whimper quietly. Only Margaret stood white-faced and silent, as if turned to stone. Rose began to shake uncontrollably as she watched the horse-drawn vehicle pull away and lumber off down the street, the girls gathered around her tearful and perplexed. She bundled them inside quickly, out of the inquisitive gaze of the neighbours, and slammed the door.

As the winter dragged on, Rose determined to keep her household going in William's absence. She strove hard to have the girls tidy and well turned out, the house clean and food on the table. The modest sickness insurance paid for William's treatment and covered the rent, but there was not enough for household bills, let alone for clothing or boots. Maggie and Danny helped out with winter vegetables and Rose sent word to Florrie that her brother was sick. She knew she would get no assistance from her estranged mother-in-law. Albert called one Saturday afternoon with a loan of five pounds until William should get back on his feet.

'Florrie would have come,' he said awkwardly, 'but she's busy with the boys and old Mrs Fawcett.'

Rose nodded, hiding her disappointment, and wondered if Florrie stayed away because of fear of contamination.

She took the girls to Mass, and prayed every day for William's recovery under the picture of the Virgin Mary that hung on the parlour wall. Once a week she got Bella to mind the children and trekked over to the hospital for a few brief minutes with her husband. He lay in a draughty room with three others, the windows open to the fierce February gales, shivering under a thin blanket. He was skeletal, his eyes huge and dark-ringed in their sockets. He resembled one of the medieval martyrs whose picture hung in the church, his face beautiful yet tortured.

William smiled at the sight of her and her heart squeezed with pain to see his pitiful condition.

'I've brought you pea soup - your favourite,' she said brightly, hiding her dismay at his frail appearance.

'Ta,' he mouthed, his chest rattling like marbles. 'The lasses?'

Rose fumbled under the folds of her cloak and took out a brown-paper package.

'Margaret and Elizabeth made you this.' She held up a small piece of hessian embroidered with their names and a pattern of flowers. He smiled again and took it in shaking hands. 'And this is from Kate.' Rose showed him a peg doll that the child had made with Elizabeth's help. They had stitched a face on to a cotton rag and tied it around the wooden clothes peg. 'It's supposed to be you,' Rose said with a short laugh, putting it into his hand.

He looked at it a moment, then slow tears began to slip down his hollowed cheeks. Rose looked at him in consternation. 'Don't upset yoursel',' she hissed, glancing round at the other patients.

She talked quickly of Albert's visit, of Maggie's help, of things the girls had done or said; anything to cover the sound of his gentle weeping. His fragility was more frightening than the rattling in his lungs. At the end of visiting, they briefly held hands then she left the icy room with its leaky roof and flimsy wooden walls that smelt of lime and sickness.

In March, the snows returned with a ferocity that they had not seen since the storms of two years ago and Rose was marooned at home for a week. She emerged, her pantry empty and no money for the gas. She steeled herself to enter Slater's pawnshop with her blue and white china tea cups wrapped in a linen tablecloth, both given as wedding presents. The children stood silently at the door, Margaret holding on to Mary's pram. With the pawnbroker's money, Rose bought bread, dripping, tea, jam and candles.

She asked Bella to put the word about that she was taking in mending and would decorate or paint people's houses now spring was starting. When she was given the job of painting the kitchen and scullery of a locksmith from church, she packed Kate off to school with her sisters and took baby Mary with her. But the locksmith's wife complained that the baby cried too much, so the next day Rose kept Margaret off school to mind Mary while she completed the job. Margaret resented this, and after she had been absent on several occasions, her teacher complained to the priest, who came round to visit.

'I can see how difficult it is for you, Rose,' said Father O'Brien. 'Is there no one else who can help out? Your sister Maggie, maybe? She has no children of her own to care for yet.'

Rose took his advice and put the suggestion to her sister. 'Father O'Brien's had words with me about keeping Margaret off school. He thought you'd be the best person to care for Mary for a bit. It won't be for long - just while William's in hospital and I get a bit money put by. Will you, Maggie?' she pleaded.

'Of course I'll help you out,' Maggie agreed quickly, giving her a hug. Rose left Mary there that day, handing the querulous baby into her sister's care and praying to the Virgin for forgiveness for the relief she felt at leaving her youngest behind.

At Easter, she visited William and took him a posy of flowers from the children and a painted hard-boiled egg that they had all decorated. She kept from him how difficult it had been cooped up all winter with the fractious, quarrelling girls - especially Kate, who was unusually wilful and demanding. She, of all of them, missed her father the most, crying out for him at night and wetting the bed. Rose had allowed her to creep into bed beside her, as much for her own comfort as her unhappy daughter's. Neither did she tell William that Maggie had been looking after Mary for over a month and that she had hardly seen the baby except on Sundays when they all went to church together.

Her life was a relentless round of getting the children ready for school and then spending every waking hour doing chores for other people for money. She took in washing and scrubbed doorsteps until her hands were raw and chapped, then sewed by dim firelight into the night until her eyes ached and black shadows distorted her vision. But she would do anything, however menial, to keep her home in Raglan Street, to cling on to the security and respectability that William had given her. She was not too proud to forget that she had once hawked vegetables around the town in a pair of her father's old boots, so she held her head high when she walked past her more fortunate neighbours and ignored their murmured comments or embarrassed silence.

But today she was cheered by the Easter celebrations at St Bede's and the sight of her daughters' faces enjoying egg-rolling and games in the park. Above all, she was encouraged by the sight of William sitting up in bed. He had been wheeled outside under an open porch. He was pale and thin, but when he opened his eyes and saw her dressed in her best green frock and bonnet, his face lit up as if the spring sun had touched him. They smiled at each other and she perched on the iron frame and let him take her hands.

'You're looking bonny as can be,' he croaked, his chest wheezing quietly.

'And you're lookin' better an' all,' she smiled, her spirits lifting.

'But your hands are all rough,' William noticed with concern. Rose pulled them away.

'It's just from washing the bairns' clothes,' she said quickly. 'The wind's been that cold. Here, smell these.' She thrust the posy of flowers at him. 'Lasses picked them for you up Simonside.'

She saw the longing in his face. 'I wish I could see them,' he whispered, 'just for a minute.'

'Maybes next time I could bring them to the gate,' she suggested. 'If you're outdoors, you could see them from here, couldn't you?'

William brightened at her words. 'Aye, I could,' he smiled. 'Just the tonic I need.' He took a few breaths then asked, 'Tell me about them.'

Rose spoke of the girls, how Elizabeth was preparing for her first communion and Margaret was teaching Kate tunes on the piano to surprise him when he came home. She did not tell him what a struggle it had been to keep the piano from being pawned. Then she stopped at the sight of his eyes filling with tears, alarmed that he was going to cry.

'So don't go gettin' yoursel' too comfy up here,' she said briskly. 'We all want you back home where you belong.'

He covered her hand with cold translucent fingers. 'Take me home with you, Rose,' he panted. 'I want to be with you - you and the lasses.'

Rose hesitated. She wanted desperately to have him home too, but not in the condition he was. He would be an extra burden on their meagre resources and it would only pain him to see how their wedding gifts had been pawned and Mary had been fostered out to Maggie. How soon before bitterness and despair would overwhelm him at his inability to help his family?

She steeled herself. 'You're better off here than in the town - the doctor said. You'll soon mend in this spring air.'

'I would mend quicker seeing you and the bairns every day,' William said, growing agitated, his breath more laboured.

'You're not supposed to gan near the bairns,' Rose said in mounting distress, 'not with consumption.'

She saw the stricken look on his face and regretted her words at once. It was the first time they had mentioned the dreaded word and it hung between them like a spectre.

Rose squeezed his hand. 'You'll get better quicker here,' she insisted, trying to convince herself as much as him. 'We'll soon have you home.' She stood to go, but he grasped her hand and would not let go. It was surprisingly strong, the cold bony fingers clinging on to her warm, roughened skin.

'Stay a bit longer,' he pleaded. 'You haven't told me about the baby.'

Rose flushed with guilt. 'She's canny. Maggie helps me out now and then.' She extracted her hand from his desperate grip. 'I must gan. Can't expect me sister to have the bairns all day long.'

'Rose,' William whispered.

'Aye?'

'I love you.'

Her heart jolted. 'William ...'

'It's true. I love you more than me own life.'

'Don't be daft . . .' Rose exclaimed in discomfort.

'Kiss me,' he croaked.

She hesitated for a half beat, then leant forward and kissed him on his dry bloodless lips. At that moment she wished she could have breathed new life and health into his emaciated body, given him some of her strength and vitality. How she yearned for the old William to hold her in strong arms or take her hand and chase the racing moon until she doubled up with breathlessness and laughter. But all she could give him was this brief kiss of her warm lips and a silent fervent prayer for his recovery.

As she pulled back, she saw the tears welling in his vivid blue eyes, so full of love for her. She knew that no one else would ever look at her in such a way, with such unconditional love. Rose felt bittersweet tears sting her own eyes.

'You get yourself well, do you hear?' she told him sharply, trying not to show her fear and longing. 'There isn't a better man in all the wide world than you, William Fawcett.'

His smile was at once tender and sad. 'Kiss the bairns for me,' he whispered hoarsely.

She nodded and turned from him quickly before her own tears betrayed her. She must remain strong for him, for the children, for herself. Rose strode away down the muddy path towards the gate and did not look back. Even so, she knew that he watched her for she could feel his gaze on her until she was through the gate and out of sight. She stumbled off down the path, blinded by hot tears that coursed down her cheeks.

'Don't let him die!' she cried out. 'Please don't let him die!'

The rooks in the sparse bare trees gave back a harsh desolate cry that turned her heart cold.

That night she woke with a start, frightened out of sleep by a dream of the grisly gibbet at Jarrow Slake. Only the face had not been Jobling's. The hanging corpse had not had a face at all. She sat up in a sweat, her heart hammering. Beside her Kate slept peacefully, her dark hair spread out on the pillow like skeins of black thread.

Suddenly, the room was full of a warm presence and the fear inside her ebbed. Rose sat on, her breath easing, and was engulfed in a comforting calm. It reminded her of the times as a small child when her grandmother would bind her in loving arms after a bad dream had woken her.

'William,' she whispered in the dark, then wondered why she should speak his name. Perhaps he was lying awake at that very moment thinking of her. She lay back down, putting a protective arm around Kate, and fell asleep again.

When she woke with the dawn, the room was cold and the feeling of wellbeing was gone. Rose got up and went downstairs to stoke up the fire. She moved around the kitchen, unable to rid herself of the dread she carried inside like a lead weight. It came as little surprise when Dr Forbes called round later that morning with news from the hospital.

'He's gone, hasn't he?' Rose said in an empty voice. 'My William's gone.'

Dr Forbes nodded sadly, wishing he did not have to bring such desolate news to this dignified woman and her pretty young daughters. 'He died in the night.'

Rose gathered the girls around her as if by keeping them close she could protect them from a fearful future. She hugged them and let them cry, but inside she walled up her own feelings, entombing her heart to cut off the pain that threatened to rip her in two. Never would she let herself love another man the way she had loved William! She could not bear to experience that depth of feeling again.

Chapter 17

Florrie and Albert brought old Mrs Fawcett over the river for her son's funeral. Rose was determined that everything would be done properly and, with William's burial insurance, she ordered a fine coffin and an open glass carriage pulled by black-plumed horses. With a collection taken among William's union colleagues she bought yards of black bombazet, a dull mix of cotton and worsted material, unable to afford the silkier bombazine. Out of this she made dresses for herself and her two eldest daughters and added black crepe trimmings to the bodice and skirts of the younger two and to Mary's bonnet.

Lizzie came home and helped her cook meat pies for the wake.

'What will you do now?' she asked bluntly.

Rose shook her head. 'I can't think beyond the day,' she said shortly, keeping to herself how she lay awake worrying over how she would feed her family. In the dead hours of the night, the spectre of the workhouse would come to her vividly. Thoughts of being incarcerated behind its blackened redbrick facade and high imprisoning railings left her gasping for breath and heart pounding. It was the last refuge of impoverished widows, fallen women, the mad and destitute. Its corridors reeked of hopelessness and shame. She remembered a rumour from years ago that Jobling's widow had ended up in there, her fate sealed by the untimely death of her luckless husband.

'I won't let it happen to me!' Rose railed at the night, as if by saying it aloud she could keep its threat at bay. She refused to believe her life was haunted by the pitman's ghost or that her fate would follow that of his widow. Their husbands had been staunch union men, but that was where the similarity ended. Disease had taken William from her, not desperate murder and vengeful employers.

But she knew she could not stay on at Raglan Street much longer. The rent was too high and the tick men would soon be banging at her door.

'Maybes you could take in lodgers,' Lizzie suggested.

'A widow in mourning?' Rose sighed. 'What would the neighbours think?'

'They can think what they like,' she declared. 'They've all got noses too high up their faces round here.'

Rose was touched by the number of people who came to pay their respects at William's funeral. St Bede's was full of friends from church and work, all with kind words about her husband. It helped her through the ordeal of the day and the spiteful comments from her mother-in-law.

'You can't have looked after him properly,' she accused acidly, 'dying of a poor man's disease. You should've taken more care of him.'

The words stabbed at Rose's heart, but she put a hand on Lizzie's arm to restrain her sister from answering back. Yet she felt a chill foreboding as she looked at the resentful woman. Mrs Fawcett offered no financial help and Rose knew she could expect none. She had battled for years to get William to stand up to his mother and had succeeded. In the end he had chosen her. But at what cost now? Rose never thought she would rue the day she won William away from his mother, until this one.

The children seesawed between tears and boisterousness, confused by the attention that was being paid to them. It seemed like a feast day, yet their father was missing and their mother was desolate. Margaret took command of her sisters, ordering them to hand round food, then keep out of the way upstairs.

'Where's me da?' Rose heard Kate ask her eldest sister.

'You know where he is,' she answered impatiently. 'His soul's with Jesus and his body's gone in the box.'

'For ever and ever?' Kate gasped.

'Aye. Now go upstairs with Sarah.'

'Won't it be dark in the box?' Kate asked fearfully.

'He can't see anything now,' Margaret replied, taking her by the hand. 'Stop asking questions.'

Two nights later, Kate woke screaming and Rose drew her into her arms before she disturbed the others.

'Mammy, Mammy, he can't see! Da-da can't see,' Kate sobbed. 'They've put his body in the box without his head - now he can't see!'

Rose rocked her. 'Hush now, what nonsense you talk. Of course he has his head.'

'But Margaret said they just put his body in the box,' Kate wailed in distress.

'Eeh, hinny,' Rose sighed, 'you've too much imagination in that head of yours. All of Da went in the coffin, head an' all. But he won't need it now. All that matters is that his soul's at rest in Heaven with Jesus and the Virgin Mary and all the saints.'

She held on to her young daughter until she calmed down. Kate sniffed and asked, 'Will he be with St Bede now?'

Rose stroked her head. 'Aye, he'll have met St Bede by now, I wouldn't wonder.'

Kate looked up at her mother and suddenly smiled. 'Da'll be glad about that. St Bede was his favourite, wasn't he? He can tell Da all about the monastery and being a monk and that.'

Rose gave her daughter a grateful hug. 'Aye, they'll be having a canny chat about it all. Now hush and gan to sleep.'

Within a month the piano, the doll's house and the rest of Rose's wedding presents had been pawned, apart from her mother's bone-handled cutlery with which she could not bear to part. She began to take in washing and gave the second bedroom over to lodgers, all the girls sharing her bed with her. But one night the two seamen returned drunk and singing after the pubs had closed and the neighbours must have complained, for the next day the rent man came round.

'The landlord says you can't have vagrants living here,' he told her brusquely.

'They're not vagrants,' Rose replied, offended. 'They're working seamen.'

'Makes no difference,' the man shrugged. 'He doesn't want his street filling up with drunkards and riffraff. They have to go.'

When Rose told her lodgers the news, one of them grew aggressive and refused to pay what was owing. So she let him go for fear he might harm one of the children. That night she discovered that her precious cutlery was missing. Her small collection of cash, hidden in the tea caddy, had gone too. She sat down and burst into tears at the cruel injustice dealt to her and the girls. How could those men have been so heartless? Now Rose despaired at how the rent would be paid at all. She was not making nearly enough from washing and mending. The walls were bare of pictures, half the furniture had been pawned and all of William's clothes and boots.

A week later the rent man came round threatening her with eviction. In desperation she got Margaret to help her write a letter to Mrs Fawcett, begging for help, not for herself but for William's children. A terse note came in reply, telling her she would not get a penny.

'God is punishing you for your sinful pride. You took my son away and turned him against me. You have too many girls for me to help, but they look strong enough to be sent out to work soon. I've put in a lace handkerchief for Margaret.'

In disgust Rose threw the letter and handkerchief into the smouldering fire. She would never belittle herself again by asking the old witch for help, no matter how desperate! Instead she hurried to Maggie.

'I've nowhere else to gan,' she said in distress. 'Would you take us in? I could get a job at the chemical works or some'at that would feed us all. The lasses wouldn't be any bother. And they could help you with the diggin' and plantin' now that Da can't manage any of it.'

'I'll have to ask Danny,' Maggie said cautiously. 'But I'm sure I can make him agree. He's quite taken to wee Mary. And I'll not see me own sister out on the street, that's for sure.'

They waited for Danny to return from the steel mill. Rose knew that she had to convince him, for he had assumed the role of head of the household, since frail old McConnell's memory was fading and he was often confused and incontinent. She could see her brother-in-law weighing up the situation in his mind. It would mean a lot of extra mouths to feed, but Rose was a strong, hardworking woman, still in her prime at not quite thirty. And the eldest girl, Margaret, was nearly ten and sensible beyond her years, she could soon be sent out to work. Besides, William had been a friend and he would not disgrace his memory by seeing his young family and handsome widow destitute.

Danny saw the advantages and agreed. He helped Rose remove her few remaining possessions from Raglan Street on the back of McConnell's two-wheeled cart and they trundled past the silent neighbours. Margaret and Elizabeth perched on top of the upturned bed clutching their last childhood possessions: the wooden lion in its cage with the lion tamer that William had made, and a photograph of them all at South Shields on a long-ago happy summer's day.

Rose and her daughters slept in the small bedroom that once she had shared with her sisters. She lay awake at night, bewildered at how quickly she had lost everything gained over so many years of striving. Only her daughters and the crumpled studio photograph whose frame had been sold were reminders of the life she had once led independently of this plain old cottage and its windswept smallholding from where she had originated.

But the children accepted their new surroundings with a cheerful fatalism that put her bitterness to shame. All except the baby, who did not seem to know her and howled when she tried to pick her up, putting out her arms to Maggie as if she were her mother. It filled Rose with guilt for having so readily abandoned her the previous winter, but it did not make Mary any easier to love.

Chapter 18

For a few months, Rose helped out on the smallholding. Over the summer holidays Margaret helped her haul the cart of vegetables into the town to sell. Elizabeth was often left in charge of the younger girls while the burden of running the home and looking after McConnell fell to Maggie. But when school started again and wintry weather threw them all together in the cramped cottage, tempers shortened and lack of money fuelled resentment.

'She'll have to gan out and find work that'll bring in more of a wage,' Rose heard Danny arguing with Maggie in the next room. 'I can't be expected to keep them all.'

'She did try, but there was nowt in the town - and she does her best with the fruit and veg,' Maggie defended.

'Aye, but you could be doing that,' Danny snapped. 'And them lasses - the older two should be out working, not ganin' to school. It's costing us precious money and what use is it? Lasses don't need an education - what do they want with readin' and writin'? She got ideas above herself, marrying Fawcett. Well, she's no grand lady now.'

Rose flushed with indignation, but she heard Maggie's placating voice. 'I'll have a word with our Rose the morra.'

Rose lay fuming. She was not going to send her girls out to work! Margaret was almost old enough to become a school monitress and her teacher had said she had the makings of a pupil teacher. She'd find the pennies to send them to school even if it meant working in the rope factory or the puddling mills, places that broke women's health faster than childbirth. But her daughters would have their education, even if it sent her to an early grave. It's what William had wanted for them and by the saints, they would have it!

The next day, after walking the girls to school, Maggie went searching for work again. She tried factories and workshops, shops and cafes, but they all turned her away. The factories had no vacancies; the shops wanted someone younger for long hours with no family to support. She was told she was too old, had no head for figures, lived too far away, looked too Irish or too obviously widowed. She heard countless different excuses that day and all the following week when she trailed as far as Tyne Dock for work.

She returned sore-footed and increasingly dejected. The only work she was likely to get was cleaning or serving in a pub, neither of which would bring in enough to feed and clothe and school her daughters. Besides, the pubs in Jarrow were rough as could be and it frightened her to think of the drinking and brawling and having to make her way home late at night on her own.

In desperation she turned to Danny. 'Can you put a word in for me at the mills?'

He looked taken aback. 'They don't take on lasses at the mill. It's men's work.'

'They do at the puddling mills,' Rose said.

'Not there!' Maggie cried. 'It's a killer of a job.'

'I'm not afraid of grafting hard,' Rose said stoutly. 'I'm as strong as any of the lasses workin' there.'

Danny nodded. 'I'll put the word out.'

But November came and went with nothing extra to spend on Elizabeth for her ninth birthday and no sign of a job. Then just before Sarah's eighth birthday, Danny came home with news of work. He did not tell Rose that a woman had dropped down dead of a heart seizure, but that is what he had heard from a man in the pub who was delivering pig iron to the mill.

'I put a word in for you,' he said. 'Gan down tomorra and see for yoursel'.'

Just before Christmas and the start of 1889, Rose began her servitude at the giant puddling mill, exchanging her widow's gown for old field clothes of Maggie's. It was so unbearably hot in that place of roaring furnaces and pounding steam hammers, that they often stripped off to their undergarments of bodices and shifts. While outside the blackened buildings and lifeless trees were frozen in a hoarfrost, inside the workers roasted in the heat of hell. All day they humped huge ingots of scrap iron and shovelled them into the blazing furnaces, their faces scorched and bodies drenched in sweat. The molten metal was pounded by hammers and the air filled with fumes as the impurities were burnt off.

When they felt like dropping with exhaustion, the foremen would give them a break long enough to down mugs of beer or occasionally milk, to give them the strength to carry on. At first Rose refused to drink the warm fermenting beer. But once, when there was nothing else and such a thirst raged in her parched throat, another woman encouraged, 'Get it down yer neck, hinny! You'll feel canny better for it.'

She sipped the bitter liquid, almost gagging on the taste. But the next time, she found herself drinking more and finding it not so unpleasant. Soon Rose looked forward to the brief respite and the thirst-quenching beer that dulled the pain in her aching limbs and back. With beer in her belly she could manage the rest of the day. But by the end of her shift, she could hardly drag herself back up the hill to Simonside. When she got home Rose would collapse on the bed and fall asleep in her dirty work clothes, too exhausted to eat, let alone talk to her daughters.

The weeks of relentless work dragged on and she hardly noticed the spring come. It was Margaret who reminded her to light a candle of remembrance on the anniversary of William's death. A year of struggling lay behind, but what filled Rose with fear was the bleak future that stretched ahead. She felt overcome with misery at her situation. All she could look forward to was a life of ceaseless grind and the charity of her sister and brother-in-law. Even with the job at the puddling mill, she did not always have enough to pay for the children's schooling, but sent them anyway. At times she wondered if she should abandon her dream of educating them and send the older ones into service. They were tall for their age and could pass for a couple of years older. Then she was filled with shame at even considering such a thing.

But she could not shake off her feeling of depression and lethargy. She saw the women around her working themselves to a standstill. Some were slowly poisoned by lead, their bodies eventually so crippled they were of no more use. Others went abruptly, crushed or disabled by sudden accident, dying of burns from carelessness brought on by tiredness and overwork. How long before she was the next victim?

When Rose had the energy to think at all, she was filled with anxiety about the future and how she would provide for her children. Worse still, what would become of them should something happen to her at the mill? But worry for them as she did, she no longer found comfort in their company. She snapped at them for the slightest naughtiness or noise and took to slapping them for no reason at all except they were an annoyance to her and a source of trouble.

Maggie watched her growing detachment from her family with alarm. When she suggested Rose should take them out for a walk after church or for a picnic, her elder sister shouted back, 'Don't tell me what I should do! I slave for them all week - not that they show any thanks. You take 'em out - they tret you more like their mam than me. Just leave me be.'

Rose stormed out of the kitchen and slammed the door to her room, leaving the girls subdued and puzzled. She refused to come out of full mourning and dressed herself completely in black when not at the mill. As the summer came, she spent the precious hours of sunlight shut away in the stuffy bedroom, asleep or praying. Her prayers were increasingly desperate as she begged for deliverance from her twilight world of despair. She was surrounded by family that she could not escape and yet she had never felt so alone in all her life.

'Oh, William! Why did you leave me?' she railed in her emptiness and anger. 'How could you have left me like this?'

One day at the mill, a carrier delivering the pigs of iron stopped and stared at her. She would not have noticed, except one of the women nudged her.

'What's he lookin' at you like that for?'

'Who?' Rose asked, without looking up.

'Him over there - gawping at ye,' she smirked.

Rose straightened up, wiping damp hair from her eyes. She saw a tall man with a lean face half hidden by a military cap. 'How should I know?' she shrugged with disinterest. 'Never seen him before.'

But the man continued to regard her as if he expected a response.

'Sure he's not yer fancy man?' the other woman cackled.

Rose shot her an angry look. 'I'm a widow. I don't have any fancy man and I never will!' She pushed past her and the next time she looked up, the labourer was gone.

Rose thought no more about the incident until a couple of weeks later, when Maggie returned from selling vegetables round the old pit cottages.

'Old Ma McMullen's pleased he's back. Bought her a new bead necklace and a teapot with a spout that isn't cracked. Over the moon, she is.'

'Who's back?' Rose asked dully, wrestling bad-temperedly with a piece of mending. Kate had gone through the knees of her stockings and Sarah and Elizabeth had both outgrown their dresses since the spring.

'John McMullen,' Maggie answered impatiently. 'I told you he was back from the army.'

Rose put down her mending. The memory of the stranger staring at her came briefly to mind. 'Since when?'

Maggie sighed, 'About a month ago. Don't you listen to anything I tell you any more?'

Rose bent her head once more. 'Nowt to do wi' me.'

Maggie carried on spooning soup into Mary's mouth. 'I don't know why I bother telling you anything,' she complained. 'Might as well talk to me shadow.

I'd get more sense out of it than you these days.'

Rose felt quick annoyance. 'Why should I be interested in John McMullen? I couldn't abide him before he went away - always drunk and swearing his head off.'

Maggie snorted. 'You used to be sweet on him - before you met William.'

Rose was furious. 'No I wasn't! How dare you say that? I've only ever loved William. I'll never look at another man again.'

'Keep your hat on,' Maggie snapped back. 'I never suggested you would. All I was telling you was a bit of news from the McMullens - they are still friends of ours even if you don't bother with 'em.'

Rose saw how she had riled her usually placid sister and felt bad. She did not know from where her bursts of anger came. She glanced across the room to where Kate was sitting on her grandfather's knee, hoping she had not heard their arguing. Their heads were bent together as they told each other stories, oblivious to anything else. Rose lowered her voice.

'I'm sorry. I know you didn't mean anything by it. I just don't like any talk of me going with another man after William.'

Maggie regarded her. 'Aye, well, maybes you don't. But it's not just yourself to think about, there's the bairns, an' all.'

'What d'you mean by that?' Rose demanded.

'I mean that mourning your dead husband won't put bread in the bairns' mouths,' Maggie said bluntly. 'And you know you can't stay here for ever - we're not managing as it is - not unless the lasses gan out to work.' Rose could tell they were Danny's words she was repeating, but Maggie went on swiftly before Rose protested at the suggestion. 'And there's some'at else.'

'What?' Rose asked, panic rising inside. If Maggie had tired of defending her, then her days at Simonside were numbered.

Maggie flushed pink as she spoke. 'Me and Danny -we're - I'm expectin'.'

Rose gawped at her sister. For ages she had longed for Maggie to become a mother too, but now she felt winded at the news. There would be even less room for her family now. She looked at Mary's sticky face and mop of unruly curls and was overwhelmed by the burden of being her children's provider. She tried to speak, but could not. Rose let out a howl that brought Kate rushing over in alarm.

'What's wrong, Mam?' she asked, putting arms around her shoulders. But Rose could not control her sobbing.

Maggie answered in a quiet, bitter voice, 'She's crying 'cos she's feeling sorry for hersel'.' She stood up and lifted Mary out of the high chair that Danny had made.

Rose looked at her sister, seeing the hurt she had inflicted. She groped for an apology.

'I'm sorry, Maggie. Don't be cross. It's grand you're going to have your own bairn.' She clutched Kate tightly and whispered in desperation, 'It's just - I - I'm that frightened. I don't know what I'm going to do!'

Chapter 19

A frostiness grew between Rose and Maggie that did not thaw, despite Rose's attempts to curb her short temper and be more helpful. But the unborn baby was an unspoken source of tension. Try as she might, Rose could not stifle feelings of resentment towards her sister for having a healthy husband in work who would be able to provide for her and the child. Danny was overjoyed that he would finally be a father and fussed around Maggie possessively, the way William used to over Rose. He would criticise Rose for not helping around the house enough and constantly order the older girls to do jobs for his wife.

Rose knew that Maggie was under increasing pressure from Danny to be rid of them before their baby was born in the spring, but Rose was at a loss as to what to do. All her energy was used up in her job. She could not contemplate having to find somewhere new to live and she relied heavily on Maggie to cope with the household chores and the children. Maybe if she could put a little bit by each week and stay until Margaret was old enough to find part-time work, she could manage.

But Rose seemed to have lost the knack of good housekeeping. She was incapable of saving anything and it was only thanks to Maggie's careful budgeting that they managed to keep the girls clothed and provide enough food to last the week without resorting to the pawn shop.

Lizzie came home for a visit, announcing that she was engaged to a gardener at Ravensworth called Peter and planned a quiet wedding in the new year.

'That's grand!' Rose hugged her tearfully. 'I'm glad for you. I wish I could help you out more ...'

'I know you do,' Lizzie said quickly, 'but we'll be canny.'

Rose felt wretched. From being the sister who always had a bit extra to give her family, she was now a burden to them.

As the leaves dropped from the trees and the mornings grew chilly, Rose fretted more and more about the future as she trudged into work. Increasingly, she caught glimpses of the tall carrier, humping scrap iron through the gates of the puddling mill. Whereas a few weeks ago she would not have given him a second thought, since the row with Maggie, Rose had been jolted out of her self-absorbed grief.

She tried to get a proper look at the man, but he never stared at her as he had that first time. She noticed a bleached moustache and eyebrows, weathered cheeks and broad shoulders under a too-tight jacket. He looked too old to be the John McMullen she had last seen at his brother Michael's wedding twelve years ago. But his thick boots and battered army hat suggested otherwise. She knew only too well how she had aged in looks since then. It was possible this sallow-faced man hiding under his soldier's cap might be the insolent John of former years.

The next time she saw him. Rose straightened up and waited. As he turned to go he caught her watching him and tipped the edge of his grubby cap at her. Something about the directness of his gaze was familiar. She nodded in return. As he went, she wondered why she had tried to catch his attention. She was not even sure it was John. Besides, she had never really liked him. Annoyed with herself, she returned to her back-breaking work.

Three days later, she caught him looking her way again. This time he removed his cap and scratched his short-cropped hair; his glance at her was bashful, but it was long enough for Rose to be sure it was John McMullen. His eyes were that startling green; the stubborn set of his mouth under the bushy moustache the same. Rose felt uncomfortable. Her heart was racing and her breath came erratically. She felt an overwhelming desire to sit down and was suddenly acutely aware that she was stripped off to her shift and petticoat. But he held her gaze and she could not look away. Neither of them smiled. Then he nodded at her, jammed on his cap and abruptly marched away.

'Who's the general then?' her friend Bridie nudged her.

'Someone I used to know,' Rose said, gripping her arms and trying not to shake. 'His father's a friend of me da's.'

'Handsome, I'd say,' Bridie winked.

'You think owt on two legs is handsome,' Rose grunted, and turned back to work before the foreman spotted them chatting.

'He's sweet on you,' her friend remarked.

'Don't be daft,' Rose cried. 'He's lording it over me! Back from the army and India and such grand places -finds me slaving for a pittance. He's always had a callous streak. John McMullen will be loving it. Well, I haven't always had to work like this - I've had a decent husband and a grand house in Raglan Street and luxuries he's never had. And I've five bonny daughters . . .' Rose stifled a sob. She despised herself for getting worked up over the likes of him.

Bridie touched her shoulder. 'Haway, don't upset yoursel'.' She glanced around. 'Did you say John McMullen? The McMullens from the pit cottages?'

Rose nodded and wiped her nose on the back of her hand.

'I'd heard one of 'em was back from the army,' Bridie murmured. 'Aye, and I'd heard they paid him a pension an' all. He's been spending it round the pubs, our Billy says. And he should know - he lives in 'em.' She took hold of Rose by the arm. 'If it's the same man, maybes you should encourage him.'

'John McMullen?' Rose said in distaste. 'He's too fond of the drink and talking with his fists.'

Bridie snorted. 'Maybes he's not perfect, but you and the bairns would be better off settling for a strong man with a bit money in his pocket. Or would you rather stay here till the work kills ye?'

Rose could find no answer to that.

Chapter 20

It took John another month to pluck up the courage to call on Rose at Simonside. He had almost gone on half a dozen occasions, washing himself carefully, polishing his boots and putting on his fading army jacket. But his brothers' ribald questioning and his own shyness had got the better of him and he had turned into the nearest pub instead.

On the long voyage back from Bombay, John had determined that he would find a wife on his return to Jarrow, someone like his mother, who would see to his needs and keep his sons in check. For John also dreamt of a large family, of children who would love and fear him, make him feel worthy in his own home. But what he returned to was a house still overcrowded with brothers and occasional lodgers, a cantankerous old father and a sick mother. He worried about his mother's bouts of coughing and the brown phlegm she spat into the hissing fire, and tried to make her feel better by buying her small trinkets and pots for the kitchen.

'All I want from you is to see you settled,' she would tell him with a weary smile whenever he gave her something. It was she who had told him the startling news that Rose McConnell was a widow and living back at Simonside.

'Left with five young daughters to bring up, the poor lass,' Mrs McMullen said with a toothless intake of breath. 'William Fawcett got the consumption - been dead two summers. Danny and Maggie took them in, but from what Danny's mother says, he's sick of the sight of them. Well, it's a lot to ask of a man - taking on some other man's wife and children - and Maggie expectin' their first one and still having to look after the old man too. He's no more than a bairn himself these days - thinks he's living back in Ireland and keeps wandering off looking for his parents.' She broke off breathlessly to cough and John did not like to tax her with all the questions that flooded into his head.

Gradually he learned that Rose was reduced to working long hours at the puddling mill and he took on a casual job, lugging pig iron so that he could see for himself. At first he did not recognise her. He was looking for the slim-waisted girl with the coils of dark hair who had captivated him as a young man. It was this image of Rose that he had carried with him through the long years of military service on the North-West Frontier.

During the Afghan campaigns, when they had marched through rocky passes, choked by the summer heat and dust, while men around him had died of thirst and dysentery, he had kept going with thoughts of her. During the bitter winters with nothing left to eat but the leather of their boots, he had conjured up her face. John had thought he would die, was convinced he would never get back to Jarrow again, and his dreams of her had been sweet torture. Only a miraculous counter-march led by fellow Irishman General Roberts had saved them all from being cut to pieces by fierce tribesmen who showed neither fear nor mercy.

Back in India, he had taken up with a local woman, an Anglo-Indian, who had been one of the camp followers and who reminded him of Rose. He knew he could never have the McConnell girl because she belonged to the respectable and worthy Fawcett. It was why he had left Jarrow so suddenly, for he could not bear to see her married happily to another. But John knew that in his bitterness he had not treated his army woman well. He had alternately used her and neglected her, leaving her behind for months at a time, punishing her for not being Rose.

Only when he had come back and found Sultana had borne him a daughter did he show her kindness and a grudging affection. He had doted on the tawny-eyed child, naming her Ruth. He had taught her to sing Irish songs. Then, three years ago, he had returned from a tour of duty at the Frontier and found them both dead from an outbreak of cholera.

He had got blind drunk for a week and nearly poisoned himself to death with the local firewater. After that, John had no more heart left for soldiering and often his stomach played up. He served his time, increasingly withdrawn and impatient with the world, waiting for his gratuity and a passage home.

Now, after years of gruelling service under a harsh sun, where anyone he had let himself care for had died of sickness or been butchered fighting at his side, fortune had smiled on him. Rose McConnell - he had never thought of her as Fawcett - was widowed and in need of rescue from the brutal puddling mill.

He had stared at her hard the first time he saw her, puce-faced and sweating in the ferocious heat. She was stout and thick-armed, her sleeves pulled back and hands filthy. Her dark hair was scraped into a severe bun at the back of her head, but wayward strands had escaped and stuck to her glistening neck and cheeks. He doubted it was her, until a coarse-faced woman at her side prodded Rose and nodded in his direction. Slowly she straightened, leaning on her shovel, and glanced over with lifeless eyes.

She pushed at her stray hair and frowned. A vein stood out on her broad forehead, throbbing with the exertion of manual work, and her chest heaved. Her breasts sagged in the shapeless dress. John felt a rush of disappointment, even anger at this woman for taking the place of the pretty girl he remembered, who had plagued his mind all these years. But it was Rose. The large, wide-set eyes, the full mouth and prominent cheekbones were recognisable. Yet despite the lines of experience and pain etched across her face, it was still attractive, still dearly familiar.

John felt a stab of pity mixed with triumph at having found her. He waited expectantly for her to show surprise or pleasure at seeing him again after all this time. But after a few seconds, she turned back to her work without a flicker of interest or recognition. He left feeling fury and hurt, humiliated by the pointing and laughter of the other women. How he hated them all! He spent the rest of the day in the pub until he was thrown out for being abusive and swearing in Urdu, and had to be frog-marched home by two of his brothers, singing drunkenly at the top of his voice.

After that, John feigned indifference to Rose and the other women when he unloaded the scrap iron from the wagons, until one day late in the autumn, when he became aware of someone watching him. It made the back of his neck prickle, the way it used to on sentry duty, camped out among the bald rocks guarding the Frontier. He looked up and saw Rose eyeing him from the open doorway. His heart thudded in shock. Gone was the dead expression of before; her look was sharp and assessing, her posture bold. In confusion, he touched his cap and fled in panic. Afterwards, he tried to remember if she had nodded at him or not.

In a state of nerves, he returned a few days later, determined to take a longer look. He lingered in the doorway, fighting the urge to run away, until Rose turned towards him. Flustered, he took off his cap and scratched his head. How was it that women managed to alarm him so easily, when he had stood and faced unspeakable horrors in battle?

She nodded at him and his stomach unknotted. It was a definite sign of recognition, even of interest. He was suddenly aware that she was only half dressed. Her bodice showed the plump tops of her breasts and the pale bare flesh of her upper arms. John felt a quickening of excitement, a familiar stab of desire at the sight of a woman's body. He turned quickly and left, nervous at the thought that she might be discussing him with the other woman. But he could not rid his mind of Rose and grew more unsettled by the day.

It was his mother who finally pushed him into paying a visit to Simonside.

'I can see something's eatin' at you,' she complained. 'Joseph tells me you're daft for some lass - you were singing about her when they had to carry you home the other night.'

John flushed with embarrassment and growled a denial.

'For the love of St Peter, go and see her,' she urged. 'It's time I had you off me hands for good.'

It was a raw December afternoon when Elizabeth and Kate spotted the man in the army jacket making his way up the track. Between them they were carrying a sack of cinders that they had scavenged from the railway siding and some fat twigs brought down by recent gales. They gawped at him as he came closer, wondering whether to stay or scamper back to the cottage in safety.

It was Kate who spoke first to the tall, stern-faced man who peered down at them as he regained his breath at the gate.

'Are you a soldier?' she asked, eyeing his appearance with interest.

'I was,' he answered.

'You still look like one to me,' Kate said. 'You've got a red coat like a soldier.'

'And who are you?' he asked gruffly.

'I'm Kate Fawcett. I'm seven and I can say me nine times table. This is me sister Elizabeth. She's ten.'

John glanced at the mute girl with blue eyes so like her father staring at him fearfully. 'Has she lost her tongue?'

'Na,' Kate answered again. 'We're not supposed to talk to strangers.'

'Not very obedient then, are you?' John grunted. 'Any road, it's your mam I've come to see.'

Kate looked doubtful. 'She doesn't speak to strangers neither. She doesn't speak much to anybody - except Our Lady and St Theresa and me da in Heaven.'

John scowled at her. 'I'm not a stranger - I'm an old friend of your mother's. Now stop yer cheek and gan and tell her I'd like a word.'

Kate shook her head. 'She's restin' with me big sister Margaret. She's poorly bad - caught a chill and won't eat anything.'

John asked in concern, 'Your mam's sick?'

'No, it's me sister. Coughing all night and keepin' us awake and—'

'Just go and tell her John McMullen's come to call on her!' he shouted suddenly, his nerve nearly failing him. Elizabeth flinched with fright and Kate froze. 'If you don't scarper this minute I'll get me bayonet out.'

Kate gave him a quick look to see where he might be hiding his bayonet. 'You haven't got a b—'

John made a sudden move forward as if he would grab her, and Elizabeth screamed. She dropped her end of the sack at once and, seizing Kate by the hand, yanked her up the muddy path. John watched them go, noticing the loping run of the inquisitive younger girl. Not only did she look like Rose, she was spirited like her mother. He laughed softly at the sound of their anxious voices shouting a warning.

'Mam! There's a soldier outside. Mam, he wants you!'

'Aunt Maggie, he's got a bayonet! Come quickly!'

Rose was roused from sleep by the girls' shouting. She had dozed off beside Margaret, a protective arm thrown around her feverish body. She was at once alert to the child's ragged shallow breathing. She put her hand on Margaret's flushed forehead and felt it hot to the touch. Her daughter opened her eyes and gazed at her trustingly.

Before she could speak, Kate burst in. 'He's waiting outside for you!'

'What's all the fuss?' Rose demanded crossly. 'Can't you see your sister's not well? And don't you go waking Uncle Danny and your grandda from their nap with all your noise.'

'Sorry, Mam,' Elizabeth said, peering in anxiously. 'He said he wasn't a stranger. He wants to see you.'

'Who does?' Rose asked, her insides lurching.

'John somebody,' Kate said.

'McMullen,' Elizabeth added.

Rose's nervousness increased. 'I can't see him now. I can't leave Margaret. Tell him to go away.'

'Mam!' Elizabeth pleaded. 'He'll shout at us again. Please see him! I'll sit with our Margaret. I'm good at wiping her face and keeping her cool.'

Rose put her hand up to her hair. It was tousled and her black dress was crumpled. She was in no fit state to be seen by a visitor, least of all John McMullen. Yet she had half expected him; looked out for him on the hill on more than one occasion. Ever since their exchange of looks at the mill, she had half anticipated, half dreaded his coming to seek her out. Now he was here and she did not know if she wanted his attentions or not.

Maggie bustled into the room. 'You can't leave him standing out there in the half-dark,' she scolded. 'I'm going to ask him in and you're going to see him.'

Rose looked at her sister and saw her stubborn expression; Maggie had reached the end of her patience. What choice did she have? Rose wondered. The girls watched her expectantly.

Suddenly Margaret whispered at her side. 'Go, Mam. I'm feeling better.'

Rose looked down at her wan face and glazed eyes and saw her trying to smile. She felt a rush of fierce love for her eldest. Margaret had been her greatest companion and help through her darkest moments, stubbornly keeping to her side even when she scolded and pushed her daughter away. It was Margaret who had raised the other girls and seen to their needs these past two years far more than she had. For her Rose would do anything, even face John McMullen

120

whom she still half feared.

Rose squeezed her daughter's hand in reassurance. 'Aye, I'll go,' she agreed.

Chapter 21

Rose felt as nervous as a young girl stepping into the kitchen. She hardly had time to glance in the stained mirror on top of the washstand, for her daughters seized her hands and pulled her after them. They were fearful and excited at receiving a soldier as a visitor and wondered why their mother had never mentioned that she knew one.

Rose pushed her wavy tousled hair behind her ears, trying to force it back into its bun. Elizabeth and Sarah hung on to her rustling skirts like limpets. But Kate skipped ahead, eager to show off to the soldier standing stiffly upright with his back to the fire.

'Here's me mam,' she cried proudly.

Rose met John's fierce-eyed appraisal. He looked taller and more gaunt in the firelight, the shadows deep in the hollow of his cheeks. Close up she could see that his once-dark hair was greying, his thick moustache brindled and faded with years under the bleaching sun. He looked distinguished standing to attention in his army coat, surveying them all with detachment down his long straight nose. But his eyes were still those of the angry young man with a passion for Ireland who had aroused her interest as a girl.

Why had he come? What could he possibly want with her after all these years? She had nothing to offer him except an empty heart and five young daughters who were too young to fend for themselves. With his army gratuity and his austere good looks he could do better than that.

While they stood looking dumbly at each other, Maggie intervened.

'Sit yourself down, John,' she smiled. 'It's grand to see you after all this time. Isn't it, Rose?' She shot her sister a nervous look. 'We heard from your mam that you were back. You must tell us all about your adventuring - the lasses would like to hear it. India, wasn't it?'

'Aye,' John nodded, and lowered himself into the chair by the fire.

'That's Grandda's chair,' Kate piped up.

John looked alarmed and half rose again.

'Stay,' Maggie urged him. 'Father's restin' in the back, he'd not mind in the least.' She gave Kate a warning look. 'You come over here and help me put jam on the bread.'

'But I want to hear about India,' Kate protested. She looked eagerly at John. 'Did you see any tigers? Our Margaret once saw a tiger at the circus, didn't she, Mam? Me da took her to see it. He made her a lion in a cage - we've still got it.'

'Kate!' Maggie cried, alarmed by the mention of William. 'Mr McMullen doesn't want to be bothered by silly questions about tigers. Now do as I say.'

Rose was jolted out of silence by Maggie's scolding of the talkative Kate. 'The lass is right, her father did take Margaret to see the tiger. There's no harm in her asking questions,' she defended the girl. 'And if there's any telling off to do, I'll be the one doing it,' she added. 'Elizabeth, you help Aunt Maggie get the tea ready. Sarah, you set the table.'

John looked with interest between the sisters. He had never seen them argue openly before. They had always been so close, the McConnell girls. But he knew all too well how easily families squabbled and fell out when they were cooped up together for too long. At once he saw Maggie as an ally in prising Rose from her hermit-like existence at the smallholding. And he knew, looking at Rose's pale, composed face, that he wanted her still.

She seemed so lost and vulnerable in her black widow's gown, yet she held herself with dignity and was quick to defend her young daughter. John admired her loyalty to her children, even if he disapproved of Kate's boldness. Like Maggie, he thought the girl should mind her tongue and help her aunt, but how Rose dealt with her daughters was up to her.

It suddenly occurred to John that if he was to win Rose, he was also going to have to take on all these girls. He had not given them much thought until now, except that lasses would be extra help around the house and could easily be put to work. How many were there? He tried to remember. Glancing quickly round he saw three. Then there was the one ill in bed. At that moment a wail went up from a wooden cot in the far corner and a small infant pulled herself up with an accusing stare around the room. Five! he thought without enthusiasm.

Yet, Rose was strong and robust and still of an age when she could bear him the sons that he now so wanted. The thought of lying with Rose made his pulse quicken.

As he struggled to think of anything coherent to say to her, he watched Maggie rush over to lift the small cross-faced girl from the cot and pacify her with soft words. He was momentarily confused. Perhaps this was not one of Rose's after all? Then Kate hobbled over and reached for the girl.

'I'll take her, Aunt Maggie,' she smiled, and almost grabbed Mary out of her aunt's arms. The girl responded to the attention and put her small arms about Kate's neck. 'This is our Mary,' Kate said, staggering back with her sister. 'She's the youngest. She's two, but she speaks canny already.'

Rose felt a pang of pity for her bright, eager-faced daughter. She could see that Kate was trying to please their visitor. She was used to the adoring interest of William and the sociable storytelling of her McConnell grandfather. She could even make Danny laugh with her antics when he had grown tired of the rest of them. Kate enjoyed male company, but the sullen look on John's face showed she was wasting her time with him. He did not seem the slightest bit interested in her children and it made Rose annoyed. If he was not prepared to be kind to them, then he was not the man for her. The sooner he stopped staring at her in that peculiar way and went the better.

Rose busied herself around the kitchen rather than have to sit and talk to John. She poured a fresh bowl of water for Margaret, but before she could retreat with it to the bedroom, Elizabeth stopped her.

'I'll take that,' she said quietly, and escaped from the tense kitchen with the bowl.

Maggie began issuing orders again. 'Sarah, go and wake your Uncle Danny and Grandpa and tell 'em it's tea time - and bring some more coal in for the fire. Kate, your hands are filthy, go and wash.'

Kate looked at her mother and Rose nodded. She disappeared into the scullery, still clutching Mary, and Maggie followed her, closing the door. Rose was suddenly left alone with John. Her heart began to thump in panic.

He stood up and stepped towards her. She must have shown her alarm, because he stopped, his face colouring.

123

'I'm sorry,' he blurted out. 'I'm sorry for yer being widowed. You and the bairns. That's what I came to say.' He glared at her as if the whole embarrassing situation was somehow her fault. 'And I'll tak them on - if you want,' he growled, his neck and face puce above the red jacket. 'I've got a pension off the army. We could live decent. You cannot stop with Maggie and Danny for ever, not with them starting a family. And I want bairns too - and neither of us are gettin' any younger. So do you want to get wed, Rose?'

She stared back at him, quite speechless. She was dumbfounded at his no-nonsense bluntness.

'I - I don't— I can't. . .' she stuttered.

What sort of courtship was this? How could he put her in such an awkward position? It allowed her no dignity, no time to think it over. Damn him, she was still in mourning for William! She would not be bullied into such an important decision by his haste or Maggie's impatience. Worse still, the thought of bearing more children filled her with horror. Rose could countenance being a housekeeper for another man, but to embark once more on the mess of the marriage bed and pain of childbirth with a man other than William filled her with repugnance. She might once have had girlish dreams about John, but those days were long gone. He could never replace her beloved William.

It came to her clearly that she could not contemplate becoming John's wife, however desperate her circumstances. At least while she worked at the mill and provided for her daughters she was free from the demands of a husband. And looking at John's hunched aggressive stance, she suspected his demands would be many.

'You don't have to answer me now,' John said quickly, worried that she might reject him outright. 'I'll not stop for tea,' he said hastily. 'I'll call on you next Sunday and you can tell me your answer.' He grabbed his cap and turned to go.

'No,' Rose stopped him, putting out a hand. He flinched at her touch and she dropped it self-consciously. 'I can tell you now.' She drew in her breath as she steeled herself to tell him. 'I can't marry you, John. In my mind I'm still married to William - always will be. I thank you for your offer, but you should be looking for a younger wife - one who can give you bairns. I've got me five lasses and I don't want anyone else's. I could be a housekeeper for you,' she said quietly, 'but I can't be a wife to you.'

His expression turned from disbelief to anger as her rebuttal sank in. His fists bunched, crushing the cap, and for a moment she thought he would strike her. Instead he just fixed her with his unforgiving stare.

'I don't want a bloody housekeeper, you stuck-up bitch!' he shouted harshly. 'You think I'm not good enough for you? Well, you're not a high-and-mighty Fawcett now. You're a common-as-muck shoveller, relying on yer sister's charity - aye, and that of her husband. But maybes it suits you to pay the rent in other ways, eh, Rose? You and Danny. Do you warm his bed too?'

Rose gasped in offence. 'How dare you suggest—'

But John could not stop himself lashing out and trying to hurt her back. He could see he had provoked her at last. 'Why else does he let you stay here?' he hissed. 'It's what people are asking round the town.'

'I don't believe you!' Rose flushed with indignation.

'Aye, well, ask Danny,' John said in savage triumph. 'I've heard him boastin' to his workmates in The Alkali.'

Rose covered her face in mortification. What was she to believe?

John was merciless. 'I could've saved yer reputation. What other fool do you think'll tak you on with all of Fawcett's brats?'

Rose was stung by his words. No one was going to insult her children or William's memory, least of all him! She glared at John with contempt.

'I'm not asking any man to take us on,' she answered proudly, 'least of all a foul-mouthed McMullen like you.'

John jammed on his cap. 'Well, that suits me.' He grabbed the door handle and jerked it open. The icy December air blew in like a slap to her face. 'Just remember, McMullens don't ask twice!' He stormed out, slamming the door behind him.

Kate ran back into the kitchen. 'What's wrong, Mam? Aunt Maggie wouldn't let me back in.' She pulled on her mother's hand. 'Where's the soldier, Mam?'

'He's gone,' she said, beginning to shake uncontrollably.

'What'd you say to him?' Maggie asked accusingly, following with Mary in her arms.

Rose could not bring herself to look at her sister. She was filled with shame at John's poisonous insinuations about herself and Danny. She felt sick at the thought of people gossiping about her situation, that Danny himself might have fuelled the gossip. She would not believe it! But she could not banish the doubts that now plagued her.

'What've you done, Rose?' Maggie demanded.

Rose faced her. 'Told him I wouldn't marry him,' she whispered.

'Oh, Rose,' Maggie remonstrated.

They stared at each other helplessly. 'I'm sorry,' Rose said, 'I just couldn't...'

'How could you be so selfish?' Maggie cried, and burst into tears.

Kate stared open-mouthed at them both, baffled by their words.

At that moment, Elizabeth ran in.

'Quick, Mam! It's Margaret—'

'What's happened?' Rose demanded at once.

'Her breathing's all funny,' the child gasped. 'She wants you quick!'

For a few seconds, Rose stood paralysed, her mind still in turmoil from the bruising encounter with John.

'Please, Mam,' Elizabeth was almost in tears.

As she stared at the girl, she heard the ghastly rattling of Margaret's breath through the open door. It was a sound that filled her with dread, a sound she had prayed never to hear again. Fear smothered her chest.

'Oh, Mary, Mother of God! My bairn!' she gasped.

Rose dashed forward, her only thought to save her beloved eldest daughter.

Chapter 22

All through that long night, Rose stayed by Margaret's bedside and bathed her face and body. She was red-hot to the touch and babbling incoherently. Rose and Maggie soaked a sheet in water and wrapped it around her to try to cool her down. Her breathing was ragged and laboured, her chest heaving and rattling with every painful breath.

They fed her sips of whisky that Danny and old McConnell were keeping for Christmas, but this made Margaret retch and spew bile down her chin and over Rose's arm. The child's eyes stared wildly, trying to fix on her mother's face, but Rose could not bear the look of terror. It mirrored what she felt inside.

The other girls fell asleep in front of the hearth, huddled together like hibernating animals and Maggie covered them up with a blanket. Rose heard Danny whispering urgently to his wife that he did not want her tending the sick child for fear that she would succumb to fever. Maggie hushed him and he eventually went to bed, but Rose's father sat in his chair talking to himself in agitation. He hated any sickness in the house since his wife had died and they had to endure his fretful ramblings.

'He's talking to Mam as if she's in the room,' Maggie said in distress.

Rose was past caring. She too felt the ghosts of the past gathering in the shadows and her panic increased.

'Maggie!' She grabbed at her arm. 'Will you send Danny for the doctor?'

Maggie looked alarmed. 'We've nowt to pay him with - Danny said.'

Rose gripped her in desperation. 'I'll pay. Look at the lass - she's hot as a fire. I don't know what else to do for her. I'm scared, Maggie!'

Maggie looked at her. 'Give us your ring,' she said quietly, nodding at Rose's hand.

Rose looked down at the thin marriage band on her calloused swollen finger. Apart from the family photograph, it was the one possession that she had kept that linked her to William. Everything else she had pawned or given to Maggie to sell, except this one token of William's love. She looked up and saw the pity in her sister's eyes. Rose clenched her jaw and yanked at the ring. What use had she for tokens now? Her daughter was fighting for her life. The ring meant nothing to her in comparison.

But it would not budge over her swollen knuckle. She tugged and twisted, nearly weeping with the pain. Maggie stopped her.

'I'll go,' she said. 'You can pay him later.'

She grabbed her shawl and went before Rose could say anything, the icy chill of the winter night howling round the door as she left. As the night wore on, Rose prayed and pleaded with the Virgin Mary to save Margaret.

Briefly, Margaret's speech became lucid. 'Mam,' she wheezed, 'are you there, Mam?'

Rose bent over her swiftly so that the child's eyes could focus on her face. She stroked her forehead. 'Aye, hinny, of course I'm here,' she smiled tearfully, overcome to hear her voice again. Hope leapt within that the fever had peaked.

'I feel cold.' Margaret shivered, even though she was drenched in sweat. 'Can

126

I have another blanket?'

'You're too hot for blankets,' Rose told her gently.

'Where're me sisters? Where's Elizabeth?' Margaret fretted. 'I want to see 'em.'

'They're sleepin' by the fire - you'll see them in the morning.'

Margaret fixed her with a troubled look. 'Why aren't they here with us? Am I dying, Mam, like me da?'

Rose's heart squeezed in pain. She held her daughter's limp hand. 'No! Don't think such a thing. Aunt Maggie's gone for Dr Forbes - we'll soon have you better.'

'Can I gan back to school soon?' Margaret whispered in hope.

'Aye, soon,' Rose answered.

Margaret's frown eased. 'I don't want to let Miss Quinlan down.'

'You won't,' her mother smiled. 'Now stop worrying and get some rest.'

But Margaret continued to stare, her blue eyes so like William's, it comforted and hurt Rose in equal measure.

'Mam? Stay with me.'

Rose's throat constricted with tears. She struggled to remain composed.

'I'm not ganin' anywhere, hinny,' she promised.

'Good,' Margaret smiled weakly. 'Tell me one of your stories, Mam,' she panted. 'The one about the weddin' - and the bride who looked like an angel. That's me favourite.'

Rose hardly trusted herself to speak, so choked was she with feeling for her sick daughter. But she gulped back the tears that threatened to betray her. She would do anything to ease Margaret's fear and pain.

After a while Margaret fell asleep and Rose began to worry over why Maggie was taking so long to bring the doctor. It seemed an age since she had gone. But she heard no footsteps or voices approach the house, only the howling of the wind.

At one stage in the black night, Mary woke and began to cry. Rose realised that it was Maggie who normally tended to her in the night and took her into bed with her and Danny. The child's whimpering jarred her ragged nerves, but she could not leave Margaret's side.

'Maggie, where are you?' she cried out in anxiety, longing for her sister to return with help.

But Mary's crying grew louder and more insistent, and she howled for her aunt. A few minutes later the door creaked open and Elizabeth staggered in with a tearful Mary in her arms.

'She wants you, Mam,' said the sleepy-eyed child.

Rose was at her wits' end. 'No she doesn't. Keep her out of here!'

Mary's wailing increased. 'Where's Aunt Maggie?' Elizabeth asked nervously.

'Gone for the doctor,' Rose said, turning back to bathe Margaret's face. 'Please take the bairn and quieten her down before she wakes everyone up,' Rose pleaded.

They went and a few minutes later she heard Mary's crying subside to a whimper and then peter out in exhaustion. Rose sank forward and rested her head on the bed. Clutching Margaret's hand and working the rosary she whispered, 'Mary, Mother of God, I'll be a better mother to the bairn, I promise. Just save our Margaret!'

She closed her eyes and carried on praying. If she could just see her daughter through the night, the worst of it might be over. . .

A hand touched her gently on the shoulder, shaking her awake. Rose looked up, needles of pain pricking her neck and shoulders as she moved. It was Maggie returned at last.

'Where've you been? Where's the doctor?' Rose gasped. Maggie looked grey-faced, her dark eyes sunken.

'I went all over Jarrow,' Maggie said wearily. 'I tried, but I couldn't find him.'

Rose turned from her in frustration. Then it struck her that Margaret's noisy breathing had eased. Her heart leapt with relief to see her daughter's restful pose. The florid flush had gone from her cheeks and her eyes were half open, looking over at her.

'Margaret,' she smiled, leaning forward and brushing her forehead.

Her hand recoiled. The girl's skin was cold and clammy to the touch. The fingers that lay on the cover were bunched into a claw-like fist, as if she had tried to grab something at the moment of death. Had she been reaching out for her? Rose clenched her teeth against the wave of nausea in her throat. She had been sleeping while her daughter died! Margaret had searched for her in the dark as the breath was sucked from her body, but she had not been there to comfort her. Had she been afraid? Had she tried to say anything to her? She would never know! How could she have fallen asleep at such a time?

Rose clutched her small cold hand and let out a scream. 'My bairn! Oh, help me, they've taken me bairn!'

Maggie tried to hold her, but she rocked back and forth, howling like a wounded animal. 'No, not Margaret! Not my Margaret! What have I done to deserve this?'

Maggie could not prise her away from the dead girl. Rose clung on to her as if she could will her back to life by warming her in her own arms.

'Rose, don't let the other lasses see you like this,' Maggie said in distress, but it made no difference. Rose was suffering in a terrifying world beyond reason, where grief stabbed at her like hot pokers. How could God have taken away her precious eldest daughter as well as her young husband? What terrible sins had she committed? What protection did she have now? If they could be snatched from her so easily, then what chance had her other children? None of them was safe!

Rose could not stop her weeping; she was shaken by disbelief and loss. Some time later, just before dawn, the younger girls crept into the room and stood around their grief-stricken mother and gawped at the white-faced Margaret lying so still with her mouth open. Rose felt their young arms touching her and patting her shoulders.

'I don't want her to die!' Elizabeth sobbed into her mother's neck, bereft without her older sister.

But Kate rubbed both their backs and said, 'Don't cry, Mammy. Margaret's gone to be with Da and the saints now. She's one of the angels, isn't she?'

Rose turned and looked at their anxious faces in the guttering candlelight. She stretched out her arms to embrace them all.

'Aye, she is,' she whispered, and pulled them into a fierce hug. They held and comforted each other with tears and soft words, until a pale dawn light spread into the room and heralded their first day without Margaret.

Chapter 23

Florrie and Albert came over the river for the funeral. It was a quiet affair on a raw December day with no pretence at a wake afterwards. Old McConnell seemed quite to have lost his mind at the sight of young Margaret's body laid out on the kitchen table and thought it was one of his daughters. Lizzie came home to keep an eye on him and the younger children, but Elizabeth insisted on accompanying her mother to see her favourite sister buried. She would not let Rose out of her sight, her pale face pinched and anxious.

At the graveside, Elizabeth shook with sobs and clung on to her mother's arm as Margaret's coffin was levered into the short gaping grave. But Rose's broad face was expressionless. Her cheeks were purple with cold, and lines of pain marked her colourless mouth, her dark-ringed eyes staring ahead blankly. She had no more tears to cry. She felt as cold and empty as the wintry cemetery in which they stood. A few feet away, the dry stalks of autumn flowers lay like fragile bones beneath the wooden cross on William's grave. Margaret had put them there on their last visit. The poignant thought made Rose crumble inside.

Oh, Margaret! Why had she left her so soon?

She had a sudden desire to throw herself headlong into the open grave, so painful was the thought of being parted from her eldest daughter for ever. She was stopped by the sound of a muffled moan close by. The priest hesitated in his words. For the first time Rose became aware of the small group of people around her. They were all staring. With a shock she realised that the stifled cry must have come from her.

'Don't cry, Mam,' Elizabeth sobbed at her side. 'Don't cry.'

But Rose could not stop the strange strangled sound that rose from the pit of her stomach and shook its way out of her throat as if she were trying to vomit. Maggie took her other arm and held on to her tightly while tearless weeping engulfed her. Only her sister's grip prevented Rose from buckling at the knees. Then the brief committal was over and Maggie took her by the arm and led her swiftly away.

Florrie and Albert made excuses about having to get back to Wallsend and did not make the muddy trek up to Simonside for the meagre cup of tea and biscuits offered them. On returning, Maggie put Rose straight to bed and told the girls to leave her to rest. The next day Rose did not have the strength to get up and Elizabeth assumed the role of eldest sister and got Sarah and Kate to church on time. All that following week, she did the same, getting the younger ones to school and helping her aunt with the washing and ironing, the way Margaret had always done.

Rose was hardly aware of this as she lay in a twilight world of grief in the icy bedroom. Maggie tried to get her to eat, but she looked with incomprehension at the food offered her, as if she had forgotten what it was for. At the end of the week Maggie lost her patience.

'Rose Ann! Are you going to lie there until you die, an' all?' she demanded. 'And what good will you be to your children then? Or don't you remember that you've got four other daughters to care for? It's them that need you now. You're frightening them with your strange ways. Get up out of that bed now!'

Rose was startled by her sister's harsh tone. Despite their recent differences, Maggie had never spoken to her with such anger before. She looked at her helplessly.

'I want to die,' Rose whispered. 'I just want to be left alone.'

'Well, I'll not let you,' Maggie snapped. 'You're not the first woman in the world to lose her husband and one of her bairns - the town's full of 'em! Think what it must have been like for Mam, losing one baby after another when we were little? But did she give up and take to her bed? No! She thought of us and kept hersel' going.'

Rose was winded by her words. 'You don't know what it's like!' she cried.

'No, I don't,' Maggie replied. 'But I do know that you're a strong person and you're brave enough to bear what's been given you. You've ten times more courage than most folk. This isn't like you to turn your face to the wall and give up.'

Rose began to shake. 'I can't do it without them,' she hissed. 'I need William and Margaret. They were the strong ones, not me.'

Maggie stood over her and gripped her shoulder. 'You can do it for them,' she urged. 'Get up out of that bed and be a mother to them unhappy bairns in the other room. Do it for William's sake - for his memory - the way he would have wanted you to - *expected* you to.'

Rose bowed her head and gave way to tears. She wanted to do as Maggie said, but she was overwhelmed with exhaustion and paralysed with fear. She could not face the world beyond these bare walls or the daily struggles of living. She dare not look her sister in the face for she knew she would find her cowardice contemptible.

Maggie stood back, seeing how little effect her words were having. 'Well, lie there and wallow in your self-pity,' she said with disdain. 'You're not the woman I thought you were, Rose Ann. You know who you remind me of now?'

Rose glanced up and saw her sister's disapproving look.

'You're just like old Mrs Fawcett, taking to her bed and not caring an ounce for anyone but herself.' With that, Maggie turned on her heels and left the room, slamming the ill-fitting door as she went.

Rose clutched herself and gasped for breath between sobs. She felt wretched at her sister's condemnation. But to be compared with William's selfish and spiteful mother! That was the most hurtful thing anyone had ever said to her in her life.

She could not lie down again. The calm dark world of isolation and grief into which she had crept had been invaded. Maggie's cruel words had shaken her and set her emotions in turmoil once again. She would find no peace lying there and she would not be compared to the older Mrs Fawcett!

Rose dragged herself out of bed, dressed and emerged in silence from the bedroom. She could not bring herself to speak to her sister, but she helped prepare tea. The girls watched her warily, expectantly. Gathered mutely around the table, their anxious, subdued faces were almost too much for her to bear. Their need for her was so great that she feared she would never be able to satisfy their wants. They were a neverending burden, Rose shuddered.

The next day, Rose went back to the puddling mills and found the gruelling, physical work a blessed relief from her tortured thoughts.

The ordeals of Margaret's birthday and Christmas passed without any celebration. There was scant money for presents, but Rose did not buy any anyway. She could not bear to walk past shops decorated with Christmas baubles, and hurried away from the sound of carollers singing in the streets. Maggie made an attempt to find a few treats for her nieces - tangerines and chestnuts and a length of rope for skipping. She fashioned a rag doll for Mary out of sacking, and made up a wardrobe of miniature clothes from an old cotton dress of Kate's that was past mending. Rose showed no interest in trying to help her.

Danny grumbled that if Rose could not make any effort for her children then neither should they, but Maggie tried to keep the uneasy peace over the holiday period. It was a dismal time. Rose was either sullenly silent or snapped at the girls if they laughed or appeared too boisterous.

'You're in mourning for your sister,' she scolded. 'Have you forgotten her already?"

Kate was the only one who answered back, baffled by her mother's reproach. 'But, Mam, Father O'Brien says Margaret's in heaven with the angels. And you said she's with Da. So she's happy, isn't she? Why can't we be, an' all?'

Rose glared at her daughter, resenting her for making her feel ashamed of her outburst. Kate was right, and she should not take her misery out on the children, but she could not help herself.

'Just show a bit of respect!' Rose snapped back, and the meal was finished in strained silence.

Perversely, Rose found escape only in her drudgery at the puddling mill. She found no comfort in her daughters, who were a constant reminder of what she had lost. Elizabeth's fair hair glimpsed from the back was just like Margaret's; Kate's quick laughter was an echo of William's. At the mill she could work herself into a mindless exhausted state where the only pain that registered was the aching of her arms and the sweat prickling her body.

Lizzie's marriage to the gardener, Peter, was delayed until after a respectable three months of mourning for Lizzie's niece and was held at the end of February. Old McConnell was now too frail to walk down to church, so Danny gave away the bride instead. Rose tried to galvanise herself for the occasion, for she did not wish to cast a shadow over the day. But she was thankful when the couple chose to leave early to return to Ravensworth and the small cottage on the estate where they were starting married life.

Rose and Maggie tried to scrape together enough food for a wedding tea, but none of Peter's family made the journey from County Durham so there was little to mark the occasion out as exceptional.

'I just wanted to keep it quiet,' Lizzie had assured them as they hurried away, leaving her sisters with the impression that she could not leave Simonside and its gloomy atmosphere quick enough.

Rose caught Maggie looking at her resentfully. 'Don't blame me,' Rose said sharply. 'I didn't chase our Lizzie away.'

Maggie said nothing, just turned away wearily. Rose noticed suddenly how large she was, her womb swollen and heavy. It struck her how often Maggie had stopped that day to catch her breath and place her hands on her aching back. Her time must be nearly due.

'Are you all right?' Rose asked her quickly.

'Aye,' Maggie grunted, and busied herself clearing the table.

'Sit yourself down,' Rose ordered, 'the lasses can do that.'

'The lasses are out playing in the dark,' Maggie said pointedly.

Rose realised that none of them was to be seen. Half the time she had no idea where they were or what they were doing; she had a pang of guilt. Maggie knew more about her daughters these days than she did.

'I'll call them in,' Rose said quickly.

'Rose,' Maggie said, stopping her at the door. They looked warily at each other. 'When me baby comes,' Maggie faltered, 'will you help deliver it?'

Rose's heart lurched at the thought of having to bring another life into the world. It would be a painful reminder of those times of expectation and happiness that she had shared with William. But looking at Maggie's nervous face she knew she must not let her down. Her sister had done so much for her and she deserved her own moment of triumph.

'Of course I'll help you,' Rose agreed. For a brief moment they both smiled, then Rose dived out into the dark to call in her children.

Chapter 24

Less than a month later, before the end of March, Maggie went into labour. She had a difficult time, and Rose watched with alarm throughout the day and into the night, while trying to keep a fretful Danny and her inquisitive children at bay. She packed the girls off to bed, but Danny refused to go further than the fireside. Fearing she might have to send Danny for the doctor, Rose shut herself in the bedroom with Maggie and prayed. In the early hours of the morning, the baby finally came and put an end to the hours of exhaustion and worry.

At the moment of birth, Rose steeled herself to hold the slippery infant and hand her into Maggie's arms.

'It's a lass,' she croaked, her eyes filling with tears as she gave a trembling smile to her sister.

Maggie's face shone with elation and joy. 'Oh, Rose,' she cried. 'A lass of our very own! Gan and tell Danny quickly.'

Rose nodded and went wearily into the kitchen, touching Danny's shoulder gently where he dozed in the fireside chair. He jerked awake at once.

'You can go to her now,' Rose smiled. 'You've a baby daughter.'

Danny's face broke into an excited grin. He leapt up and kissed Rose on the cheek. Rose tensed at the contact, the coarse words of John McMullen flooding into her tired mind. She knew her brother-in-law would never take advantage of her, that he had just enjoyed boasting about having two women in the house. But she no longer felt easy in his company. She pushed Danny away from her.

'Save that for Maggie and the bairn,' she told him stiffly, and turned away.

He almost ran from the room. Rose went and stood by the flickering fire and rested her head against the mantelpiece. She felt utterly drained and very old. The two years without William seemed like ten. She had been slaving in the puddling mill for almost a year and a half, yet she could hardly remember a time when she had not worked there. Her former life in Raglan Street seemed like someone else's.

As she stared into the fire, trying to remember what it felt like to be happily exhausted, holding a new baby in her arms, she heard Danny's excited voice through the open door.

'Of course we can!' he exclaimed. 'She's right bonny -just like her mam. No other name would do.'

'But what about ...?' Maggie sounded uncertain.

'I'll not have that sister of yours ruling our lives any longer.' Danny was adamant. 'This is our home and our baby. We'll call our lass what we like.'

Rose held herself stock-still, her heart beginning to hammer as she realised what they were talking about.

'We're calling her Margaret,' Danny declared. 'Margaret Kennedy.'

Rose felt thumped in the stomach at his words. They were going to call their girl *Margaret*. How could they do such a thing? It was all she could do to stop herself crying out in anguish. The baby had not reminded her of any of her daughters, but now suddenly hearing that precious name, Rose nearly crumpled to the hearth. How could she carry on living in this place where she would have to hear her dead daughter's name mentioned every day? It would tear her apart!

Rose managed to make it to the door and slip outside into the cold damp darkness. She gulped for air, but the panic in her chest would not subside. She felt hemmed in by the blackness, the smell of dank earth at her feet, the brooding cottage at her back that felt more like prison now than home. But then it no longer was her home, she told herself brutally. Danny was right: this place belonged to him and Maggie. She and her children were only there on sufferance, at the mercy of their charity. Even her own father was a stranger there; he no longer knew or cared where he was. Besides, her sister and brother-in-law had every right to call their daughter Margaret if they chose. Hadn't her own Margaret been called after Maggie too?

'Oh, Margaret!' she cried out in the dark. But not a soul heard her as her words were whipped away on a raw wind blowing off the river.

Far below, a lurid glow lit the town from the furnaces that never slept - the ceaseless workings of the mills. Despair and desolation swept over her at the realisation that this was her lot in life from now on. A life without purpose, world without end.

Long days of back-breaking work, then the toil uphill to be faced with the drudgery of making ends meet for her ever-needy daughters. Compounding this was the guilt of impoverishing Maggie further and the fear of Danny's growing resentment. How long before he forced them to find somewhere else to live? She should have gone long ago, but could not face the thought of coping alone again, especially now without Margaret's help.

Margaret. Above all, would be the pain of loving a new Margaret who wasn't her Margaret - could never be hers.

Rose stumbled forward, not knowing where she was going, only that she had to get away. She went without a shawl to pull over her head in the wind, but she did not feel its bite as she fled down the muddy path and out of the gate. It banged behind her, but she did not look back. On she hurried, past the fallen-down pigeon loft where she had sheltered as a girl with the youthful William. A sob caught in her throat as she thought of it. But the pigeons were long gone and the fields were being swallowed up by grimy tenements advancing uphill from the overcrowded town. It no longer felt like the haven it had once been. There was no longer refuge on this hill, only relentless grind and pointless striving to get out of the mire.

The mud sucked at her boots and squelched as she pulled them out and ran on. Through empty streets she went, panting for lack of breath, but still she forced herself on. By the rank smell around her, Rose knew she had reached the Don. She followed it down, past the gaunt ghostly outline of the ruined monastery and the empty rectory where the Liddells had once lived. It had been abandoned by the clergy for a more manageable house in Croft Street. If only the kind couple had still been there to turn to in these desperate times!

Rose's mind crowded with memories of William and the Liddells and past times of happiness. Out of breath as she was, she felt her steps now had some purpose, as if someone - some presence - was leading her on.

'I'm coming,' she gasped. 'Wait, I'm coming!'

A few minutes later she was standing on the banks of Jarrow Slake. The tide was in. Its putrid molten blackness lapped at her feet, opening up before her like a deep, bottomless void. She could hear the creaking and groaning of seasoned timber as it bobbed on the high water. The sounds that had terrified her as a girl, that she believed were the cries of Jobling's ghost, held no fear for her now. Jobling's gibbet had gone sixty years ago and even if his ghost haunted this desolate place, she did not mind. Ghosts no longer frightened her. Rather, she longed for ghosts, for the restless souls of her beloved William and Margaret to come and claim her.

Rose knew that the only way she could gain peace of mind was to join them, to step into the Slake and cross to the far side, to the hereafter. Part of her knew that what she proposed to do - to take her own life - was a mortal sin. But what sort of life was it? What use was she to anyone? Her daughters would be better off without her. Maggie was a far better mother to them than she was. Rose had given her girls every last ounce of her strength and love, but now they had sucked her dry. She had nothing left to give them. She was as insubstantial as a husk blown away on the wind. The world would not miss her.

But William and Margaret did. They were impatient to be reunited. She could hear them moaning on the wind, calling to her in the mournful cry of the seagulls in the dawn. This was why Jobling's spectre had called through the elements all these years. He was beckoning his widow to follow. He would not rest until they were together again.

Rose felt sudden urgency with the growing light. She must have been standing there for quite some time, because it had been dark as pitch when she had arrived. She was chilled to the bone in her thin dress. The Slake was turning grey and less mysterious, its enticing sigh lessening with the falling of the wind. It was time to go or her chance would disappear with the coming of the new day. Already, the vivid image of William and Margaret waiting for her was fading.

'Wait for me!' Rose cried.

She stepped off the bank and tumbled forward into the filthy frothing water. Her skirts floated up around her for a moment, then turned heavy and began to drag her down. She screamed at the impact of the icy river around her legs and thighs. Then the breath froze in her chest and she could not breathe or cry out. Fear gripped her. She was going to drown in this foul water, all alone. There was no William there waiting for her, she realised in panic. She was taking her own life and she'd go to Hell for doing so. Rose would be divided from William for the rest of eternity!

As she went down, the water enclosing her waist and breasts, she found her voice and screamed for help. Her mouth filled with stinking water. She spluttered and flung her arms above her head, trying to cling on to one of the floating planks.

There was a splash further up the bank, but Rose could not turn her head to see if it was human or animal. She went under again. Her mind filled with thoughts of her daughters waking and finding her gone, their sleepy faces turning to panic. She didn't want to die! Too late she realised how much she wanted to live, wanted to hold her children in her arms once more. What madness had tricked her into taking such a drastic step? Her foolish, fanciful obsession with Jobling's ghost had finally been her undoing. The long-ago tragedy was claiming another life.

Suddenly someone gripped her by the hair and pain shot through her scalp. Then they had hold of her arm. She was yanked towards the bank, as strong arms went around her chest and hung on to her.

Her rescuer hauled her on to the slimy bank and rolled her, spluttering, on to her side. She retched and spat out the foul water, her chest heaving in relief. It was several moments before she had the breath to look up. A dark figure leaned over her, panting with the exertion. His sour breath smelt of whisky.

'You daft bitch!' he cried. 'What you doing down here—' He broke off as recognition dawned on them both. 'Rose!'

Through her strands of wet hair she stared back at the astonished face of John McMullen.

Chapter 25

For a long moment they simply stared at each other. How was it that the treacherous Slake had thrown them together once more? Rose had felt drawn to its brooding, malign presence, its promise of oblivion. She had yearned for its nothingness, for the pain inside to stop.

Yet at the point of drowning, she had been seized by a desperate desire to cling on to life. She wanted to see her daughters again, to smell the earth of Simonside, to see the sun set and the moon rise. She longed for the comfort of human touch. All this she knew in a few short seconds of struggle in the evil Slake.

How strange that she should have been rescued by John McMullen, a man she half feared and had always connected with Jarrow Slake since the day he had tried to frighten her with Jobling's ghost. He seemed to embody its dangerous depths, its hypnotic pull. He gazed at her now with his fierce look, and she braced herself for some brutal remark about throwing her back in the water now he could see who it was.

So Rose spoke first. 'I slipped,' she panted.

He snorted in disbelief. 'You were standing there for ages, then you jumped.'

'You were watching me?' Rose exclaimed.

'I could see you as I came down the bank,' John mumbled.

'What you doing out here at this time in the mornin'?' Rose asked, noticing his dishevelled, unshaven appearance.

'I was ganin' to ask you the same,' John grunted.

He was not going to tell her that he had got so drunk the night before that he had lost his way home and stumbled into the monastery ruins, finally finding shelter in an outhouse of the old rectory under a pile of sacking. Waking stiff and cold, he had wended his way down the Don, cursing the thudding in his head until he caught sight of the lonely figure standing by the Slake. It seemed to mirror his own feeling of isolation, of being cut off from the people around him, however crowded his surroundings.

Ever since his return from India he had felt himself different, set apart by his journeying and soldiering. He had no words to describe what he had experienced: blinding sun on rock, the smell of heat, raging thirst, the chatter of a foreign tongue around the village oven, the terrifying sound of an enemy charge.

Much of the time he had fought tedium rather than tribesmen, had longed for cold rain, a green riverbank, a coal fire. But he had also lived with danger, felt the gut-wrenching fear and exhilaration of living on the brink of death and surviving. It was not the debilitating danger of poverty, the long-drawn-out anxieties of slump and fever that faced people on Tyneside for years on end. His had been a glorious danger written about in the London newspapers; he had been one of Lord Roberts's heroes in the Afghan campaigns.

But what good had it done him? The faraway war was long forgotten, as was their gruelling march across parched merciless terrain from Kabul to Kandahar. They had marched till they dropped, half mad with fatigue and hunger. Roberts, from his horse, had forced them onwards. He had become a national hero, rewarded for his daring. But the men, John thought bitterly, had been pensioned off and forgotten about.

Where once he had hankered after Jarrow and to be able to boast around its pubs, now all he craved was one hot day in the sun, listening to the banter of his fellow soldiers. At times he longed for that heightened sense of living, the headiness of existing for the moment, rather than the drabness of civilian life. He seemed forever cursed with not being able to have what he wanted, with being in one place and hankering after another.

Catching sight of the forlorn figure on the banks of the Slake, John had been struck by their common unhappiness. Here was another desperate soul, he felt sure of it. Yet his first impulse was to turn and avoid a meeting. It was just some broken woman who had had enough - let her throw herself in if she wanted. He watched the woman pitch forward, half fascinated to see how long she would take to drown. But when she had started to shout and struggle against death, John had acted instantly. Some instinct deep within, or maybe it was just his training, made him jump in after her and pull her to safety.

What a shock it had been to find Rose Fawcett in his arms! This woman who plagued his thoughts, who attracted him yet rebuffed and humiliated him with her rejection of marriage. Would he never be rid of her?

Rose could not answer his question of why she was there. She was too ashamed to admit that she had tried to take her own life. What a coward she was! But she could see from the harsh look on his wolfish face that he already knew. It would give him further cause to despise and mock her. She hung her head.

'Well, Rose?' he demanded. 'What were you thinking of? With all them lasses depending on you! Were you ganin' to leave Maggie with all your troubles?'

Rose nodded, unable to face him. He let out an oath.

'What kind of mother are you?' he asked angrily. 'It's not as if folk haven't tried to help you! But you're too proud for that, aren't you, Mrs Fawcett?' he said scornfully. 'You threw my offer to wed back in me face – but you'd risk your mortal soul by hoying yoursel' in the Slacks instead!'

Rose looked up. She was shaking so violently with cold and remorse that she could hardly speak through chattering teeth. 'Ay-aye - I-I know,' she whispered, meeting his hard look. His frank words were more than she could bear. 'I d-didn't know what else to do—' She broke down sobbing.

John's chiselled face showed no flicker of sympathy. 'I never thought you'd be the kind of lass to give up and desert your bairns - and you from good Irish stock. You must've gone soft, being married to Fawcett.'

Rose was aghast. 'Don't you speak ill of the dead,' she hissed at him. 'William was a good man, the best husband and father there ever was!'

John was riled by her words. He hated to think of Rose so happy with his old rival. 'He was weak,' John growled. 'Mam said you had to gan skivvying for the Anglicans whenever he got sick. And look at you now! He's left you and the bairns with nowt - and you with your Irish spirit knocked out of you.'

'Don't you preach at me,' Rose cried in fury. 'You've never been married or had to watch your bairn get sick and not be able to stop her dying! You don't know what it's like to lose someone so dear. You've always just thought of yourself and where your next drink's coming from. I've lost a grand husband,

and Margaret - me canny, canny lass.'

She covered her face in her hands and wept in distress. Moments before, she had been relieved to see him, grateful at her deliverance. Yet within minutes John had succeeded in upsetting her again. He was hateful for his unkind words! What use was it trying to make such a heartless man understand the depths of her grief? Rose crouched over her knees as if she could protect herself better from his verbal assault, hoping he would get up and leave her alone.

The last thing she expected was to feel his hand on her shoulder. She flinched in shock, looking up in alarm. Her distrust of him must have shown, for he quickly pulled back. But his expression had changed. John looked shaken by her outburst. Without a word, he slipped off his crumpled jacket and held it out to her. Rose did not move or attempt to take it. John edged forward and wrapped it around her cold wet shoulders.

'You'll catch a chill,' he said gruffly.

What he yearned to say to her was that he did know how she felt. Her grief-stricken words had stirred up the deeply buried pain over his dead Sultana, but more especially his sweet daughter, Ruth. Was it ever possible for such a deep wound to heal? Looking at Rose's haggard, tear-swollen face, John doubted it. In that moment, he felt the loss as keenly as on the day he learned of their deaths. He looked at Rose and wanted to shield her from the raw hurt and despair that tore at her heart too.

Overcoming his fear at touching her, of being rebuffed, John tightened his jacket further about her and put an arm around her back. He tensed and waited. But Rose did not shrink away from him in disgust. She continued to weep and look at him with large despairing eyes. He pulled her into his hold and gently stroked her matted hair.

'I'm so unhappy,' Rose sobbed. 'I miss them that much!'

'I know,' John whispered and held her tighter, 'I know.'

Rose was perplexed by his sudden kindness, suspicious even. But she was too exhausted to care why he had stopped haranguing her. It was such a relief to feel someone's arms enfold her and give her warmth. She had not felt a man's arms around her in so long; she had forgotten how comforting it was. And John's were strong and protective, his hold surprisingly tender. She leaned her head against his shoulder and closed her eyes.

John thrilled at the feel of Rose in his arms, the trusting weight of her body against his. He dared to kiss her lightly on her hair.

'I'm sorry for the things I said to you,' he said in a low voice. 'It's a terrible thing to lose a bairn - the worst kind of thing. And I had no right to say them cruel words about your husband. It was just me jealousy.'

'Jealousy?' Rose questioned. 'Why should you have been jealous of William?'

John gave a groan. 'Oh, Rose lass! You must have known how much I cared for you? Wasn't it obvious at our Michael's wedding when we danced together? I kissed you, remember?'

Rose did and it was not a pleasant memory. He had tasted of stale whisky and made her feel nauseous after William's sweet kiss.

'But you were just drunk,' Rose said, embarrassed by the turn of conversation.

'Maybes,' John grunted, 'but I thought the world of you, drunk or sober. I hated the way Fawcett could say clever things and make you laugh and smile at him.' He murmured into her hair, 'I thought that night that maybe you did care for me a bit - dancing with me and letting me kiss you. That's why I came up Simonside with that bunch of flowers,' John admitted ruefully. 'You weren't in, but you must've found them. They were the only flowers I've ever picked for a lass - or ever will. Daft of me! No doubt you and your sisters had a good laugh over it.'

Rose sat up and stared at him, the memory of the wild flowers on the doorstep coming back to her. She had thought they were from William. It was those flowers that had spurred her on in her courtship of her husband! But all the time they had been from John. He had unwittingly thrown her and William closer together by his romantic gesture.

'I never knew they were from you,' Rose whispered.

He looked at her sharply, but he could see the astonishment on her face. John sighed. 'Well, it doesn't matter now. Wouldn't have made any difference any road, would it? You were Fawcett's lass, I could see that. That's why I joined the army - wasn't going to stop around to see the pair of you wed.'

Rose shook her head in disbelief. 'You never joined the army because of me?'

'Aye, I did.' John flushed, suddenly embarrassed by his admission. He was seldom so loose-tongued when sober. Rose could make him do and say things that no other woman had ever done.

Rose could not help but be flattered by his candid confession. To think that the taciturn youth who used to tease and frighten her had been sweet on her all along! Her sisters had seen it, but Rose had dismissed their ribald comments as nonsense. She thought of her and John's first walk together back to Simonside with the bag of cinders, and how her interest in him had been sparked by his passionate talk of Ireland. As a young lass, before her heart had been won by William, had she not also been interested in the darkly handsome John? Rose blushed to think of it.

Sitting so close to him now, with his brawny arm still heavy on her shoulder, she realised that he still had brooding good looks, despite his weather-ravaged face. His jaw was strong and angular, his nose long and straight, his eyes a mesmerising green. Her pulse began to beat more rapidly at the thought of their proximity.

'I never said thank you for you saving me life,' she said hoarsely, 'but I'm glad that you did.'

He scrutinised her face. 'Aye, so am I.'

For a minute, neither of them spoke, but both were aware that the atmosphere had changed. There was a heightening of feeling between them.

'How will you manage, Rose?' he asked quietly.

'I don't know,' she whispered. 'I just know I can't be separated from me bairns. I'll do anything to keep us from the workhouse and being split up. That would kill me for sure.'

He fumbled for her hand and held it firmly in his. She felt her numb fingers tingle in his warm grip.

'Marry me, Rose,' he rasped. 'Let me look after you and the lasses. I have me faults, I'll grant you - I'm not a saint like Fawcett - but I'll do me best for you lass, that I promise.'

Rose felt tears sting her eyes. She was touched by his fond words and earnest expression. Hope leapt in her heart. Perhaps John could give her and the girls a secure future, as well as a rough, bashful love. By the saints, she could hardly be any worse off than she was now! She imagined how relieved Maggie and Danny would be at such a marriage. But what of the girls? There was no reason why they should not grow fond of John as a stepfather in time. Maybe all he needed was a good wife to love him back, to curb his wilder nature, and then the fighting and drinking would be things of the past. She would take courage from such a thought.

Rose smiled at him tremulously. 'Aye, John, I will,' she agreed. 'I'll marry you.'

He stared at her in amazement. 'You will?' he demanded.

Rose nodded and smiled more broadly.

John gave a cry of triumph. Laughing, he seized her chin in his rough hand and planted a lusty kiss on her lips.

Chapter 26

Rose and John were married in a quiet ceremony at the beginning of May. Rose was still in mourning for Margaret and so wore her black dress of bombazet, trimmed for the occasion with white lace at the collar and cuffs, taken from Lizzie's wedding dress. Her only piece of jewellery was a mourning necklace woven with strands of Margaret's fair hair.

'Won't John mind you wearing widow's clothes?' Maggie asked anxiously.

'That's what I am,' Rose answered brusquely. 'Anyways, it's me only smart dress. He won't have to mind.'

And John didn't. 'Doesn't matter what you wear, lass,' he assured, 'as long as you wed me.'

Rose was charmed by his eager attentiveness to her in the days before they were married. He would appear at the garden gate, scrubbed, shaven and dressed in his army jacket, his hair wetted and combed into place. He brought small gifts - a lace handkerchief for her, a twist of lemon drops for the girls - and stayed to tea. Rose was delighted that he came sober and without the slightest hint of drink on his breath. They would walk out beyond the smallholding, across the fields to the stream, with Sarah and Kate scampering behind at a distance, and talk of the future.

'I've found a place to rent,' John told her proudly one evening.

'Where?' Rose asked, turning to him in excitement.

'House in Albion Street,' he grinned. She tried not to show her disappointment. It was in a crowded part of the town, hemmed in by the coke and steel works.

'It's got four rooms,' he added quickly.

Rose brightened. 'Four rooms? Tell me about it.'

'Parlour at the front, kitchen at the back and two bedchambers upstairs. One for the lasses, one for us,' he said, pinching her cheek.

Rose flushed. 'Can we afford it?'

'Course we can,' John said indulgently. 'I've got me army pension and I can pick up carrying work easily enough.'

'I suppose I could stay on at the mill for a bit till we get sorted,' Rose suggested half-heartedly.

'No you won't,' John was adamant. 'I'll not have my wife slaving in that place. You'll stop at home and keep house for me and the bairns. I'll do the providin'.'

Rose felt utter relief at the thought of never having to face the furnace of the puddling mill again. Daily she felt the poisonous, debilitating fumes weakening her body, leaving her breathless and limp. At times, violent pains stabbed her stomach and when these subsided, lethargy would settle on her like a winding sheet. Just in time, John had saved her from complete exhaustion and an early death, she was sure of it.

'We'll need furniture.' Rose began planning ahead eagerly. 'I've got little to bring from here - just the bed and the feather mattress, a few pots and candlesticks.'

'I'll take care of that,' John nodded. 'We'll get some stuff from the store - a dresser and a canny oval table with chairs. Me brothers'll help shift it.'

Rose slipped her arm shyly through his and smiled. She had no idea John had this much money to spend and it made him the more attractive. 'To have me own home again -I can hardly believe it. I cannot thank you enough for taking on me and the bairns.'

John leant towards her and lowered his voice so the girls could not hear. 'There's only one way you can show your thanks, Rose Ann, and that's to be me wife - truly me wife in every way.'

Her heart began to thump at his words and the way he looked her over keenly with his vivid eyes. It made her uncomfortable the way he could be so proper one moment and suggestive the next. The consummation of their marriage had never been mentioned, though Rose remembered only too well that it had been the reason for her refusing his proposal before. He had been furiously disdainful of her offer to be his housekeeper but not lie with him. She remembered with unease how he had said he wanted her to bear him sons.

But since his rescue of her from the Slake and the eager kiss that had sealed their betrothal, Rose was not so averse to the idea of sharing John's bed. She felt the stirring of interest in such intimacy that she had thought never to feel again.

'I've said I'll be your wife,' she answered quietly.

He smiled in satisfaction and she knew he wanted to kiss her, but she pulled away, too aware of the girls chattering behind them. She saw annoyance flicker across his face.

'Haway, Rose,' he urged, 'just a little one.'

'Not here,' she murmured, seeing that Sarah and Kate had stopped to watch them with interest. Elizabeth stood further off, trying to contain a fractious Mary.

He turned on them crossly. 'What you lookin' at?'

The girls were startled, then Kate piped up, 'Are you ganin' to kiss me mam?'

Sarah giggled; Elizabeth looked anxious. Rose exclaimed, 'Kate, don't be so cheeky!'

'And what if I was?' John demanded, stepping nearer. 'Your mam and me are going to be wed and we'll do as we please.'

Kate smiled, undaunted. 'She used to kiss me da, an' all.'

John's face clouded and for one awful moment Rose thought he was going to strike her daughter. She half stepped forward to intervene, when he suddenly relaxed and barked with laughter.

'Well, in a week's time I'm ganin' to be your da,' he said, ruffling her hair. He glanced at Rose as he added, 'And I'll be the only man she'll be kissing from now on.'

Only one matter marred the preparations for Rose. Florrie and Albert refused to come to the wedding. She received a terse note from Mrs Fawcett, written in Albert's hand, condemning her for remarrying. In her mother-in-law's eyes, she was betraying William and committing a sin by taking another man. A respectable widow should never remarry and she disowned Rose for doing so. She and Florrie would have no more to do with her or her family.

Rose crumpled up the note in fury. 'It's all right for her!' she railed at Maggie. 'She can afford to be a respectable widow with a posh son-in-law to keep her. I've got no other choice. If she cared that much about her son's precious memory, she would have tried to help me out when I needed it. But she's never stopped punishing me for winning William away from her. When did she ever lift a finger to help her own grandbairns? She washed her hands of us years ago!'

'Don't upset yoursel',' Maggie comforted. 'She's never had a good word to say about us McConnells - why should she start now? It doesn't matter what she thinks.'

'But Florrie too?' Rose said in distress.

'She'll just be going along with it to keep the peace,' Maggie reasoned. 'It's her we should be sorry for - having to put up with a mam like that every day.'

Rose's anger subsided. 'Aye, you're right,' she sighed. 'I just thought we could have kept friends.'

Maggie put a hand on her shoulder. 'You'll not be a Fawcett much longer. That's all in the past, so stop dwelling on it. It's the McMullens are your family now.'

Rose felt a deep pang of longing for her old life, for the name she had borne so proudly and that still linked her to William. But her sister was right, she had to put all that behind her and make the best of her new life with John. At least his family did not judge her harshly and his mother was as kind and welcoming as could be.

So on the eve of her marriage, Rose plunged her left hand in cold water and rubbed fat around her knuckle to help ease off William's wedding ring. Unable to part with it completely, she tied it to a piece of string and hung it around her neck, out of sight under her bodice where she could feel it touching her breast close to her heart.

The marriage ceremony was over swiftly, without fuss, but the McMullens were not going to be done out of a celebration. They brought jugs of beer and jars of whisky up to Simonside and danced outside until the stars came out. Rose's father thought he was back in Ireland, broke into song and then wept like a child. He had no idea whose wedding it was.

'Shouldn't we be going?' Rose tried to coax John away. 'The lasses are falling asleep.'

'Aye, in a minute,' John answered, giving her waist a pinch, then helping himself to one more drink.

Finally the beer ran out and, amid much noise and confusion, a party set off down the hill towards the town, a procession of John's brothers carrying Rose's bundles of clothes, bedding and sleepy-eyed children. All except Mary, who had crawled into Maggie's bed and been found fast asleep.

'Leave her be,' Maggie suggested. 'You can fetch her the morra.'

Rose accepted, not relishing the thought of waking her youngest and provoking a tantrum. They arrived noisily in Albion Street, Rose embarrassed by the loud laughter and ribald jokes of her new brothers-in-law as they pushed an unsteady John through the front door of Number 54. To her dismay, one of them produced a bottle of whisky and the drinking continued in the kitchen, where the fire was still to be laid and lit. The men did not seem to notice.

Rose sent the girls outside to use the privy and went upstairs to lay blankets on the beds. Soon she had the three girls bedded down in their old feather bed, while she made up the narrow brass bed that John had secured from the Kennedys. 'We'll have a new one soon,' he had promised.

'They're makin' too much noise for us to get to sleep,' Elizabeth fretted.

'I like to hear voices,' Kate yawned. 'It's homely.'

'Everything's covered in black dust, Mam,' Sarah complained. It was true. Rose had spent hours scrubbing floors and ledges two days ago, but the grime had blown in once more under ill-fitting windows and doors.

'Hush now,' Rose bade them. 'Tomorrow you can help me clean out the house - we'll have it looking grand in no time.'

There was a loud thud from below followed by cursing and laughter.

'What's that, Mam?' Elizabeth asked, wide-eyed.

'Just the McMullens carrying on,' Rose said disapprovingly, then checked herself. It wouldn't do to be too critical of them now that they were family. She didn't want to show John in a bad light to her daughters for they were under his authority now. She felt a small prick of misgiving as she added, 'Everyone's entitled to a bit of carry-on at a weddin'. It's tradition.'

Rose didn't go back downstairs, but made ready for bed. When John failed to appear, she blew out the candle and settled to sleep in the hope that he might have drunk too much to climb the stairs. Let him sleep it off on the large uncomfortable wooden settle that he had won in some wager on his return from India and that had been cluttering up his mother's house ever since. She did not relish his drunken attentions or whisky-reeking breath tonight, she thought as she drifted into a pleasant state of semi-sleep.

A clatter on the stairs and a thumping on the wall behind her head shook Rose wide awake. It was pitch-black and the voices below had ceased. Feet stumbled outside the bedroom door.

'Where've you gan, lass?' John shouted. 'Where y' hidin'?'

She sat up, alarmed he would wake the children. 'Hush! I'm in here,' she answered in a loud whisper.

John laughed and pushed at the handleless door. 'Are you warming the bed, Mrs McMullen?' he chuckled.

'Haway and shut the door,' she hissed. 'You'll wake the neighbours with your shouting.'

'Bugger the neighbours!' John cried, and lurched towards the bed. Belching roundly, he plonked himself down and contemplated his feet. 'Rose, me boots seem a long way off.'

Rose sighed and hauled herself out of bed. 'Here, let me help you.'

He let her undress him, hiccupping and laughing like a schoolboy when it came to removing his trousers and braces. Lunging at her in the dark, he pulled her to him.

'Gis a kiss,' he urged, enveloping her in beery fumes.

Rose wrinkled her nose in distaste. 'You smell like a brewery.'

'Aye, and taste like one, an' all,' he laughed. 'But then I've seen you down a mug of beer like mother's milk at the mill. So don't go turning your pretty nose up at me.'

Rose decided it was best to say no more, but lie back and get on with it. She closed her eyes tight shut as John covered her mouth in a slobbery kiss and held herself still as his hands cupped around her breasts and squeezed them

146

hard. His breathing came harder as he kissed his way across her face and licked inside her ear. He whispered things to her that made her hot with embarrassment. Drink had loosened his tongue and bawdy thoughts about her.

'I've waited years for this,' he rasped, as he tugged at her nightgown and hitched it up around her thighs. 'You're mine now, Rose, the way you should've been years ago.'

John climbed on top of her and took her swiftly, grunting with pleasure and effort. Rose was reminded of one of her father's pigs, but tried to rid her mind of the image in case she snorted with laughter. It was over quickly and John collapsed back on the bed with a triumphant sigh. He laid his head on her breast, one arm thrown over her belly.

'It's done,' he murmured. 'Now it's your job to give us a bairn.'

Within seconds, he was asleep and snoring gently like the drone of a bee.

Rose lay staring in the darkness, wide awake. It felt strange to have the weight of a man's head on her chest and the heat from his body next to hers. She had grown used to Kate's restless movements in bed beside her and Elizabeth's troubled sleep-talking.

But now she was Mrs McMullen, a married woman again. It had to be better than the lowly, vulnerable status of widow. For she had a house to call her own once more; she had escaped the servitude of the puddling mill and had a man to provide for her children. She put a tentative hand on John's head and stroked his thick wiry hair. What kind of a man had she married? Rose wondered. She had yet to discover.

But the feel of his strong body lying contentedly next to hers was not unpleasant. She was no longer battling in the world alone. Her guardian angel, whom she had come to doubt, was looking after her still. With that comforting thought, Rose closed her eyes and allowed herself to sleep.

Chapter 27

That summer Rose was happier than she had been for an age. The long period of uncertainty since William's death seemed at an end, the raw grief for her former husband and eldest child had subsided to the bearable. To her surprise, she realised that this was partly owing to John's regard for her.

Her new husband could not do enough for her. If she liked the look of a piece of second-hand china or a tablecloth in a shop window, he would buy it. When a poster advertising a touring troupe at the Albert Hall caught her eye, he took her to see them. Even though they sat far up in the highest tier of the theatre, Rose enjoyed the music hall acts and John sang snatches of the songs for days afterwards.

He filled their small house with singing. On warm evenings when the kitchen door was thrown open to let out the stifling heat from the range, his lusty voice would carry down the back lane where the children played and Rose sat peeling potatoes.

'I love a lassie, a bonny, bonny lassie, She's as sweet as the lily in the dell!'

Rose would blush and laugh and throw a potato at him where he stood washing in the scullery basin, stripped to the waist, showing his taut chest and thick muscled arms. She was silently proud that this good-looking man was hers and that her fears at his waywardness had been unfounded. She had seen no evidence of his reputation for being drunken or boorish since their marriage and she quietly congratulated herself for bringing a calm, sober influence to bear. It had just been a matter of keeping his brothers at bay and John occupied with domestic concerns.

He was not in regular work but there seemed to be plenty of money from his army pension. Some weeks he would pick up a labouring job but mostly he was content to do small jobs around the house such as making a cupboard for the girls' clothes and painting the ceilings. He was not as skilful as William had been, but he was workmanlike and once set to a task would carry on until it was finished. To Rose's delight, John was gruffly affectionate with the girls. He played the army officer and marshalled them into helping him with chores: stirring paint, polishing boots and filling the tin tub for the weekly bath. There was much giggling and splashing on a Friday night in front of the kitchen fire. John teased Elizabeth the most because, at nearly eleven, she had grown painfully modest and refused to bath with her sisters.

When her turn came, she erected a defensive wall of shirts and blankets over the clotheshorse so that no one could see her naked. The house echoed with screams of protest and shrieks of laughter from her sisters if John peered over the screen.

'Tell 'im to stop peekin', Mam!' Elizabeth squealed.

'John,' Rose would scold half-heartedly. 'Let the lass alone.'

But Kate and Sarah egged him on. 'Gan on, Father. Make our Lizzie scream again!'

Rose liked it best when they all gathered around the hearth after tea, she with a piece of mending and John with the last cup from the teapot. He would hand his newspaper to Elizabeth and instruct her to read it to him, saying the print was too small for his eyesight. Rose knew that he could not read a word of it, had even less learning than she, but would never have wounded his pride by saying such a thing.

Kate would sidle up to her stepfather and rest an elbow on his fireside chair, hoping he would pull her on to his knee as William had used to do. But John rarely touched the girls, apart from the occasional bashful ruffle of the hair or pinch of the cheek. At times Rose saw again in him the awkward, callow youth of her girlhood, the John to whom girls were a mystery.

So Kate and Sarah would have to content themselves with squatting on the wooden fender and listening to his tales of Irish heroes and legends. As daylight dimmed and the flickering firelight cast eerie shadows across his gaunt face, the girls would listen entranced to his stories.

'Tell us the one about the leprechaun,' Kate urged one evening when Rose tried to send them to bed. 'Please! Just one more.'

John winked at Rose. 'It's only right they should learn about dear old Ireland - it's in their blood.'

She relented and let him tell his stories one more time, remembering how as a girl she had revelled in her grandmother's ancient tales. There was something comforting in the sound of the rhythmic rise and fall of John's words over the hiss and pop of the fire.

Only when Kate demanded stories about his time in India did Rose see a flash of John's temper.

'There's nowt to tell - not for a bairn's ears, any road,' he snapped. 'What happened there's best forgotten.'

Rose shooed her daughters upstairs with a hissed warning. 'Your father doesn't like speakin' about his army days. It still gives him nightmares. Don't you go bothering him with your questions, Kate, do you hear?'

She did not know why he was so sensitive about India, but sensed in him a deep hurt of which he could not speak. Perhaps she would learn in time.

Soon afterwards, John followed them upstairs and waited impatiently for Rose to join him in bed. His appetite for intimacy seemed never to be satisfied. Sometimes he would wake her in the middle of the night, aroused and eager. He made love with quick urgency, with hardly a word spoken and then sank back to sleep just as swiftly as he had awoken. It was as if he were releasing the pent-up desire of years. Rose did not look on these brief, passionate episodes with the same enthusiasm, yet she was flattered that his want for her was so great.

Only in one matter did they disagree and it caused the single cloud that hung over those contented summer months. That was the question of what to do with Mary. When Rose went back to Simonside to fetch her youngest daughter, the stubborn infant stamped her feet, threw herself on the ground and screamed so loud the rooks in the chimney flew away in panic.

'Me stoppin' here!' she wailed. 'Me stoppin' with me mam!'

Rose looked on in dismay. At first she tried to coax the child. 'Haway, hinny, come to Mammy. We've got a canny new house to live in - I want to show it to you. Your cot's already there and your father's got you a new rag dolly all of your own.'

But when Rose tried to pick her up, Mary turned puce-faced and screamed all the louder. She kicked against her mother, then bit her on the arm. Rose gasped in shock and let go. Maggie tried to intervene.

'You naughty lass,' she scolded. 'You mustn't hurt your mam. You have to gan with her, Mary.'

The hysterical girl clung to Maggie as she lifted her towards Rose and refused to look at her mother. 'You're me mam!' she sobbed into Maggie's breast. 'Won't gan wi' *her*.'

Rose's upset turned to anger. 'I'm your mam whether you like it or not. You'll stop that noise at once and come with me, you little devil! You're not going to spoil things for the rest of us.'

She grabbed Mary roughly and wrested her from Maggie's arms. The girl kicked and screamed and squirmed to be free, but Rose hung on to her, astonished at the strength in the wiry little body.

Maggie followed them anxiously to the door. 'You could leave her a day or two more,' she offered.

Rose clenched her teeth. She could not bear the thought of having to go through such a battle again. 'No,' she snapped. 'John wants to give her a home. She'll come with me now or not at all.'

The sisters exchanged helpless looks, then Rose was hauling the resisting child down the rutted path and out of the gate. All the way down the bank, Mary's shrieks of protest and sobbing rang in Rose's ears. Ashamed and furious, Rose hurried on, not daring to glance about her at the people who stopped to stare at the spectacle. She prayed that she did not run into the priest or a teacher from the girls' school and would have to explain why Mary was in such a state. At that moment she hated her daughter for loving Maggie more than her and for making her feel such a bad mother.

She said terrible things to her youngest that day, hurtful words that later she felt sick at heart for having uttered.

'Your father'll lock you in the cupboard when he hears how bad you've been,' she threatened. 'And you can stay there for ever, for all I care! Your Aunt Maggie's spoilt you rotten. Well, you'll not get any favours from us, you little brat. And if you carry on screaming like this I'll give you away to the gypsies the next time they come selling round the doors.'

By the time they reached Albion Street, both of them were shaking with temper and exhaustion. She pushed Mary through the door and banged it shut on the gawping neighbours. Mary hammered on the door to be let out, but could not reach the handle. Rose was thankful that the girls were at school and that John was out on some errand of his own. She went to the scullery, poured out a cup of water and threw it over the distraught child. Mary froze in shock. She turned and stared at her mother with red, swollen eyes, her cries subsiding. Rose stood wheezing, the storm of anger that had raged in her dying at the sight of her daughter's fearful face. She was seized with remorse.

'I'm sorry,' she whispered, holding out her arms to the child.

But Mary just stood petrified and whimpered, 'Mammy, Mammy, Mammy.'

By the time John returned, Mary was curled up on the hearth asleep, her thumb half in her mouth. Rose was in the yard grimly pounding washing in the poss tub.

'It's not washday, is it?' he smiled in surprise.

'No,' Rose answered curtly, bashing the poss stick with all her might.

'Where's the lass?' he asked cautiously.

Rose nodded towards the kitchen.

'Rose,' John said quietly, 'what's the matter?'

Abruptly Rose stopped and bent her head. She felt her shoulders begin to heave as a deep sob rose up from the pit of her stomach. 'She hates me,' she sobbed. 'Me own flesh and blood! Not even three years old and she hates me guts.'

Instantly John was putting his arms about her and pulling her to him. 'Don't talk daft,' he chided.

She cried into his shoulder. 'It's true - our Mary's never loved me. It's Maggie she wants to stop with, not us.'

'Well, it's us she's got,' John said firmly. 'I said I'd tak on all your bairns and that's what I'm ganin' to do. She's too young to know her own mind, she'll settle given time.'

Rose leaned against him, praying fervently that John was right. Her fondness for him grew. He wanted to care for them all, was more prepared than she was to take on the wilful Mary. But deep down she worried that it was already too late to win Mary's trust and love. The small, unhappy girl seemed to know her own mind only too well.

For a short time, Mary seemed to calm down and accept her new surroundings, particularly when her sisters were there to make a fuss of her. But when Rose was left alone with her, she would become moody and sullen or fly into a tantrum over the smallest upset and cry for an hour at a time. When the weather was fine, Rose tried to tempt her with trips to the park, but these would always end in a tearful scene and Mary being dragged home in disgrace. Eventually, Rose gave up taking her out and dreaded going anywhere with her in public. The girl responded to neither punishment nor treats.

John began to tire of her temper and stubbornness too. She refused to play with the rag doll he had bought her and tore up the paper windmill he made. Mary wandered around clutching her worn and grubby peg doll that Maggie had made for her one Christmas and gazed at them with dark reproachful eyes.

Once, John grew so impatient with her for not doing as she was told, that he seized her peg doll, strode to the back door and hurled it down the back lane. Mary threw herself at the door, screaming like a banshee. Her sisters looked on in alarm, but Rose hushed Kate when she tried to protest.

'She has to learn to behave herself,' she told her daughters, though silently wished John had not been so hasty.

But her husband could not bear the noise and stormed out of the house and did not come back until dusk. To Rose's dismay he was smelling of drink. By this time Mary was asleep in her cot and Rose was not going to tell John that Kate had spent the evening scouring the lane till she found Peggy the peg doll.

'Maybes we should send her back to Maggie's?' Rose suggested as they lay in bed.

'No,' John was adamant. 'I'm not ganin' to let the little bugger beat me! She's my responsibility now. She'll not get her own way so easy with me as she has done with you and your sister.'

'Aye, but it's me who has to put up with her ways, while you're out and about spending money,' Rose complained.

'That's my business, not yours,' John replied sharply. 'I give you plenty for housekeeping.'

'Some weeks,' Rose muttered.

'Every week,' John protested. 'You should spend it with more care.'

'You're one to talk!' she snorted.

'Don't you go telling me what I should or shouldn't be doing, woman!'

Rose turned away in annoyance. For a while they lay not speaking, each resentful of the other. Then she felt John reaching for her, his breath warm on her neck.

'Haway,' he said, relenting, 'let's not fall out over the bairn. Listen, it's the Hoppings next week. We'll all gan together - make a day of it. What do you say?'

Rose was about to say no; she had sworn never to go back to Newcastle's Town Moor since Margaret had gone missing and caused her and William such panic. But she checked herself, aware that John did not like any mention of her former husband.

'Aye, that would be canny,' she said instead. 'The lasses will be over the moon.'

'Grand,' John said in satisfaction, nudging closer. He kissed her cheek and squeezed her waist. Swiftly, his hands hitched up her nightdress and began his familiar fumblings. Soon there was no more talk.

Then three days later, on the eve of Race Week, Mary went missing. Rose had left her for five minutes while she went to the corner to buy currants to put in the rock buns she was making for their Saturday picnic. When she returned there was no sign of her.

In a panic she searched the house, then doubled back across the yard to peer into the gloom of the privy. When there was no sign of her, she picked up her skirts and ran up and down the lane, peering into backyards and shouting breathlessly to neighbours to search their own kitchens for the child.

'Skinny, brown hair - she'll be carrying a peg doll,' Rose panted.

But no one could find her, nor even recall seeing her. When John came back from visiting his mother, they spread the search. He went into the neighbouring streets, calling into pubs and small house shops to ask if anyone knew where the missing girl was.

'Mary McMullen,' he told those who asked her name, 'she's me youngest bairn.'

All afternoon they searched the surrounding streets, even venturing into the middle of town in the faint hope she had climbed on to a cart and been carried further afield. Rose was half demented at the thought of her being run over by the heavy wheels of some goods wagon or spirited away by passing tinkers.

'I'll never forgive mesel' if she's come to any harm,' Rose cried at John in distress. She burned with shame to think of the way she had scolded and resented Mary, taken a hand to her far more often than her sisters. Now all she wanted to do was find her and hug her and never let her go.

It was Kate, returning from school, who suggested where they should look.

'She'll have gone to Aunt Maggie's,' she said straight away.

'Maggie's!' Rose cried in disbelief. 'She couldn't possibly know the way.'

'A lass of her age?' John was dismissive. 'She could never walk that far, even if she did.'

But, at a loss as to what else to do, they all trekked the mile and a half up to Simonside. Maggie was at the gate looking out for them.

'I was going to come and fetch you once Danny got home,' she said in agitation. 'I couldn't leave our Margaret - and Mary - well, she won't budge.'

'She's here!' Rose cried, relief engulfing her. 'Is she all right?'

Maggie nodded. 'She's sitting on her grandda's knee eating plums.'

John exploded, 'I'll give her bloody plums, the little bugger! We've been running round the whole of Jarrow looking for her!'

He strode forward, trying to barge past Maggie, but she barred his way, pushing him back with both hands. 'You'll not gan in there shouting and frightening her,' she said firmly.

He glared at her, astonished to be spoken to so frankly by Rose's younger sister. But Rose knew that Maggie could be mulish too; she would stand her ground, especially where Mary was concerned. Rose stepped between them and put a hand on John's arm.

'The lass is safe, that's all that matters,' she said quietly. 'If she wants to stay with Maggie, what's the harm? I can't be doing with fighting over her any more.'

John swore with incredulity. 'For God's sake, Rose ...' He chewed and pulled on his moustache, a sign, Rose knew, of his agitation. But she looked at him pleadingly.

'Let her stop here for a bit longer, till she knows you better and we're more settled.'

His look was thunderous. 'Don't you blame me for that little beggar's bad ways! If she were mine, I'd give her a hidin' into next week for the trouble she's caused.'

'But she's not,' Rose said impatiently, then instantly regretted her words.

He narrowed his eyes at her accusingly. 'No, she's Fawcett's bitch and your problem, isn't she? You do what you want with her.'

He shook off her hold, turned on his heels and marched off down the path without a backward glance.

The women watched him go, Rose trembling at his harsh words. She felt wretched. Somehow she had mishandled both John and Mary and she had the uneasy feeling that she would pay for it some day. Your chickens always come home to roost, her granny had used to say.

Rose sighed and turned back to Maggie. The girls scrambled for the door, eager to be out of the way of wrangling adults and to see their infamous little sister.

'There's a storm brewing in that one,' Maggie warned, nodding at John's retreating back.

Rose gave a mirthless laugh. 'Maggie, hinny, I'm used to weathering storms.'

Chapter 28

John's anger at Rose for leaving Mary at Simonside did not last longer than a night, though it was a long disturbed night. He came back drunk from The Railway pub, singing raucously about his homeland of Ireland, and broke a plate trying to help himself to mutton pie from the pantry shelf.

'Haway to your bed, man,' Rose cajoled as she picked up the shattered plate and wondered if it could be mended. 'It's late.'

'I'll come when I'm ready,' John snarled, shovelling the uncut pie into his mouth and scattering crust over the oilcloth. He hummed loudly as he ate.

'Keep the noise down,' Rose chided, sweeping up behind him, 'you'll wake the lasses.'

John snorted and focused bleary eyes on her. 'So we've still got some bairns under the roof, have we? Not dumped them all with your sister, eh? Call yoursel' a mother!'

'You know I haven't,' Rose answered tersely, stung by his sarcasm. The day had left her overwrought and tired out. She could do without his petty needling comments.

'Mary, Mary, quite contrary, how does your garden grow?' he taunted before ramming in another mouthful.

'Stop it!' Rose reproached. 'I'll not leave her up there for long - just till she's a bit older and can understand what's what.'

'What's what?' John sneered. 'That her mam cannot teach her manners or how to respect her new father?'

'She's still a baby,' Rose protested.

'That's when they need tellin',' John declared. 'We had respect for our mother and father knocked into us before we were old enough to run away or answer back. If you don't take a strong hand to that Mary now, it'll be too late.' He belched, then added, 'Mark my words, that lass'll give you the run around when she's older.'

'Maybes,' Rose sighed, suddenly too tired to care.

She straightened up and looked at his tousled appearance. It had been an anxious day for him too, she conceded. John had searched as frantically for Mary as if she had been his own daughter. He had found her only to lose her once more to his sister-in-law, a bitter disappointment and blow to his pride as her new stepfather and provider. And Rose was learning just how much that pride meant to John, how quick he was to take offence, how easily his passion was roused.

Drained as she was, Rose knew there was one way left of sweetening his mood. That was if he hadn't drunk too much, she thought drily.

'I'm away to me bed,' she said, holding his look. 'Come with us, John man.'

He regarded her as he sucked the crumbs from his moustache and wiped his mouth across his sleeve. All at once, a boyish grin spread across his face, lightening the look in his eye.

'Why, that's the best bit of sense you've talked all night, Mrs McMullen,' he answered as he took an unsteady step towards her.

Rose smiled and turned quickly for the door. She wasn't going to let him get his hands on her before she had seen him safely up the stairs. He cursed and laughed and stumbled after her, chasing her into the bedroom. The short June night was already giving way to an indigo dawn when their tussling in the bed had ceased and Rose finally got some sleep.

With Mary gone, the tension in the house evaporated. John and Rose took the older girls on the train to the Hoppings fair in Newcastle and Rose walked arm in arm with her husband, thinking they looked a proper family to the outside world. Arriving at the huge echoing Central Station, the girls clutched their parents' hands and stared about them, their eyes wide in wonder at the size and grandeur of the city buildings. The younger ones had never been this far from Jarrow and even Elizabeth had been too young to remember her one and only visit with William.

The girls revelled in the rides and the gaudy side stalls on the Town Moor, while John won a coconut with a powerful shot and bought them all some cinder toffee to share out. Just as they were making their way back to the town, a gypsy woman called out in an Irish voice, 'Come here, lady! Come and buy a fancy piece of Irish lace and I'll tell you your fortune. Come and get a piece of Irish luck, lady!'

Rose would have ignored her and walked on, but John tugged at her arm and turned to smile at the red-haired young woman sitting on an upturned box. She was sharp-featured, with shrewd, lively eyes under fair brows, and knew John was the key to custom. She beckoned to the girls and Kate went closer with curiosity. The gypsy stroked the child's lustrous chestnut hair.

'Sir, you've a fine clutch of pretty daughters, so you have! Buy your lady this piece of lace for the baby she's carrying. It's luck you'll have if you buy from the Irish!'

John flushed with surprise and pleasure. Rose could tell he was captivated by the woman's blarney and pretty smile.

'You're right there, lass. I'm Irish mesel',' John preened, 'a McMullen.' He nodded to Rose. 'But what's this you're saying about me missus expectin'?'

Rose squirmed with embarrassment and remonstrated, 'John! I'm not expectin'. How could a stranger know, anyways?'

The young woman gave her a quick sweeping look and laughed. 'I've the gift of second sight, lady! I can tell by just lookin' at you. Buy this pretty bit of lace for your baby and you'll have the son you want and a christening within the year.'

John removed his cap and scratched his head, letting out a whistle. 'That's grand talk, grand talk! Isn't it, Rose Ann? A lad and a christening! By heck, another John McMullen to carry on the line,' he crowed. 'Would you like a baby brother, Kate?'

Kate, who was listening in open-mouthed fascination, turned to her mother. 'Are we ganin' to have a baby brother, Mam?' she asked in excitement. "Cos he can have Mary's cot.'

Rose put a hand to her mouth, quite flustered. 'No! There's no baby coming - not yet.'

John laughed and put an arm around her waist possessively. 'There will be if the lass says so,' he grinned. 'We'll have the luck of the Irish, you'll see.'

He paid up swiftly for the piece of homespun lace and handed it to Elizabeth for safe-keeping. 'Here, you can look after this until your baby brother comes,' he winked. Turning to the gypsy he asked jovially, 'And what else can you tell me missus about the future?'

'Come here, lady! Let me see your hand,' the girl said, waving her closer.

'I don't hold with such things,' Rose said primly.

'Haway and show the lass your hand, Rose Ann!' John insisted, pulling her back.

'Go on, Mam,' Kate said, enjoying the commotion.

Reluctantly, Rose offered her palm and let the girl rub a grubby thumb across it. Her young face creased in concentration as she studied Rose's calloused hand. After a minute of this, John grew impatient.

'Haway and tell her! How many bairns are we ganin' to have?'

The young woman glanced up, her eyes hooded. She shrugged vaguely. 'Nothin' much to tell.'

Rose was relieved. An uneventful life from now on would suit her fine. She withdrew her hand, but John was suddenly scornful.

'You'll get nowt from me for that. Call yoursel' a fortune-teller? I've heard better predictions from me brother's canary.'

The gypsy looked at him sharply, her pretty eyes narrowing. 'Very well,' she muttered, seizing Rose by the hand and gripping her round the wrist. 'You've had more than your share of sadness - there's loss and death.' Her look was grave. 'And there are hard times still to come.'

John snorted impatiently. 'You could say that about anyone round here. You're tellin' us nowt we don't already know. Haway, Rose, let's gan.' He pulled her away.

But the Irish woman stood up and grabbed at her arm. 'You're heading into the storm - there are rocks ahead and a time of wandering like tinkers. But you mustn't give up. The lives of others are tied to yours.' Her urgent look filled Rose with foreboding and she snatched her hand away.

'You're talking gibberish!'

'No!' the gypsy cried. 'You must keep afloat in the storm and choose your course wisely. Only if you do that will you come through the worst into the sunset. The angel child is waiting for you there to sweeten your old age.'

For a brief moment, Rose had a picture of Margaret standing waiting for her in a doorway, her hair bound in ringlets and head tilted, a quizzical smile on her lips. An angel child.

But the image was shattered by John's angry cursing. 'Load of rubbish! Storms an' angels. D'you think I'm daft? Here, you can have your cheap bit of lace, an' all. I want me money back, you thieving little bitch!' He tore the lace from Elizabeth's hands and thrust it menacingly in the woman's face. 'Give us me sixpence!'

She pulled the coin from a cloth purse around her neck and spat on it. 'I don't want it - there's blood on it - the blood of foreign men!' She tossed it at him. 'You're full of fight, but you've the heart of a coward,' she mocked. 'You're the sort of man who picks on the weak.' The look she gave was venomous. 'May the son that sleeps in your wife's belly be the one to stand up to you. May he bring you not a minute's peace till the day he dies!'

Rose saw the look of shock on John's face ignite into fury. She grabbed the arm that he raised before he could strike the fortune-teller.

'Stop, John!' she cried. 'Come away from her! She's just mischief-making.'

He tried to throw her off, but Rose was strong too and clung to his side. She pushed him away. The gypsy did not flinch or take her look from his face. Rose's heart thumped in fright. It was as if the woman was cursing her husband with her all-knowing eyes and mysterious words.

The girls crowded round their mother, confused and upset by the angry exchange. Elizabeth began to cry. Two men appeared from out of a makeshift tent and stood silently beside the red-haired woman.

'Please, John!' Rose hissed.

At the sight of the men, John hesitated, then started shouting abuse as he walked away. He cursed the woman and told her she was a disgrace to old Ireland. As they jostled past people in the crowd, he pointed at her and shouted out that she was a charlatan and a thief.

By the time they had trekked back into the city and fought their way on to a crowded train, Rose was feeling quite unwell. She silently railed at the spiteful woman for ruining their day out and souring John's humour. The children sat jaded and subdued, no one answering Kate's questions about the strange lady.

'Are we not getting the baby now?' she asked as they disembarked at Jarrow station.

'Shut your gob about it!' John shouted. 'I don't want to hear mention of that witch again - or any of her daft rubbish.'

Because of John's anger at the gypsy's words, Rose said nothing about the creeping tiredness that swept over her each afternoon, or the bile that rose in her throat as she prepared the girls' tea. The smell of meat pies sent her rushing to retch in the scullery sink. Long before the end of the summer, Rose knew she was pregnant again, and must have been for some time by the spreading of her waist.

Eventually, John noticed how her breasts were swelling and how she could only drink her tea as weak as dishwater. Rose was nervous at his response, her mind still plagued by the gypsy's ominous words and malicious cursing. She dreamt often of a ship being wrecked on the black rocks off Shields and her children, sodden and shoeless, searching for shelter.

But John was overjoyed. 'A bairn of our own!' he cried, hugging her thickening body. 'That's grand news! Wait till I tell me mother and Father O'Brien.'

'So it doesn't worry you?' Rose asked cautiously. 'After what that lass said ...?'

He gave her a sharp look. 'I told you never to mention her again,' he warned. 'I'll not have you being scared by her talk - or the baby harmed. We're going to have a son, Rose, I know it. Maybe even twins or triplets - it runs in me family. A whole crop of lads.'

Rose felt weak at the thought, but said nothing. Silently, she prayed that it would not be a son, if only to break the hold the gypsy's words had over her. She wanted to prove the prophesy wrong, so that none of the other nightmarish images of storms and rocks and tinkers would come true either.

As the autumn wore on and Rose felt the baby grow and turn in her womb, the memory of the incident on the Town Moor dimmed. By late October, when she was lumbering breathlessly down the back lane watching out for the girls returning from school, she had shaken off her feeling of dread. It had been mere coincidence that the Irish girl had guessed she was carrying a baby, nothing more sinister.

Then, as the raw east wind blew in from the North Sea in late November, Rose's new peace of mind was shattered. One Monday, she lifted the cracked Jubilee mug from the mantelpiece and fished inside for threepence to send with the girls to school. She kept all her housekeeping money in Margaret's old mug, the only one of the set not pawned after William's death. It was empty. Yet on Friday it had held a fortnight's rent money and enough to see them through the coming week. Every Thursday, John shaved and put on his jacket and went to collect his army pension and put a share of it in the mug for the household bills. How much he kept for himself she never knew and felt she couldn't ask.

Rose searched around the hearth to see if the money had spilt when one of the girls had reached up for a taper or match. Not a farthing could she find anywhere. She turned accusingly on Sarah, who was nearest.

'Have you been pinching from the mug? 'Cos if you have I'll have your guts for garters!'

'No, Mam,' Sarah protested. 'I never!'

'Elizabeth? Kate?' Rose demanded, her voice rising. 'Where's me money?'

Kate stared at her nonplussed, but Elizabeth's look was anxious, almost guilty.

Rose lunged forward and grabbed her by the arm. 'What've you done with it?'

She cried out, 'You're hurting me! I haven't touched the money, honest.'

Rose hardened herself against the girl's frightened look. She'd die of shame if one of her daughters had taken to stealing. 'You know some'at, don't you?'

'Aye - no - I don't know much.' She winced at Rose's rough handling.

'Mam,' Kate tried to intervene, 'don't hurt our Lizzie.'

'Tell me what you do know,' Rose ordered. 'Cos there's no money for school till you do. I'll have you scrubbing doorsteps till next year if you don't spit it out. And heaven knows what the father will say!'

'It's him,' Elizabeth whispered, tears springing to her eyes. 'The father.'

'What d'you mean?' Rose was baffled.

'I saw him take the money out the mug,' she confessed. 'On Saturday, when you were having a nap upstairs. I thought he'd just taken a couple of pennies for his baccy.'

Rose felt sick. 'A couple of pennies? There's nowt left!'

'I didn't know he'd taken it all, Mam,' Elizabeth said in distress. 'Please don't tell him I told you. Please, Mam.' She burst into tears.

Rose looked at her in dismay, quickly putting her arms around her daughter.

'Haway, hinny, it's not your fault. He must've had his reasons.' She wiped Elizabeth's eyes with her apron. 'You get yourselves off to school and tell Miss Quinlan I'll pay her the morrow.' She pushed her gently away. 'Off you go, or you'll be strapped for being late.'

After the girls had gone, Rose moved restlessly about the kitchen boiling up water for the weekly wash, her heart pounding uncomfortably and her hands clammy. She waited for John to emerge, thinking back to Saturday afternoon. He had been out until early evening and had come back with the smell of drink on his breath, but not drunk. She had not seen him the worse for drink since the episode over Mary in the summer.

When he strolled into the kitchen, she had a bowl of porridge warming for him on the stove and a pot of tea brewing.

'I seem to have run out of housekeeping already,' she said as lightly as her trembling voice would allow. 'Can you lend us some more? I need suet for dumplings the night - and the lasses had to gan to school without their pennies."

'School,' John muttered. 'What's a big lass like Elizabeth doing still at school? She should be looking for a place.'

Rose hid her irritation. 'She's just turned eleven. Miss Quinlan thinks she's bright enough to be a monitress - even a pupil teacher in time. I want her to stay on.'

'And I say she should be earning her keep at her age,' John said bad-temperedly, snatching the porridge bowl from Rose.

'With a bit more learning she could bring in a better wage,' Rose pointed out, wondering why he was being so belligerent all of a sudden. 'In the meantime we're managing canny on your army pension.'

It was something about the defensive hunch of his shoulders, the way he avoided her look, that made Rose's stomach lurch in alarm. She put protective hands on her womb as it tightened and her baby stirred. Her heart raced like a train.

'John?' she gasped. 'What's wrong? Tell me what you've done with the rent money.'

Still he would not look at her, but she saw the red flush rise from his neck into his tense jawline.

'I'm off to see about a job at the mill the day,' he told her by way of an answer. 'You'll have the money by the end of the week. You'll just have to manage till then.'

She gawped at him. 'Manage with what? You'll have to give us a bit of your baccy money or some'at.'

'Haven't got owt,' he growled.

'But your army pay. .. ?'

He looked at her for the first time, his eyes defiant. 'Gone.'

Rose felt faint. 'Gone? What d'you mean? Has someone nicked your weekly pay?'

'No, woman!' he barked in irritation. 'Not just this week's. It's all gone - spent - there's nowt left.'

But - but I thought there was plenty. . . ?'

'You cannot complain,' he answered bullishly. 'I've spent every penny on you and your lasses. You can't say I haven't been good to you.'

Rose pressed her moist fingers against her throbbing forehead. 'But the baby,' she gulped, her throat drying and pulse drumming in panic. 'We need things for the baby.' She looked at him accusingly. 'You should've told me the money was running out.'

'I never said it would last for ever!' He banged down his spoon. 'Look around you, Rose. You're the one wanted all this - that's where all the money's gone. Keeping you like a stuck-up lady, trying to keep up with Fawcett!' He sprang up and toppled back his chair. 'Well, I'm not William bloody Fawcett! I'm John McMullen and proud of it. I'm as hard-working as the next man and I'll soon have a job. You'll have to manage the housekeeping better than you do - me mother brought up thirteen of us on a lot less.'

Rose was indignant. 'You'll not blame me for your spendthrift ways! I didn't ask for half of the second-hand furniture that clutters up this house. And I'm not the one who spends Saturday in the pub and gambles on the horses!'

John glared at her. 'Watch your tongue! It's my money and I'll spend it how I see fit.'

'Aye, and spend it you have!' Rose derided. 'There's nowt left to spend, remember? Now how are we going to clothe the baby when it comes?'

Mention of the baby seemed to rile John all the more. He grabbed at the tablecloth and whipped it off the table, sending the bowl of porridge crashing to the floor.

'Here, you can sell this!' he cried, waving it in her face. 'And this!' He kicked a horsehair stool the girls used. 'And that weddin' ring you keep around your neck and think I don't notice.'

Rose took a step back, her hands going protectively to her throat. 'Stop it,' she whispered in fright.

'And after you've been down the pawnshop,' he snarled, 'you can see about a job for that lazy daughter of yours. If she's so good with bairns, she can bring in a wage lookin' after someone else's. She'll not grow up with ideas above herself in my house, do you understand?'

Rose looked at him appalled. His face was puce with anger, the veins standing out on his high forehead, his moustache flecked with spittle. Never had she seen him so furious, but to have such anger directed at her shook her to the core. If she had not been pregnant, she might have stood up to him and carried on answering back. She was no coward and the trials she had undergone and survived had made her a harder person. The foremen at the puddling mill had learnt she was not one to be pushed around.

But she felt vulnerable standing there, breathless and heavy with her unborn child. She could not risk the danger of John's wrath any further. Her eyes defied him, but she said as calmly as possible, 'Aye, I understand.'

For a moment they stood staring at each other, an atmosphere of anger and mistrust settling around them like the dark dust of the town. Then John strode to the back door without a further word, grabbing his jacket and cap from the nail. He flung open the door and marched out, leaving it wide. An icy wind gusted into the room.

Rose felt paralysed but knew she had to keep moving to keep the demons of fear inside her at bay. She bent to pick up the bowl, which miraculously had not smashed, and began to scrape up the cooling, sticky porridge. He'd get it again tomorrow, she promised herself defiantly.

An hour later, she had made up a parcel of household linen and crockery and left the house, dressed in her heavy cape and black widow's bonnet. Rose determined not to go to Slater's in the town where she might be recognised, but set out instead for the long walk into South Shields. No doubt there were those who thought it just a matter of time before she would be resorting to the pawnshop - the price for marrying a McMullen. Rose knew her former mother-in-law would have said so. Well, she would not give the people of Jarrow the satisfaction of seeing her haggling at the 'in and out'.

By the time she reached Shields, Rose was so exhausted she would have taken anything for her offerings. But the pawnbroker took pity on such a heavily pregnant customer, and she got nearly the asking price for her bundle. She would have to put the rent man off, but she had enough for the week's food. And there was threepence left over for the girls' schooling, Rose thought with fierce satisfaction, as she turned for home.

Chapter 30

The walk to the pawnshop in Shields proved too much for Rose. The next day she could hardly climb out of bed. Her legs had swollen to double their normal size and sharp pain stabbed between her legs. Despite the cost, John called out the doctor. He ordered complete bed rest and waived his fee.

'I've a house and bairns to look after,' Rose fretted. But John was full of concern, his temper of the day before cooled.

'Elizabeth can help out while you're restin',' he insisted. Soon he was keeping the older girl off school to take her mother's place running the home.

Rose felt guilty, but enjoyed having her easy-going daughter in the house.

'Don't worry, Mam,' Elizabeth assured. 'I can do me lessons at home till you're better.'

At the beginning of December, John secured regular work carrying pig iron to the puddling mill and Rose's worrying eased a fraction. Still, she had to send Elizabeth to the pawnshop twice more, with parcels of clothing and trinkets that John had bought her in the first flush of his passion.

'As soon as this baby's born, I'll be right as rain,' Rose told her eldest, 'and you can gan back to school. Back end of January.'

Elizabeth's smile looked uncertain, but she said, 'Aye, of course, Mam.'

So it came as a complete shock to Rose when she went into labour one dark December day, shortly after Sarah's tenth birthday. She was on her own in the house; John was at work, the younger girls were at school and Elizabeth had walked into Shields for some cheap fish.

At first, Rose refused to believe what was happening to her. She had lain shivering and sweating all morning, not feeling well, and then the griping in her stomach had turned abruptly to sharp contractions.

'It's not time,' she cried out loud in the cold, bare bedroom. 'Me baby's not fully made!'

But there was no one to hear her and no one to help, when half an hour later, water gushed from between her legs and soaked the bed. Then the pains really began - red-hot searing pain that wrapped around her belly like iron manacles and squeezed until she nearly passed out.

She had to get help! Somehow she had to get off the bed and attract someone's attention at the window or bang on the wall. Rose took deep breaths to calm herself, but her chest felt heavy and her breathing sounded loud in her ears. She had to keep her head and do things nice and easy, she told herself. No harm would come to her and Elizabeth would be back soon to fetch help. There was nothing about childbirth that she did not already know, so there was no need to panic. But the pain! Mary Mother! She had forgotten what agony.

Rose gripped the side of the bed and hauled herself on to her feet between contractions. Her legs were still swollen and her ankles buckled under the sudden weight. She fell forward, banging her head on the metal bedframe. For a moment she was stunned, then crumpled forward, not knowing whether to clutch her head or her belly. She crouched on all fours like an animal, gasping for breath and trying to swallow the bile that rose in her throat. Then another spasm seized her body and she cried out for mercy.

When the worst of the pain passed, she crumpled forward on her arms and started to weep.

'I can't go through this again,' she sobbed. 'Just let me die.'

She remembered now how she had sworn never to bear another child after Mary. And that was three years ago when she had not been worn down by the puddling mills and living hand-to-mouth. Now she felt she had the body of an old woman and this child within her - this McMullen - was pummelling and tearing her to pieces.

'I hate you, John McMullen!' she shrieked at her dismal surroundings. 'You're killing me. I'll never have another bairn. You'll not come near me again, not *ever*.'

With her tirade went the last of her energy. Rose remembered little of what happened next or how long it took for the baby to come. All she was aware of was hot relentless pain, her panting and screaming like a wild animal and the pressure of the baby between her shaking legs like a dead weight.

She gave birth there, on the bare wooden floor, her nightgown soaking and blood-stained. Rose looked down through a blur of tears and sweat at the crinkled bloodied scrap between her knees and saw a shock of dark hair. It gave a small choking cough and instantly she leant forward to clear its mouth. The baby spluttered, then started a quiet whimpering. Rose felt a wave of relief and pulled the bed shawl that was dangling over the bed to wrap around her tiny newborn.

It was only then that she noticed it was a boy. In her exhaustion she had not thought to look, had in fact not cared two pins what sex it was, only that her body was rid of it and they were both still alive. Sudden unexpected tears pricked her eyes. She had a son! How William had always longed for a boy to cherish alongside their bonny girls.

Rose sat back and cradled the infant, oblivious now to the mess and stench around them. She gazed at the trembling baby with his mass of sticky black hair, and kissed his soft forehead. Then it hit her. This was John's son, not William's. He was skinny and dark - so obviously a McMullen. How could she have thought otherwise? The ordeal had left her dazed and confused, and her mind was as shaken up as her body.

Rose leant back against the bed and wept. She wept with regret for the past that could never return, for William who would never be the father of her son. She wept with fear for the babe in her arms and the uncertain world into which he came. The words of foreboding uttered by the gypsy returned to haunt her: storms and rocks ahead and wandering like a tinker. They seemed far more prophetic since the discovery that all John's army gratuity was gone.

John! At least he would be pleased with this day's work. At the thought of him, Rose attempted to stir herself, but found she could not move. Cramp seized her legs and kept her pinned to the floor. She winced and jerked in agony and the baby wailed at the sudden movement. Her throat was parched and she could no longer cry out.

It was in this state of distress and mess that Elizabeth found her mother. She came up the stairs answering Rose's hoarse call for help. Stopping abruptly in the doorway, she gasped in horror at the scene.

'Mam! Are you all right? What's happened?'

'What does it look like?' Rose cried weakly. 'Where've you been all this time?

I could've died here on me own.'

'Mam,' Elizabeth sprang into the room. 'You've had the baby! What should I do? Gan for Aunt Maggie?'

Rose shook her head. 'It'd take too long. The hard bit's done with. You must help me now.'

'Me?' her daughter gawped.

'Aye.' Rose gasped as the cramp took hold again. 'Bring me a drink of water - and a knife and candle.'

'Knife? What for?' Elizabeth asked in alarm.

'For cuttin' the cord.' Rose was blunt. 'Then stoke up the fire and bring some newspaper - we'll need to get this cleared up and burnt before your father comes in.'

Elizabeth crept closer. 'Is it a lass or a lad?'

'Lad,' Rose whispered.

The girl's face lit up. 'Can I hold him, Mam?'

'After you've done what I say,' Rose murmured. 'Quick, hinny, I don't feel too grand.'

Rose was amazed at how efficiently her quiet, nervous daughter dealt with the crisis. Within a short time, the cord was severed, the afterbirth rolled into paper and thrown on the fire downstairs. She held her mother's head gently as she helped her to sip water and coaxed her out of her dirty nightdress when all Rose wanted to do was lie back and sleep.

'It's too cold for you up here,' Elizabeth declared. 'I'll get you down in front of the fire. You can lie on the settle with a blanket.' She had the baby cuddled gently in her arms. 'He's that tiny!' She kissed him, then frowned. 'He's cold an' all. Mam, I think we should put him by the fire.'

Rose made an effort to sit up, alerted by the worry in the girl's voice.

'Give him here!'

But Elizabeth kept hold of her brother. 'I'll carry him down and come back for you.'

Rose was too tired to argue. When Elizabeth returned for her, she was surprised at how strong her daughter was. She was tall and wiry, the way Rose had been at her age, and it suddenly struck her that Elizabeth was almost full grown. Because she had always seemed so immature compared to Margaret, Rose had continued to think of her as a young girl, protected her, and even mollycoddled her. But she was a willing and competent helper. As Rose sank on to the settle after the breathless exertion of descending the stairs, she was comforted by the thought that her second daughter would be of increasing help to them all.

She woke to the sound of the younger girls traipsing in from school and throwing off their boots at the back door. There were squeals of amazement as they caught sight of their older sister sitting by the fire cradling a small bundle.

'Mam's had a little lad,' Elizabeth told them proudly, 'and I helped her.'

'Can I have a hold?' Sarah asked excitedly.

'Let me!' demanded Kate as they crowded round.

They tussled and the baby let out a querulous cry.

'Haway and bring him over here,' Rose ordered, 'it's time he was fed.'

All three of them carried him over and stood watching as Rose undid her bodice. She felt suddenly awkward. 'This isn't a holiday,' she remarked. 'You can get the table set and the tea on for Father coming in.' She looked at their reluctant faces. 'Then you can hold him,' she bargained.

When John came home he was greeted by a cacophony of noise from his stepdaughters, all trying at once to tell him the news. He stared beyond them at the sight of Rose lying on the settle in the firelight, a tiny swaddled creature latched like a piglet onto the end of a large pendulous breast. His heart surged in excitement.

'Rose.' He lurched forward. 'We've got a lad? Tell me we've got a lad!'

She grunted, 'Aye, he's a lad. Couldn't wait for his proper time - had to come early, didn't he?'

John punched the air and let out a whoop of joy. 'That's grand. That's bloody grand!'

'John,' she remonstrated but smiled despite herself. It was so good to see him happy and his look almost tender under the grime. She felt ashamed at all the terrible things she had screamed about him while in the grips of labour, for she did not really mean them.

He leant forward and kissed her roundly. 'We'll call him John, of course.'

Kate frowned. 'He looks too small to be called John.'

Her stepfather looked at her baffled. 'You talk a lot of nonsense, you do.'

Kate persisted. 'John's a big name - a grown-up name. It'll sit too heavy on that tiddler.'

Rose looked at the two of them and laughed. Then John shook his head and laughed too. 'Well, you can call him Jack, if you want,' he conceded. 'Is that light enough for you?'

Kate beamed. 'Aye, I like that - Jack. That suits him canny.'

John leant over Rose, touching the snuffling baby with rough, dirt-ingrained hands. She noticed how he could not resist brushing his fingers against her breast and she caught the look in his eye. It made her feel suddenly bashful to be feeding the baby in front of him. He had touched her in the dark many a time, but she had never let him look at her naked body.

Rose pulled her shawl over her open bodice and covered herself and the baby. The less he thought about such things the better. There would be no more of that carry-on for a long time, if she could help it. He had his son. Let him be content with that.

Straight after tea, John went back out. 'I'm away to tell me mother the good news - likely she'll want to call round and help.'

Rose felt weak at the thought of visitors, but said nothing. She succumbed to sleep even before she heard him bang the back gate.

Mrs McMullen called round later in the evening, hobbling in on her arthritic legs and praising the saints for the new life in their midst. She installed herself in the fireside chair with baby Jack in her arms and gave out orders. John, it appeared, had gone celebrating.

'Sarah, you're a strong girl - fetch another bucket of coal for the fire. We can't have it going out tonight of all nights. This little man has to be kept warm - he's no bigger than a rat.'

Rose bristled at the unkind comparison. 'He's not so small,' she protested, still wrapped in her shawl on the settle. She thought she couldn't move even if the house was burning down around her.

'He'll need plenty feeding if he's to thrive,' her mother-in-law said, making clucking sounds at her grandson. 'Maybe you should give him an extra bottle or two while your milk's coming in.'

Rose thought how they had no money to go buying milk or bottles, but she was not going to tell their business to John's mother. She would only fuss and make things bad between them.

'I'll feed him mesel',' she answered stubbornly. 'I fed all the others well enough.'

'Well, you try again now,' Mrs McMullen said, rising stiffly from the chair. 'His little lips are sucking the air.'

'I'll carry him.' Elizabeth was at her side immediately, taking the baby from her shaking hands. She bore him over to her mother like a piece of precious china and delivered him safely into her arms. Rose smiled gratefully as she put Jack to her breast once more.

Sarah returned with a pailful of dross and threw it on to the fire. At once the flames were smothered and plunged the kitchen in darkness. Smoke billowed out, making them choke. Jack spluttered at Rose's breast and lost his hold.

'Sarah!' the women scolded in chorus.

'You said a bucketful,' she cried. 'There's no proper coal left.'

'She's right, Mam,' Kate came to her sister's defence, 'there's just dust.'

Rose's eyes smarted in the smoke, but she said quickly, 'It won't spoil. Might as well bank up the fire for the night, hinny. Pour a bit water on and the fire'll still be in come the morrow.'

'One of you girls will have to marry a pitman,' Mrs McMullen cackled as she groped for her shawl, 'then there'll be plenty coal for all of us.'

'Not me,' protested Sarah.

'Never!' Kate giggled. 'They're all dirty and the wives are washing clothes all the time.'

Rose laughed drily. 'Your father would never allow it, any road. Doesn't think much to pitmen.'

'Doesn't think much to a lot of folk,' John's mother snorted. 'But no one should be looked down on for working hard, whether it's under the earth or over it. Long as it puts bread and potatoes on the table.' She peered at Rose in the dark. 'How come there's money for John to go wettin' the baby's head, but not for coal?'

Rose was glad of the darkness to cover her blushing. 'We just forgot to get some in - this all happened so sudden. Don't fret yourself.' But the old woman tutted.

Then Kate piped up, 'Father took the coal money from the mug, didn't he, Mam?'

'Is that true, Rose Ann?' Mrs McMullen demanded.

Rose's heart sank. 'Just the once - but he paid it back when he started at the carrying.'

John's mother sucked in her breath. 'It's gone, hasn't it, the money?'

'Aye,' Rose admitted. 'But we'll manage.'

'Don't let him drink it all away,' her mother-in-law warned. 'Fight him for his wages if you have to - it was like that with his father till the boys were old enough to help out.'

Rose was indignant. 'John's not like that - not any more. His wild days are over. He's got responsibilities and bairns.'

The older woman quickly put a reassuring hand on her shoulder. 'Aye, maybe he's changed. You're good for him, Rose Ann, I'll give you that. I've never known him so happy. But you were always a good girl.'

Rose felt suddenly tearful to be spoken to so affectionately and as if she were still a young lass. 'Ta, Mrs McMullen.'

Just then, they heard the sound of singing growing louder in the back lane. Rose's insides lurched as she recognised John's voice belting out across the yard. But his mother acted swiftly.

'Elizabeth, light the gas lamp. Sarah and Kate, get yourselves up to bed and stay there. Go on, the pair of you!'

They scrambled for the door and thudded up the dark stairs, galvanised by the sense of panic in the room. The gas flame flared just as John banged in the back door, singing at the top of his voice:

'Sing us an Irish Comaylia
sing us an Irish tune,
for Patsy Burke has buggered his work,
all by the light of the moon!

'Where's me lad? Where's me little Jack? Scoffing at his mother's tittie! Lucky Jack!' John staggered across the room and bumped into the table.

'Sit yourself down,' his mother ordered, taking him by the arm and steering him to the large wooden chair by the fire. To Rose's amazement he did as he was told. 'Elizabeth, get your father a piece of bread and dripping to soak up the drink in his belly.'

'Bring me a beer!' John shouted, collapsing into the chair.

'You've drunk enough to fill the Irish Sea, by the look of it,' his mother declared. 'There'll be no more beer drunk the night.'

John tried to struggle out of the chair. 'Rose! Bring him over here and let me look at the little darlin'.'

'You leave them alone.' His mother was firm. 'He needs his feed and she needs to rest.'

'I need a drink an' all.' John leered drunkenly at his wife. 'Rose, have you got a little bit for me?' He laughed until his mother smacked him sharply across the head.

'None of your dirty talk! You'll get that food down you, then off to bed.'

He rubbed his head and sank back in a sulk. 'Bloody women,' he muttered, snatching the crust that Elizabeth cautiously held out to him. This provoked another cuff from Mrs McMullen.

Rose watched them in silence, thankful that her mother-in-law was there to handle her husband. She had never had to deal with much drunkenness. Her father had only imbibed at weddings and funerals, and William had hardly touched a drop. True, she had witnessed plenty drunken brawling in the streets, even among women, but had walked away rather than intervene. Yet she knew enough to know that it was a fine line between a happy drunk and a fighting, swearing one. What tipped them over was anyone's guess. So she watched warily, her pulse quicker than was comfortable, and tried not to disturb Jack's attempts at sucking.

Distracted by the food, John slumped into a reverie and stared at the smoking fire.

Rose said quietly, 'Elizabeth hinny, you walk Granny McMullen up the end of the street. It might be icy out.'

But the old woman shook her head and murmured, 'I'll see him to his bed first - then I'll know you'll get a good night's sleep.'

'Ta,' Rose said gratefully.

She felt a wave of fondness for this brave, kind woman, bent and scraggy as an old crow, yet full of wisdom and generosity. Glancing at her husband, almost comatose by the fire, she thought she would do well to learn whatever her mother-in-law could teach her on handling a McMullen. Jack nipped at her breast and she winced in pain. In a rush of realisation it came to Rose that she now had two McMullens on her hands.

Chapter 31

It was only through exhaustion that Rose slept at all on the hard, ungiving wooden settle. She was hardly aware of the baby nuzzling during the night, but by her soreness in the morning, she knew that he had been. When she woke, Elizabeth was already up and moving about the room, stoking up the spitting fire with some damp wood she had found in the scullery, left over from John's attempts at making shelves.

Her daughter lifted Jack gently from her side and, wrinkling up her nose, said, 'By, this one smells ripe.'

'I'll change him in a minute,' Rose said wearily, closing her eyes again.

'I can do it,' the girl answered brightly. 'I've seen Aunt Maggie cleaning baby Margaret - and I used to help with our Mary, remember?'

Rose looked at her. No, she did not remember. But then she had been worried sick with William's illness when Mary was a baby and she had blotted out the memory of those anxious days. She supposed Elizabeth must have helped her, or helped Margaret. The thought gave her a guilty pang about Mary. She certainly could not cope with the child at the moment.

As if her daughter could read her mind, Elizabeth said, 'I'll go up and tell Aunt Maggie the day, shall I?'

'There's no hurry,' Rose said quickly. 'She'll not be expectin' such news. A day or two won't make much difference.'

Elizabeth glanced up from where she was unwrapping Jack by the hearth. 'Don't you want Aunt Maggie to come and help you?'

'She's got enough troubles of her own to cope with,' Rose sighed.

'What about Aunt Lizzie?'

'It's a long way for her to travel at this time of year - and she's still working at the castle - can't drop everything just for us.'

Rose did not know why she was so reluctant to call in the family to help. Perhaps it was because she still felt so beholden to Maggie and Danny for saving them from the workhouse after William's death and for keeping Mary. This time she wanted to show everyone that she could manage without their charity. She and John and their young family would manage together.

Rose smiled over at her daughter. 'Anyways, I've got you, hinny. You're being a grand help - thank you, lass.'

Elizabeth smiled with pleasure and set to work cleaning and changing her baby brother. Afterwards she went upstairs to chase her sisters out of bed and knock timidly on the door of her stepfather's bedroom as her mother had bidden her. When he did not reply she hammered louder and called out his name. Eventually he stirred, emerging unshaven and red-eyed, reeking of stale beer.

Downstairs he snapped at Rose to pour him some tea while he dowsed his head in cold water in the scullery. No one told him the basin of water had just been used in the cleaning of his son's soiled bottom and he did not seem to notice.

Elizabeth dealt with him calmly. 'Here's your tea, Father. And there's bread and dripping on the table.'

John grimaced. 'I'm not hungry. By, the beer at The Railway must've been bad.' He clutched his stomach but gulped at the tea thirstily. Rose wondered if he had forgotten all about the birth of his son.

He drew back his chair. 'I'll be off.'

'Don't you want a hold of your lad before you go?' Rose asked reproachfully. She pulled aside her shawl to show him the sleeping baby.

He looked alarmed. 'Me?'

'Aye, you,' Rose smiled. 'You are his father. Gan on,' she encouraged.

He came over cautiously and stood looking down at them, his large rough hands hanging limp at his sides. Rose held the baby out to him.

'Here, put him in the crook of your arm. That's it. See how snug he fits.'

John's furrowed brow relaxed into a look of amazement. 'He's no weight at all, is he? Light as a feather.' He stood stock-still as if to attention, his arms frozen in position.

Rose could see the wonderment on his face at the feel of something so small and delicate and alive in his hold.

'Me own flesh and blood,' he murmured in awe. His look met Rose's and for the first time she could recall, she saw tears well in his eyes.

'Feels grand, doesn't it?' she asked softly. He simply nodded, unable to say anything for the sudden lump lodged in his throat like a boiled sweet. Rose did not know how long he might have stood there, if she hadn't said, 'Don't be late for work, John man. We need your wages more than ever.'

Abruptly, he handed the baby back.

'I'll take him,' Sarah cried.

'It's my turn!' Kate insisted.

'You two get yourselves off to school this minute,' Rose ordered, holding out her arms for Jack.

There were howls of protest at which John growled, 'Do what your mam says or I'll smack you. The bairn's not a toy.'

'Elizabeth gets to hold him all the time,' Kate continued the protest.

"Cos she's a sensible lass and you two are as giddy as foals,' John derided. 'Now off with you.' He raised a hand in mock threat and the girls grabbed their jackets from the nails halfway down the back door. He laughed at them and chased them out of the back door with a shout to Rose of, 'See you the night!'

Rose sighed thankfully as peace descended on the house. She planned a quiet day getting used to dealing with a baby again and sending Elizabeth out on errands.

'See if you can get a bag of coal on tick from Henderson's - tell him about the baby,' she instructed. 'Say John's in work again and he'll be paid Friday. We'll need to put a wash on an' all if we get the coal.'

But the day did not go as Rose planned. The baby tried frantically to feed, but the more he tried, the more he slipped off her nipple. By the end of the day he was exhausted and crotchety and she was sore and tearful. That night she stayed downstairs, but suffered more of the same. The next two days were no better. By the fourth day she was snapping at the girls, achingly tired and her breasts were swelling painfully as they filled with milk. More alarmingly, Jack seemed to have given up the fight to feed and lay sleeping for hours on end, sometimes lying so still that Rose shook him awake in alarm and set him mewling like a kitten.

170

The following evening, both she and John were at their wits' end. Worried by his wife's weepy state, John went round for his mother.

'St Theresa! The bairn's not gettin' enough to eat,' she fussed. 'He's a tiddler to start with; he can't go missing meal times.'

'But he's not interested!' Rose wailed. 'I've never had trouble feedin' before - but this little devil...'

Mrs McMullen studied the baby closely, nudging her little finger into his tiny mouth. Then she pulled back Rose's bodice and looked at her engorged breasts. They were painfully swollen with milk, the skin stretched tight as a drum and the nipples cracked and inflamed.

'He's too small to latch on to the size of them,' she exclaimed. 'Rose Ann, they're as hard as cabbages! Put a pin to them and they'll burst.'

Rose flushed at her frankness, only too aware of John hovering close and staring at her. She pulled her shawl about her, feeling her neck and face burning with embarrassment. The girls, sitting at the table, had stopped drawing on John's newspaper to listen and gawp.

'Not in front of the lasses,' Rose hissed.

Mrs McMullen made an impatient sound. 'They'll all have to go through this soon enough. It won't kill them to know.'

'Please!' Rose said, tears springing to her eyes.

Her mother-in-law turned to the girls and said briskly, 'Away and play in the lane for a few minutes.'

Kate, who had looked on in horrified fascination, complained, 'But it's dark and cold outside.'

'Play under the gas lamp,' she replied. 'Or go upstairs to bed.'

Kate and Sarah scrambled for the outside door. Elizabeth followed reluctantly to keep an eye on her boisterous sisters.

When they had gone, Rose asked in desperation, 'What shall I do? The bairn's not going to die, is he?'

'Not if he gets fed,' her mother-in-law reassured. 'But we need to get the swelling down, so his wee mouth can suck again.'

'I'm that sore,' Rose whimpered.

'Rub your milk around the cracks when we get some out and they'll soon mend. The more you feed the more you'll toughen up. Don't you remember all this?' The older woman gave a wry smile.

Rose shook her head. 'It was never this bad.'

'That's 'cos he's so small, no doubt,' she nodded, 'and you're too big for him.'

'So what do I do?' Rose asked, sniffing away her tears.

Mrs McMullen said nothing for a moment. She looked round at John and seemed to be considering something. Rose thought she was going to banish him from the room too and felt relief. Most men would have left them to their women's worries long before. But not John. She couldn't believe he was enjoying her discomfort, but he made her edgy standing there silently staring.

'John will have to do it,' his mother decreed.

Rose's heart thumped in alarm. 'Do what?'

'Suck the milk from you, of course!' Mrs McMullen said as if she was dull-witted. 'He's got a mouth for suppin', that's for sure.'

Rose was appalled. 'You can't mean—'

'Why ever not? He's your husband. It's no time to be shy, Rose Ann.' She was blunt. 'That baby needs your milk if you don't want to be burying him next week instead of christening him.'

'Mother,' John spoke for the first time, 'is there no other way?'

Rose glanced at him and saw that he was as flustered by the idea as she was. His neck was scarlet under his open shirt and he scratched his head in a sign of embarrassment.

His mother put her hands on her hips with impatience at them both. 'Aye, I could go and get Dr Forbes or Dr McKay to do it instead. But likely you wouldn't want another man to do such a thing to your wife?' she ridiculed. She turned and hobbled towards the door.

'Don't go for the doctor!' John cried. 'I'll do it.'

She nodded. 'I'll stand outside with the girls for five minutes. That's all you'll need. So get on with it.'

She went, leaving Rose and John blushing furiously at each other. Between them Jack murmured and whimpered like a forlorn, unhappy puppy. Why was she so upset by the idea? She had lain with this man and done the most intimate of acts countless times. Even through her pregnancy his lust had not dimmed. That was it, she thought. This to John would be an act of lust, a taking of forbidden fruit, a mother's milk. Whereas she now saw her body only in terms of providing nourishment for her precious baby, she knew he would gain sensual enjoyment from it. He was that sort of man.

But what did it matter? Rose thought wearily. She was at the end of her tether, lying in a sweat of agony and fear. All she cared was that her son lived. Rose closed her eyes against the indignity.

'Haway and get it over with,' she hissed at him.

For a moment he did not move. Then she heard him kneeling in front of her, his breathing growing more rapid. She flinched when he touched the first of her swollen breasts, his hand tightening around it while his lips fixed around the nipple. He sucked. Nothing happened. He opened his mouth wider and pulled more of her in.

She cried out in pain, but he held on and squeezed as if it were a cow's udder. Suddenly she felt small jets burst from her nipple as the milk found a release. The mixture of pain and relief was exquisite.

'Oh, thank God!' she shuddered.

John grunted in surprise as his mouth filled with the warm liquid. He gulped and sucked harder, kneading her breast rhythmically, intoxicated by the experience. He felt triumphant, better than being drunk. He had never felt so close to Rose as at that moment. He loved her, desired her, cherished her, and would never let another man touch her in all his life!

She pushed his head away. 'That's enough,' she said sharply, 'they'll be nowt left for Jack.'

John sat back and wiped the drips of milk from his moustache. Rose swiftly reached for Jack and shoved him on to her breast. The baby searched for a moment, aroused by the scent and taste of milk on her skin, then latched on.

Rose felt joy and relief flood through her at the sound of his slurping.

'He's taking it!' she cried.

'By heck, so he is,' John grinned. 'Just like his father.'

Rose felt uncomfortable at the comparison. 'Ta for your help,' she said awkwardly.

John studied her. 'I've the other to do yet. Haway and let's get on with it.'

Rose gritted her teeth while he bent to the task again. It was like feeding twins, she thought as the two of them pulled on her hungrily. The relief that it brought was indescribable. Once the first sharp pain had passed, she was astonished to find herself almost enjoying it. She would never admit it to her husband, but the feeling was not unpleasant. She felt bountiful and content and, for a moment, powerful, to have them sucking at her breasts together.

Rose put a hand lightly on his bowed head. John was hers. He would never do such things for any other woman and it gave her a warm, triumphant thrill. He loved her and she had grown to care for him. Now they were bound to each other for good by the baby who snuffled between them. If there were storms ahead, they would face them together.

Chapter 32

That winter was dogged by worry over baby Jack. He was small and sickly and did not thrive in the way Rose's other babies had. She knew that the puddling mills had sapped her former strength and left her with a body that ached and wheezed in the winter cold, then swelled uncomfortably in the summer heat. She blamed her damaged health for her son's premature birth and his listless start in life.

The priest came swiftly to christen the baby at home and Mrs McMullen shook her head with worry whenever she called. 'He's got the look of an angel already,' she clucked, and muttered about accepting God's will.

Relations grew tense between Rose and John. He looked on anxiously, chiding her for not feeding Jack enough or failing to keep the kitchen warm.

'You're neglectin' him, Rose Ann.'

'No I'm not.'

'You let the fire go out!'

'Only when there's nowt to buy coal with,' she retaliated.

'You're a bad housekeeper - you should make the money go further.'

'I do the best I can with what little you give me,' Rose said reproachfully.

'Don't blame me,' he grumbled. 'I bring back a man's wage.' He gave her a stern look and jerked his head in Elizabeth's direction. 'You know what I think.'

Rose glanced at her daughter squatting on the wooden fender by the fire, absorbed in a book borrowed from Aunt Maggie. She knew how happy Elizabeth was to have returned to school. Yet it would be so easy to give in to John's pressure to send the girl into service, for she was tall for her age, capable and eager to please, and would soon find a place. It would mean one less mouth to feed and extra money every fortnight once she was earning. But death had cruelly robbed Rose of her ambitions for her beloved Margaret and she was not going to be thwarted a second time. No amount of badgering from John would sway her. Above all, she was determined that her eldest should do better in life than she had.

'No,' Rose was adamant. 'The lass has just been made a monitress. Likely she'll be a pupil teacher by the spring - Miss Quinlan said as much.'

'You shouldn't be filling her head full of fancy ideas,' John complained. 'What do you want her to be a teacher for any road? No man'll want to marry her, that's for sure.'

'She'll be able to stand on her own two feet and fend for herself without being beholden to a man,' Rose answered quietly but with an edge to her voice.

John gave her a surly look. 'Well, if you won't see sense over the lass you can stop your complaining about lack of money then,' John said harshly, spitting into the fire and startling Elizabeth. 'I'm the only one doing an honest day's graft around here.'

'And what do you think I do all day long?' Rose remonstrated. 'I never stop. There's no nine-hour day for us women with a house full of bairns!'

Elizabeth glanced between them anxiously, aware that they were arguing over her again. Her two sisters fell silent and stole out of the room, preferring to play in the dank back lane than listen to the adults wrangling.

Rose and John continued to snipe at each other until the baby began to whimper. Then both of them reached to calm him.

'I'll see to him,' Rose said testily.

'Haway and give him here,' John insisted, holding out his arms.

Rose gave in without much protest, silently thankful that her husband was willing to pacify the unhappy infant. The baby's crying alternately filled her with panic and jarred on her frayed nerves. But John was surprisingly patient with their son and was soon pacing the small room, clutching him tightly and whistling Irish tunes until the wailing subsided.

This was how many of their arguments ended, petering out in concern over the child, bringing them together in shared worry. Jack was the cause of most disputes between them, but also the remedy. Rose felt fiercely protective of her tiny, delicate son, struggling to hold on to life, and she recognised the same passion in John's rugged, concerned face. But the New Year came with no improvement. If anything, the baby's weight was dwindling and during the short, raw days of January he contracted a cold which made him almost impossible to feed.

Rose, frantic with worry, stayed up nursing him by the fire, calling on the saints for help. She had no energy left for her daughters and scolded them if they came too near or coughed over their brother. Her only thoughts were for her son and keeping him alive. Somehow he symbolised her new start in life with John, this second chance of some security and a home life. If Jack died, Rose feared the rough tenderness and care that had grown between her and John would die with him, wither in the bitterness and guilt of losing their shared child.

She knew how much Jack meant to her husband. He was fiercely proud of this son he had waited so long for and thought he might never have. John rarely talked of his former life in India, but Rose knew it had been hard and at times he had thought he would never return alive. She also suspected Jack was extra special because he had no link with William. When John looked at her daughters, Rose knew he was reminded of her first husband. However much he laid down the law to them in his own home, he knew he would never truly be their father. But Jack was different, prized and unique. He could not be replaced, for she never wanted to go through childbirth again. He must live!

Yet as the days dragged on, Rose could see her baby weaken and was filled with terror at the sight of him fading before her eyes. In panic one February day, she bundled up the moribund infant and ran through the streets to Dr McKay's house.

'He's out on his rounds,' the housekeeper told her with a disapproving look.

'Please tell me where he is,' Rose begged.

'I can't do that,' the woman said primly.

'You must,' Rose choked. 'Me baby's dying!'

The stout woman hesitated, then said grudgingly, 'I'll ask him to call as soon as he returns. Where is it you live?'

'Albion Street,' Rose said hoarsely, trying not to cry. 'Fifty-four. Ta, missus.'

She trailed home, buffeted by a strong westerly wind, her hopes ebbing with each step. When the doctor finally called it was dark and they were all gathered near the fire in the gloom. Dr McKay unwrapped the baby, examined him and shook his head.

'I'm sorry, there's nothing I can do, Mrs McMullen. He was born too early, hasn't got the strength of the fully formed. A common cold could see him off.'

Rose crumpled in defeat and Elizabeth put comforting arms around her. But John was indignant.

'Not fully formed? He's a damn McMullen! Of course he's fully formed. There's nowt wrong with him that a bit of feedin' up and a bit medicine for his chest won't put right. Call yourself a doctor? I'm not paying you owt for talking like that about my son!'

Dr McKay drew himself up and snapped closed his leather bag. 'You don't owe me anything, Mr McMullen. But no medicine I could give him would make any difference.' He turned to Rose. 'Best call for Father O'Brien - only prayers might save him now.'

When the doctor left, John paced the floor like a caged animal, hiding his fear with angry outbursts while Rose cried quietly over her silent baby.

'Damn doctors! They're quacks the lot of 'em! Killed off more soldiers with their meddling than the Afghans. Wouldn't let one near me even if me leg was hanging off!'

'Stop your shouting,' Rose whimpered in distress. 'Give the bairn a peaceful end, for pity's sake.'

John strode across, knocking a chair out of the way, and seized her by the shoulders.

'Don't say that!' He shook her hard, so that she almost dropped the near-lifeless infant. 'Our Jack's not dying! He's not going to die, do you hear me?'

Rose glared back at his stormy face, maddened by his obstinacy. It was obvious the boy was dying, so why was he torturing them all by denying what was happening? She wanted peace and quiet, to hold her little son close and give him comfort in his last hours. All John's ranting wouldn't alter a thing, only make the final night more difficult to bear. Well, she would make him see how futile his blustering words were.

Struggling to stand up, Rose thrust Jack at him. 'Here, you take him then!' she hissed. 'You think you're God and can stop bairns dying. You save him!' He staggered backwards, clutching the small bundle in astonishment. She pushed past him. 'I'm off for the priest. My lad's ganin' to Heaven with a blessing on his head!'

Rose fled for the back door and rushed out into the blustery dark. At once she was caught in a squall of rain. It whipped at her face and uncovered hair, but she did not care. At the top of the street she heard footsteps coming after her.

'Mam! Wait, Mam,' Elizabeth panted behind. 'You shouldn't be out in this without your coat and bonnet. You'll catch your de—' The girl broke off suddenly.

Rose turned to see her daughter anxiously holding out her black cape and bonnet. Her heart melted to hear the familiar scolding that she was constantly giving her younger girls. Swiftly, Elizabeth put the cloak around her shoulders and helped her tie on the hat as if she were a helpless child. Rose could not trust herself to speak for fear she would start to cry and never stop.

'I'll come with you, Mam,' Elizabeth said, slipping her arm through her mother's.

'Ta, hinny,' Rose managed to whisper, and together they bent into the wind and rain and headed for the priest's house.

Father O'Brien left his half-eaten supper and came with them at once. They were all drenched by the time they reached Albion Street. John was still pacing the room with Jack in his arms and Rose felt a pang of remorse for the angry words she had flung at him. His face was haggard and pinched with worry and he flinched at the sight of the priest at the door.

To Rose's relief, he made no protest as Father O'Brien took the baby from him and began to pray. They stood about tensely, Rose gripping the hands of her other children, who were crying softly at the sudden solemnity of the final rites. She felt bitter bile rise in her throat at the thought of what was to come. Another child to bury, the fleeting happiness of a son in their midst gone like the moon disappearing behind black clouds. Why her? Why them? Why wouldn't the Virgin preserve her little lad? Jesus lived to be a grown man, why couldn't her son? she demanded angrily. What had she done to deserve this?

As the words of the priest tolled like sombre bells, Rose recalled the prophecy of the gypsy that she would bear a son but that storms would follow. Then the Irish woman had cursed John, willing that his son would stand up to him and give him not a minute's peace till the day he died. Till the day the boy died. She had thought it odd at the time, but she was sure that was what the woman had said. Had she predicted that their son would die before John? But then Jack had not lived long enough to stand up to anyone, poor little scrap. Rose bent her head, ashamed that she should have put so much store on the fey words of a tinker. Nevertheless, she would take what storms lay ahead, if only they would let her son live! Please save my child! she pleaded wordlessly as Father O'Brien handed Jack back to her.

The priest went out into the night, leaving Rose and John staring at each other across the fireside. His gaunt face looked as expressionless as if it had been cut from stone. Wearily, Rose turned and settled the baby in his drawer that served as his cradle and placed it on the hearth. While her back was turned she heard the outer door slam and John's heavy boots ring across the yard.

He's off to drown his sorrows in drink, she thought dully. No doubt this is how things will be from now on.

'Kiss your brother good night,' she told the girls quietly.

'But what if he gets me cough?' Kate asked uncertainly.

'It won't matter,' Rose murmured.

'Will he be dead in the morning?' she asked.

'Maybes.'

All at once, Kate burst into tears. 'I don't want him to!' she sobbed.

Rose put her arms around her. 'I know, hinny. Maybe he'll be spared. Either way it's out of our hands.' She bent forward and kissed Jack tenderly on his pale lips, then ushered the girls swiftly upstairs. The three sisters huddled together in bed for warmth.

'Mam?' Kate asked across the dark room. 'If Jack dies, can Mary come and live with us instead?'

Rose felt her stomach twist at the sudden mention of the neglected Mary.

177

She hardly gave her a thought these days, especially with so much worrying over Jack.

'We'll see,' she gulped, and closed the door quickly before Kate could ask any more awkward questions.

As she descended to the kitchen again, she heard the back door bang and found John already back, a jar of whisky in his hand.

'If you're ganin' to drink yourself daft, you might as well stay down the pub,' Rose said tartly.

He hardly looked at her as he placed the jug on the hearth and blew on his hands to warm them. Then he bent forward and lifted Jack out of the drawer. The baby did not stir as John sat back in his fireside chair. Rose looked on appalled. She could not bear to stay and watch him make a fool of himself, slugging back whisky and singing mawkish songs about Ireland and crying over their dying baby. Without another word, she went back upstairs to the girls' bedroom, creeping in beside them for comfort and wrapping her arms around Kate's warm body. Below she could hear John beginning to sing. She buried her head under the blanket and tried to stifle the sobs that choked her throat.

Alone, John held the listless baby on his knee and talked and sang to him about Ireland.

'One day you'll be proud to be a McMullen. Maybes you'll wear the uniform like your father and march under the Colours. You may be the runt of the litter now, little lad, but one day you'll stand your ground and fight with the best of them. I'll teach you to talk with your fists if anyone insults the name of Ireland or McMullen or the Pope!'

Every so often, John bent to the jar warming on the hearth, dipped in a finger and moistened the baby's lips with whisky. Then he lifted the jar to his own lips and took a swig. As the fire died down and the room darkened and chilled, he wrapped Jack in his jacket and walked up and down the kitchen, cradling his son tightly in his arms to keep him warm.

Through the small hours of that dark February night, John continued to pace the floor, singing, talking and feeding Jack tiny sips of whisky. As long as he kept moving and talking, John could keep at bay the frightening spectre of the black-robed priest coming to bury his son, of his wailing mother and Rose's grief-stricken empty face. He remembered how despair over Margaret's death had so maddened his wife she had thrown herself into the Slake. It filled him with terror to think that she might give up all hope in life if Jack were to die. He knew how painful it would be to lose his son - he had been astonished at the strength of his love for this tiny child - and fear of losing him had churned up his smothered grief for the loss of his daughter, Ruth.

But to lose Rose would be to lose everything. With her he felt important, needed, the head of the household, the provider. With her he was a husband and father, with a home of their own. Rose was well liked, respected, still handsome despite the rigours of the puddling mills, and he still could not believe his luck that she had finally married him. To see her smile at him warmed his very guts. The sound of her laughter was the sweetest sound in the world, better than a hundred sentimental songs.

She had no idea how much she meant to him, he was sure of that. He would never have the words to express what he felt deep down and would die of shame rather than admit them to her. But when she looked at him with contempt, as she had done that evening, it filled him with a bleak shame and rage.

'I'll show your mam, bonny lad,' he croaked. 'I'll not let you die. By heck, you'll live, you little bugger!'

Finally, John sank with exhaustion and drink into the chair once more. He hardly had the voice to sing or the strength to keep his eyes open. He stuck his little finger into the baby's mouth one more time and felt a faint flutter in response. It was the last comforting gesture he remembered before falling asleep.

Rose woke to the sound of John shouting her name in alarm. It was still dark, but from the sounds outside of early deliveries and the scrape of men's boots, morning had come.

'Rose! Rose!' he bellowed. 'Rose, help me!'

She heard him take to the stairs. Her heart hammered in dread now the moment had arrived. She had prayed half the night that this morning would never come, railing at the Virgin Mary for taking her son away so soon.

'I'm here!' Rose called out, the girls beginning to stir around her.

John burst through the door, a bundle of blankets and his jacket in his arms. His face was grey and creased with lack of sleep.

'Rose - the bairn,' He almost threw the bundle at her.

She looked down and gasped. Jack's tiny face was tinged with pink and puckering as if on the point of crying. His mouth opened and made a sucking motion, then he gave out a bleating cry of protest.

Rose shrieked, 'He's still alive!'

John nodded vigorously. 'I woke up and he was suckin' on me finger! The lad wants feedin'!'

Rose's eyes flooded with tears as she looked between John and the baby. 'Aye, he does!' she exclaimed. 'I never thought I'd see him open his eyes again.' She gulped down a throatful of tears. 'What did you do?'

John grinned proudly. 'Gave him a taste of McMullen medicine.'

'The whisky?' Rose asked, shocked.

'Aye,' John grunted. 'Last night was no time for signing the pledge.'

Rose shook her head and laughed in disbelief. As the girls woke up around her and cried with excitement that their baby brother had been spared another day, Rose tentatively began to feed him. Jack snuffled and latched on to her breast. For the first time in days, he took her milk. She felt dizzy with relief.

Glancing up from the bed, she caught John's look. It was dazed, triumphant and, she thought, suffused with love for her. Then he gave her a quick bashful smile, cleared his throat and said gruffly, 'Haway, lasses. Gan downstairs and give your mam some peace.'

As he turned to the door, Rose said softly, 'Thank you, John.'

He hesitated, nodded without looking round and walked out of the room. She knew he was too full of emotion to say anything and she let him go. But she was filled with warmth towards him, knowing that more than Jack's life had been saved that night. Their marriage had held firm. Rose was thankful. Her prayers had been answered and she would light candles and rejoice.

Yet she had bargained with Our Lady. In return she had promised to weather whatever future storms were thrown at her, Rose remembered with a touch of unease. She looked down tenderly at her suckling baby and hoped fervently that the price of saving him would not be too high.

Chapter 33

By March, Jack was putting on weight and thriving at last. He soon grew out of his small drawer and Rose felt confident enough to let him sleep in Mary's old cot close to the side of her bed. With the stirrings of spring, she felt her spirits lift and a new surge of energy. She organised her daughters into helping her spring-clean the house, scrubbing the walls and floors and polishing the windows to rid them of the winter grime. Rose offered to do the same for her neighbours, who in return paid for whitewash for her kitchen walls and dark green paint for the windowsills.

They washed the curtains and blankets and hung them out to dry in the lane, until Kate rushed in screaming, 'Mam, the sheep are eating the washing!'

'Sheep?' Rose said incredulous, pausing in her sweeping of the linoleum floor. 'Is this one of your fancy tales?'

'No, Mam,' Kate insisted, grabbing her mother's hand and heaving her towards the door. 'There's a pack of sheep out the back!'

'Flock of sheep,' Elizabeth corrected, running in behind her. 'She's telling the truth, Mam.'

Rose dashed out still clutching the broom. A drover, who did not know the town, had got lost on the way to the docks and his flock of sheep had scattered in fright at the sound of a whinnying dray horse. Some of them had taken refuge down the back of Albion Street and were nibbling at the mossy bricks and Rose's moth-eaten patchwork quilt.

'Get away! Shoo, you little beggars!' She ran at them yelling and waving her arms. 'I'll have you for me tea if you don't scarper!'

The neighbours and local children came out to watch the spectacle of Rose and her daughters whooping like Red Indians and chasing the bemused sheep down the lane with the long-handled broom.

John heard about it before he reached home when he stopped for a glass of beer at The Railway. He came back chuckling, 'I hear it's mutton for tea the night, eh? Must have sheep stealers in your blood, Rose Ann!'

'I didn't steal any,' she protested, 'just threatened to boil them.'

'Mam was the only one knew what to do,' Kate said proudly.

'Aye, the neighbours might laugh, but nobody came out to help.' Rose was indignant. 'And will you look at this!' She held up the corner of the blanket she had patched with a scrap from his old army trousers. 'Ate right through it.'

'Should've kept the beast in compensation,' John snorted. 'Wish I'd been here to see you.' He grabbed her round the waist and gave her a squeeze. 'Me Little Bo Peep!'

'Give over!' she said, struggling free. 'You're worse than the bairns down the lane - they've been making sheep noises at the back door all afternoon.'

John laughed and began to whistle 'Ba Ba Black Sheep'. Soon Kate and Sarah were joining in with raucous singing. Elizabeth tried not to laugh, glancing at her mother's cross face.

'You did look funny, Mam,' she said with a half-smile, 'chasing that sheep with the brush. That farmer lad looked scared for his life, an' all.'

Rose suddenly saw the funny side and laughed. 'Aye, he did, didn't he? I think I had a touch of spring fever!'

'Poor lad,' John teased. 'He'll gan home telling them Jarrow's full of mad women.'

Rose covered her face with embarrassment and laughed into her hands. Tea time was punctuated with jokes and laughter about the incident, with John comparing her to a wild cowgirl or shepherdess.

'Your mother always was a country lass at heart,' he smirked with the girls. 'Gans mad at the sight of animals.'

Not only did Rose have to endure the cheeky noises of the neighbouring children pretending to be sheep whenever she went out the following week, but even Father O'Brien teased her about it when he called.

'It's a grand job to be the finder of lost sheep, Rose,' he smiled. 'You're a lesson to us all.'

But Rose took the teasing in good heart, for it made her happy to see her family in such high spirits.

The air of excitement was maintained when Kate and Sarah rushed in from school one day gabbling about a circus setting up on the pit heap.

'It's huge, Mam,' Kate gasped. 'Can we go?'

'It's American,' Sarah reported. 'Cowboys and Indians - we've seen the horses. Please, Mam, can we go?'

'You'll have to ask your father,' Rose said cautiously.

Every meal time for the following week, they badgered John to let them go to the circus and Rose watched with interest. He was not one for buying treats for the girls, not since the days of their courtship when he had tried to win their approval with small twists of sweets. Not that they ever had much to spare for such things, but she knew that he kept back enough each week for his own tobacco, newspaper and a drink or two on a Friday night.

At first he resisted. 'What you want to see them Americans for? They're a strange lot. And them Indians are half naked - shouldn't be seen by young lasses. No, I'm not wasting money on them.'

Rose tried to intervene. 'Why not let them go, John? It's not as if they've ever been. Only Margaret went when she was a bairn. We took—' She broke off abruptly, realising by his scowling that she had said the wrong thing. After that she kept quiet, keeping the happy memory of that long-ago trip to herself. But the girls were more persistent.

Each evening they came back from reading the posters with more information.

'Mexican Joe's the ringmaster,' Kate said. 'He wears this great big hat like a lampshade.'

'I like the look of Mustang Jim - he rides a white horse,' Sarah sighed.

'I want to be Violet, the Dashing Rider of the Prairies!' Kate cried. 'She's really bonny.'

But John grew impatient with their constant pleading. 'I haven't got the money,' he snapped, and disappeared behind his newspaper. They all knew by now he could not read it, but anyone who disturbed him snoozing under his paper got a sharp slap of his large hand.

Then, as the end of March neared, two incidents happened to change John's mind. One windy night a fire broke out in Ormonde Street, gutting a house where two families lived and leaving them with only the clothes in which they escaped. John's local newspaper reported that Colonel Joe Shelley of the American Circus had offered the bereft families a free show as well as having a whip-round and raising them nearly seven pounds.

'That's generous of them, isn't it?' Rose said pointedly, eyeing her husband. 'They must be kind folk.' John merely grunted.

The following day, the girls came home late and got a telling off from Rose for worrying her.

'Where've you been?' she demanded.

'Watching the funeral,' Kate sniffed.

'What funeral?'

'Mustang Jim and Violet's daughter,' Sarah explained. 'Died a few days ago - just a young lass. The whole circus was there.'

'That's right, Mam,' Elizabeth said breathlessly. 'I've never seen such a sight. They were all on horses - Indians and cowboys and army lads - all following the hearse.'

'Apache Indians,' Kate added, her eyes wide and glistening. 'And all for a young lass!'

'Mustang Jim was crying.' Sarah trembled as if she would cry too.

'Poor man,' Rose sighed, her anger dissipated at the thought of the circus couple losing their daughter. Then unease stirred. 'What did the lass die of?' She was ever alert to the scare of some epidemic breaking out.

Elizabeth shrugged. The next day the newspaper had a picture of the strange funeral procession and revealed that the young girl had been killed in a riding accident.

'To think they had just lost their lass, yet they still bothered about the families in the fire,' Rose said in admiration. 'What canny folk.'

John said little about it and Rose wondered at his callousness in the face of such tragedy. But the next day he returned home with a brusque command, 'Haway, we're all ganin' to the circus.'

The girls yelped with delight and rushed to wash their faces and comb their hair. Rose smiled at her husband quizzically.

'It's like you said - canny folk,' he mumbled. 'They looked after strangers, didn't they? Us ganin' is like paying our respects to them and their lass.'

Rose was moved by his words. So often when she felt angry with him or thought the worst of this mercurial man, he would surprise her with some kindness, some spontaneous generous gesture that gladdened her heart. Stepping forward, she put a hand up to his cheek in affection. 'Aye, it is. You're a good man, John.'

He grunted impatiently and moved away, but she knew by the way he blushed that he was pleased.

'It's a wonder they can perform so soon after losing their bairn,' Rose reflected.

'They've a living to make,' John said bluntly, 'just like the rest of us.'

That evening they walked through the gaslit town, arm in arm, while Elizabeth carried the sleeping Jack, and Sarah and Kate skipped ahead in excitement. In the large torchlit tent, Rose sat close to John as the noise of gunfire crackled around them, horses thundered over the cinder-covered ground and Indians whooped their war cries.

183

'Sounds like your mam rounding up the sheep,' John joked with the girls.

All the way home, Kate never stopped chattering about the magical experience until finally, coaxed into bed, her sisters ordered her to be quiet. Rose had pushed from her mind that trip to the circus long ago with William and Margaret and the talkative Alexander. But hearing Kate's bubbling enthusiasm reminded her of the small boy and she felt a pang of regret for that far-off time. What had become of the Liddells' restless small cousin? She would probably never know. She did not even know where the kind Liddells were any more, let alone the hapless boy, passed from relative to relative.

As she settled Jack in his cot, she pondered whether her dark-haired son might turn out as inquisitive and lively as Alexander. How well he and William had got on together! But she smothered such thoughts; it was dangerous to make comparisons or try to conjure up the past. It was John who waited for her now. She glanced at her husband watching her in the flickering candlelight and knew the look on his face well. For the past month, since John had saved Jack's life, they had resumed lovemaking. Rose got into bed, blew out the candle and waited for him to reach for her, guiltily praying that she would not fall pregnant again.

One day in April, Rose heard a strange piece of news from Maggie. Her sister had brought Mary down to the town for one of her infrequent visits to see her mother and the women were sitting at the open kitchen door, stitching scraps of cloth into a new clippy mat for the hearth. Mary was playing with the old wooden cage and lion that Rose had managed to keep when everything else she and William had once possessed had been pawned several times over. Beside her, on the old clippy mat, Jack kicked and gurgled contentedly. Out in the yard, one-year-old Margaret was sleeping in the bogie that Danny had made into a pram for his daughter.

'Have you heard old Jobling's widow died at last?' Maggie asked as she prodded a hole in the hessian with a metal spike.

Rose looked up nonplussed. 'Jobling's widow?'

'Aye,' Maggie said, pausing in her work. 'Jobling that got hung on the gibbet down the Slacks for murdering that magistrate—'

'I know who Jobling is,' Rose said impatiently. He had haunted her life with his grisly image ever since her granny had filled her head full of tales of his ghost. But the gibbeting had been long before she was born, in the days when her grandmother had been young and before Queen Victoria had come to the throne. 'Do you mean to say his missus has been alive all this time?'

Maggie nodded. 'Aye. Seemingly she's been in the workhouse at Shields for years. Ninety-six she was - that's a grand age, isn't it?'

Rose shuddered. 'A long time to be widowed. Must've been nearly sixty years fending for hersel'.' It made her couple of years of widowhood seem insignificant in comparison, gruelling though they were. She recalled her granny telling her how Jobling's widow had lived so close to the Slake that every day she could not avoid seeing the horrific spectre of her husband's tarred corpse swinging in the breeze. It must have sent her half crazed! She remembered uneasily how thoughts of Jobling had unhinged her after Margaret's death and led her to throw herself into the treacherous Slake.

Maggie looked thoughtful. 'Aye, and to end up in the workhouse with no one else to look after her. .. She must've had a hard life, poor woman. But then that place is full of widows—' She broke off abruptly, looking awkwardly at her sister.

Rose put out her hand in reassurance. 'You're right - and I'd have been one of them if it hadn't been for you and Danny. I'll never forget what you did for me and the bairns - what you're still doing.'

She looked uneasily at Mary. The child had grown a good inch since she had last seen her. She was skinny and lithe with straight brown hair, a thin stubborn mouth and a guarded look in her nut-brown eyes. She still clung to the grubby peg doll that Maggie had made her and was busy giving it rides in the lion's cage while the lion was discarded in the coal scuttle.

'You don't have to worry about her,' Maggie said quietly. 'You've four bairns to take care of- we've only Margaret. Mary's canny company for me - specially when Da doesn't know who I am any more.'

Rose felt another wave of guilt. 'Are you managing all right with him?'

'Course,' Maggie assured. 'And Lizzie visits when she can. But I'll be surprised if he lasts another winter,' she sighed.

'I'll take Mary back when she has to start school,' Rose promised, thinking that could still be two years away. Time enough for her to really settle with John and the baby first. By then Elizabeth and maybe Sarah would be working, and there would be more room and time for Mary.

Just then, Mary looked up and glared as if she understood Rose's reluctance to take her back. The girl stood up and tugged on Maggie's arm. 'I want to go home. Don't like it here.'

Maggie tried to hush her. 'I'm talking to your mam. You play with your brother Jack.'

'No,' she shouted, kicking the chair in sudden temper. 'He's not me brother and he's smelly.'

'Watch your manners,' Rose warned. 'And you'll stay to see your sisters after school.'

Mary stuck her tongue out at Rose. 'No! You're not me mam so you can't tell us what to do.'

'Mind your tongue!' Rose smacked her swiftly and Mary howled in protest.

Maggie stood and picked up Mary, pinning her under a strong arm and shouting to be heard. 'Sorry, Rose, when she gets like this it's best to take her away.'

She left with the red-faced child screaming and struggling to be free. Maggie wheeled the bogie with her free hand and marched out of the yard. Rose stood at the back door cringing at the sound of her daughter bawling all the way down the lane.

'Got a temper on her, that one,' one of her neighbours commented, having come out to view the commotion.

Rose nodded and flushed, unable to admit it was her own daughter. Besides, it was none of the woman's business, she thought defensively.

But the visit had an unsettling effect on Rose. Although the days grew warmer and lighter and the children were able to play out for longer, she could not stop thinking about the ancient Mrs Jobling, living all those years after her husband had been hanged, incarcerated in the workhouse in a twilight existence. How long had she been there? Maybe all Rose's lifetime. And her only escape had been death. Whenever Rose thought of it, she shivered as if a chill river breeze blew at her back. Every day she prayed that she and John were kept in health and he in work so that they could support themselves and their children. It was all she asked.

On Whit Monday they took the girls to see a huge procession of horses from all around the county, processing through the town. But the festival was marred by torrential rain and they retreated early, soaked through. John caught a cold and declared it was the last time he would waste a day's holiday standing in crowds with her children when he could have been snug and dry in the public bar of The Railway.

As the summer progressed, Rose noticed that John's visits to the pub on his way home from work were growing more frequent. It puzzled her until she heard from her mother-in-law that John's brother Pat was back after a couple of years in Ireland.

'So that's why he's coming home spouting off about Ireland and Home Rule all of a sudden,' Rose laughed shortly.

Mrs McMullen nodded. 'Pat's a supporter. John'll be trying to prove he's a better patriot than his brother. They're more Irish than the Irish, my boys, for all they speak like Jarrow men.'

When Rose asked him about it, John was dismissive. 'It doesn't concern you, Rose. We talk politics - it's men's business.'

Rose was annoyed. 'I've a right to know the company me husband keeps. Are you drinking with your brothers again?'

'I'll not be questioned like a criminal by me wife,' John blustered, which confirmed Rose's suspicions.

'We can't afford it,' she complained. 'Why can't you come home straight from work like you used to?'

But John avoided her look. 'I've got important business to see to, political business. There's a chance we might even get Charles Parnell himself to come and speak.'

'Parnell, the Irish leader?'

'Aye.'

Rose was dubious. 'Wasn't he mixed up in some divorce? Aye, I'm sure that's the one. Father O'Brien preached against him last year. Not that you would have heard him,' Rose added pointedly.

John was quickly riled. He might not attend church regularly, but he was still a staunch Catholic. 'Parnell's still a nationalist and leader of the Home Rule movement and I'll go and hear him whether the priest likes it or not!'

'This is all Pat McMullen's doing, I suppose?' Rose scoffed. 'All dreamed up in the front bar of The Railway.'

'Don't talk daft,' John snapped. 'I don't need Pat to tell me what to do. There are lots of us supporters. We're planning a rally in Newcastle and I intend to gan to it.'

Rose was dismayed. She had thought this was all an excuse to go drinking, but he sounded serious about getting involved in politics - Irish politics at that. That was more worrying. John had always been passionate about his homeland, but it didn't do to shout too loudly about being Irish when it came to finding work and getting on in life. She had witnessed enough discrimination to know that. Only the other week, the tick man from the Pru had refused to let them pay into a burial fund because of their surname. And hadn't she herself hidden behind the name of Fawcett in order to secure a much-needed job with the Liddells all those years ago? Besides, nobody liked an agitator, least of all employers.

'You're not ganin' to make trouble, are you?' Rose asked in concern.

'Stop frettin',' John said impatiently. 'And don't meddle in things that don't concern you.'

Rose could get no more out of him but as the summer wore on she had the suspicion that he was keeping something from her. She could tell by the way he avoided her look and lost his temper over trivial matters, snapping at her and the girls if the table was not set to his satisfaction or the fire poker was put back in the wrong place.

Worry nagged at Rose like a bad tooth, but she could not discover what was wrong. At night, lying awake listening to his snoring after one of his 'meetings', she imagined him involved in some Fenian plot. She saw him being transported to the colonies for agitation or, worse still, hanged for treason. She would be like Jobling's widow, left to fend for herself.

Then Race Week came and John announced he was going through to Newcastle.

'Will you take the lasses?' Rose asked tentatively, remembering how last year's trip had ended in fierce argument with the gypsy.

'No,' John was brusque. 'We're having a procession - the Home Rule supporters. There might be bother.'

Rose's insides felt leaden. 'Don't go, John,' she pleaded quietly. 'You've never had any truck with politicians and demonstratin' before. Why start now when you've a family to support?'

But this only incensed him the more and he barked at her, 'Don't tell me m' business, woman! I'm doing this for Ireland and me people. The English have me sweatin' and toilin' for them six days a week. The British army had me pound of flesh for long enough, an' all.' He stuck his fists up aggressively. 'Now these are ganin' to be used for Ireland!'

He strode to the door, jamming on his cap. Rose went after him, full of fear.

'Don't go fightin', please, John, man!' She held on to his arm.

But he shook her off roughly. 'It's time we stood up for ourselves. Leave off me, Rose Ann!'

Rose gulped back the panic in her throat. 'It's that useless brother of yours, put you up to this, isn't it?' she accused, following him outside. 'It's all right for Pat - he has no wife or bairns to think about. But you have.' She ran after him as he marched out of the yard, not caring if all the neighbours heard. 'Damn you, John McMullen!' she bawled. 'What use are you to me locked up in Newcastle gaol the night?'

She could not believe she was behaving in such an unseemly way, screaming after him down the lane. But a familiar sickening terror was churning in her stomach: the terror of losing her husband, the roof over her children's heads, her tenuous security once again.

'Mam, *Mam*,' Elizabeth pulled on her arm and tried to coax her back inside and out of view of disapproving neighbours. 'It's a day out at the races, that's all. Just a bit march through Newcastle and then a few drinks, I wouldn't doubt. He'll not come to any harm.'

As Rose looked at her daughter's fair face, creased in concern for her, the anger in her subsided. How could a girl her age be so wise? Elizabeth had seen John's protesting for what it was - an excuse for a day out drinking more than likely.

'You've an old head on young shoulders,' she said quietly, touching her daughter's face affectionately.

With an indignant stare at the neighbours who stood cross-armed on their back steps, Rose retreated into the house and slammed the door shut on the outside world.

It was late by the time John came home, crashing in at the back door and cursing as he tripped over a pair of boots in the dark. Rose had sat up dozing on the settle, waiting for him. Her relief that he was safely home turned swiftly to annoyance at his drunken state.

'What time do you call this?' she demanded, rising from the seat and reaching for a spluttering candle. 'It's gone midnight.' She held the dying candle higher. 'Look at you! Your jacket's torn - and where's your cap?'

He lurched at her, but banged into the table instead and swore loudly at her as if it were her fault.

'I'll not be blamed if you can hardly stand,' Rose said in derision. 'Or hardly speak except to take the saints' names in vain.'

He tried to focus on her with bloodshot eyes, his breath reeking of whisky. 'Don't speak to me like that, woman,' he slurred.

'I'll speak how I want if you choose to come rolling in on all fours like an animal,' Rose jeered. 'What a fine specimen of an Irishman! Have you won Home Rule today?'

'Don't mock me,' John raised his voice in aggression, pushing the table between them out of the way. 'No one makes a fool out of a McMullen!'

'No one's making a fool out of you 'cept yourself,' Rose muttered, thinking how old and haggard he suddenly looked.

John grabbed the stool with which he was steadying himself and raised it above his head. He waved it wildly. 'You'll not speak to me like that in me own home,' he roared.

'It won't be our home if you carry on drinking all your wages like you have done this past month,' Rose cried. 'If we get put out on the street it'll be from your drinking, not my bad housekeeping.'

He gave a howl of fury and brought the stool crashing down on to the table. The legs cracked and splintered. Rose jumped back in fright, nearly dropping the candle in its tin holder. Hot wax splashed over her hand and she gasped in pain.

John turned to her, clutching the remains of the stool. 'Well, I've some'at to please you, you ungrateful bitch! You can make a bit extra out of our new lodger.'

'What you talking about, you drunken fool?'

He glared at her in triumph. 'Pat's moving in with us.'

'Pat?' Rose repeated incredulously. 'He's not stopping here!'

John came at her, jabbing the stool at her chest. 'If I say he is, he bloody is!'

'No, John,' she protested, fending him off. 'I don't want lodgers in the house with the lasses. We'll manage on our own.'

'With what?' he cried. 'There's no more work at the pig carrying.'

Rose stared at him, horrified. 'What d'you mean?'

'You heard,' he snarled. 'They've laid me off. The work's drying up - the mill's on short time again. It'll be a hard winter, they're saying.'

Rose's heart thumped like a steam hammer. 'When did you know?'

'Week ago,' John said, his shoulders suddenly slumping. He dropped the broken stool.

'The money for the races?' Rose asked bewildered.

John's look was empty as it met hers. 'I had a lend off Pat.'

Rose felt breathless. 'And we're supposed to pay him back by giving him a bed?'

John nodded. 'And he'll pay for his keep.'

'Where's he working that he can afford to keep the pair of you in whisky?' Rose demanded.

'Down Tyne Dock,' John answered in a flat voice. 'Loadin' iron ore off the boats.'

She stared at his bowed, dejected head. The fight of moments before had gone out of him. She was filled with both sadness and contempt. He was once more at the mercy of slackening trade, turned away from work through no fault of his own; yet he had kept from her the gravity of their situation, turning instead to his drinking friends and wild dreams of Irish freedom.

When she managed to speak, there was a bitter fatalism to her voice. 'Pat can sleep on the settle. If there's work at Tyne Dock you can try for it too. Monday, you'll gan down the dock gates with your brother.'

She turned from him, swallowing the bitter bile in her throat, and made for the stairs. She tried to stem the panic that threatened to overwhelm her - and the belief that they were finally heading into the storm the gypsy had predicted.

Chapter 34

On Kate's ninth birthday, the schools broke up for the summer holidays. She brought two friends home, promising them cake and home-made lemonade.

'There isn't any,' Rose said sharply to her eager-faced daughter. 'I never said there would be.'

'But we always have cake on me birthday,' Kate said in disappointment.

'Not this year - we can't afford it. Why'd you bring the lasses here?'

She felt ashamed that she had nothing to give them apart from tepid water and bread smeared with dripping. Maggie had brought her eggs the day before so that she could make a cake, but John had ordered that she boil them for breakfast for Pat and himself. Rose had seethed with annoyance, but since Pat had moved in, John had been lording it over her. If she argued back, her husband would shout at her foully in language that she did not want the girls to hear. It was easier to bite her tongue and try to keep the peace, so long as Pat was their lodger.

With dismay she realised that John's brother was very content with his new lodgings, being waited on by her and Elizabeth, receiving the largest share of their meagre rations. Yet the paltry amount he contributed to the housekeeping hardly covered the cost of feeding him, let alone the rest of them. There was too little left when he and John returned late from the docks.

Rose knew that the work was gruelling, shovelling iron ore from the boats for ten hours a day. The men would return home soaked to the skin from standing thigh-deep in cold and filthy water, their clothes stinking and stained red from the iron ore. For their efforts they were paid a mere three shilling and sixpence, but by the time they had stopped off at the pub on the way home, Rose barely saw half of it. She knew that for John these drinking sessions blunted his exhaustion in the way that quaffing beer at the puddling mill had done for her. But it was she who was left to dry off their work clothes while they demolished what food there was in the house and sent one of the girls out to fetch another jug of beer from The Railway. While Rose worried over how to make ends meet, she grew resentful of John's drinking with Pat, especially when there was not enough to treat her daughter and friends to a plain cake for her birthday.

Rose could hardly bear to look at Kate's disappointed face. She came to a swift decision. 'You mind Jack for half an hour,' she ordered, 'and I'll fetch some'at nice for your tea.'

At once, Kate's face broke into a happy grin. She flung her arms around her mother's thick waist. 'Thanks, Mam!'

Rose fleetingly touched her soft brown hair before pushing her away. 'Haway, you'd think I'd promised you the crown jewels,' she protested in embarrassment at her daughter's open affection in front of her school friends.

Kate laughed and turned to pick Jack from the hearth where he was sitting chewing on a stale crust. She hauled him into her arms and staggered outside, calling to her friends to follow.

'We'll play houses with our Jack,' she cried. 'I'll be the mam.'

Rose grabbed her thick black cloak with its stiffly embroidered collar and hurried out of the house. Half an hour later she had handed it in to Slater's pawnshop and received enough in return to provide a handsome birthday tea.

From the co-op she bought ham and cheese, jam, scones and currant buns, as well as a large cherry cake - Kate's favourite. She dithered over whether to save the remaining pennies to put towards the gas, then doubled back into the shop and spent them on ginger beer and lemonade. She'd worry about the bills next week.

Kate's eyes bulged at the sight of the meal spread out for them that tea time and Rose could see with what pride she welcomed her friends to the table. Maggie called in with Mary and baby Margaret and was equally surprised.

'Don't say a word to John, but I pawned me coat,' Rose whispered. 'Just hope the weather stays fine for a week or two.'

Maggie gave Kate a pair of mittens she had knitted for her niece. 'They'll come in handy for the winter,' Maggie explained, smiling at Kate's baffled look. 'And this is for you an' all.' She handed over a book she had traded eggs for at a second-hand stall in the town. Kate flicked through it; saw too many words and not enough pictures.

'Ta, Aunt Maggie,' she smiled. 'I'll let our Lizzie read it first.' She handed it straight to her sister.

Rose could not help a wry smile. It rankled that her sister could give her daughter presents when she could not. But Kate did not seem to mind. Being able to share a feast with her friends, to have the lively company of her sisters and playmates, seemed enough for Kate.

The children went outside again to play and Rose enjoyed a quiet cup of tea with her sister, sitting in the doorway catching the evening breeze. Maggie was the first to hear them coming, the thud of boots up the lane. She jumped up and grabbed Margaret, calling to Mary to come.

'I'll go out the front,' she said nervously. 'Call up soon with the bairns, now they're on holiday - they can give a hand in the field.' She flung the words over her shoulder as she retreated out of the seldom-used front door.

Rose hardly had time to call a goodbye. Behind her she could hear John shouting at the children in the lane and Pat's loud fog-horn laughter. For the first time it struck her how eager Maggie was to avoid the McMullen men. She was always away by the time they marched in, cussing the girls and ordering her about like a skivvy. When Rose thought about it, none of her neighbours called in any more for a quick word or to help her on her clippy mat.

Something was changing under her roof. The family closeness and teasing intimacy of the past year had evaporated since Pat had moved in and John had gone to work at the docks. Now the place jarred with shouts and swearing, the sound of legs being slapped by leathery hands and the swaggering of drunken men. No wonder Maggie was quick to leave and others were frightened to venture over the doorstep. But Rose felt anger rather than fear, and it was directed at her overbearing brother-in-law. Pat was to blame for this. He seemed intent on creating discord between John and his family. She could smell the drink on them the minute they tramped in the door.

Pat shouted for Kate. 'Come here, lass!' he commanded. 'I've something for you.'

Kate came to the door, glancing at her mother cautiously. Rose shook her head, but John waved her in.

'Haway and do as your Uncle Pat says,' he barked. He grabbed Kate by the arm and pulled her into the kitchen, pushing her forward. Rose tensed. He was growing too rough with the girls.

Pat beamed at her, showing the gummy gap where four rotten front teeth had been knocked out in a fight on St Patrick's Day. He was shorter than John, stocky and thick-necked, his hair almost gone. His muddy brown eyes were frequently bloodshot from grit and drink, and his face was flushed and perspiring from the three-mile walk home.

'Come and sit on me knee,' he said, slapping his sodden thighs. Kate looked at him appalled.

'Not while you're still in those stinkin' trousers,' Rose intervened. 'And you shouldn't be sitting in the chair either.'

'Stop fussing,' John said with a dismissive wave of his arm. 'Gan on, Kate. See what he's got you.'

Kate edged forward and bravely tried to smile. Pat pulled her on to his knee and put his filthy arm about her. 'Never had a lass of me own,' he said, putting his head close to hers.

'She might have nits,' Rose said suddenly, and saw with satisfaction how Pat leant quickly away.

'If she has, you'll chop her long hair off,' John said, irritated by Rose's lack of co-operation. 'Haway, Pat man, and give her the present. It's from the two of us,' he said proudly.

Rose watched dumbfounded as Pat pulled something from his pocket and placed it in Kate's hand. It was a battered pack of playing cards tied together with string.

'There, isn't that grand, Kate?' John prompted.

Kate nodded, a little unsure. 'Ta very much, Uncle Pat. Can I go and play now?'

Pat laughed, squeezed her and planted a kiss on her lips that made Rose queasy. 'Off you go then,' he conceded. As Kate slipped from his knee, Rose saw the girl wipe her lips on her arm.

'Don't I get a kiss an' all?' John asked in mock hurt. Kate leant up and kissed him on the cheek, then bolted for the doorway where her friends and Sarah were watching at a distance.

When they had disappeared, Rose rounded on the men indignantly. 'You didn't buy those cards for the lass, you bought them for yourselves. So you two can play cards late into the night while you sit there boozing!'

John seemed taken aback by her outburst. He gawped at her in surprise. But Pat tutted and shook his head as if dealing with a naughty child. 'Now, now, Rose Ann. A little gratitude, a little gratitude. That's no way to speak to the man of the house.'

She was infuriated. 'I didn't ask for your opinion,' she snapped. Turning to John, hands on her ample hips, she berated him. 'You never said you had any money spare for the lass's birthday. We could've got her some'at she wanted - a spinning top like the other bairns in the street. What do you think it's like for me, her own mam, having nowt to give her? I even had to pawn me coat to put tea on the table today! How long is this ganin' to go on? With him sitting there like the Viceroy of India taking everything we have!'

Behind her she heard Pat tutting again and saying, 'Haway, John, I wouldn't stand for a woman talking to me like that.'

Rose swung round to give him a piece of her mind and that was why she did not see the punch coming. But an instant later, she felt as if an iron hammer had been swung against her ear. It exploded in pain as she staggered back, caught off balance, and went crashing to the floor, hitting her arm on the table as she fell. The half-eaten cherry cake toppled after her.

For a moment she lay there dizzy and wondering what had hit her. Her ear buzzed and throbbed with pain. She looked round vacantly, trying to remember what had just been said. Rose caught sight of John's haggard, sweating face peering down at her. He was clenching and unclenching his fists. She stared at him in sickening realisation. He had hit her. He had dared to hit her, his own wife! Revulsion and shame engulfed her.

John stepped towards her and for a fearful moment she thought he would strike her again. She flinched from him, but he just stood looking over her, his eyes as hard as flint.

'Rose?' he growled. 'Rose Ann! Get up!'

Just then, Elizabeth came in from the yard, Jack in her arms. 'Mam, are you all right?' She hurried over, plonking her brother on the floor.

Rose's instant response was to cover up what had happened, to protect her daughter from the violence, to deny it had ever happened. She still could not believe that it had. Other women were beaten by their men behind closed doors, but not her! And not her John! He was a man with a temper, a fighter on the street maybe, but not the type to hit women. She had married a soldier, one of Lord Roberts's brave campaigners, not a coward or a bully.

'I had a dizzy spell, that's all,' she said, brushing off Elizabeth's attempts to help her. 'Hit me head off the table.'

The girl glanced up at her stepfather.

'Aye, she fell,' he mumbled.

Pat rose and came over. He looked down at Rose with a satisfied glint. 'Should be more careful, Rose Ann,' he said evenly, and she heard the mockery in his voice. 'Come on, John. We've that meeting remember.' He prodded the fallen cherry cake with his dirty boot. 'There's nowt left for us to eat here. I'll treat you to hot peas on the way.'

Rose watched her husband hesitate. His jaw was clenched as if he were biting down on words that were trying to escape. But what he wanted to say to her she never knew. For with an impatient grunt, he turned from her and strode after his brother.

Rose stared after him, feeling some small flame of hope smother inside her and go out. Heavy-hearted, she dragged herself up from the floor. She felt light-headed as she stood, sounds from far off jangling in her ears. She touched the tender spot where John's fist had caught her. The bruising was swelling. Elizabeth came with a cold damp cloth and held it to her mother's face. After a minute Rose pushed her away and said she was fine.

Somehow, Rose managed to go about her chores without showing her pain or giving in to the tears that pricked her eyes. She retrieved the cherry cake and put it in the pantry. Kate's friends went home and Rose packed the girls off to bed, only half listening to their chatter about what they would do with the holidays. Rose thought with a leaden heart how she would have to get them working rather than playing out in the street. Already her mind was grappling with how she would cope with this new situation. By the saints, she would not allow her family to fall apart because of Pat's boorish, bullying influence!

Only when Rose finally collapsed into bed did she give in to the bitter sorrow that gnawed at her insides like a rat. She wept with humiliation and anger.

Bending over the cot where Jack lay sleeping untroubled, she hissed, 'Don't you turn out like those McMullens. Don't you dare!'

Chapter 35

After John's callous attack nothing was quite the same. Rose suspected his outbursts were to satisfy his older brother, yet she was wary of his temper now. They desperately needed money and she saw no end to John and Pat's spendthrift drinking. Yet she still resisted John's attempts to have Elizabeth sent into service.

'She's not yet twelve,' Rose pointed out; 'it wouldn't be legal. We'd have the priest on our backs for truancy.' Usually mention of the priest would stop John's badgering.

Over the summer she sent the girls up to Maggie's to help in the field and sell vegetables around the town. They learned how to use the McConnells' old sewing machine and made a few pennies mending and altering clothes for customers too. Sarah and Kate got jobs scrubbing doorsteps for the more well-off in the surrounding streets and Rose made elder-flower juice and sold it from their kitchen window.

But much of this extra income evaporated when the girls went back to school at the end of the summer. They continued to scrub doorsteps in the chill early morning before lessons, but with autumn came the need for more fuel and candles, and Rose's debts began to mount. Yet still she stubbornly resisted pressure from the men to have Elizabeth sent out to work. She clung to the ambition that her eldest would make something of herself. The thought kept her going when she trailed to the pawnshop each Monday morning or chivvied her inebriated husband to bed late at night. Besides, Rose had grown to depend on her eldest for company as well as help around the house. She had taken the place of Margaret in her affections.

While she welcomed Elizabeth's growing maturity, the signs of her womanhood were a cause for concern. Her daughter was tall for her age and bashfully pretty with her fair hair and soft skin. Increasingly she noticed Pat's lascivious looks and the way he tried to touch her as she served him at table. Elizabeth had taken to carrying water up to the bedroom to wash rather than risk Pat surprising her as she bathed in front of the fire.

Rose wanted to talk to John about his brother's unhealthy interest, but she dared not provoke another row over Elizabeth. It might only add fuel to his argument of sending the girl away rather than Pat. So all Rose could do was keep a watchful eye on her brother-in-law and protect her daughters from his groping hands and ribald remarks. How she longed for the day when they could be rid of him!

Then nature conspired against Rose and all her plans began to unravel. Fever broke out all over Jarrow that autumn. In particular, measles spread quickly around the infants' schools in the town and by November every one of them had closed. Children roamed the streets, shivering in shop doorways like packs of skinny dogs, some barefoot, wondering what to do with their freedom.

Rose put her girls to work doing the washing and ironing, baking bread and minding Jack, but still she found they were always under her feet. She prayed for the epidemic to wane and the schools to open up again, but by Christmas they were still closed. They had little to spare for the celebrations, but managed to give the girls oranges and a penny each to spend on sweets. To Rose's relief, Pat stayed round at his mother's over the festivities and they enjoyed a quiet Christmas together.

John made an effort to stay sober and they walked up to Simonside in the glistening frost and roasted chestnuts with Maggie and Danny. Lizzie was visiting with her husband, Peter, and even old McConnell perked up at the company and began to sing. They swapped news and everyone clapped when Jack took his first tottering steps across the room. Rose enjoyed the day and felt a surge of hope that things would improve come the New Year. If only she could get rid of Pat's malign influence, she felt sure John would become his old self again.

But once home, drudgery and arguments over money weighed them down as before. John's bad temper returned with his long, relentless days at the docks and the tramp uphill to Jarrow at the end of them. Sometimes he was turned away with no work at all and his black moods would deepen. Worse still, Pat was back and the schools remained firmly closed. Scores of children were still laid low with measles.

With Pat goading him, John began rowing again over sending Elizabeth out to work. It was Elizabeth who finally took the decision out of Rose's hands, unable to bear the warring between the adults any longer. She came back one grey January day to say she had found a place with a clock repairer's family, recommended by her teacher.

'McQuarrie they call them. The missus needs someone to mind the bairns while she's in the shop and he's out calling on the big houses. I'm to do the washing and cleaning, an' all.'

'How much will they pay you?' John asked at once.

'Two shillings a week - and me bed and board.'

'Better than nowt,' he grunted.

Rose was stunned. 'You'll be living in then?'

Elizabeth nodded. 'One day off a fortnight.' She saw the look on her mother's face and added, 'Maybes I could bring the bairns round to see you some days - when the spring weather comes. They look canny - the lad's six and his sister's four. The missus is expecting again soon.'

Rose turned and busied herself at the kitchen table, trying to hide the desolation she felt at her daughter having to go 'to place' after all. After all these years of striving to give her an education, her dreams of Elizabeth becoming a pupil teacher had come to nothing. She was to skivvy for others instead. How William would have hated it!

When the day came for Elizabeth to go she refused to let her mother accompany her across town.

'I'm old enough to go on me own,' she insisted, as Rose fussed with her hair. Rose was hurt to think her daughter might be ashamed to introduce her to her more well-to-do employers. But as her only decent clothes were constantly in and out of the pawnshop, she supposed she did look shabby.

So Rose was brusque, belying what she felt inside. 'We'll see you in a fortnight. Keep yourself tidy and remember to say your prayers.' She wiped a smut from the girl's face with a wet finger.

Suddenly Elizabeth flung her arms around her mother's neck, tears flooding her eyes. 'Will you be all right, Mam?'

Rose steeled herself against the emotion that threatened to choke her. 'Course I will. No crying now, hinny.' Briefly she pressed her daughter to her breast and then let go. Sarah and Kate hovered nearby, unusually subdued. 'Say goodbye to your sisters.'

The girls mumbled self-conscious farewells, then Elizabeth picked up Jack, kissed him and tickled him under his chin to make him giggle. Handing him over to Rose, she turned swiftly for the door. They followed her silently into the lane, but Kate could not contain herself. She ran after her older sister, shouting, 'I'll see you to the end, our Lizzie!'

Rose watched them go arm in arm down the muddy lane, Kate keeping up with her sister's leggy strides with her strange limping skip. There would never be enough money for an operation on her foot, Rose realised with a pang. At the end, Elizabeth slipped free, turned, waved one last time and disappeared round the corner. Kate stood in the raw wind, her dark hair blowing wildly, waving to a figure that Rose could no longer see.

Unable to bear the sight, Rose said to Sarah, 'Gan and fetch your sister back, hinny.' Then she turned and went inside with a heavy heart.

The two weeks until Elizabeth's first day off dragged like a month. Rose was largely cooped up at home with the younger children. It seemed to rain incessantly so that the kitchen was festooned with damp washing for days on end. Rose and the girls had to tidy it away in the evening, dumping it in a wet pile in the corner, so that Pat would not complain about it hanging over his bed or John pull it down in annoyance.

'If that school ever opens again you'll have forgotten all your lessons,' she grumbled to the fractious girls. With breaks in the wet weather, Sarah and Kate ventured out to find firewood or nuggets of coal along the railway line, anything to get out of the house.

The day of Elizabeth's holiday arrived at last and Rose had a tray of scones baked for the occasion. But by mid-afternoon on the Sunday there was no sign of her. An hour later it was dark and Rose knew she would not come so late. Pat was the only one who had an appetite for the special tea which he tucked into, then slumped in John's chair by the fire and fell asleep.

Overwhelmed with disappointment, Rose cried at John, 'They've no right to keep her there on her day off!'

But he shrugged fatalistically. He had been round to collect his stepdaughter's wages from the McQuarries the day before and they had all feasted on herring and potatoes as a result.

'She's settling in canny. Maybes she's taken a walk up to see Maggie instead.'

Rose was indignant. 'She wouldn't do that! Not on her first day off.' She could not stop fretting and started questioning John all over again. 'How did she look? Are they treting her well?'

'I told you before,' John answered impatiently, 'she was canny. Mrs McQuarrie said she's gettin' on grand with the bairns and she couldn't manage without her.'

Something struck Rose about his answer that had not the previous day. 'Mrs

197

McQuarrie said? But I thought you'd seen Elizabeth herself?'

John frowned hard in concentration over the game of patience he was playing with Kate's birthday cards. He did not look up. 'Well, not in person. She was busy upstairs.'

Rose looked at him in disbelief. 'You came back without even a word to the lass? I thought you'd seen her. You told me she was looking grand. I knew I should've gone mesel'!'

'Stop your fussin',' John snapped. 'She's a sensible lass. She'll be all right.'

'How do you know if you never saw her?' Rose accused. 'I'm ganin' over there first thing tomorra to see for mesel'.'

'Don't you go interferin' and causing bother with the McQuarries,' John was quick to dissuade her. 'It's her first job and the lass has only been there a fortnight. Give her time to settle in, Rose Ann. You'll only make it awkward for her, turnin up unexpected.'

Reluctantly Rose agreed. She did not want to be the cause of trouble between Elizabeth and her new employers. If Mrs McQuarrie had said she was doing well, she must take the woman's word for it.

But she could not help crossing town the following week to try to catch a glimpse of her daughter. She stood in the rain for half an hour at the end of the street watching the house, but no one came or went. She thought this strange for a house with a workshop. Still, she was reassured by the look of the place with its polished door knob and clean windows. At least Elizabeth was working in a respectable, quietly prosperous neighbourhood, the kind that foremen and small shopkeepers could afford. It reminded her of Raglan Street where she had lived with William.

The McQuarries' workshop must be at the back, for the only indication that a clock mender lived there was from a discreet sign in the window. Rose stood in a frenzy of indecision, wondering if she should call in pretending to have something to repair. But her courage failed her and she trailed back home in frustration.

Nevertheless, she was not going to allow John to fetch the wages the next week. It was high time she met these McQuarries. On the Friday before Elizabeth's next day off was due, she dressed carefully in her Sunday dress and cape, which she had reclaimed from the pawnshop with a pair of brass candlesticks and the fire poker. Leaving Jack with his sisters, she set off for the McQuarries'.

She hammered on the front door three times before it was answered. Rose hoped it would be Elizabeth, but instead a small man with spectacles peered out.

'Mr McQuarrie?'

'Yes, what do you want?'

'I'm Mrs McMullen. I've come for Elizabeth's wages - and to see the lass.' She looked squarely into his narrow-set eyes.

She noticed his slight agitation, the way he pulled at his waistcoat and cleared his throat. Rose tried to see past him into the dark interior. There was no sound of children or anyone else.

'I'll not be paying a full two weeks,' he muttered. 'She's not worked them.'

Rose was perplexed. 'What d'you mean? She's not been home. She must've worked them.'

He cleared his throat again noisily. 'Been in bed, sick. Mrs McQuarrie's had to take the children to her sister's. It's not been convenient - not with her preparing for her confinement—'

'Sick?' Rose cut him off. 'What's wrong with her?'

'Caught the measles.'

Rose's heart thumped in alarm. 'Measles! Why didn't you send her home?'

'It's nothing to do with me,' he said indignantly. 'She told the missus she didn't want to go home and risk passing it on to her family. My wife was very considerate, letting her stay and putting up with the inconvenience of moving in with her sister.'

'Where is she? I want to see me lass!' Rose pushed past him easily.

'You can't barge in here.'

'I'm taking her home. Tell me where she's lying,' Rose demanded.

'She's in the attic,' he answered testily. 'We'll not have her back after this.'

Rose ignored him and hurried up the narrow stairs in front of her. 'Elizabeth! Hinny, where are you?'

At the top were two bedrooms. Through one door she could see a rocking horse. She shouted again. A small croaking cry answered from the children's room. Rose dashed in. The beds were empty. She could see no sign of her daughter. Then she heard a painful coughing from a half-open door into the eaves of the roof. Rushing forward, she yanked back the small door and peered in. The girl lay on a mattress in a space no bigger than a cupboard. The air smelt fetid yet cold. Rose sank to her knees.

'Oh, Mary, Mother of God! What's become of you?' She felt her forehead. It burnt like fire.

'Mam?' Elizabeth croaked. 'Is it you, Mam?'

'Aye,' Rose gulped, hardly able to speak. As she lifted her up, she could see the angry rash of small red spots on her face. Her neck looked swollen. 'I'm taking you home. Can you stand, hinny?'

Elizabeth winced at the light from the open doorway and tried to shade her eyes. She sank back heavily in her mother's arms.

'Just try,' Rose pleaded. 'Put your arms round me neck and I'll lift you.'

Struggling with all her effort, Rose managed to half drag her daughter out of the squalid roof space that passed for a room. But the girl had no energy. She knew she was too heavy for her to carry more than a few steps. Rose got her on to one of the children's beds. It made her blood boil to think how her lass had been abandoned to her fever in that hateful cupboard, while the pampered McQuarrie children had been removed.

'How could they have left you like this?' she cried out loud.

Elizabeth squinted at her in confusion. 'Mrs McQuarrie? You're back, miss. Is David better?'

Alarm leapt inside Rose. The girl was delirious with fever.

'It's Mam,' she said gently. 'I'll need to fetch your father to help me carry you home. You lie here, hinny, and rest. I'll not be long.'

'This is David's bed.' Elizabeth smiled and closed her eyes. 'He must be better now.'

Suddenly it hit Rose. One of the children must have been ill first. Anger igniting inside her, she stormed downstairs, nearly knocking into Mr McQuarrie in the gloom of the hall.

'Was your lad sick with the measles an' all?' she demanded.

'David, yes,' he said, startled by her question.

'You should've had him isolated! But you had my lass living in that hole next to him. I bet you had her looking after him, didn't you?'

'Don't blame me,' he defended. 'The girl knew he had measles when she agreed to take the job. That's why my wife needed her. She couldn't risk nursing him in her condition.'

Rose nearly hit him in her fury. That was why Elizabeth had told her not to come on that first day. She might have discovered there were measles in the house.

'If she was here I'd give her a piece of my mind! Using my lass like that - it's unforgivable!' She stood over him threateningly. 'I'll be back to fetch her with me husband. You better let us in or he'll knock you into next week.'

She fled back across Jarrow, wheezing and panting with the exertion, praying that John would be home and not waylaid in some dockside bar. Mercifully he was back. No doubt he had come home promptly with the thought of going to fetch Elizabeth's wages. Rose breathlessly gabbled out her story as quickly as her racing pulse would allow.

John's anger was instant. 'How dare they tret the lass like that?' He was off before she could regain her breath, marching into the dusk.

When Rose caught up with him at the house he was hammering on the door and shouting foul curses at the terrified McQuarrie.

'Please, John, stop or he'll never let us in,' she urged. Finally she persuaded the clock repairer to unlock the door. Rose pulled John up the stairs while McQuarrie shut himself in the parlour.

John swore at the sight of Elizabeth's limp, feverish body. He picked her up gently, but she did not seem to recognise him. Rose swiped a blanket off the bed and wrapped it around her. Downstairs again, John aimed a kick at the closed parlour door.

'Come out, you bloody coward! You owe us two weeks' wages! If you don't pay up, you'll have the McMullen brothers meeting you down a dark lane.'

McQuarrie opened the door long enough to thrust two shillings into Rose's hand and then slam it shut again. 'Now go away. If I see any of your kind round here again I'll call for the constable.'

John cursed him loudly and kicked over an umbrella stand on his way out for good measure.

It was pitch-dark by the time they got Elizabeth home and up to bed. Rose ordered the younger girls to stay away from their sister.

'You can sleep in our bed the night,' she told them. 'And see that Jack doesn't find his way in there either.'

That night, John did not go out drinking with Pat. He sat by the fire staring into its dying flames while Rose kept vigil by Elizabeth's bed. Once in a while she would come down for fresh water to bathe the girl's itching limbs and burning face. Neither of them spoke, but drew comfort from the watchful presence of the other, while Pat snored on the settle.

In the early hours before dawn, Rose reappeared. 'She's sleeping more peacefully now.'

John nodded. He stood and stretched stiffly. 'I had measles as a bairn - so did five of me brothers. We all survived.'

'Aye,' Rose nodded. 'So did Maggie.' But silently she worried at the delirium she had witnessed. Maggie had been unwell, but never that feverish. Not for the first time she wondered how long ago Elizabeth had contracted the disease. She was so weak and confused she could have been lying in that attic for days. Who had tended her? Had McQuarrie pushed in food and water as if she were a dog in a kennel? Rose felt ridden with guilt.

She flopped into the chair John had just vacated. It was warm from his body. She closed her eyes in utter exhaustion.

'Please God, Jack doesn't catch it,' she whispered.

'Aye,' he agreed, staring into the fire once more. 'Rose,' he added in a low rumble, 'I'll see to our Pat.'

She opened her eyes and looked at him questioningly.

'He's stopped with us long enough,' he said awkwardly. 'I'll ask Mam to take him back if you like.'

Rose's heart leapt. Finally he had come to his senses! If Elizabeth's illness had brought it about then maybe some good would come out of this terrible carry-on.

'Aye, that would be grand,' Rose smiled at him for the first time in an age.

He smiled back bashfully. 'Shall I tak the lass up a cup of water?' he offered.

'Ta,' Rose nodded. She did not have the strength to move from her seat. She would try to doze for a few minutes.

She heard him fill the cup from the jug in the pantry and cross the room. Footsteps on the stairs. She was almost asleep . . .

A bellow like a bull made her sit bolt upright in fright. She was out of her chair in an instant. John was shouting her name like a mad thing. She hurried up the stairs, finding him roaring at the top like a man possessed.

'She's gone! Rose Ann, help! I think she's gone!'

'What do you mean, gone?' Rose demanded in incomprehension.

'Dead, woman!' John cried.

Rose fell in the room, choking with panic. She knew it was true before she touched the cooling body on the bed. She recognised the smell of death all too well. But it did not stop her denying it, shaking Elizabeth hard as if she could bully her back to life.

'She's not dead,' Rose screamed. 'Wake up! You're not dead. I just left you for a few minutes, you little beggar!'

It was John who finally pulled her off the dead girl. 'Don't, Rose Ann,' he pleaded. 'She can't hear you. I'll gan and fetch the priest.'

She rounded on him in shock and bewilderment. 'You and your bloody priests! What good are they to me now? My lass is dead! What can the priest say? Can he tell me why God keeps taking away me bairns - me husband - all that I ever cared for? Can he?' she raged at him.

John shrank away from her as if she whipped him with her words. 'Don't blame me!' he protested.

The words stung her. She had heard them so recently from the cowardly McQuarrie. Men were all the same, forever shirking responsibility.

201

She lashed out. 'I do blame you! You were the one forced my lass to gan into service. You let her go slaving for those terrible people. She should have stayed on at school and got her education. Look what you've done to her!' Rose yanked at the girl's lifeless arm.

John stumbled from the room with its guttering candlelight, fleeing from the raw smell of fear and grief. Alone, Rose collapsed sobbing on the bed, pulling Elizabeth to her for comfort. She did not think she could ever let go.

Chapter 36

To pay for Elizabeth's coffin and burial, Rose had to pawn her wedding ring from William. It had hung under her clothing, a warm nugget of metal next to her heart, the only material possession left to prove she had once been the wife of a skilled workman, a brethren of St Bede's, a respectable man. It had hung there like a talisman warding off evil, an insurance against destitution, a charm that would bring her good luck in time. It would only be sold, she had promised herself, for something special like a daughter's wedding.

She had not discussed it with John, for she knew he had no money to give her. It was the only thing that had spurred her to leave Elizabeth's room where she had shut herself away to mourn. The bed still smelt of her, the imprint of her head was still on the pillow. Neither Maggie nor John's mother had succeeded in getting her to come out. But worry over a decent burial made Rose emerge from the cold, dark bedroom, wrap herself in her cape and set off alone to Slater's. She spoke to no one save the pawnbroker.

After her outburst against John the night her daughter died, she had hardly spoken a word to anyone. Rose's speech had dried up like a parched stream. At first, shock had left her lost for words. Then it became easier to say nothing, almost a relief not to have to speak. All around her she heard idle chatter or softly spoken platitudes, each as meaningless and empty as the next. She listened, but it was as if she was not really there. She was walled in by silence, cocooned from the world by her refusal to communicate. Rose could understand why some nuns took a vow of silence. John could plead, coax, rant or rail at her and it made no difference. For the first time, she was immune to his sharp tongue and swearing.

So she did not tell him she was going to sell her wedding ring, the one John had hated to see kept close to her breast because it provoked his jealousy of her first husband. Instead she went straight round to a local joiner who also did a sideline in coffins and paid for one. Then she went home to prepare Elizabeth's body. It still lay where John had left it the day before, on a board over the china sink where the fluids dripped through.

'We didn't like to touch her till you came,' Mrs McMullen murmured. From the smell of barley stew on the range, Rose realised her mother-in-law must have been left in charge.

She nodded at the bent old woman and together they bathed Elizabeth's body and wrapped her in a sheet ready to place in the coffin. She went about the other preparations for the funeral with the same methodical detachment, still hardly able to believe that she was burying yet another sweet daughter. Inside she felt as numb and cold as death itself.

A week after Elizabeth was buried, notices appeared around the town to say the infants' schools were opening again. The measles epidemic was over. Somehow Rose galvanised herself into starching clean pinafores for Sarah and Kate, and finding coats and boots to fit. For the last month they had taken it in turns to wear the same pair of boots, as Kate's own had become too small.

Without a word, Rose handed out Elizabeth's clothing. Sarah got her work dress, worsted jacket and shoes. The sleeves and hem had to be taken up three inches and the shoes lined with newspaper to make them fit. Kate got her dead sister's woollen stockings, chemise and hat. The Sunday dress was pawned to pay for the funeral meats and the girls returning to school. Rose resented her younger daughters' suppressed excitement at receiving the clothes and anticipation at going back to school. Yet she envied them the callousness of youth that accepted tragedy and recovered from it quickly. Life for them went on.

She knew they missed their sister, but she was also aware that they helped themselves to more at meal times, as if they expected there would now be a little bit more to go round. One extra portion to share. One less to clothe. More room in the bed. Rose saw it in their faces. This was how Elizabeth's death really affected them.

'Don't cry, Mam,' Kate kept repeating, 'our Lizzie's with Margaret and me da and the angels now. Father O'Brien said she couldn't be in a better place.'

But Rose would not be comforted. She found no solace in the priest's words or Kate's attempts to cheer her. Instead she found herself almost hating her daughter for being able to laugh with Sarah, for humming to herself when she helped around the kitchen, for the way she swung Jack on to her hip and tickled him like Elizabeth used to do.

Perversely, Rose fostered this resentment in her heart. It made it easier to bear the future. If she stopped loving her other children so much, then it would not hurt when they too were taken from her. For Rose was certain that they would be. That seemed the only certainty in life now - that her children would be taken away from her. One by one. Little by little. Until she was left like a barren husk with nothing to look forward to except her own oblivion.

The only consolation in those bleak spring days was that Pat moved out. Where before he had delighted in her angry words and arguments with him and John, now he could not bear her ghoulish silence. It unnerved him. Rose did not know if it was John who told him to go or whether he went of his own free will, but at long last she was rid of him.

'That should give you some'at to smile about,' John grunted. But Rose said nothing. She did not think she could make the effort to smile about anything ever again.

John continued to pick up casual work at the docks and did his best to resist the temptation of a thirst-quenching beer at one of the numerous pubs along his route home. For a while he managed to stay clear of his brother Pat and those who would inveigle him in for a drink or a game of cards. Although he would never admit it, he knew that they could ill afford for him to spend half his meagre wages before he reached Jarrow and the safety of Albion Street.

John worried about Rose and her strange silent depression that hung over them all like a funeral pall. He could not accuse her of neglecting the other children, for they were always as cleanly and smartly turned out as they could afford. But she had taken Elizabeth's death very badly. Her expression was set in stone. He looked into her dark eyes and they were like deep empty pits. Her mouth was permanently drawn in a tight, bitter line as if her lips had been sewn together. Sarah and Kate were more subdued around her, but she did not seem to notice. It was as if she were not there at all.

At times it drove him mad. He shouted at her for petty misdemeanours such as not putting the dripping away in the pantry so that it melted in the growing summer heat. But it made no difference. She ignored his criticisms and bursts of temper as if he were of no more consequence than an annoying bluebottle buzzing around the kitchen. In the bedroom it was worse. Rose would not let him touch her. She lay with her back to him and if he tried to shake her awake, she would fling off his hold.

One night she cried, 'Leave me be! How can you even think of it?'

The disdain in her voice made him shrink back. 'You can't deny me for ever,' he complained. 'It's your duty as me wife. The priest'll have some'at to say.' He knew that would rile her, but he preferred her to argue with him than the dreadful silence she imposed between them.

'The priest can say what he likes,' she hissed. 'But I'm bearing no more bairns for him to bury!'

'I have needs,' John growled.

She gave a mirthless laugh. 'Needs? Oh, aye, I know all about your needs. Most of them lie at the bottom of the bottle.'

'Don't laugh at me,' John warned, 'or I'll gan back to the bottle sharp enough if that's the only place I'll find some comfort round here!'

'Aye, you drink away the roof over our heads,' Rose mocked, 'and the food out of the bairns' mouths. That's why Elizabeth had to gan out to work, wasn't it? Because you couldn't provide for us like a man. You preferred to gan drinking and meddling in politics with that good-for-nothing brother of yours.'

In fury, he hit her cheek with the back of his hand. 'I do provide for you, you ungrateful bitch! If it weren't for me you'd be dead from the puddling mill or thrown in the workhouse by now - you and all Fawcett's brats! No one else would have taken you on. So don't you blame me for the lass's death. You should've managed the housekeeping better. You were quick enough to spend her wages an' all. And you never bothered to gan with her and find out what sort of folk she was working for. Just because that precious teacher of yours had spoken up for her and got her a place, you didn't think to ask. Isn't that the truth of it, Rose? It wasn't my fault, it was yours.'

She crumpled into a protective ball, nursing the cheek that stung from his knuckles. Oh God, he was right! She did blame herself. She tortured herself every waking minute with the thought that she had not had the guts to confront the McQuarries earlier. Had she done so, Elizabeth might still be alive. But John was hateful to say such things! She despised him for his accusations and his cowardly punch. She was disgusted that while she mourned all he could think about was his own bodily satisfaction. Well, he would not get it from her! She'd fight him off with every last inch of her strength, for she swore her body would never again carry another life within it. That was one way at least in which she could stand up to him.

'Aye, it's my fault,' she admitted in distress. 'She's dead because of us both. But we'll not do any more damage, the pair of us. I'll burn in Hell rather than bear any more bairns, do you hear? No more babies, John, no more!'

John was horrified. He had never heard her so venomous. He did not know from where such hate came. How could she blame him for her daughter's death? He had not given Elizabeth the measles or mistreated her. But deep down he knew he had failed Rose. He had wanted to provide for her and the girls and yet he had not been able to give them what they wanted - constant security and meals on the table.

But then they were no worse off than half of Jarrow. People like them never did have the luxury of security. That was the preserve of the well-off, like the Fawcetts, who thought themselves above the rest. Well, Rose and her lasses had been ruined by her marriage to Fawcett, not to him! They had come to expect too much in life - a posh house, money for new clothes and fancy education for lasses. It was Fawcett who had let her down, not he!

John fuelled his hurt pride and indignation with such thoughts. It made him feel less guilty for the way he had struck out at her. He had not liked the glimpse of the man he was becoming under the goading influence of Pat, too ready with his fists and his temper against his wife. But Rose better not push him too far. He wanted things to be the same between them as they had been before Pat had moved in and spread his poison. John had seen too late that his brother had done so out of jealousy. Pat envied him for having a wife like Rose and pretty stepdaughters and a son to call after himself.

John knew he must make Rose respect him again before it was too late. If only he could find a way of filling the void that Elizabeth had left. He longed for Rose to smile on him again, to allow him back in her arms, to be close once more. Husband and wife.

Chapter 37

That summer, old McConnell died. As Maggie said, he had left them in spirit long before. Many years ago, his mind had passed back across the water to Ireland where he lived among the ghosts of his past. Many of the Irish community came to the smallholding at Simonside to pay their respects and take a swig of whisky.

John drank long and deep, for there had been precious little to break the monotony of dock work and a drab, penny-pinching existence these past months. He had a wife who hardly spoke to him and stepdaughters who were growing up with too many fancy ideas and opinions in their heads. They were far too quick to answer him back rather than do as he ordered, and their mother never checked them. Even young Jack paid him little attention when he came in from work. He was tied to his mother's apron strings and fussed to death by his sisters. As John tossed back yet another dram, he determined that Jack would not be turned into a sissy. He would teach him to fight and stand up for himself like a McMullen, by God he would!

Rose watched her husband getting drunk with the men. Soon he would be singing. At least her father would have approved, she thought drily. She looked around the low-ceilinged room, with its smoke-blackened walls and dowdy furniture, and was reminded of happier days. She could imagine her mother sitting by the fading light of the small window, weaving a basket out of twigs for her to carry vegetables in. Her sisters were sprawled by the hearth, their fingers entwined with string in some game of their own making. The acrid smell of her father's pipe would mingle with the reek of fire smoke. And what was she doing? Rose saw herself sitting by the open door looking at an orange ball of sun setting in the west, the smell of honeysuckle and hay on the stiffening evening breeze. She was gouging the black grit from under her nails with a paring knife to try to make them pretty for Sunday when she might see William ...

'Rose?' It was Maggie who broke into this reverie. 'Fancy a walk outside?'

Rose nodded and followed. It was a cold dank August night, not like the summer of her imaginings. She could hear Kate's loud voice over by the hazel tree where she and Sarah were trying to show Jack how to swing. Margaret was gazing up in delight, but Mary was protesting tearfully that it was her tree and her go. The older girls were ignoring her.

'Careful with him,' Rose called out. 'Don't drop—'

Jack slipped from Kate's arms and landed on top of Mary. Both of them howled in protest. Both women began to hurry over, but before they were halfway across the field, Maggie stopped Rose.

'They're all right,' she panted. 'See how the lasses take care of them.'

Rose watched, undecided, as Kate swiftly picked up Jack and cuddled him. Sarah was doing the same with Mary, raising her up in brawny arms and pacifying the wailing child. As they stood, Lizzie came waddling out behind them, heavy with her first unborn, to see where they had got to.

'That's a bonny sight,' she greeted her sisters. 'They look a right little family together, don't they? No one would know by looking that Jack's just a half-brother.'

Rose gazed and saw that it was true. Her three remaining daughters had her darker colouring, with their thick brown hair. Gone were the two fair-haired girls who had taken after their father. The dark-haired Jack had a look of his half-sisters, the same small nose and oval curve of his jaw.

'Mam would have liked to see the grandbairns playing under the tree,' Lizzie mused, slipping her arms through her sisters'.

'Aye, but Da would've been chasing them off for trampling across the cabbages,' Maggie laughed.

'What'll happen to the place now?' Rose asked quietly. She had overheard Danny talking about moving down into the town.

Maggie sighed. 'Landlord wants us out. We can't make a living here any more. Danny's never been much of a gardener - I'm that glad he kept on his job at the steel mill. And it's hard work on me own, since Da's been housebound.'

Rose was dismayed. 'You should've said. Me and the lasses could come up here more and help out.'

Lizzie nudged Maggie. 'Have you told our Rose?'

'Told me what?'

Maggie hesitated.

'Haway, Maggie,' Lizzie urged. 'You might as well tell her all in one go.' Lizzie did not give her sister time to hesitate and blurted out, 'She's expectin' again. Danny doesn't want her slaving up here through the winter over a few tatties and turnips. They're looking for somewhere in the town. It'll mean you'll have to take Mary back.'

Maggie slid Rose a cautious look. 'We can move in with Danny's sister for a bit - but there won't be much room. And you did say you'd take her back when she started school. It's just with another bairn on the way—'

Rose's heart was leaden. They were hardly managing as it was. Try as she might, she could only look on Mary as an extra burden. But she hid her disappointment at the news.

'Of course I'll take her back,' she assured. 'I should've done so long before now. You've been that good to our Mary.'

'See!' Lizzie exclaimed. 'I told you she'd not mind. And if you're living nearer each other you can still see plenty of the bairn. Can't she, Rose?'

'Aye,' Rose agreed. 'I'll probably have to tie her up like a goat to stop her trotting off to see her Aunt Maggie all the time.'

It was said in jest, but she knew it would be difficult for the girl to settle with them after all this time. She wondered, with a feeling of dread, what John would make of the new arrangement. He had grown so surly and bad-tempered with the girls recently, ordering them around like servants and shouting at them if they stopped to play with Jack.

But surprisingly, he made no objection. Rose put it down to the amount of whisky he had consumed. As they wended their way back downhill, he was almost enthusiastic about Mary coming to live with them.

'Bout time, Rose Ann. She's your lass, not Maggie's. It'll do her good to get away from your sister. Spoils her rotten. Got a temper like a mule, that one. We'll knock some manners into her soon enough.'

He rambled on about the child all the way home. Rose did not contradict him or answer back. She thought that by morning he would have forgotten every word he had said. But to her amazement, when she returned from church the next day, there was Mary, sitting swinging her legs and glowering at her across the rough kitchen table.

'Went to fetch her mesel',' John crowed. 'Wasn't going to have Maggie making a song and dance about leaving her here. Just walked in, took her under me arm and said I was off.'

Rose gawped at them both. 'What did Maggie say?'

'Didn't have time to say much,' John laughed, pleased with himself. 'Just like a raid on the Afghans!'

Rose regarded her youngest daughter nervously. At least she was not screaming at them - yet. 'Well, hinny,' she said, 'are you hungry?' Mary said nothing, so Rose carried on. 'We've a broth on for dinner. No meat this week. But there's rhubarb pie and custard for pudding - the rhubarb's from Aunt Maggie's allotment. You come over here and help me.'

Mary did not move. John stood over the girl and Rose tensed, sure he was about to lose his temper.

'Haway,' he cajoled. 'Your mam's made a canny dinner. You be a good lass and do as she tells you.' He lowered his voice conspiratorially. 'And if you are she might give you a taste of it before the others.'

Rose was sure she saw him wink at the child. Dumbfounded, she watched Mary slip off her chair and sidle round the table towards the range.

'Good lass!' John cried, leaning over and rubbing the top of her head.

Rose gave Mary a long-handled spoon and told her to stir the pot. Moments later, the older girls rushed in with Jack swinging between them. They stared at Mary solemnly standing on tiptoe, stirring the soup.

'Where's Aunt Maggie?' Kate asked eagerly.

'She's not here,' John answered. 'Your sister's stoppin' with us from now on.'

Kate shrugged philosophically and turned back to fussing over Jack. Sarah was more enthusiastic.

'That's grand,' she smiled, and went over to tweak Mary's button nose.

John, pleased with his morning's work, relaxed into his chair and continued to drink the jug of beer Danny had sent him away with. He had done the right thing. There was Rose talking more than he had heard in months, directing Mary at the range, a mother and daughter reunited. And all thanks to him! Rose looked content, her face less drawn and tense than usual. She was still a handsome woman. Mary would be the saving of her. She would fill Elizabeth's place and make Rose care about her family again - about him. How could she not take to the pretty pouting Mary? That lass had spark! Yet he would make sure Mary did not waste too much time at her lessons like the others had. What she needed to learn she could pick up from her mother during the week and from the priest on Sunday.

It filled John with a sense of wellbeing to have the room full of children for whom he was responsible, busying themselves getting ready for Sunday dinner. The room smelt pleasantly of cooking barley and beans. He was mellow with beer. Today was a day of rest with no nagging that he should be out jostling at the dock gates for work. Sunday dinner was the crowning moment of the week. He was head of his household and the world beyond the kitchen fug mattered nothing for a few hours.

Chapter 38

Rose wondered at her husband's ability to surprise her. She would never have guessed he could have doted so much on her moody, wilful youngest daughter. At barely five years old, Mary was as obstinate and temperamental as John could be. Small and skinny as she was, the girl had the power of a steam engine. She drove all opposition before her. She pushed Jack over if he got in her way, whined at her sisters until they gave in to her and refused to do what Rose told her unless she wanted to do it.

But, perhaps because their temperaments were so similar, Mary got on best with John. Whereas the older girls were wary of their stepfather and kept out of his way, Mary ran to the door when she heard his footsteps tramping through the yard and followed him while he struggled out of his boots and filthy jacket and washed himself in the scullery.

He trained her to fill his clay pipe with tobacco (on days when there was any) and allowed her to shuffle his playing cards before he settled down to a game of patience. If either Kate or Sarah heard him bark their name, they scarpered down the lane to avoid some chore or being sent on some errand. But when he called for Mary, she came trotting to his side, holding on to his jacket if they walked outside or leaning between his knees while he played cards indoors.

If Mary stamped her feet in a fit of petulance or screamed at her mother, John would be the one to calm her down.

'Leave the lass be,' he would chide Rose. 'You're too hard on her. She's tired out after all that learnin'.'

Rose would sigh with frustration. What use was it battling with the child if he came along and took her side every time? It annoyed Rose that he could be so hard on the other girls while favouring Mary. But guilt at having neglected her youngest daughter for so long made her bite her tongue and try to be more patient. At the very least, Mary's coming had shaken her out of the silent gloom that had oppressed her for the past months. It was impossible to keep quiet when Mary was a constant source of vexation.

Rose knew that Kate shared this irritation. Kate could not fathom why Mary should want to pinch and nip her and try to get her into trouble. She would retaliate by chanting, 'Mary, Mary, quite contrary!' over and over, until Mary ran at her screaming or John grabbed and slapped her.

Rose thought twice about intervening. Kate would have to learn to put up with her difficult sister and John was her stepfather and had a right to chastise her. But she guessed that Kate was hurt by this new rival in the household. Before, she had been the one to make John laugh. Before Elizabeth died, it was Kate who would slip on to his knee when she sensed he was in a good mood and ask him to tell her stories of Ireland or occasionally his time in the army.

'Tell us about marching with General Roberts,' she used to urge. 'Did you really have to eat the soles of your boots to stay alive?'

'Aye,' John would grunt, 'and we drank water as green and poisonous as the Slake - but none of us died of it.'

'He must've been a magician,' Kate would cry. 'Tell us more, Father, tell us!'

She was the only one who dared ask him about his past life. The only other time he mentioned his service in India and Afghanistan was when he was drunk. Then he would brandish the poker and shout and swear like a heathen. But Kate's place had been usurped by Mary and she gave up trying to please her stepfather. She took Sarah's lead and kept out of his way, or answered him back if she dared.

As for Mary, she refused for a long time to call Rose her mam. At first Rose was hurt, but then it ceased to bother her. That was the way Mary was, and there were far more pressing worries by the autumn.

Trade, which had been sluggish all year, slackened further. The rumour-mongers passed on dire predictions that this winter would be worse than the last. All along the river, factories and docks began to close their gates. Large groups of men stood around stamping numb feet, hunched in threadbare jackets in the slim hope they might be offered a half-day's work. John walked miles each day along the Tyne to try to find a few hours of carrying or shovelling. Rose watched in sickening alarm as his boots wore out and the fierce look in his eyes dimmed to despair at his idleness.

Rose tried to stave off their financial ruin, making trips almost daily to the pawnshop. She would take in bedding in the morning to reclaim boots for the girls to go to school. When they came home, she sent Sarah down with the younger girls' boots to get back the bedding. The bread knife would be exchanged for the paraffin lamp (they could no longer afford to pay for gas lighting) and the washboard would be swapped for the kettle.

Gone was John's best suit, the girls' starched pinafores and Rose's Sunday dress and cape. Kate wore through Elizabeth's old stockings and Rose had nothing with which to darn them. She could no longer take the children to Mass, for they looked like street urchins in their bare feet, and she had nothing respectable to wear. Jack was still wearing baby dresses because she could not afford to put him in breeches.

The children had constantly runny noses and racking coughs in the icy house that they could no longer afford to keep warm. She watched them anxiously for signs of fever, for rumour was spreading of an outbreak of typhoid in the town. Finally, they were threatened with eviction.

'We can't afford to stop here any longer,' she told John on a raw November day that never grew light under the gunmetal-grey sky. 'The rentman's coming back at the end of the week with the bailiffs if we don't pay up.' She saw the muscles in his gaunt face tense and thought he would resist with fighting words.

But John spat into the cooling grate where they had just burnt the clothes prop and nodded. 'We'll move in with me mother till I find us somewhere else.'

Rose was glad he did not look at her, for she thought she might burst into tears. To think she was reduced to sharing that flea-ridden, stinking cottage with the McMullens. It had filled her with revulsion as a girl selling vegetables around those old sunken cottages where the filth oozed through the walls from the earth middens. No landlord had attempted to improve them over the years for their Irish tenants, Rose thought bitterly. Even the town council had resisted improving the sanitation, for the rate-paying councillors saw it as a waste of their money. Now Rose and her children were to be among the very poorest, who counted for nothing in the eyes of the respectable. She was engulfed in humiliation.

But she could suggest no other course of action. Simonside was no longer a refuge. Maggie, who was about to give birth any day, was still living with Danny's sister. Lizzie lived in a tied cottage and was too far away to help. Contact with the Fawcetts had been severed and she would die of shame if they ever got to hear of her fallen circumstances.

That night she lay awake in their bedroom that no longer had curtains or mats on the floor. She watched the yellow glow of a streetlamp illuminate the icy patterns of frost on the inside of the window and wondered if she would ever have a bedroom to call her own again. Jack lay bedded between them for warmth, snuffling in his sleep through his blocked nose. This was the room in which he had been born. It was from upstairs that she had lain listening to John pacing the kitchen below, saving their son's life with sips of whisky.

For a brief time, this had been a house of noisy laughter, chatter about Wild West circus people and runaway sheep. She could still hear Elizabeth's soft voice reading out articles from John's newspaper and Kate standing on the fender singing songs she had learnt at school. But these happier days had been eclipsed by the tragedy of Elizabeth's death, the coarsening of John's behaviour when Pat became their lodger and these relentless days of making ends meet.

Still, Rose thought as she closed her eyes and reached for the comfort of Jack's warm body, this had been home. Albion Street. Tomorrow or the next day, she would be back under someone else's roof, at the beck and call of others. She prayed that it would not be for long.

Chapter 39

Rose and John sold what furniture they had left, apart from the settle to which, bafflingly, John had become too attached to sell. He and Pat lugged it round to their parents' cottage. Slater's sent round a cart for their beds, kitchen table, chairs and dresser. Two days later, they bundled up their bedding, clothing, pans, kettle, knives, poss stick and tub, and crept out the back way before daylight. Later, Rose discovered that Kate had hidden the old lion cage and wooden figures in a pillowcase.

'I took it for Jack,' she told her mother, when she found it under the bed at the McMullens'. 'He'll want some'at to play with, won't he?'

Rose dismissed her first thought - that it might have fetched enough bread and pea soup for a week. She was glad of Kate's generous gesture. It was something to remind them in their new dismal surroundings that they had been part of a better-off class. It became a symbol for Rose of a more leisured time when she had not been a drudge for the McMullen men, or had to live cheek by jowl in a dirty hovel.

The small cottage, still home to several of John's brothers including Pat, was hopelessly overcrowded. John's bedridden father occupied the main bed in the kitchen all day. The room stank of his incontinence, as well as the stench from a dozen unwashed bodies and the overflowing midden. Brendan, who was 'simple' and unable to live by himself, slept on a truckle bed in the corner, while Pat used the settle. Everyone else slept in the loft, reached by a rickety ladder.

John and his family were given one bed for the six of them and sometimes Rose had to turf out a sleeping McMullen in order to put her children to bed. Each morning they woke up itchy and scratching from flea bites. Soon Rose gave up combing out nits from the girls' hair, for she could not rid them of head lice. Sometimes she could see them crawling in their matted hair as her daughters bent over the washtub. They scratched until their scalps bled.

John's mother did not complain at the extra burden on her out-of-work household, but she was increasingly arthritic and Rose wondered how she had managed before without her help. Despite the number of men hanging around the house with nothing to do, the bulk of heavy chores fell to her and her daughters. They queued at the standpipe in the freezing cold for a trickle of water. They scrubbed filthy clothes in tepid scummy water that turned their hands raw and chapped. Sometimes Kate would cry with the pain in her hands as they stuck to the metal tub and tore off her frozen skin.

Since the move to East Jarrow, the girls had stopped going to school. Their boots had been pawned and they went about barefoot like tinkers. When the truancy officer tracked them down, Rose bundled them up to the loft and told him they were sick. He took one look into the dark cottage and took her at her word, hurrying away quickly with a handkerchief pressed to his nose.

John's brothers would disappear all day, where, Rose did not know. She suspected they gathered in the warmth of soup kitchens or pub doorways. Occasionally they came back with a hare or some shreds of offal scraped from a slaughterhouse floor, still clinging with sawdust. At times one of them would come back with news of free food being distributed at a church hall. Rose would send the children hurrying, so at least they would have a warm meal in their bellies that day.

Where once she would have balked at sending them to queue in public for charity, she became hardened to it. At the slightest rumour of free food or clothing, Rose would drag the children behind her in search of the source: the Mechanics' Hall for a parcel of clothing; Salem Baptists' Chapel in the High Street for children's breakfasts; Lockart's Cocoa Rooms in Ormonde Street, where she had danced on her first wedding day, for a bowl of soup. She pushed and shoved and shouted to get them first in line. She would scrap like a vixen with other women over the last stale loaf. Pride was a luxury that went with money in your purse, Rose concluded bitterly.

Her self-esteem dwindled with each tramp to the pawnshop, each charity handout, each time she stood waiting at the standpipe overhearing the pitying whispers of other women. She no longer cared how she looked or whether her children could read and write. Her only thought was surviving that winter, getting to the end of the week, seeing her children still alive at the end of the day. It was a brutal, joyless existence. But it was existence.

Soon the numbers of needy in the town were so great that the money raised by subscription could not begin to cope with such distress. The Churches, unions and small businesses struggled to help, but as the depression continued, the donations dwindled and the supply of charity became less frequent.

There were stirrings of unrest in Jarrow when news spread that the council had refused the offer of a three-thousand-pound loan from the Local Government Board to provide relief work for the unemployed. Pat and John came back from a mass meeting held on the pit heap.

'The council's scared of the shopkeepers who vote them in,' Pat fulminated. 'Don't want to be landed with paying back the loan for the next twenty years. They'd prefer to see us starve to death!'

'We waited to hear what the Mayor had to say,' John said stonily. 'He washed his hands of us. Told us to gan to the parish Guardians for work.'

Rose knew what that meant: outdoor relief from the workhouse for those still strong enough to stand and wield a pickaxe. It was the final indignity.

'So why don't you?' she asked him sourly.

He just looked at her as if she had cursed the saints and the Virgin Mary. John was too proud for that. He would see more honour in stealing bread from a rich man and being hanged for it than submitting to the humiliating questions of the pious Board of Guardians. She could never see him grovelling to them for their meagre work and a pittance for pay. She did not really want him to. But Rose could not let it rest. It enraged her that he should waste his time in fruitless protest, when they all knew that those with power in the town, who held the purse strings, would never listen to the likes of them in a month of Sundays.

'We're living on charity as it is,' she said bitterly. 'Or would you rather me and the bairns went out thieving next?'

John did not answer her. But if looks could have struck her down, she would have been unconscious on the dirty brick floor of the McMullens' kitchen. He stormed out of the cottage and did not speak to her for a week.

So on some of those short, bleak days, when Rose feared there would be nothing to eat, she sent her two older daughters out to beg for food around the big houses of South Shields. She led them out of Jarrow, so there was little chance of them being recognised or bumping into their teachers or the priest. At the turnpike road she pushed them towards Shields.

'Stay together,' she ordered. 'Be polite and steer clear of the police. Now off you gan.'

Kate stood mutinously on the rutted road, her face as white as alabaster, her lips purple and pinched.

'Mam, I don't want to go,' she whined, shivering in her grubby dress.

'You'll get nowt else to eat the day if you don't!' Rose scolded. 'So don't come back till you've some'at to show for it.'

'Haway,' Sarah encouraged, 'it's better than stopping at Granny's all day.' She pulled a moth-eaten blanket around both their shoulders and chivvied her sister towards the smoky outline of South Shields. Kate gave her mother one last reproachful look, then huddled into Sarah's hold and limped away.

Rose stood alone, watching her daughters disappear into the distance, their bare feet cracked and legs covered in sores. She fought off the desire to go with them, to protect them from hostile rejection and slamming doors. But she knew that they would stand a better chance of receiving charity on their own than if they begged with an adult, especially Kate with her crippled foot. Oh, she could not spare Kate! Who could not be stirred by pity at the sight of two young lasses hungry and frozen on their doorstep?

Rose remembered children begging one Christmas at her own door in Raglan Street and how she had felt contempt and anger at the parents for having sunk so low. Now she was doing the same to her own flesh and blood. She felt total disgrace at having to subject the girls to such an ordeal. William would turn in his grave!

The sight of her once-pretty daughters trudging on frozen feet to beg on the doorsteps of those still in work was seared into her heart for ever. As the grey, lowering sky pressed down on them, heavy and threatening with snow, Rose broke into loud, racking sobs. She would never forget it! Never forgive herself!

Just when Rose thought they had sunk to the depths of shame, John returned one day with a terrible look on his face.

'What is it?' Rose asked.

'I've got work,' he said almost inaudibly.

Rose's stomach lurched. 'Work? That's grand—'

'I've been to the parish,' he cut her off. 'I've ...' He struggled to finish his sentence. 'I've signed on at Harton.'

Rose felt winded. 'Harton?' she gasped. 'The workhouse?'

His look was haggard. 'Aye. Start the morra.'

'How much?' Rose whispered.

'Shillin' a day.' His voice was leaden. 'I told them Guardians you and the bairns were sick - so you didn't have to sit and answer all their nosy questions.'

Suddenly, the shame that Rose felt at the thought of them going begging to the parish turned to pity for her husband. She knew what a blow to his pride it must have been to be so humbled by strangers. There was no lower level to which they could sink, except imprisonment in the workhouse itself. Outdoor relief was one precarious move away from that. Rose shuddered at the horror.

She stepped forward and touched his arm. 'John thanks. I -'

She was too overcome to tell him how at that moment she was proud of him. He had walked himself into the ground every day to try to find work to support them. She could see in his face how it gnawed away at his spirit to have to live under his parents' roof again and go begging around the streets for work. Now he had put himself through the final indignity of going cap in hand to the Board of Guardians to plead for the chance to break rocks or some such hard labour usually reserved for convicts and criminals. It hurt to see him so bowed.

But mixed with her pity was a surge of relief that he had not let himself be beaten. He would submit to this back-breaking work rather than see his family starve to death. She had half expected him to give up and kill himself with drink. But John was strong. He had spirit, she'd give him that. By God, he had spirit!

Rose could not find the words to tell him so. They looked at each other for an instant with a flicker of the old affection. Then he grunted and turned from her, and the moment for speaking what was in her heart was gone.

Chapter 40

1895

A year and a half later. Rose and John moved their family to Tyne Dock on the edge of South Shields. Number 25 Napier Street was a narrow terrace wedged between the railway station and the dock. It was noisy and gloomy under the permanent pall of smoke from the railway, but it was two rooms to call their own.

How they had survived Rose could not tell. Prayers and bloody-mindedness most probably. Others had not. Both of John's parents were dead, buried within five months of each other. Rose had wept for her brave, compassionate mother-in-law, but lit a candle in thanks to the Virgin for ending the exhausted woman's misery in that hovel she had tried to make home for them all.

The family had broken up, moved in with other brothers or disappeared from the area to try to seek work. As for her and John, they had come close to starvation. John had nearly worked himself into an early grave with the punishing, relentless rock-breaking. For his pains he had received a shilling a day, not in money but as a voucher to be exchanged for food at a local shop. At least he had not been able to drink a penny of it, Rose had been thankful.

But it had taken its toll on them both. John had the stooped, skeletal figure of an old man. His hair and moustache had turned completely white in the past two years. Rose had stayed alive on a diet of bread and water, occasional gristly meat, dripping and burnt scrapings from the bottom of pans of barley soup. She had put herself at the end of the queue at every meal, watching that her children got fed before John's brothers devoured the mean pickings.

Her breasts sagged and the skin over her belly hung in withered folds. Her neck was scraggy and her eyes had shrunk back into dark sockets. Her monthly bleeds had stopped for a whole year. She had lived in a fever of anxiety about being pregnant, even though John had hardly touched her. Then with the move, the bleeding had started again, more heavy and painful than ever before. Compounding her discomfort, her legs were often large and swollen, puffy to the touch as if water had collected in them like rain barrels.

It made it difficult to chase after Mary or Jack when they were up to some mischief. Her youngest two had been used to amusing themselves in the squalid lanes of the old pit cottages while the adults had grown listless with hunger and the fight for survival. They had become as independent and out of control as weeds. Rose was horrified to hear four-year-old Jack's high-pitched voice spouting oaths like his father and uncles.

'Wash your mouth out,' she would scold, cuffing him.

But he would stare back at her with large, hurt eyes, wondering what he had done wrong.

Mary was the only one at school now, for Sarah had been living in as a general maid for an undertaker and his family since the summer of '93. His was one of the few businesses that had done well in Jarrow through the slump, his grim trade boosted by a flurry of smallpox victims that year. At twelve, Sarah's wages had been paltry, but her employer had given her bed and board, which

Rose looked upon as a gift from the saints. She delighted in seeing her daughter fill out again and the shine return to her hair and eyes.

The following year, when Kate turned twelve, she too was sent into service. This coincided with the family's move to Tyne Dock and she was sent to work for a butcher in nearby Stanhope Road. Rose turfed the girl out of bed at six in the morning and half an hour later she was starting her long stint of washing and cleaning for the butcher's large household. Not only did she have all the family laundry to wash, bleach, rinse, wring, hang out and iron, there were the blood-stained aprons and overalls from the shop too.

When Kate came home complaining she could not see over the large wooden washtub, Rose took her back and asked them to make a stool for her daughter to stand on. There was no question of Kate packing in the arduous job. She was lucky to have it and Rose needed every penny of the two shillings and sixpence she handed over at the end of the week.

Rose knew how her daughter hated the work. She spent most of Sunday asleep, but on her half-day off a fortnight, Rose kept her busy with mending, for Kate was neat with her stitching and Rose's eyesight was not as good as it had once been. But Kate never complained. Rose could not but admire the girl's stoical nature, her ability to look on the bright side of life despite their poverty. Although Rose never said so, it was like a shaft of sunlight piercing the gloom of their bare home to have Kate walk in at the end of a long day, humming a popular tune she had picked up on the street.

Rose found precious little to sing about amid the grime of Tyne Dock. For a long time they had orange boxes for chairs and mattresses made out of sacks of lumpy flock on the floor for beds. John was picking up casual work once more at the docks, but he was not as strong as he used to be and was sometimes passed over for younger men. This fuelled his temper, which these days was as quick to ignite as tinder. He picked arguments with anyone who glanced at him in the street. He shouted at the children, kicked dogs out of his way and made lewd comments at other men's wives. Sometimes Rose wondered if the past hellish years had unhinged his mind.

With wages in his pocket once more, John took to the drink like a fish who had been thrown back in the sea after too long on dry land. He could not get enough of it and it took little to get him roaring, cursing drunk, for he no longer had a head for holding his drink. With fire in his belly and a numb mist in his head, Rose knew he thought himself invincible. He was the Irish patriot, the war hero, the heroic fighting figure of Irish legend.

He came home singing his head off and waking up the children in the dead of night.

'Up! Gerrup the lot of you and face old Ireland across the sea!'

If they ignored him, he would throw orange boxes around the kitchen and smash them against the walls. Mary would scream and Jack would wet himself as he clung to Rose and whimpered as quietly as possible.

'I'll teach you to respect me, you little buggers! Gerrup and sing!'

'John, leave us alone, it's the middle of the night,' Rose would hiss, rising from the mattress they shared with Jack. 'Come to bed, John.'

But sometimes she could not pacify him and they had to stand to attention beside him. On one occasion he terrified Rose with his strange words and threatening gestures. He seemed to think he was General Roberts himself, waving the fire poker over their heads like a sword.

'I'm the bloody general and you'll march till I tell you to drop! You're all on half-rations till we get to Kandahar. Now sing to keep your spirits up!'

Rose clutched Jack tightly as he stared in sleepy-eyed confusion at his father. The small boy could not tell if this was some game of soldiers or the start of a fit of violence that would end with his mother's pictures of the Virgin Mary and St Hilda being dashed from the wall. They marched on the spot, Mary and Kate shivering with cold in their petticoats while John shouted incoherently and sang snatches of army songs.

Then abruptly, with spittle still on his chin from singing, his expression switched from belligerence to terror. He grabbed Mary by the arm.

'They're coming for us, can't you see them?' John peered fearfully into the shadows.

'Who?' Mary asked in alarm.

'John, don't be daft, there's no one there,' Rose protested, frightened by his staring look.

'There! Behind there - waitin' to cut our throats!'

Rose was still not sure if he was play-acting and deliberately trying to scare them. Or was he quite mad? She felt helpless at the thought that her husband was losing his sanity.

'Quick! Retreat,' he gasped, pushing Mary towards the back door.

They would all have been out in the cold if Kate had not intervened.

'It's all right, Father. They've gone now.' Swiftly she took a stick of newspaper and lit it from the fire. She held it aloft. Briefly light flared, illuminating the dark corner beyond the range. It was empty. 'Look, see?'

Rose hardly dared breathe, let alone move. She feared Kate's action might provoke him to violence, he was so unpredictable. But it broke the spell that seemed to have bewitched John.

'I knew there was no one there,' he growled. 'D'you take me for a fool?'

'No, Father,' Kate said earnestly. 'You were right to be careful.'

He stared at her suspiciously, as if trying to weigh up if he was being mocked. Perhaps he could not remember what he had been doing this past half-hour, Rose wondered. But Kate's words seemed to mollify him.

'Aye, I was, wasn't I?' He let go of Mary and she escaped back to the mattress in the front room.

By degrees, they persuaded him to go to bed. Finally he gave in. John stumbled through the open door and fell heavily on to the mattress. Within minutes he was unconscious. The girls helped Rose undress him, giggling now at his bizarre behaviour, dizzy with relief that the menacing moment was over.

After that, it was Kate that Rose relied on to handle John when drunken madness took him over. Only Kate seemed able to calm him and coax him to lie down. She sang along with him, humouring his drunken delusions and stroking his head. During these night-time ordeals, Rose felt a rush of contempt for her husband. How could he behave like this in front of his stepdaughters? And what kind of example was he setting their only son? Jack was a sensitive lad, for all his foul-mouthed mimicking. He took things to heart and cried easily at Mary's casual teasing or John's ridicule.

'You'll turn him into a pansy-boy!' his father would sneer if he caught Rose cuddling Jack and drying the boy's tears. He would not let her pick him up if he fell and scraped his knees.

'Leave him! He needs toughening up. A bit of blood and pain will make a man of him.'

Sometimes Rose would defy him and go to Jack's aid. 'He's still a baby,' she would protest. But John only took it out on Jack the more, goading him for being a mammy's pet.

'Why don't you put him in dresses? We've nowt but lasses in this house!'

Rose wondered what had become of the man who had doted on their baby son and walked the floor with him cradled in his arms? She looked at John's hard, unforgiving face and saw a stranger.

Whatever affection the girls had once had for him Rose knew was wearing thin. Now and again, Mary would try to wheedle a halfpenny out of him for sweets, if she gauged her stepfather was in a good mood. She was the only one who could manage it, for he still seemed roughly affectionate towards her in sober spells.

Sarah rarely came home, except to give her mother money, fearing her stepfather's interrogation. By Christmas of that year, she had turned fifteen and had suddenly grown full breasts and hips. John appeared obsessed with her moral behaviour, threatening her with a beating and eternal damnation if she 'got herself into trouble'.

'She's a good lass,' Rose answered indignantly. 'Our Sarah's been brought up respectable, even when we had nowt to our name. She'll not do anything daft.'

'We don't know the half of it,' John said, eyeing the girl suspiciously, 'living in Jarrow. We don't know who she sees or what she does.'

Sarah rolled her eyes with impatience. 'Chance would be a fine thing! I get no time off to meet anybody. And when I do, I come here, don't I?'

'Well, you keep it that way,' John scowled. 'I'll have none of you lasses bringing shame on the McMullen name. You'll be out on the street if you do.'

Rose gave Sarah a warning glance that told her not to answer him back. It did no good. To argue only made him carry on longer with whatever petty obsession was worrying him.

Often it was Kate who attracted John's critical attention. Rose could not understand why as she was the most patient with him. He teased her about her crooked foot.

'You'll not get a husband if you can't walk straight up the aisle.'

At first Kate would laugh off his remarks, but this only encouraged him. He continued to bait her until he provoked her into anger or tears.

'Still it'll come in handy having a cripple if we have to beg on the streets again, won't it, Kate?'

This always brought a response. 'Tell him to stop it, Mam!'

Rose saw the girl's eyes swimming with tears. Kate hated any allusion to her having begged on the streets. Rose knew the experience had scarred the girl deeply.

'John, that's enough,' Rose remonstrated.

John laughed at them. 'Bloody women! Can't take a little joke. Look at your long faces.'

Rose's defence was to ignore him until he tired of his name-calling, but Kate could not. Bafflingly, she attempted to win him round. Of all her children, it was Kate who continually tried to gain his approval. She was the one who sang songs or told jokes she had learned from the butcher's sons to try to entertain John and make him laugh. If he gave her a grudging smile or a rare word of praise, her pretty face would beam with delight. Rose did not know why she bothered. Perhaps Kate, more than the others, missed having the father who was taken from her so abruptly. John was a poor substitute, but he was better than nothing.

Whatever the reason, Kate's willingness to please her stepfather became an irritation to Rose. Why should he receive such favour when he did nothing to deserve it? She was the one who looked after them all! Even when she turned to Kate during John's drunken outbursts, she resented the way her daughter could cope when she could not. She knew that John never remembered what he had said or done, or that Kate had been the one to help him. But Rose watched them and saw flickers of tenderness in John's bloodshot eyes when he babbled nonsense to Kate that he no longer showed her.

It wasn't right! Rose thought with disgust. But deep down she knew her resentment was fuelled by guilt that she had to rely on her thirteen-year-old to do the job that only an unlucky wife should endure: undressing a drunken husband and putting him to bed.

It wasn't long before Rose began to get complaints from the neighbours upstairs about the midnight ranting and banging about in their flat. The neighbours were a quiet couple who kept to themselves and never made a sound, except for the thud of boots on the stairs when the husband returned from working on the railways.

The woman was timid and would scuttle back across the yard they shared, with anxious looks towards Rose's back door. She had once been caught coming out of the toilet closet by John and he had made a bawdy remark about what she had been doing inside. Rose had overheard him and cringed with embarrassment. The woman had flushed puce and bolted for her back steps.

Now she would not speak when Rose bid her good morning. But eventually her husband spoke up.

'You kept us awake again last night,' he complained to Rose one tea time. 'The missus isn't well - she's bad with her nerves. And Mr McMullen's making her worse. We can't afford the doctor, you know.'

'I'm sorry about your wife,' Rose said stiffly. 'But it's only a bit of singing. Doesn't do any harm.'

'Well, you might be able to put up with it, but we shouldn't have to. We had a decent family living down below before,' he muttered. 'Your lot run wild.'

'Don't you speak about my family like that,' Rose was indignant. 'They're good bairns and me husband's allowed to let off steam a bit after a hard day's work.'

'Hard day's drinking, more like,' he mumbled.

'What did you say?' Rose demanded.

'Nowt,' he said. 'So are you going to keep the noise down or am I going to have to complain to the landlord?'

'Complain to the Pope if you like!' Rose replied. 'But don't come whining to me about your problems - I've enough of me own.'

He stomped up the stairs muttering about her, so she shouted after him, 'And tell your missus to stick her head under the pillow next time! Nerves indeed. I'll swap my nerves for hers any day of the week.'

The trouble with the neighbours grumbled on for several months, but it was always Rose who bore the brunt. The railwayman never had the courage to confront John directly.

In some ways Rose was glad that her husband had a reputation as a hard man. It meant that people were wary of getting on the wrong side of the McMullens. It helped when the tick men came round for overdue payments for rent or gas or groceries. They gave Rose an extra week's leeway rather than run the risk of being booted down the street by her cantankerous husband. She saw it in their eyes: not just the fear of John but the glint of respect for her for being strong enough to put up with such a man. Not that she had any choice. So she hid her sensibilities behind a tough exterior and let people think her hard too.

Gone were the days when Rose would cross the street to avoid confrontation or a cross word. The shy McConnell girl was long gone. Even the respectable Rose Fawcett, who feared debt and the disapproval of neighbours, had vanished along the way. Rose McMullen faced the outside world with a stubborn jut of her chin and a bold look in her dark-ringed eyes. She challenged anyone to say they were better than her and usually nobody did.

But one day John came home from the pub to find her arguing in the dark hallway with the railwayman.

'What's all this?' he demanded, suspicious at once.

'Nothing, John,' Rose said quickly. She knew if he heard the complaints from their neighbour, he'd see red and go for the man.

'Didn't look like nothing. You were rowing.' He lurched forward. 'What you been doing with me wife?'

'Don't be daft!' Rose laughed.

'We've just been having words,' the neighbour admitted, retreating a step. But John lunged and grabbed his arm.

'You've been carrying on with me missus behind me back, haven't you?'

'No—'

'You have, you dirty little bastard!' John yanked him off the stairs. The man tried to resist.

'Get your hands off. There's no need—' he gabbled in fright.

'You dare to touch her?' John bawled. With just one drink in his belly, he was livid.

'He didn't.' Rose took hold of his arm, but John shook her off angrily and shoved her away.

'No one touches my wife and makes a fool of me!' he thundered at the terrified neighbour. With one strong punch, the man was reeling backwards and crashing to the floor. John was on him, kicking him with his hobnailed boots and screaming oaths at him like a madman.

Rose had never seen him this angry with someone he hardly knew. She could not believe he would be so jealous over her and all because of a misunderstanding. She hovered anxiously, wondering what to do. Just then Mary ran in from the street with Jack at her heels. She froze in shock at the sight of her stepfather kicking and swearing at the writhing figure on the ground.

'Get inside,' Rose commanded, seizing both children and pushing them to safety. 'And stay there!' She slammed the door shut behind them.

Turning to John, she grabbed at him and tried to shove him away. 'You'll kill him! That's enough, John! He's done nothing to me—'

'Whore!' he shouted, glaring at her with wild eyes. Then, with the swiftness of lightning, he drew back his fist and punched her full in the face. Rose reeled back, stunned by pain. For a second she thought she had been blinded. She could see nothing. She covered her face as the agony spread.

The shouting stopped, but Rose could not look up. The bridge of her nose throbbed so bad, all she could do was clutch it and moan. She heard the railwayman groaning as he got to his feet and dragged himself back upstairs.

'I never touched her,' he spat from the safety of his own door. 'She's a foul-mouthed baggage - you deserve each other.'

Rose felt tears of humiliation sting her eyes. But she was damned if anyone was going to see her cry. Least of all this beast she was shackled to, who called her a whore and used his cowardly fists against her! And after she had defended John for months against their quarrelsome neighbours. How she despised him now!

'Rose?' John stood over her. 'Rose, are you all right?' He touched her on the shoulder, but she flinched away from him. 'I'm sorry,' he whispered. 'I don't know what came over me. That man - I just thought - I couldn't bear anyone touching you ...'

She looked at him coldly over her protective fingers. She could feel the warm blood from her nose trickling between them. She wanted to die of shame.

'Leave me alone,' she said through clenched teeth.

He hesitated, then his tone changed. 'Haway, let's get you inside,' he said, as if she were a child he had found fighting in the street. 'You shouldn't have been arguing in the first place.'

Rose stumbled into the flat and made for the sink. She dowsed her face in water from a tin dish. It ran red in seconds.

'What's wrong?' Mary asked.

Jack ran to her and pulled at her skirt. 'Mammy? Let me see! Mammy's hurt.'

'She's all right,' John snapped. 'Stop fussin'. Mary, keep your brother away.' He steered Rose into the only chair they possessed and pulled the dirty cotton muffler from round his neck. 'Here, hold this to your nose. It'll stop the bleedin'. Mary, make your mam a cup of tea.'

While Mary boiled some tea leaves in a pan and added some condensed milk and sugar, Jack climbed on to his mother's knee. She held him with her free hand, the other clamped over her pulsating nose. Just let John try to take the lad away from her! She could hardly bear to look at her husband. Mary came over with a cup of weak, sweet tea and stood beside her while she drank it.

Perhaps the sight of them huddled together around their mother, excluding him, was too much for John. Or maybe his thirst got the better of him. For moments later, he had straightened his cap again and was banging out the door before Rose's tea was finished.

When Kate came home, she was less easy to convince that Rose had merely slipped and hit her face on the newel post at the bottom of the stairs. She noticed the tense look on her mother's face when her stepfather could be heard returning, and pondered at the silence that descended on them like hoarfrost.

Rose did not go out for two weeks. Her nose was broken and both eyes puffed up and blackened like a prizefighter's. She sent the girls out for any errands and answered the door to no one. She waited indoors, imprisoned by her shameful looks, as the swelling went down and the bruising turned from purple to yellowy-brown.

When she looked no more than jaundiced, she told the girls to pack up their belongings. She went out with Kate's last wages and paid a week's rent on a room in a tenement five streets away.

That evening she told John firmly, 'I'm not stopping here after what happened. I'll not have them neighbours looking at me the way they do.'

He blustered for a while, telling her she was being foolish and not to mind the bloody neighbours. But during those two long weeks of hiding, Rose had had too much time to dwell on what people thought. Shatteringly, she had lost her confidence to brazen things out. When John had felled her so unexpectedly, her spirit had taken a blow too.

'We'll start over - where folk don't know us,' she insisted quietly.

John shrugged and gave in. She knew he had no real choice in the matter if he wanted her to provide what meagre home comforts their stretched resources could manage. Rose's one trump card that she still held through all the agony of her humiliation was that John now needed her as much as she needed him.

She had daughters who could provide a little for her now, so he was no longer the sole breadwinner. But since his mother's death, she was his only home-maker. She and her children gave him the esteem of being a husband, a father, the head of a household; someone who could hold his head up in the street and look the priest in the eye. Well, Rose would choose where that household would be. It was a small triumph. But Rose still had the spirit to cling to small triumphs.

Chapter 41

1899

A time of wandering like tinkers . . .

How often had Rose thought of the gypsy's words over the past five years? They had moved house as many times in as many years. Sudden 'flits' had become so routine that she had kept the household in a state of semi-preparation for flight. She kept pots and pans stored in a crate rather than put up shelves; their clothes were packed in boxes which saved on buying a wardrobe.

It was hard to remember the names of all the poky streets they had briefly inhabited. What was the point? They were like temporary camps before being evicted for non payment of rent. Or Rose would take it upon herself to move them when John's abuse of neighbours grew too much to bear.

But the last address she could recall: Frost Street in East Jarrow. Number 38. Because it was there that she heard of a flat for rent in the New Buildings. Rose had long hankered after a home in the New Buildings. They lay on the edge of East Jarrow like Naboth's Vineyard, a coveted group of tenements surrounded by open ground that could almost pass for countryside. Rose had watched them going up in the late 1880s as she toiled between Simonside and the puddling mill, and envied the chemical workers at St Bede's for whom they were being built.

They were clean, model homes amid fields that Charles Gidney's workers could return to, an easy half-mile walk away (and upwind from) his sulphurous-smelling factory. At some stage, the philanthropic owner had run out of money and the development had never been finished. But three rows of solid, large-roomed dwellings had been completed and it was now possible for other workers - dockers and railway hands - to rent them. Some were little short of grand. One terrace of self-contained houses had bay windows and flights of steps leading up to their front doors. Rose no longer dreamt of the impossible, but she secretly had her heart set on one of the more modest upstairs or downstairs 'houses'.

She encouraged her daughters to work hard and please their employers so that they might be rewarded with better wages. Kate had stopped working for the butcher in Stanhope Road soon after the family's flight from Napier Street. The girl adapted wherever they went, grafting hard for a series of upper-working-class families. Then a year ago, her reputation for hard work and her willing, pleasant manner had landed her a job with the Pattersons, a well-to-do family in South Shields. Rose could see how happy her daughter was.

'I'm to help look after the bairns during the holidays, an' all, Mam,' she told her mother eagerly. 'He's a real gentleman, Mr Patterson. And the missus - you should see the clothes she wears. She gans all the way to Newcastle to shop!'

Rose was filled with gladness to hear Kate's excited chatter and to see her pretty face light up. For her middle daughter had just turned sixteen that summer and she was growing bonnier by the day. Somehow, despite the years of hunger and demanding physical labour, Kate had the soft, delicate skin and rounded figure of a lady. Her rich brown waves of hair framed her pale brow and oval face. Her blue eyes were startling under long brown lashes and arched eyebrows. Her full mouth was always animated in chatter or open wide with quick laughter.

Sarah was heftier and bigger-boned, but not unattractive with her wide-set eyes and easily blushing pink cheeks. At eighteen she was a good cook and a hard worker, and was employed as a cook's help in South Shields. Rose sometimes wondered if her daughters had ever begged at the houses in which they now worked. But they never said so. It was a time that they never ever talked about to her, nor she to them.

Work had picked up steadily in the shipyards while the McMullens had moved restlessly around the streets of Tyne Dock and East Jarrow. Palmer's were building ships again for the Navy: warships like Rainbow and Pegasus, and the battleships Resolution and Revenge. The docks seethed with activity and disputes. John grumbled at the number of stoppages over job demarcations and wages, for they were never on his behalf, an unskilled ageing labourer. But Rose was thankful he was working at all. On good days he made five shillings a shift. On good weeks he brought home twenty-five shillings, minus his beer money, and they would eat ham for tea on Saturday and brisket for Sunday dinner.

So when Mary turned twelve in the autumn of '99, Rose lost no time in finding her a job too. As luck would have it, a family who lived in one of the houses in Simonside Terrace, among the New Buildings, was in need of a general maid. They took one look at the slim, neatly dressed Mary and started her the next day. It was through Mary working at the Simpsons' that Rose got to hear about Number 6 William Black Street becoming vacant.

'We can't afford it.' John was dismissive.

'We can now that our Mary's working too,' Rose pointed out.

'It's too far from the docks,' he objected.

'You used to walk much further from Albion Street.'

'I was younger and fitter then,' he snorted.

'You're still a strong man,' she said, pandering to his vanity. 'And it'll be grand for our Jack - get him away from the smoke and dust. You know how it lies on his chest.' What worried her more was that her son, only eight years old, was running around with rougher lads of twelve. There was no Mary now to keep him in check, and Kate and Sarah just indulged him when they were home. She was not going to have him grow up with the same wild ways as his father and uncles. But this she could not say to John.

'You fuss too much about the lad,' her husband complained.

Rose hid her impatience. She was not going to lose this chance of a step up in society; she had scrimped and gone without for long enough.

'Maybes I do,' she admitted. 'But think how handy it would be for Mary, working just round the corner. She'd be back home to help all the sooner.' She slid John a look. He still liked to come home and have Mary run around him fetching things. Rose knew the girl only did so in the hope of some favour, but who could blame her? She saw him purse his lips, so she persisted. 'Course, it may be too late - already spoken for, most likely. I know Maggie and Danny had their eye on it. It's a popular place to—'

'Maggie wants it?' he interrupted. 'And Danny Kennedy?'

'Aye. They've been looking out for such a place since last winter.' Rose waited. One of John's many petty jealousies these days was of her sister and husband. He had always been far more envious of Mary's closeness to Maggie than she ever had. Rose did not mind when Mary chose to stay over at her aunt's house and play with her cousins. But John would berate Rose for allowing the girl to stay a night under someone else's roof.

'We don't know what she gets up to when she's not here!'

More than that. Rose knew that John resented Danny for being more skilled than he and commanding a better wage. Besides, Danny had once been a good friend of William's, so he was no friend of John's.

'Maybes we could look into it,' John conceded.

It was all the encouragement Rose needed. Within the month they had vacated Frost Street and moved into the three-roomed dwelling in William Black Street. Rose was content for the first time in years. They had their own dry closet which they did not have to share with strangers, and a water tap in the yard that dispensed with long trudges down muddy back lanes. There was a separate scullery in which they could wash in privacy, a bedroom for her four children and an alcove in the kitchen big enough to take a bed for her and John.

Mary was happy in her new job, keen to mimic the genteel airs of Mrs Simpson and study the ways of a more prosperous household. She took pleasure in dusting the china ornaments and polishing the brass door knobs and fingerplates. She liked to handle the cut-glass cruet set on the gleaming dining-room table and run her fingers over the smooth, cool marble mantelpiece. Best of all, on the pretext of laying the bedroom fires, Mary delighted in opening the cavernous mahogany wardrobe and breathing in the aromatic smell of mothballs. She wanted to touch the lace and brocades of Mrs Simpson's clothes and run her fingers through her fur stole, but never quite dared.

Within weeks, Jack's health had improved and Rose was happy to watch him through the dilapidated fence opposite their street, playing in the farmer's field and helping lift potatoes. As long as he kept away from the Slake, which lay below them, Rose did not worry.

Even John seemed less truculent, if not happier, than he had done for a long time. He ceased to complain about the tramp uphill from the docks, and even occupied his evenings raising chickens in the long back yard. He began to accumulate furniture again; large unfashionable pieces that he bought second- or third-hand in the town. Kate encouraged him. To Rose's dismay, her daughter had a similar weakness for ungainly, ostentatious furniture and would tell John if she heard of a house auction in Shields. They came back with solid, uncomfortable chairs and a table that was so big they had to saw the legs off to get it in the house. A dresser followed and a curious contraption that was a desk by day and pulled out into a bed at night.

'Father says Lord Roberts most likely had one of these on his campaigns in India,' Kate announced as they demonstrated it with a flourish.

Rose looked at them as if they had gone mad. 'What do we want with such a thing?'

Jack drew closer, intrigued. 'Won't Lord Roberts be needing it in Africa?' The boy was developing a fascination for the far-away war against the Boers in South

Africa that had flared up that autumn. He and John had named the chickens French and Buller after two of the generals.

'It's not really his,' Kate laughed, and gave her brother an affectionate hug.

'Leave the lad alone.' John looked annoyed and pulled his son away roughly. 'You can sleep on this, our Jack. You're too old to be sharing a bed with your sisters.'

Jack cried, 'Champion! I'll be like a soldier on me own camp bed.'

'Good riddance, I say,' Mary declared. 'It's like sleeping with an eel the way he wriggles in bed.'

Only Kate looked abashed. 'He's no bother. Like a little warming pan, aren't you?' She hugged him again, but Jack saw his father's disapproving look and shook her off.

'Gerroff, Kate man.'

Afterwards, Rose pondered the incident. Jack was coming up for nine and he was sprouting like a runner bean. John was right - he was no longer her baby. But why did her husband's remarks about Jack being too old to share a bed with his sisters trouble her? She thought he was making too much of a fuss as usual. The lad was, after all, still a young boy. There was nothing improper about him sleeping with his older sisters. Jack was far too young to be a nuisance to the girls in that respect. Yet John did not think so.

The more Rose thought about her husband's reaction, the more she realised that it was his attitude towards her daughters that gave her concern. She began to notice the way he looked at Sarah and Kate with knowing eyes that lingered too long on their maturing bodies. She caught him hovering at the back door when one of them was stripped to her underclothes, washing in the scullery.

John veered between telling them bawdy jokes and reprimanding them for coming in later than he thought they should from work or shopping.

'Where've you been? Who've you been talking to? Have you been giving anyone the eye?'

He constantly questioned them as if he did not trust them. Or was it that he did not trust himself? Rose was filled with a new alarm. She had never seen John as a threat to her daughters in that respect. She had only been concerned with keeping his wandering hands off her at night. His brother Pat had worried her with his lascivious interest in Elizabeth when he had lived with them before, but John had always been circumspect. When in drink, he was quite capable of saying the most disgusting and lewd remarks about their neighbours and women in general, but it was all talk. He had never pestered the girls, and since their move to the New Buildings, John had managed to curb the worst of his drinking as well. Rose decided she was worrying about nothing.

Then, with the turn of the year and the advent of a new century, John grew morose and his drinking increased. It was an unsettling time - a time of change - yet no one was sure what form that change would take. The old queen was still on the throne, but the war with the Boers was going badly and the nation was gripped by the distant struggle. It seemed like a bad omen for the twentieth century.

On New Year's Eve, Rose took the family over to Maggie's, where some of the Kennedys were gathered, and had a small party. John got roaring drunk around the pubs of Tyne Dock and came home ranting about the end of the

Empire. Rose's only consolation at his drunkenness was that he was too incapable of forcing himself on her in bed.

When news reached the country that Lord Roberts's only son had been killed in the conflict, John and Jack went around wearing black armbands. The hero of the Afghan campaigns was put in command. Larger numbers of militia and yeomanry were needed and young men flocked to the call.

'I wish I could go,' Jack declared in frustration. John had taken him to watch the volunteers march through Shields on their way to the station and distant glory.

'It's a dog's life.' John spat into the fire. 'Half of them won't come back.'

'But you were a soldier,' Jack said in admiration.

John shot Rose a resentful look. 'Aye, well, I was a fool. I should've stopped at home.'

Rose knew that he blamed her for his going away, just as she was to blame for all his trials in life. She retaliated. 'If it was such a mistake, then why fill the lad's head full of nonsense about joining up?'

'I didn't,' he snapped. 'Just took him to see the daft buggers who do.'

But she suspected John was secretly envious of the young men who could march away to the beat of the drum and leave behind their drab lives in an instant.

'Well, I thank the saints he's too young to gan to war,' Rose sighed.

'I'm not glad,' Jack said grumpily. 'I hope the war gans on long enough so I can join the army and fight the Boer.'

John gave a harsh laugh of satisfaction. 'Listen to the little runt! I'll make a fighter out of him yet, Rose Ann.'

A chill went through her at the thought and she was reminded once again of the gypsy's curse.

May the son that sleeps in your wife's belly be the one to stand up to you. May he bring you not a minute's peace till the day he dies.

She would not let Jack become a soldier and risk dying young, or let John turn him into a bullying McMullen.

As 1900 progressed, John's obsession with the war continued. When the country went wild with celebration at the news of the relief of Ladysmith in late February, he sulked and lost his temper, as if good news did not fit his mood of doom.

'You're just like your brother Pat and them Nationalists,' Rose accused, 'only cheering when the Boers are winning.'

'No he's not.' Jack came to his father's defence. 'You're right pleased with General Buller for getting back Ladysmith, aren't you, Father? You don't know what you're talking about, Mam. You're just a silly woman.'

Rose was pained to hear John's words trip off her son's tongue.

'Aye, you tell your mother,' John said, taking delight in Jack's derision of Rose. It was time he had an ally in this house of women who thought they could do what they wanted without his say.

'Don't be cheeky,' Rose said smartly and threw John an angry look.

Rose was hurt by Jack's increasing rebelliousness against her and siding with his father, but at least it disproved the gypsy's threat that Jack would be a constant trouble to John. More worrying was John's growing jealousy over the girls. He was becoming stiflingly protective, until they could hardly glance at a man in the street without provoking his wrath. If he caught them outside chatting with anyone older than Jack, he would shout at them to get in the house, then turn on the astonished neighbours and give them an earful of abuse about the laxness of their morals.

There was little Rose could do about his fretfulness, except humour or ignore him.

Just before Easter, Kate came home bursting with excitement.

'The Pattersons have asked me to gan on holiday with them!'

'They haven't!' Rose exclaimed.

'Where?' demanded Mary.

'The Lake District,' Kate squealed. 'They want me to look after the bairns. We'll be staying in a hotel. Can you imagine!'

'Bet you'll be put in the attic and have to eat with the kitchen staff and won't get any time off to see anything,' Mary pouted.

'I don't care,' Kate said, dismissing her sister's envious outburst. 'The bairns are canny. I don't mind stopping with them if the Pattersons want to gan out.'

Rose smiled. 'That's grand, hinny.'

'They like walking, Mam,' Kate continued, 'and Mrs Patterson says there's a steamer on the lake we can go on.'

'I hate ferries,' Mary said, 'they make me sick.'

'You've never been on one,' Kate laughed.

'Have so! Aunt Maggie took me on the ferry to North Shields once. And they make me sick.'

'It's a good job you're not ganin' to the Lake District then,' Rose said drily.

'I wouldn't want to,' Mary declared.

But she lost no time in telling her stepfather when he came in. 'Kate's boasting about ganin' with her posh people on holiday. And we can't even afford a day trip to the seaside. Tell her to stop ganin' on about it, Father.'

Rose watched in irritation as John began to work himself up.

'What holiday? No one thinks to ask my permission whether you can gan so far away. Who do these people think they are, taking a young lass away from her family like that?'

'They're respectable people, that's who,' Rose answered.

'She'll be staying in a hotel an' all.' Mary needled his anxiety. 'Full of strangers - and what about the stable lads and the porters?'

'Hotel?' John cried. 'No, I'll not have you ganin' to any fancy hotel!'

'John,' Rose tried to calm him, 'it's not going to cost us anything.'

'Oh, it'll cost us. She'll come back with ideas above herself and there's no knowing where that will end.'

'I won't, Father,' Kate protested.

'She already does think she's better than us,' Mary said maliciously, 'just 'cos she works in a big house in Shields.'

'I don't!'

'You're not going,' John barked.

'Mam?' Kate appealed to her mother.

'Don't you gan crying to your mother. She'll keep her big trap shut! I'm the one who says what can happen in this family, do you hear?' John thrust his puce face at his stepdaughter.

Damn her for looking so pretty! Defying him with those large blue Fawcett eyes. He would show her who was master. He would show them all! John scowled at Rose. She was to blame. They took their lead from her and she showed him nothing but contempt these days. He saw it in the dull resentment of her faded brown eyes, the downturn of disapproval in her bloodless lips. Was it possible that she had once smiled on him and kissed him with a willing, fulsome mouth? He tried to remember what it was about Rose that had attracted him all those years ago. He wanted to conjure up those dark good looks that had plagued him half his life, but could not.

She was forty-one or two, but looked much older. John saw only a lumpen woman in a shapeless apron whose grey face was creased with fatigue and disappointment. Well, it was not his fault! He had saved her from a worse fate; Rose would've been dead by now if it hadn't been for him. And what had he gained by it? A millstone around his neck. A wife who did not want him in bed and a houseful of daughters who drained him of every penny he ever made and tempted him to distraction with their plump figures and soft skin.

'You can't stop me,' Kate cried, 'I'm ganin' whatever you say! The Pattersons have asked me and I'm not going to let them down.'

Instantly, John slapped her hard across the cheek. 'Don't you speak to me like that!' he thundered. 'You'll do as I say, you little bitch!'

Rose moved to intervene but he raised his hand in threat and she faltered. She knew the cruel power of that fist and she hated him for it.

'You'll do as I say an' all, woman,' he shouted. Rose glared at him but said nothing, too frightened of his violence.

John stormed out of the house and went off to find Pat or another drinking friend with whom he could fulminate about the lack of respect of young women and the godlessness of the age. He came back late that night, fired up with whisky and indignation, dragged Kate out of bed and beat her for daring to defy him - this time with his belt.

After he had fallen asleep, Rose slipped out of bed and went through to the other room to comfort Kate. They were all awake, shaken and subdued by the abruptness and savagery of the outburst. Sarah had her arm around her sobbing sister. Jack stared with anxious eyes over his blanket from the desk-bed. Even Mary was looking sheepish at her part in stirring up trouble. Rose held up a candle to see if John had marked Kate. Luckily his aim had been impaired by drink and the lashes from his belt had landed as much on the bed as the girl. She dabbed a weal on her bare shoulder with a damp rag. Kate winced and whimpered.

'He's a bastard,' Sarah hissed.

'Don't speak about your father like that,' Rose chided half-heartedly.

'He's not me father,' she answered. 'I remember me real one - Da would never have laid a hand on us like that.'

'Your father doesn't know any better,' Rose tried to explain. 'He was brought up hard among lads. He thinks he's doing it for the best.'

'He stares at us an' all,' Sarah complained, 'when we're dressin'.'

Rose felt uncomfortable. 'He wouldn't—' she began, then stopped herself. She did not know what he would not do in one of his drunken rages. She could no longer ignore John's unhealthy fixation with her maturing daughters. Somehow she had to protect them from his increasing violence and latent lust before he did any real damage.

'I want to go with the Pattersons, Mam,' Kate whispered, still defiant.

Rose felt the bile in her throat rise at the thought of what John had just done to her. 'You will, hinny,' she promised. 'I'll see that you do.'

Rose waited a few days and then instructed Kate to come home with a letter from the Pattersons asking John for permission to take her away with them. It was written in flourishing handwriting on thick notepaper and sealed in an envelope with a wax seal. Rose watched John open it, preening with self-importance.

'So, what's it say?' he asked Kate suspiciously.

Kate read out the formal request asking for her to accompany their children on the holiday. It was polite and deferential to him as the head of the family and as Rose had hoped, it worked. He gave his permission. But he spent the days before Kate went warning her of the dire consequences of speaking or looking at young men, so that right up until the moment Kate went, Rose feared he would suddenly change his mind.

That Easter, with Kate away, Rose steeled herself for a more onerous task. She had decided the only way to keep John's interest from straying to her daughters was to give in to his pestering at night. She had put up with his whispered demands and his filthy words when she rebuffed him. He could no longer threaten her with the priest, for Rose had long ceased to care if the Catholic Church thought her a bad wife. She had stopped going regularly to Mass when she no longer had decent clothes to wear. She had seen to it that Jack received instruction from the priests at school and that they had all had their first communion. Beyond that she would not be reproached by the Church and least of all John, who never darkened a church door, for all his sermonising.

So the next time her inebriated husband fumbled for her in bed, Rose did not push him off. She allowed him to paw her breasts and pull up her nightgown. She turned her face away from his sour, whisky-fumed breath and prayed it would all be over swiftly. Perhaps because John was so surprised by the easy capitulation, he was quick to satisfy himself. Within minutes he was asleep, half slumped across her, snoring heavily.

Rose lay, not daring to push him away, fighting down the revulsion she felt. She told herself it was worth it if it kept his attentions away from her daughters. No matter how bitter she felt at the hardships she'd endured these past years and the changes for the worse in John, her children were what kept her going. For them she would submit to the indignities to which John subjected her. For them she would go to Hell and back. And one day they would escape their stepfather and poverty and make her proud.

Kate came back from her holiday in the Lake District bubbling over with the experience. She regaled them with stories of the children and eccentric characters at the hotel and places she had seen. It had quite opened her eyes to a world she had not imagined existed.

'You wouldn't believe the height of the mountains,' she gasped.

'I've seen bigger in Afghanistan,' John said scornfully.

But not even her stepfather could dampen Kate's enthusiasm.

'And the water - it was that clear and fresh, you could see right through it!'

Kate's delight at what she had seen reminded Rose of her rare trips beyond Jarrow to the countryside around Ravensworth. She could still remember being entranced as a child at the sight of long green grass and trees heavy and rustling with leaves. It had been a glimpse of Heaven. She saw the same wonderment in her daughter's face - and something else - a growing confidence in the seventeen-year-old. She had tasted freedom and Rose could tell she hungered for more.

A few weeks of relative peace followed with John and Jack caught up with following the progress of Lord Roberts's march north after taking Bloemfontein. Jack looked out for billboard headlines on his way back from school and reported them to his father. He had copied a map of South Africa on to brown paper from a globe in his classroom and traced the progress of the British troops whenever reports on the war filtered through.

It was a Saturday morning in late May when the extraordinary news reached Tyneside. Rose had thrown open the back door and levered up the sash window to let air into the hot kitchen. The smell of fresh baked scones and bread wafted out on the warm breeze. John was down the bottom of the yard feeding the chickens and Jack had last been seen vaulting over the black tarred fence with his toy rifle, made from scavenged pieces of wood. For weeks he had been re-enacting the heroic sacrifices of Spion Kop and the relief of Ladysmith.

Somewhere down on the river a hooter went off. Then a factory siren wailed. Rose and John looked up at the same time. She saw the alarm on his face and knew he was thinking the same thing. An accident had happened, maybe an exploding boiler or a fire. John stood up and went to the back gate. As he did so, a red flare soared up from the river and speckled the air above them. Several more hooters began to blare along the riverside.

'What the bloody hell's ganin' on?' he cried. 'Are we being invaded?'

Rose picked up her long skirt and apron and hurried down the path towards him. There was now a cacophony of noise rising up all around them. Ships' bells were being rung as if for action stations. Rose's pulse hammered in alarm.

Just then, Jack came hurtling up the back lane waving his dummy rifle above his head.

'They've gone and done it!' he screamed in agitation. 'They've broken through!'

'What in the name of—' Rose stretched her arms out to calm him. 'Who's broken what?'

'We have!' Jack squeaked, hardly able to speak.

'What's happened?' John barked. 'Spit it out, lad.'

'Mafeking,' he panted. 'Mafeking's been relieved!' He whooped and punched the air with his rifle.

'Is that what all this song and dance is about?' Rose asked in bewilderment.

'Aye,' Jack grinned. 'Happened Thursday or Friday. They're saying down at the station London's ganin' crackers at the news. Can we have a party, Father?'

John just grunted. 'You scarper before I find you a job to do.' Then as an afterthought he fished in his pocket and pulled out a penny. 'Gan and get yourself some'at to celebrate.'

Jack took the penny as if he had just been given a sovereign. 'Ta, Father. Ta very much!' He ran off with the speed of a fire-cracker before John changed his mind.

John shook his head. 'Well, bugger me! He's gone and done it again. Lord Roberts - he's a bloody wizard.'

Only later did the newspapers reveal that it was Colonel Baden-Powell who was the hero of Mafeking, bringing deliverance to the railway town after seven months of siege. But to John it was still the brilliance of Roberts, that talisman of the British army that was turning the conflict in the country's favour, conjuring victory out of humiliation. Rose could not decipher whether her husband loved or hated the field marshal, but that day he basked in the glory of it all as if he had had a hand in it.

The town was gripped in a fever of celebration and John was not going to miss out. Factories closed and brass bands marched with children parading behind them playing kazoos and waving flags. The pubs did a roaring trade and by the afternoon there were people openly singing and dancing in the streets.

Sarah came home excited. 'They've given me the rest of the day off, Mam. Can I go into Newcastle with Clara? Her Auntie Bella lives there now - we could stop with her.'

'I'll not have you stoppin' with strangers,' John said at once. He had returned from several hours' drinking and was dozing in his chair. But he was not too drunk to give his opinion.

'They're not strangers,' Rose defended. 'The lasses have been friends since school. And Bella used to help me out with the bairns when we lived at Raglan Street.' As soon as the words were out she knew it was the wrong thing to say. Bella and Raglan Street were part of her past that was anathema to John.

'I don't know them,' he snapped. 'And Newcastle won't be safe on a day like this. It'll be heavin' with strangers and bad 'uns.'

'We'll just be looking round the shops,' Sarah said, 'and having our tea with Auntie Bella.' She looked pleadingly at them both. 'Please. I hardly ever get time off and it's a special day - one for celebrating.'

Rose forced herself to keep quiet, knowing that if she gave her permission, John would perversely refuse it. It was best to say nothing and let him make the decision.

He stared at Sarah suspiciously. 'You sure you're not meetin' some lad?'

'Course I'm not,' Sarah exclaimed. 'It's just me and Clara.'

'Cos you're too young to start courtin' and when you do it'll be on my say-so.'

'Aye, Father, I promise.' She stared at him expectantly. 'So can I go?'

John pulled a face. 'Aye, go on. Just this once, mind.'

Sarah's face broke into a smile of relief. She gave him a quick kiss on his cheek. 'Ta, Father.'

But before she could fix on her boater and dash out the door, he added, 'You're to come home the night, mind you. There's no stopping in Newcastle on a Saturday night.'

Sarah glanced at Rose in dismay, but Rose cut off any protest, fearing that John might forbid her to go at all if she argued back.

'You'll do as your father says,' Rose warned. 'Be back here by nightfall.'

Chapter 43

Those words of warning rang in Rose's head hours later when the sun began to set over the blackened stacks of the coke works and factory chimneys to the west. The evening shadows were growing longer up the lane and creeping across the back yard. Rose went out to look, pretending she was paying a visit to the outside closet. She peered away down the hill for any sign of Sarah returning along the Jarrow Road. There were still plenty of people meandering home along it, but none of them looked like her daughter.

Rose's heart began to pound. John had gone out again after sleeping off his early drinking. Please God, let Sarah return before him! Kate and Mary had taken Jack along to see the bonfire at the end of Lancaster Street on the other side of the New Buildings and she could hear the noise from where she stood. But families were beginning to return to their houses and children were being called in. It was not nearly dark yet, and Rose drew comfort from the thought.

An hour later, she went out to fetch the younger ones home. Through the dusk she could see the lights of Newcastle away in the distance. Now and again, fireworks would pepper the indigo sky with sparks of light, then fade like shooting stars. For once the evening sky was clear and the moon rose and brightened like a ship's lantern as the sky darkened.

'Haway, our Jack, it's high time you were in bed,' Rose said when she found him squatting by the bonfire. His face was weary but still aglow with excitement in the light of the flames.

'Can't I stop?' he complained.

'Get yourself home now, before your father finds you still out,' she ordered, pulling him up. She looked round for Kate and saw her in the middle of a group of young friends, telling some story that was making them laugh.

'Mary, tell your sister I want her home,' Rose said, anxiety clutching her. Kate was quite capable of staying out late and forgetting what time it was. But where could Sarah be? She was usually so sensible.

When Rose got back there was still no sign of her eldest. She busied herself getting Jack to bed and tidying up the house for the morning. She laid a cloth on the table and put out cups and plates for Sunday breakfast - there would be bacon and freshly baked bread. Rose banked up the fire and sent Kate to the tap to fill up the kettle. Her daughter could tell she was fretting.

'She'll have stopped with Auntie Bella,' Kate said.

'She was told to be home.' Rose was short with her.

'The trams'll be busy the night,' Kate pointed out. 'Our Sarah might have had to wait—'

'Don't make excuses for her,' Rose cut in. 'She should've been back before now. I'll have some'at to say when she walks in that door.'

For the next hour, she paced in and out of the house, hovering at the back door or walking to the top of the street to see if Sarah was in sight. But when one of her neighbours stopped her to ask if she had lost something, Rose hurried indoors, not wanting her business known. The time of the last tram came and went. She watched the clock, counting down the fifteen minutes she thought it would take for Sarah to walk up the bank from the tram stand. She listened out for the girl's steps but heard only a distant tug on the river and the sound of someone singing through an open window.

Sarah was not coming home. Rose felt nauseous. Perhaps something terrible had happened to her? She had been set upon on her way home. Pushed in the river. Crushed in a crowd. She had fallen in with bad company, as John had feared. At best, Sarah had defied them and deliberately stayed over at Bella's. How could she be so stupid? Rose see-sawed between anger at her daughter's disobedience and terror that something awful had happened to her.

Several times, she reached for her shawl with the intention of setting out to look for Sarah, then realised the futility of such an act. Newcastle was a good hour's walk away and she would not know where to begin searching. Perhaps she should go to the police station? Or walk into Jarrow and see if Clara had returned? But then Sarah's friend was expected to stay over at Bella's, Sarah had said. Rose wrung her hands in a fever of indecision. In the end she decided to go to bed, praying that Sarah was safely at Bella's.

As Rose had dreaded, the next person to walk - or rather stagger - in the door was John. It was gone midnight and quite dark. He lurched around, bumping into furniture and cursing that the light was out. Rose lay still, pretending to be asleep. He began to sing again. The others were safely shut away in the bedroom, at least she had seen to that. She wondered how long they would stay asleep with the noise he was making.

Rose watched her husband guardedly. It was just possible that he was so drunk he would not notice that Sarah was not there. He might have forgotten she had gone to Newcastle at all or she could pretend that the girl was asleep in the other room with her sisters. Better for him to discover her absence in the morning when he was hungover than when fiery with drink. Or maybe Sarah would come home on an early tram and slip in the house before he awoke. She prayed for such a miracle.

John stumbled towards the bed. 'Where are you, Rose?' he slurred.

'Here,' she whispered. 'Come to bed.'

He nearly fell on top of her as he crashed against the bed. He swore, then yanked at the bedclothes.

'Gerrup,' he ordered. 'Out. It's Mafeking. We've got the Dutch peasants on the run. Dance wi' me!'

'John,' Rose protested, 'it's the middle of the night.'

'Dance, woman!' he cried, trying to drag her out of bed. 'Everyone up and dance!' Abruptly, he turned and lurched off across the room. Before Rose could haul herself up, he had barged into the other room.

'Leave them be!' she called after him in panic.

But it was too late. She could already hear him shouting at Jack to stand to attention and the girls to get up and dance. He pushed them through the door and clapped his hands in time to some imaginary tune in his head. Rose could just make out the pale, apprehensive faces of her children, but could do nothing to reassure them. John lunged at the fire with the poker and stabbed at the dross to stir up some flame to light the room. A lurid red glow flickered over his face.

'Dance, you little wasters!' he cried, laughing at their sluggish attempts. 'Get your knees up!'

Kate and Mary spun each other round. Jack stood yawning widely, half asleep on his feet. Rose went over and pulled him towards her, guiding him to her bed. 'Sit here, hinny,' she murmured, pressing his tired head to her bosom.

It was a mistake. With just Kate and Mary turning circles to his command, John realised the room was too empty. There was someone missing. Through the alcoholic numbness that slowed his thoughts, it came to him.

'Where is she?' he demanded, his humour souring instantly. The girls carried on dancing. He grabbed at Kate's arm and shook her roughly. 'I said where is she? Where's your sister?'

Nobody spoke. John pushed her aside and lurched back into the bedroom. He poked the bedding with the fire iron and swore at the empty bed. Rose stood up, her heart hammering, and pushed Jack behind her. John came storming out of the bedroom.

'Where's that little bitch got to?' he bawled at her.

'She's not here, John,' Rose said, her throat so tight she could hardly speak. 'She must've missed the tram. Maybe they were too full after all the celebratin'. She'll have stopped with Bella - she'll be all right.'

He stepped forward unsteadily, his face full of fury. Rose just had time to anticipate his clumsy move and dodge out the way before he brought the poker crashing down. It clattered to the floor, missing her by an inch. Kate screamed in fright.

'Are you all right. Mam?'

'Aye,' Rose gasped, side-stepping John's attempt to grasp her. She ran round the table. 'Get out the house,' she cried at the girls. 'Take your brother!'

They could hardly hear her for the shouting and cursing of their stepfather. He chased after Rose like a man demented, ramming the table and hurling chairs out of the way to get at her. Kate grabbed Jack and ran for the back door, pushing Mary in front of her.

Rose seized the heavy iron skillet from the range and held it in front of her like a shield. 'Don't you touch me!' she screamed at him. 'I told the lass to be back. You heard me!'

'You encouraged her to go,' he shouted. 'Always going against me! She'll be whoring on the streets of Newcastle. You've a slut for a lass! I should've taken the belt to her long ago - but you're soft as clarts. This is your doing, you old witch!'

'Don't you blame me,' she yelled. 'You're the one that's driving her away with your drinkin' and cussin'. It's no surprise she's not come back - she might never come back! And who would blame her?'

'By God, I'll tak the belt to you, an' all!'

'Never!' Rose spat at him. 'You'll not touch me. You're nothing but a drunken, foul-mouthed pig who picks on them that can't fight back. But I'll fight yer this time!'

John picked up a plate from the table and threw it at her. 'Gerr-out!' he roared. 'I'll kill yer!' He grabbed the bread knife from the table and held it aloft. Kate, still hovering in the doorway, screamed.

Rose froze in shock at the madman before her. His face was contorted, a

238

gaunt devilish mask in the firelight. He was going to kill her! Without thinking, she hurled the skillet at him then bolted for the door. She heard the pan clatter against the table but did not look round to see if it had hit him. Rose tripped over the doorstep, pushing her children ahead of her.

'Run!' she gasped and fled down the brick path, panic choking her.

She knew she could not outrun John if he came after her. For a second she wondered what neighbour would give them shelter, but even in that moment of gut-wrenching fear, she could not bring herself so low as to beg for refuge in the middle of the night.

Rose reached the bottom of the yard. 'In the netty,' she ordered, hurling her children into the shed that housed the dry closet. She slammed the door shut behind them and fumbled with the iron bolt with shaking hands. She rammed it shut just as she heard John staggering down the path after her. He shouted oaths and hammered on the door until she thought he would knock it down. But she and Kate leaned against it with all their weight and prayed it would not give way. Mary and Jack huddled on the wooden seat and sobbed in fright.

John kicked and thumped the door and railed at her for several minutes, but did not break in. Finally the blows subsided and the threats lessened until he tired and gave up. Rose heard him trudge back to the house shouting at some screeching cat on a neighbouring roof. She did not move till she heard the back door bang shut and then silence.

Her heart pounded. She felt too ill to speak or reassure the terrified children. Rose waited, not trusting that he had really gone, but heard nothing more. After a while, she slipped back the bolt and peered out. All was quiet. Yet she did not dare go back to the house to make certain he had fallen asleep. Rose retreated into the musty, rank-smelling closet and closed the door again.

Her legs gave way and she sank to the floor, sobbing with relief that she was still alive. Kate put comforting arms around her.

'It's all right, Mam,' she crooned, 'it's all right. Father's wrong. It's not your fault. It's nobody's fault.'

Rose was shaking all over, her hands clamped over her mouth to stifle her weeping. The neighbours must have heard the row, but they would not hear her crying like a bairn! She must be able to walk past them in the morning as if nothing had happened. They must not guess that she had spent the night locked in the outhouse like a dog. She hardly took in Kate's gentle words of reassurance, only that she was there being strong for her when she felt as weak and helpless as a newborn.

It was Mary's disapproving tone that forced her to take hold of herself. 'Our Jack's dirtied himself,' she said with distaste. 'He stinks.' She shoved him away from her.

Rose struggled to her feet with Kate's help. She saw Jack's forlorn, skinny figure standing shivering in his shirt, his shoulders shaking with silent sobs.

'It's running down his leg, Mam,' Mary said in disgust.

Rose reached out for her unhappy son.

'Sorry, Mam,' Jack whimpered.

Rose touched his cheek with her hand. 'I know, hinny. Let's get you cleaned up.'

Kate was already handing her some sheets of torn-up newspaper. Between them they stripped the boy and wiped him down, ignoring Mary's protests at the stench.

'Divn't listen to her, kidder,' Kate said kindly, wrapping her shawl around her half-brother. 'Bet plenty of soldiers shit their breeches fighting the Boer.'

Rose gathered her youngsters around her and told them they would wait a little longer to make sure their father had fallen asleep. But she must have done so herself some time during the short hours of the night, for she woke to find herself slumped against the wooden box seat, stiff and aching. Mary was huddled in the corner, while Jack lay curled in the crook of Kate's arm. Daylight was poking in through the cracks around the door. She dragged herself up, her insides clenching at the thought of what the day would bring. Quietly, she roused the exhausted children and together they crept out of the closet.

Chapter 44

To Rose's relief, there was no one yet up on this early Sunday morning to spot them tiptoeing back up the mud track to the house. Only an expectant squawk from the henhouse broke the silence. They found John slumped asleep in his chair by the hearth, still dressed, his face pinched and unshaven. Rose thought how old he looked, vulnerable even.

But when he stirred with the sound of her making ready for breakfast, his habitual sour expression returned. He watched her with bloodshot eyes and she could tell he was trying to recall the events of the night. Kate, now dressed, was sweeping up the broken cups and resetting the table with what was left.

'Me and Mary can drink out the jam jars,' she murmured to her mother.

John scowled at them and went to douse his face in the pantry. They listened to him groaning as the shock of cold water hit him. No one spoke. They sat at the table, eating in silence, Rose hardly able to force down the food for the dryness in her throat. Jack and Mary scarpered as soon as they could after breakfast. Jack went to feed the hens.

'I'll gan for the newspaper,' Mary offered, and was gone before anyone objected.

Rose and Kate exchanged tense, guarded looks as the time ticked on and church bells began to ring for morning worship. John returned to his chair by the fire without a word to either of them. He sat in brooding silence and Rose knew with a sickness in her heart that he had not forgotten or forgiven.

She would have warned Sarah not to come in the house, if she had spotted her returning first. But the young woman returned so quietly, while she was in the front room making up the bed with Kate. The first they heard was John's sudden bark. Rose saw Kate jump with fright. She rushed into the kitchen.

'Where've you been?' John shouted. 'You were told!'

'I spent the night at Bella's,' Sarah said breathlessly. 'I'm sorry. I couldn't get on the last tram. People were hanging off it...' She threw her mother a pleading look.

'We were worried sick,' Rose whispered.

'You could've walked home,' John snarled, rising out of his chair. 'You haven't been at Bella's at all, have you?"

'I have, Father,' Sarah insisted. 'Me and Clara. Bella wouldn't hear of me walking home with all the crowds.'

'That's what I thought,' Kate piped up from behind. 'Didn't I say she'd be safe at Auntie Bella's, Mam?'

John whipped round. 'You keep your big mouth out of this.' He glared at Rose too. 'And you.' He swung back to Sarah. 'How do we know where you were? You can't keep your promise to your mother, so why should we trust you?'

'Honest, I was,' Sarah said, holding her ground.

'You went into town, didn't you?'

'Aye, but—'

'You went looking for lads.' John advanced towards her, his finger pointing.

Sarah took a step back. 'No I didn't.'

'Look at you - all done up like a tart.'

'Mam, tell him to stop.'

'Your mother will stay where she is,' John snarled. 'She's let you gan wayward for long enough. Well, I'll not have a slut for a daughter!' He yanked at the large buckle at his waist and pulled the long thick worn leather belt from his trousers.

Sarah's face froze in alarm. 'I'm not your daughter,' she shouted back at him. 'You can't beat me!'

This riled him further. 'You don't tell me what to do in me own house!' He drew back the belt and lunged for her. Sarah sprang back, but he half caught her and brought the belt down on her back. Sarah cried out.

Kate screamed, 'Stop him, Mam!'

Rose went after her husband. 'Don't, John, please don't!'

She took him by the arm, but he threw her off violently and sent her sprawling on the floor. It just gave Sarah enough time to wriggle free.

'Run!' Kate cried at her sister.

Sarah fled out into the yard with John just behind her, roaring obscenities, belt bunched in his hand. She might have got clear away, if Jack hadn't let the hens out. The boy emerged from the henhouse with a handful of eggs to see Sarah and his father bearing down on him. Sarah tripped over a chicken and fell flat. John knocked Jack out of the way to get at her. The eggs smashed and feathers flew as the screeching birds flapped in panic around them. At the bottom of the yard John cornered Sarah.

His face was scarlet with fury. He lifted his belt and brought it down, buckle first, on the girl's back. Sarah yelled, throwing up her arms in protection. John pulled back his belt and hit her again, bellowing oaths at the top of his voice, disgusting words that made Rose cringe with shame. She watched in horror from the doorway, quite incapable of moving, as her husband whipped her eldest daughter like a stray dog.

Sarah crumpled under the blows, as the hard metal of the buckle bit into her skin and bruised her soft flesh. She wept in terror and pain, as her torturer beat her with his leather strap and his stinging words. She was vaguely aware of Kate screaming her head off at their stepfather, to no avail.

Rose could not say how long the assault went on. It seemed like an eternity, though it could only have been half a minute. It was long enough for the neighbours to come out of their houses to listen and stare. Through the open gate where Jack had gone chasing the terrified birds, she could see the gawping faces of people in Phillipson Street opposite. Children were climbing on to a back wall to watch the spectacle. This was better than the travelling fair, the boxing ring. They were a freak show; The Notorious John McMullen and his whip.

Rose stood there helpless, dying inside of the disgrace. Fear and anger flooded through her in equal measure. Fear of John; anger at Sarah for bringing this upon herself - upon them all. Fear of the neighbours, of being cast out of this paradise and doomed to wander the earth with this tyrant who bullied them all with his bitterness and hatred of the world. Anger at John for the shame he brought. Anger at herself for ever having married him. Sick anger for doing nothing to stop him.

Eventually something made him stop. He stood back, panting, flecks of spittle on his chin. His wrath was subsiding, his anger sated. Sarah lay curled in a ball like an animal, whimpering. She was still alive - Rose registered relief through her numbness. John wiped his mouth on the back of his hand, then calmly began to fasten his belt around his waist.

'Let that be a lesson,' he mumbled.

He stalked back up the path, brushing past Rose. He avoided her bitter look. Grabbing his jacket and cap, he marched back past her and out of the back gate, without looking at anyone. She hurried down the path to Sarah where Kate was already bending over her sister and holding her.

'She's black and blue, Mam,' Kate said in disbelief.

'Get her inside,' Rose said in a strained voice. She could hardly speak.

Between them, they half carried the weeping Sarah into the house. Rose unbuttoned the girl's dress. She winced at the sight of the wheals across her shoulders and back. Even her neck and jaw were livid with the marks from his buckle. Nobody spoke as Rose set about bathing the wounds, too shocked at what had happened for conversation.

Finally, wincing with pain as her mother pulled the dress back over her bruises, Sarah hissed, 'I hate him! I'm not stopping here any longer, Mam. You'll not make me!'

Rose paused for a long time, considering. She looked at Sarah's tear-swollen face, then at Kate's perplexed one. She felt overwhelmed with guilt at having allowed such a beating to take place. Why had she not defended her daughter? Better that she had put her own body between the girl and that evil belt! She had failed her - failed them all - and brought humiliation on her family by her lack of action. No doubt the neighbours were gossiping about it at this very moment, shaking their heads in disapproval at such carry-on in a respectable street. They could not stay. None of them could stay now.

'We'll go to Aunt Maggie's,' Rose said quietly.

Her sister would give them shelter for a night or two while she thought things through. She saw the relief on her daughters' faces and felt encouraged. Whatever she did now, she must do her best for them.

Briefly, Rose laid her hand on Sarah's head. It rested there for an instant, like a benediction, a promise. She would never betray her children like that again. She would protect them by whatever means possible, so that one day - and she knew deep down that day would come - they might be able to protect her.

Chapter 45

Rose stayed at Maggie's cramped two-roomed house for a month, while John disappeared on a drinking spree. Sometimes he would turn up after dark, bawling at her from the street below, cursing her for leaving him. It lasted till the Boers were defeated at Diamond Hill and Roberts declared the war in South Africa won. Rose knew at some stage his black mood would blow over like a storm and he would wash up as wreckage on the doorstep. But by the time he did, they were deep in debt once more and unable to afford the rent in William Black Street. Not that Rose could have faced going back there.

One morning, as she had predicted, John turned up at Maggie's door looking haggard and contrite.

'Landlord's hoying us out,' he told Rose.

She looked at him with disdain. 'What am I supposed to do about it? It's you that's made us homeless with your drinkin'.'

She saw his jaw tense but he did not try to deny it. His bloodshot eyes looked utterly weary.

'I'll find us somewhere,' he promised. 'Just come back, Rose. I'll not touch you - or the lasses.'

She did not trust him. That was why she had found Sarah a job in Hebburn where she could live in with a draper's family and not have to come home at night. He would never horsewhip any of her children again.

She told him brusquely, 'Come back when you've found us somewhere,' then shut the door in his face.

Rose did not know where she found the courage to stand up to him, but since that moment a month ago when she had slammed the door at William Black Street firmly behind her, she had felt stronger. That part of her life was over. Never again would she stand by powerless and let John bully and frighten them as he had done these past years. Maybe it was the only way he knew, but it was not her way. She had been brought up with a sense of worth, both for herself and for her fellow beings.

Sometime during those dark years of depression when she had had to send out her own daughters to beg for food, she had lost her self-respect. It had seeped away so gradually that Rose had hardly been aware of it. Until that dreadful morning when she had watched John beating Sarah to within an inch of her life and done nothing. Then her self-loathing had hit her like a blow to the stomach.

Two days later, John returned. 'I've found lodgings,' he told her, 'a couple of rooms. Pat's offered to help us move.'

'Where?' Rose demanded.

John looked wary. 'Straker Street.'

Rose's heart sank. Straker Street was opposite the stinking chemical works. It was a slummy street of cramped houses and factory gates that straggled through East Jarrow. Its ugliness was only partly relieved by the stark Methodist chapel and the brash new tram depot.

'Not Straker Street,' she answered stubbornly.

John looked at her with desperation in his faded eyes. 'It's just temporary. And I'll stop the drinkin'. Here,' he dug into his pocket and brought out a half-crown, 'tak it. I'm workin' again. You'll get all me wages.'

She looked at it lying in his calloused palm. His hand was shaking like an old man's. Rose hesitated. She wished she had the luxury to throw it back in his face. But she didn't. She needed that half-crown, needed the wretched lodgings in Straker Street. Maggie and Danny could not keep her any longer. It was expected that she should return to her husband at some point. It would be a scandal if she didn't. For richer for poorer. She had taken her vows. She looked at him and knew she had no choice.

'Haway, Rose,' John chivvied, 'you cannot stop here.' When she said nothing, he added, almost whispering, 'Lass, I want you back - you and the bairns. Help me, Rose.'

Rose was astonished; he had tears in his eyes. It was the first time she had heard him really plead to her or ask for her help. She did not know whether to feel pity or despise him more for it. Yet she could not help feeling touched at the sight of a hard man like John on the brink of tears because of her. Perhaps at that moment he really meant it. Rose could not tell. All she could do was hope it was true.

'I'll come,' she said with a defiant lift of her chin. 'But we move out of Straker Street as soon as we can afford it, do you hear?'

'Aye, bonny lass,' John rasped, his grim face breaking into an unaccustomed smile.

'And the boozin' stops,' Rose added firmly.

'Not another drop past me lips,' John promised. 'I'm signing the pledge.'

Rose and the girls hated Straker Street. The air was thick with noxious gases which invaded every corner of their damp, poky dwelling. At times when the wind blew off the river, the fumes from the chemical works were overpowering. They burnt the throat and clogged the lungs. Rose used to tie a damp cloth around her mouth and nose when she hung out the washing. She had seen the sallow-faced workers streaming out of the Lake Chemical factory doing the same, and copied them.

Kate tried to make the best of it, bringing home small trinkets at the end of the week to brighten the drab mantelpiece or a piece of gaudy cloth to cover the scratchy horsehair chairs. But Mary complained constantly.

'I cannot stand the smell any longer. Mrs Simpson says I stink of rotten eggs when I come in the house. I hate it here! Why can't we move? I wish I could live with the Simpsons.'

Rose tired of hearing her, but could not blame the girl. Some days the atmosphere was suffocating. She felt increasingly ill and lacking in energy. At times she found it hard to haul herself out of her chair where she dozed half the afternoon. Her chest felt tight and her breathing sounded like a pair of bellows. The swelling in her legs grew worse.

But what worried her the most was the effect living there was having on Jack. His bouts of wheezing and breathlessness had returned. His dark eyes were ringed with black smudges while his pallor was tinged with yellow. Usually one for running around outdoors from dawn until dark, he spent half the winter confined to bed with recurring colds, chills and a persistent wheezing cough.

John had been quiet and subdued for months, going to work and returning

245

to eat and sleep. He hardly touched a drop of drink - just the occasional small glass of beer - but it did not sweeten his temper. Rose knew he had tried to curb his outbursts of anger, but it was in his nature to be moody and he was beginning to pick on Kate again. That January Queen Victoria had died and the country had been plunged into mourning. To Rose's surprise, John had taken it badly though he had never had a good word to say for her when she was alive. It was as if one more mooring in his life had been severed, one last solid anchor lifted, cutting him further adrift from the old certainties.

When Jack came in from school one day and collapsed on the floor, unable to breathe, Rose was frightened into action. With Kate's help, she managed to calm the boy and get him to bed. They gave him a steam infusion, holding his head over a bowl of boiling water, enveloped in a blanket. Jack emerged wheezing and gasping, his eyes wide in terror.

'This place is killing him,' Rose declared to John, 'it's killing us all.'

John just looked at her with a deadened expression. 'Aye, we're all headin' in the same direction.'

With a shock, it struck Rose that John was giving up. He had the world-weary look of a defeated man. He no longer cared how they eked out the rest of their miserable existence or in what manner they died. He was merely going through the motions, biding his time. Rose realised that if anyone was going to save them from the hell of Straker Street it would have to be her.

That Sunday she dressed as best she could and took Kate and Mary to Mass. She prayed as hard as she had ever prayed in her life. Amid the smell of burning wax and musty bodies, she pleaded to the Virgin for Jack's life as he lay listless on the bed at home.

'You saved him once before - let him grow to be a man - please let him live!'

Rose prayed for deliverance for them all, a way out of the slow, suffocating death that was sapping their will to carry on.

On the way home, bowed down with her troubles and feeling no relief from the bout of frantic praying, Rose was surprised by Kate's sudden suggestion.

'Mam, let's take a walk up Simonside - blow out the cobwebs.'

Rose resisted. 'I haven't the strength.'

'We'll take it steady,' Kate replied, slipping an arm through her mother's.

'I should be gettin' back to our Jack ...'

'Father's keeping an eye on him.' Mary joined in the pressure, for she had no desire to hurry back to East Jarrow. 'He'll manage a bit longer.'

'Haway, Mam,' Kate smiled, and the two girls steered her away from the town.

Within minutes Rose was glad they had bullied her into the walk. The stiff breeze at their backs helped push them up the bank. At the top, the air tasted fresher than Rose had ever remembered it. Around them were small signs of spring - purple crocuses sprouting in a ditch, tight resinous buds forming on a straggle of trees. Up here a thrush was trilling noisily, drowning out the clangs and sighs from the riverside far below.

'Look, Mam,' Kate pointed, 'Grandda's old home.'

'Aunt Maggie's house,' Mary corrected at once.

Rose looked up and squinted through the pearly light which dazzled after the greenish gloom of Straker Street. With sadness she saw that the old cottage stood forlorn, its roof fallen in and its door off its hinges. It was derelict. The once-cultivated field around it was a mass of bricks and planks and paraphernalia of the builder's merchant who now used the plot. A dog ran to the fence and barked at them territorially.

'It's all gone,' she sighed.

'Let's gan on,' Kate said gently.

They skirted round the former smallholding and kept on walking, each of them wrapped in her own thoughts yet content with each other's company. They followed a lane which petered out in a field, crossed it and found themselves beside the main railway line. In one direction it stretched all the way to Newcastle and in the other disappeared towards Tyne Dock and South Shields. A short distance away stood a signal box and across the track lay two short rows of railway cottages.

Someone had fashioned a crude bench out of a railway sleeper and placed it near the signal box. Who it was meant for Rose had no idea, but it beckoned her tired legs. Without a word she crossed the track and plonked herself down on the rough seat. With the bank at her back it was sheltered and warm in the weak spring sunshine and smelt not unpleasantly of grass and axle grease.

The girls sat down beside her, Kate closing her eyes and tilting her chin to the sun like a contented cat. Rose thought how bonny she had grown. At eighteen she was blooming into the prettiest of them all. She must not waste her life away in Jarrow! Rose felt a rush of conviction. She would see that Kate got away from the drudgery that had pulled her down like the muddy backwater of the Slake, drowning the potential that had been in her to better herself. Kate would do it instead.

As Rose wrestled with the problem of how, she suddenly thought of Lizzie. She would ask her sister to keep an ear out for any jobs at Ravensworth. There was slim chance that the aristocratic Liddells would take on a lass from Jarrow, but there was no harm in trying. Perhaps Kate should be sent to Lizzie's for a while anyway - get her away from the unhealthy conditions of Straker Street and John's critical comments. It might be the making of her, just as Rose herself might have flourished if she had stayed with her dear granny at Lamesley and not been brought back to Jarrow all too soon.

Rose's musings were suddenly disturbed by the distant hoot of a train. Above them she heard a clank in the signal box. They all bent forward to look down the track. The rhythmic puffing of the steam engine could be heard long before it rattled into view round the bend. The passenger train thundered past them, covering them in a cloud of smoke. By the time it cleared, the train had vanished, whistling breathlessly down the line.

A tall, wiry man emerged from the signal box and walked towards them. He touched his cap.

'Morning, ladies. Grand day,' he greeted them.

Kate smiled back at once. 'Aye, a grand day.'

'You from Shields?' he asked.

'Jarrow,' Kate told him. 'Just taking the air.'

Mary sniggered. 'Listen to you, all hoity-toity!'

Kate blushed but the signalman smiled. 'Good on you.' He was about to walk on when he looked closer at Rose. 'Are you all right, missus?'

Rose's pulse was fluttering and she felt breathless and faint all of a sudden. 'It was the smoke - I feel a bit funny. Maybes a glass of water ... ?'

'Haway with me,' the man said quickly, 'my missus'll give you a cup of milk straight from the cow - that'll settle your dizziness.'

Kate and Mary helped Rose to her feet and they followed the railwayman along to the first terrace of cottages. The front garden was neatly cultivated and the sweet smell of wood smoke drifted through the air. Inside it was dark at first, but as Rose grew accustomed to the dimness she saw a plain, well-kept kitchen with a lean dog stretched across the hearth asleep. She was ushered into a high-backed chair and a small, birdlike woman bustled over with a tin mug of milk.

'Drink this, hinny,' she urged. 'It's a long way to walk if you're not used to it.'

The milk tasted warm and still had the faint earthy smell of the cow about it. Rose was transported back to her early days at Simonside and her mother standing over her watching in satisfaction as she drank the milk she had just squeezed from their cow. Rose felt a pang of longing for those simple far-off days when her mother had looked after them all. She nodded gratefully and listened to Kate chatting to the couple, telling them how they had once lived at Simonside.

It was only as they were going that the wife mentioned it.

'Number One's empty since old Matty Moore passed on. It's in a bit of a state, mind you - birds nesting in the chimney and that - but it's sound enough. These houses were standing here long before the railway came – old wagon way afore that - and they'll be standing long after we're gone, I shouldn't wonder.'

'Will you show us?' Rose asked on impulse.

'Happy to oblige,' the railwayman offered.

The house on the end had a large overgrown patch of garden. Brown brambles grew up the side of the pitted brick wall like stubble on a pock-marked face. Rose peered through the windows but they were so filthy she could not see in. They went in cautiously. The doors inside creaked and something scuttled across the stone floor at her feet. Mary screamed, but the old railwayman laughed.

'Only a field mouse. Bet you get them twice as big down by the river.'

There was a stone sink in the corner and a dusty black range with a round oven.

'Have to draw water from the well,' he told her. 'But rent's cheap - be half what you're paying in the town.' He followed her gaze up the loft stairs. 'Two rooms up there - cosy as a nest in winter - heat from the chimney warms 'em, see.'

They emerged back into the sunlight. Kate watched her mother's severe expression. She could see that she thought it unsuitable. There was too much work to be done and it would be too far from the docks for Father. Yet strangely, Kate felt at home here, for all it was primitive and neglected. She loved the countryside and did not mind its strange noises, smells and muck like Mary did. And she had warmed to the kind signalman and his friendly wife. She braced herself for disappointment.

Rose turned to the railwayman. 'When could we move in?'

He smiled as if he had expected such an answer from her all along. 'I'll have a word with the foreman the morra. Soon as you want, I wouldn't wonder.'

Kate cried with delight. 'Can we, Mam? I don't mind the walk up from Shields.'

'Well, I do,' Mary protested. 'It's a hovel.'

Rose stood and looked at the cottage. It was like coming home. It filled her with the same warmth and feeling of safety that Simonside once had. Jack would love it. John would hate it. Rose did not care. She would have it. She had had her fill of the town.

Rose turned to Kate and nodded. 'Aye, we'll take it.' Kate linked arms and grinned. 'Champion! Jack'll be like a pig in muck up here.'

'It's horrible, it smells!' Mary grumbled, screwing up her face in disgust. But Rose took no notice.

Two weeks later, they had shaken the miasma of Straker Street from their clothing and hair and moved into Number 1, Cleveland Place.

Chapter 46

1904

Rose prepared excitedly for the girls coming home for Christmas, or to be exact, Boxing Day. With the luxury of Jack's new wages from the docks, she had bought a leg of pork from a local farmer and a bagful of vegetables from Harry Burn, the friendly railwayman at the end of the terrace. She had to be careful when she spoke to him, for ever since Mrs Burn had died the previous winter, John was suspicious of her conversing with the widower.

It amazed Rose that John could still be jealous over her. She had long ago stopped looking in the stained mirror that hung in the scullery where Mary used to preen every morning and apply her Pond's cold cream. At forty-six, Rose knew her looks and figure were gone. She had the slow painful gait of a much older woman and had given up trying to mount the stairs to the loft a year after they had moved in. The marital bed stood in the corner of the low-ceilinged kitchen and Jack had the run of the loft, except when his sisters came home on rare holidays.

Rose felt her stomach lurch in anticipation. It was over a year since they had all been together. She had decorated the room with streamers of coloured paper and holly that Jack had helped her pick from along the railway cutting. She glanced at the clock yet again.

Sarah would be here first from Hebburn with the mince pies that she had promised, and to help her mother cook the festive dinner. Rose had not seen her eldest since she had turned twenty-four. Sarah was courting and happy; everyone knew except John.

'When can I meet the lad?' Rose had asked in the summer.

'I'm not bringing him back here,' Sarah had declared. 'Father would kill me - or him.'

Rose had no answer. Sarah's sweetheart was a miner and John thought them the lowest form of life. He was suspicious of men who chose to crawl underground for a living and never see daylight. He cursed them for their readiness to strike for better conditions, calling them lazy, whereas William would have blamed the pit owners. John only cared that the disruption in the coal supply could bring the mills and yards grinding to a standstill and make men like himself idle.

'It's the fault of the pitmen we have no work on the river,' she had often heard him rail, whether there had been a strike or not. 'They can't be trusted.'

Once she might also have disapproved of Sarah being courted by a miner, thinking the match too lowly. They were a breed apart, rough and dirty and kept closely to themselves. Rose had grown up with such views. But Sarah's stories of her pitman and his family were quite different. She spoke of kind, generous folk and a spotless kitchen despite the grime that the men tramped in. Besides, Rose had learnt from experience that you could not judge a man by his outward appearance. Her head had been turned by the sight of an army coat and a strong handsome face, and look where it had got her. She did not object but worried for Sarah if John should find out.

Rose had to accept that she could not offer hospitality to Sarah's young man.

Anyway, the romance might come to nothing so it was not worth riling John's temper over the matter. For her husband's ill humour had got no better over the three and a half years they had lived at Cleveland Place. His attempts at sobriety had not lasted long, and when in work he would often get no further than the pubs on Learn Lane, a stone's throw from the dock gates, forgetting about his long walk home. Many were the times she had had to send Jack searching for him late in the evening, for she was too lame to go herself and would not have suffered the indignity of entering a public house.

Jack, a tall, wiry youth, was often repaid with a 'smack in the gob' for his efforts in trying to prise his belligerent father from the cosiness of some bar. John's favourite haunt was the notorious Alexandria, known locally as The Twenty-Seven because it served as the next stop after the twenty-six staithes along the docks.

Rose would try to comfort her son after such bouts of violence. 'Your day will come,' she promised him. 'He'll not be the stronger one for ever.' The saints forgive her, but she almost willed the moment to come when Jack would stand up to his father and give him a taste of his own medicine.

Sometimes Rose worried about Jack. He had become increasingly moody and withdrawn since his sisters had left home, especially Kate, who had always been openly affectionate with her half-brother. But faced with John's constant criticism at his lack of hardness or teasing about girls, Jack kept to himself, disappearing on his own to trap rabbits or fish the streams. He would shadow the local farmer when he went out to shoot crows and once or twice the man had let Jack have a go with the gun. Jack seemed to gain more pleasure from this than any amount of socialising. The boy had a good aim and had once returned from a fair with four coconuts that Rose had not known what to do with. Rose often wondered if she had been right to bring the family out to their semi-rural retreat. Perhaps Jack needed more company; he was turning into a loner. But better that than a fighting, cussed drunk like his father. Not one day did Rose regret the move for her own sake. Even in the depths of winter when she had had to break the ice on the pail to get water for the kettle and struggle through the snow to search for tinder, she had thanked the saints for her primitive cottage.

Like an animal in hibernation she had rested her bruised spirit, slowly reawakening to the world with a new inner strength. She delighted in spring rain, summer birdsong and autumn sun as if she was experiencing them for the first time. While she tended her garden, the earth seemed to nurture her in return. During these solitary years when she had often been on her own for long hours at the cottage, Rose had rediscovered a sense of worth. She kept hens and grew giant rhubarb and strong onions. She exchanged these with her neighbours for jams, relish or firewood. She bartered produce with itinerant pedlars for buttons, hairpins and Emerson's Bromo Seltzer, which she forced on John when he complained of sore head, stomach or bowels.

Rose would take Jack with her blackberry picking along the railway line and gather elderflower and wild mint for cordials. Her son would return from his wanderings with crab apples, nuts and the occasional rabbit or wood pigeon for the pot. On rare occasions, John would come home early and in a good mood, and they would eat together and walk out along the embankment to view the trains, and Rose wished life could always be that tranquil.

Certainly, it had been easier this last year without Mary in the house. At sixteen she had grown as sharp and quick with her tongue as her stepfather. Gone were the days when John would indulge the girl and defend her from her mother's censure. He found her as difficult and volatile as Rose did. Mary was as prickly as a briar and not afraid to speak her mind. Her job with the Simpsons had not lasted. Rose had hoped that her youngest daughter would be content to stay at home and help her, as she was finding heavy chores increasingly difficult. But Mary chafed at her confinement in the remote cottage and resented doing the back-breaking washing and water carrying.

'I've been trained as a lady's maid,' she declared grandly to her mother. 'This'll ruin me hands.'

In desperation, Rose had begged her sisters and daughters to find employment for Mary as far away from home as possible. It was Kate who had saved the day. The inn at Ravensworth, close to where she was working, needed a chambermaid. When Mary heard that this was no common hostelry, but the hub of social life for the staff at the castle, she lost no time in boarding the train for Lamesley.

Rose glanced at the clock again. Kate and Mary might be at Lamesley station at this very moment, waiting for the train to take them to Gateshead and then on to South Shields. They would get off at Tyne Dock station and walk up the hill. Jack had gone down to meet them and carry their bags.

It had been one of the best decisions of her life to send Kate to Lizzie's. Rose felt sure of it. Shortly after their move to the cottage, Kate had said a tearful goodbye to them all and gone to live with her aunt. It was not long before she had been noticed around the estate and put to employment. At first Kate had gone to work at Farnacre Hall on the estate. There her easy nature and willingness for hard work had been spotted by Lady Ravensworth herself and soon she was working in the castle. It was more than Rose could have wished. Kate had told Rose that the old earl himself took a passing interest in her because she came from Jarrow.

'He spoke to me, Mam!'

'He never!'

'Aye, said a cousin of his used to be rector here - Canon Liddell,' Kate told her on a visit home. 'He spoke highly of him - says he worked himself into an early grave for the people of Jarrow.'

'He's dead?' Rose asked in shock. 'Canon Liddell's dead?'

'That's what he said.' Kate gave her an enquiring look. 'Did you know him, Mam?"

Rose felt a pang of sorrow. 'Aye, I did,' she answered quietly. 'Worked for him and Mrs Liddell a long time ago. He was a real gentleman, just like your da. They were two of a kind,' Rose said sadly.

'Did me da know him an' all?' Kate asked eagerly.

Rose nodded.

'That's grand!' Kate exclaimed. 'A real gentleman, eh?' Her face was suffused with pride as if she had just discovered some aristocratic blood in her own ancestry.

Afterwards, Rose noticed, Kate held herself with a new dignity and spoke with assurance in a voice that had subdued the rough edges of her speech. Rose was secretly proud of her daughter's ability to improve herself, despite John's teasing and Mary's mimicry.

So it was a blow to Rose's ambitions when the old lord died in the summer of 1903 and his widow moved out of the castle. With the coming of the new earl and his wife, some of the dowager's staff had been dismissed, including Kate. As luck would have it, help was needed at the Ravensworth Arms, where Mary was now working, and Kate had been able to stay on in the area, serving as barmaid at the inn. She had stubbornly resisted John's decrees that she should come home and be of more help to her mother. Rose was finding it harder to manage on her own, but she refused to let Kate be bullied back by her stepfather. She would rather struggle on uncomplaining, knowing that her daughters were happy in their new lives.

It was worth it on the rare days off to see Kate blooming and full of life, her hair loosely gathered on the nape of her neck and swept back from her forehead in the latest style. Last March she had surprised Rose with tickets to the Theatre Royal in Jarrow to see a farce, The Cruise of the Saucy Sally, part of a grand naval and military night. She even persuaded John and Jack to go too.

'Haway, when's the last time you had a night out?' Kate cajoled. Rose thought back to those distant days of early marriage when a more romantic John had treated her to an evening at the Albert Hall.

'Your mother couldn't walk that far.' John was dismissive.

'Aye, I could,' Rose said stoutly, not prepared to be denied.

'I'll borrow the cart off Mr Burn,' Jack offered, keen to listen to the military bands. 'He'll not mind.'

Between them they managed to win John round to the idea and they had all ridden in style in Harry Burn's vegetable cart, the kind neighbour driving them himself and picking them up afterwards. Rose's head had been full of the songs of the show for weeks afterwards and she had delighted in hearing the solemn Jack whistling them while he dug the garden for her.

All was quiet in the house now as Rose waited for her family to gather. John had disappeared to buy a newspaper which probably meant she would not see him until dinner was on the table. But by half-past ten, Sarah had arrived and was bustling around the dark kitchen, shoving the meat into the oven and heaving the chopped vegetables into a large pot to simmer on top of the range.

If Rose could have run, she would have done so when she heard Jack's whistling and footsteps approaching up the garden path. She hobbled to the door and flung it open. Kate and Mary were there, pink-cheeked and chattering, their breath billowing in frozen clouds. Jack was behind them almost hidden by a mound of Christmas parcels.

'It's Kate's fault,' Mary said, by way of a greeting, 'she spent every penny of her Christmas wages at the village bazaar. You wouldn't believe the rubbish she's got.'

'Happy Christmas, Mam!' Kate cried, ambling towards her with her quick limp and nearly knocking her over in an exuberant hug. Rose was sometimes embarrassed by these shows of affection, but today she did not mind.

'Haway inside, hinnies,' she said. 'Sarah's got the dinner on. Jack, you open that bottle of ginger wine - I've been keeping it hid from your father. Take your coats off and let's have a good look at you!'

She surveyed her daughters in their neat dresses and boots, their hair well groomed. What a picture they looked! But she could not help fussing.

'Mary, are they feedin' you enough? I've seen better-fed scarecrows.'

'I'm run off me feet all day long, that's why,' Mary complained.

'They feed us plenty, Mam,' Kate assured her.

'Well, you look well enough on it, our Kate,' Rose remarked. 'Mind you, you've rings around your eyes. Are you gettin' enough sleep? They don't keep you up all hours, do they?'

'I don't mind the hours, Mam. I like me job,' Kate smiled.

'She's lovesick, that's what,' Mary said drily.

Kate blushed. 'Give over, our Mary!'

Rose eyed her more closely. 'So that's it - I could tell there was some'at. Who is he then?'

'Nobody!'

Sarah joined in. 'Mr Nobody?'

'Are you courting?' Rose asked excitedly.

'No!'

'Yes you are,' Mary contradicted. 'He's a gentleman an' all. Our Kate's quite turned his head.'

'A gentleman!' Rose gasped. 'What sort of gentleman?'

Kate hid her face in her hands in consternation. 'He's just an acquaintance.'

'Hark at her - he's just an *acquaintance*,' Mary mimicked.

'He's friendly, that's all - it's in his nature,' Kate blustered. 'He's like that to all the staff.'

'Just happens to call round on your day off,' Mary smirked.

'So you are courtin'?' Sarah cried.

'Not properly—'

'But this lad - he's special to you?' Rose asked.

Kate looked at her with shining eyes and Rose knew that it was true without her having to speak. There was an expectation in her flushed expression, a quickening of the voice as she talked about him.

'He's not from round here, but business brings him to the castle now and again. He's travelled - even been to the Continent. Full of learning and stories, Mam.'

'Blarney, more like,' Mary snorted. 'You're not the first lass he's taken an interest in, from what I hear. Quite a reputation as a ladies' man, for all his fine airs and posh clothes, has Mr Pringle-Davies.'

'That's just gossip,' Kate protested. 'He's a real gentleman - related to the Liddells themselves.'

'And I'm the Queen of Sheba!' Mary laughed.

Kate took a swipe at her sister.

'The Liddells, eh?' Rose gasped in astonished delight. 'What did you say his name was?'

But before Kate could answer, they heard a shout on the path outside. John was back.

'Quick, get the table set,' Rose ordered, deciding she could question Kate later. 'Jack, more coal on the fire.'

Kate said in alarm, 'Don't say anything to Father, will you?'

'I thought there was nowt to tell?' Mary baited.

'You say a word and I'll pull your hair out!' Kate threatened.

'She'll not,' Rose warned. 'We'll not have today spoilt with silly tittle-tattle or give your father the excuse to lose his temper.'

But by the sound of John's singing, she gauged he was in a good mood. He came banging through the door, clutching two bottles of beer, to find them all bustling round industriously.

'Now isn't that a grand sight?' he crowed. 'A family making ready for the master! Is me dinner ready, Rose Ann?'

'We've all the presents to open first,' Kate said, pointing at the pile on the hearth. She loved the present-giving more than anything. The more she gave the more it made up for those barren Christmases after Jack had been born when there had been no treats and no gifts.

'We'll eat first.' John was firm. 'Jack, pour me a beer, son.'

With a look from Rose, Kate did not argue further. They gathered around the oval table, John in his high-backed fireside chair, the others on an assortment of chairs and stools. Once it was all served up and John was digging into his food, Rose sat down with satisfaction. The table was laden with good things to eat and the smell of roast pork and steaming potatoes filled the warm kitchen. Her family tucked in eagerly, their faces flushed, their chatter light-hearted. She wished she could savour this moment for ever.

After the mince pies and custard, John pushed back his chair and eased his belt.

'By, that was a good dinner, lass,' he said with satisfaction, and Rose thought how that was praise indeed from her taciturn husband.

'Please, Father, let's open the presents now,' Kate pleaded. She was almost bursting with the effort not to tear open the parcels at once.

John gave a grunt of agreement. 'What've you got us then?'

Kate scrabbled among the pile. 'This is for you, Mam. It's a hat so you don't have to keep wearing that old bonnet.'

'You're not supposed to tell her till she's opened it,' Sarah laughed.

'I like me old bonnet,' Rose said, looking doubtfully at the brown paper package.

'Put it on, woman, and let's have a look at you,' John said indulgently.

Rose unwrapped the parcel and found a neat, flattish green hat like a stunted boater with a large bow of pale green ribbon tied at the front.

'It's not quite the latest fashion - Mrs Fairish in the village wore it a few years,' Kate explained. 'But no one round here will know that. I remember you having a green hat when I was a bairn,' she smiled.

'You remember that?' Rose said in amazement. 'You were a baby.' A green hat and a green dress that had been her pride and joy when married to William. She had never worn anything as elegant since. Rose put the hat on.

'Suits you,' Sarah said.

'It'll blow off in the wind,' John snorted.

'You can use one of me hatpins,' Mary offered.

'It's bonny,' Rose said, her voice suddenly wavering. She took it off quickly

255

and busied herself wrapping it up again, in case anyone saw the glint of tears in her eyes. It would not do to get sentimental about the past and all over a silly hat.

'I'll find a hatbox for it next time,' Kate promised.

'Haway, what else have you brought?' John asked impatiently.

Kate handed out the other presents, stockings for Sarah, a clothes brush for Mary and a book for Jack.

'What's that?' John asked suspiciously, eyeing the second-hand book.

'It's all about the Boer War,' Kate said, unable to keep the surprise.

Jack read out the title slowly,' With Roberts to Pretoria by G. A. Henty.' He looked up at Kate and gave one of his rare smiles. 'Ta, our Kate. That's champion.'

'What use is a book?' John scoffed. 'And about that bugger Roberts an' all.'

'I thought Lord Roberts was your hero?' Kate asked in dismay.

John snorted. 'He might be a good commander,' he conceded, 'but he treated us lads like muck - drove us till we dropped. It's us soldiers should get the glory, not the generals on horseback. It's easy to shout orders.'

'You should know,' Mary murmured, and Rose tried not to smile.

But John's hearing was not what it used to be and he missed the remark.

Kate heaved her final present from the floor. 'You'll not be wanting this then.'

'What is it?' John eyed the flat parcel, the largest of them all.

'It's a picture of—'

'Don't tell me!' he shouted. 'Give it here.'

Kate helped him untie the string. Everyone crowded round. It was a painting in a heavy wood frame: a British general on a horse with an African servant holding the reins.

'By, that's grand!' Jack exclaimed in admiration.

'Who is it?' Sarah asked.

'That's what I said when Kate bought it at the bazaar,' Mary smirked.

'Lord Roberts, of course,' Jack said impatiently.

'Which one?' Mary laughed. 'The soldier or the servant?'

'Don't be cheeky,' John said, flicking a hand at her. He sat back and looked at it. 'Stand over there and hold it up.' Jack and Kate did so, Kate holding her breath for some sign of approval.

'Well, John?' Rose grew impatient. She could see how much it mattered to Kate. She must have spent a small fortune on it.

John sucked in his cheeks, then nodded. His face broke into a smile. 'Fancy me having a grand picture like that.'

'You like it then?' Kate asked.

'Aye, it's a canny picture.'

Kate gushed in relief, 'It used to hang in the big hall - but the new mistress didn't like it and gave it to the butler. His missus didn't like it either - so she gave it to the bazaar. Think of that, it once hung in Ravensworth Castle.'

Rose could see John swelling with pride before her very eyes. Kate had played cleverly to his vanity.

'Pity there's not enough room to hang it above the fireplace,' Mary said cattily. 'I told Kate that but she wouldn't listen.'

'We can move the dresser and hang it over there,' Rose said quickly, not wanting Kate's moment spoilt.

'Dresser be damned!' John cried. 'We won't need to. I nearly forgot.' He slapped his knee, looking pleased with himself.

'Forgot what?' Rose asked.

'My Christmas present to you,' John grinned. 'I heard about it this morning.'

'Heard what?' Rose was nonplussed. He had not bought her a present at Christmas for years.

'Where is it?' Kate asked in excitement.

'Down in the town,' John chuckled. 'We've got the chance of a place - Leam Lane - right next door to The Twenty-Seven. No more tramping up here in the pouring rain for me and the lad. And it'll be much easier for you to manage, Rose. We'll hang Lord Roberts over the mantelpiece in Learn Lane. What d'you say?'

There was complete silence. Rose was appalled. But she could not say that she was completely taken by surprise. John had been itching to get them back to the town where he felt more at home. Jack was just an excuse. So was her health.

'We're canny here,' she answered. 'I can manage.'

'No you can't,' John snapped, displeased with all the long faces around him. 'I thought you'd be happy at the idea. Close to the shops, no stairs, a tap in the back yard. Better than living like peasants up here.' He glared round the room. 'Tell your mother it's the best thing for her. Unless one of you wants to come home and run this place for her?' he challenged them.

Rose saw them all look away, one by one. She would not ask it of them and John knew that. She knew that she had no choice. He was right: she struggled to manage as it was. Leam Lane would be far more practical for all of them, especially for John and Jack, working at the docks.

'Well, it's all arranged,' John said brusquely. 'We'll move come the New Year.' He glanced around. 'Look at your twisty faces - you'd think we were headed for Botany Bay! Jack, open that other bottle and let's drink to better times - to living in Shields. We'll hang the old dog Roberts over the fireplace, eh, our Kate?'

Rose caught the look of horror on her daughter's face. She seemed on the point of tears.

Kate sprang up. 'Hang it where you bloody well like. I don't care!' Then she fled to the door and rushed outside into the dusk, slamming it behind her.

'Kate? *Kate*. John shouted after her. He looked at Rose quite baffled. 'What's got into her?'

Rose was surprised too by the girl's response to the news. It would hardly affect her away in Lamesley. Rose had spared her the need to come back.

'Sarah, put the kettle on,' she sighed. 'I'll go after her.'

Chapter 47

Rose found Kate at the bottom of the garden, shivering by the fence. The last glimmer of silvery light in the west touched her downcast face. Her cheeks were wet with tears. Rose was puzzled by why she should be so upset; Kate hardly let anything get her down.

'You shouldn't worry what he says about Lord Roberts,' Rose chided. 'He was pleased with the picture, I could tell.'

Kate shook her head. 'It wasn't the picture.'

'Us moving then?' Rose questioned. 'You're upset at us moving.'

Kate sniffed. 'Aye.'

Rose sighed. 'It had to come sometime - I knew we couldn't stay on here for ever. Your father's right, I can't manage and it'll be easier for Jack—'

'Jack!' Kate cried. 'It's always what's best for Jack.'

Rose was taken aback. 'He's just turned fourteen - he's still a young lad - and he still lives at home. You don't,' Rose said pointedly. 'It's not like you to be jealous of our Jack.'

Kate looked at her with soulful eyes. 'Oh, Mam, I'm sorry. It's not our Jack either.'

'Then what?' Rose pressed. 'What's bothering you, hinny?'

'It's Leam Lane - Shields - we don't belong there. And next to The Twenty-Seven - that terrible place!'

Kate could not begin to explain to her mother how much she was afraid of it. It was part of the nightmare of her childhood, begging on the streets for food. When the doors of the well-off had been shut in her face she had gone down to Tyne Dock and stood outside the dock pubs begging the men for the remains in their bait tins. Grubby bread and treacle wrapped in newspaper, that's what Leam Lane and The Twenty-Seven meant to her.

'We've managed in worse places,' Rose said defensively. 'There're still decent folk live round there, don't you forget that. Don't judge a book by its cover.'

'That's as maybe,' Kate cried in desperation, 'but I could never bring him home to such a place!' It was out before she could stop herself.

Rose stared at her, first in disbelief, then with shock as realisation dawned. 'Your gentleman,' Rose whispered, 'you're talking about him, aren't you?'

Kate bit her lip, furious with herself for speaking her thoughts. They were wild thoughts, dreams that might come to nothing. And because of her impetuous words she had hurt her mother, she could tell by the wounded look on the older woman's face.

'You're ashamed of us,' Rose said, feeling numb inside. 'You're ashamed of your own mother.'

'No, Mam!' Kate cried, grabbing her mother's arm. 'Not of you.' Her pretty face was pleading. 'Please believe I'd never be ashamed of you. It's just Leam Lane and -'

Rose felt tears sting her eyes. 'I know - your father,' she finished for her.

'He's not me father,' Kate said in a voice full of rancour.

Rose pulled away. 'He's kept a roof over our heads all these years - including yours. He at least deserves your respect for that.'

Kate shook her head. 'You did that, not him.

Rose looked at her daughter and felt overwhelming sadness. A huge gulf separated them and it was of her own making. She had encouraged Kate to go away and better herself, yearned for the day she would return with a ring on her finger, having won the heart of a respectable, prosperous man. How could she blame her for wanting to distance herself from the grubby, noisy poverty of Tyne Dock? Wherever they lived, Rose realised too late, Kate would probably shun them. That must be why she had been so coy about telling them she was courting. She wanted to keep her admirer and her new life quite separate from her old.

'Is he so very grand?' Rose asked quietly, searching her daughter's face.

Kate hardly dared meet her mother's look. 'Yes,' she whispered.

Suddenly Rose was filled with foreboding. Had Kate set her sights too high? Was she involved with someone too far above her station for safety? On impulse she stepped towards Kate and pulled her close, gathering her arms about the girl's slender shoulders.

'Oh, lass, I fear for you!'

'Oh, Mam, don't!'

Kate clung to her mother as she had not done since childhood and wept. She had thought never to feel her strong hug again. Her mother seemed to have forgotten how to touch them these past years. But it felt so good now! She felt strength flow from the older woman to her and give her courage.

'I know you'd like him. He's kind and funny and so handsome. I don't know what he sees in me.'

'Don't you do yourself down,' Rose declared. 'You were meant for better things than skivvying. You hold your head up high when you walk out with this Mr— what do you call him?'

'Pringle-Davies.' Kate blushed.

'Aye, Pringle . . .' What was it about the name that was familiar? Rose struggled to remember. There was something Kate had said about him before that had sparked off a half-memory. No, it had gone. It did not matter now. Having Kate holding on so affectionately was weakening her resolve to let her daughter go.

With difficulty, Rose pulled away. She would not break down in front of Kate. She had not stayed strong for her all these years to betray herself as weak now. Rose gulped back the tears in her throat. How she wanted to protect her daughter!

'You're right,' Rose said hoarsely, 'don't let him come here. If you've a chance of happiness, lass, take it. By God, you take it!'

They looked at each other, both shaking with the cold and the emotion that clawed at their insides. Kate reached forward to touch her once more, but Rose drew back. She did not trust herself to embrace the girl again; she would not have the strength to let her go.

'But whatever you do and wherever you go,' Rose added stoutly, 'don't you ever be ashamed of who you are. You've had good parents - God-fearing parents who've brought you up to do right, however poor we've been.' She raised her hand and lightly touched Kate's cheek as if in farewell. 'Remember you were born a Fawcett - you were your da's favourite. I've given you that - so be proud of it. Make me proud of you, lass!'

She withdrew her hand swiftly and turned away.

'Mam,' Kate rasped, 'don't go!'

But Rose kept on walking towards the cottage. They both knew that in that moment of truth when Rose had laid bare her feelings, she was also letting go. Rose did not look back; she could not in case her resolve wavered. She would rather her daughter went back to Lamesley and never saw her again, disowned her family, if it meant a chance at happiness with a man above her station who could give her security. Although the pain of separation would be raw, she would give up her daughter for William's sake - for her beloved William's memory!

As she reached the door, Rose heard Kate sob, 'I will, Mam - I'll make you proud!'

Rose glanced round and gasped to see Kate's features caught in the golden light of the winter sunset. Her tear-stained face looked beatific. There was no other way to describe it. At that moment she had the face of an angel.

The gypsy's words rang in her ears. At the end of her life she would be blessed with an angel child. Kate would give her that angel child, Rose was certain of it. Ever since she had first seen Lord Ravensworth's daughter married and in her childish mind confused her radiant face with that of the moon, Rose believed she had been looked after by a guardian angel. How else to explain how she had survived all that she had been through? It was all for a purpose. All roads had led here to this moment of clarity. Kate was her chosen one. She would carry on where Rose could not. In time she would bring her greater joy. Rose smiled at her daughter, then opened the door and went inside.

Kate was left trembling in the dark, weeping at the weight of responsibility she felt pressing upon her. She had seen it in her mother's eyes, heard it in the way she spoke of Kate's real father. Her mother had freed her from her stepfather's dominance, but in return there was a price to pay. Rose expected the world from her.

Kate looked up into the late afternoon sky, already dark. There was just a glimpse of a new moon hanging over the copse, lifting like the sail of a ship. A new beginning. Kate took heart from the omen. She turned and looked behind her, to the south where Ravensworth and her other existence lay.

'Oh, Mam,' she whispered in the frosty stillness, 'I wish I had as much faith in myself as you do - and as stout a heart.'

Then she thought of the man she loved, the man with auburn hair and dark eyes that danced with dangerous merriment. The man with the deep voice that flattered and teased and told her she was beautiful. The man of a hundred tales who claimed his mother had been a Liddell who had eloped with a coachman named Pringle. The man who tempted her to recklessness too.

'Alexander.' She whispered his first name tentatively, blushing at her daring. A wave of tender longing swept over her.

'*Alexander,*' she called out more boldly, as if she could conjure him to her. 'Soon we'll be together again!'

Then, before facing the others, she blew a kiss in the direction of Ravensworth. For after today, Kate knew more than ever, that was where her heart and her destiny lay.

***

THE JARROW LASS is the first in a Trilogy. A CHILD OF JARROW and RETURN TO JARROW continue the story of Rose and her family through the first half of the 20th century.

Praise for A CHILD OF JARROW and RETURN TO JARROW:

'The Jarrow Lass was inspired by Catherine Cookson's grandmother. This follows into the next generation, with Cookson's mother and the childhood of the great novelist herself. It is a winner.' **The Bookseller.**

'Brings early 20th century Jarrow vividly to life. A smashing read.' **Lancashire Evening Post**

'Her finest yet - a wonderfully moving, deeply emotional tale'.
The Daily Record

'This is a story to burn itself into your mind.' **Northern Echo**

'Penmanship of the highest quality ... This is a story of warmth and despair, based on facts and places and with excellent characterisation. It is a delicate yet strongly-woven book of biography and imagination. Rich in narrative, which twists and turns on every page. It touches many raw nerves of human experience.' **The Newcastle Journal**

'It is powerfully and skilfully written, and keeps you interested until the end.'
The Sunderland Echo

***

Janet welcomes comments and feedback on her stories. If you would like to do so, you can contact her through her website: www.janetmacleodtrotter.com

Lightning Source UK Ltd.
Milton Keynes UK
UKOW041206300312

189896UK00002B/5/P